THE INHABITANTS II: WELCOME HOME

A NOVEL BY

KEVIN FLANDERS

ALSO FROM KEVIN FLANDERS

Please check out the following novels from the author.

WELCOME TO HARROW HALL

BURN, DO NOT READ!

INSIDE THE ORANGE GLOW

LASER TAG

GRIDLOCKED

For more information about upcoming works, visit www.kmflanders.wordpress.com.

Prologue

Saturday, December 18, 2010

It's a few minutes before shift change, 2335 hours. I'm ready to begin my first ever law enforcement shift with the Hollisville, NH, Police Department. I've got a good meal in me, Julia's spaghetti and meatballs, although I took it easy on the meatballs this time to make sure I'm light and loose for work.

At times I thought this might not happen for me, Zach King, a smalltown kid who dressed as a cop for three consecutive Halloweens. Not long ago I feared I'd graduate from the Academy and wind up working a mall security detail, or at a college busting up parties, or at an abandoned mental hospital, on the lookout for teenagers trying to get in. More than anything, it was fear of falling short of expectations that sometimes kept me on edge, fear of not measuring up to the Old Man, who's been a distinguished cop for thirty years.

And now it's my turn. I have to make my family proud.

I arrive at the station early, get dressed. It feels weird to see myself in uniform and know I actually made it. This is really happening – it's not just some dream I'm gonna wake up from and realize I'm still twelve years old and I've got a math test today. I'm a cop, just like Dad and Uncle Vince. It's all real – the uniform, the badge, everything! My field training officer, Sgt. James Fitzgerald, is really welcoming me to the Hollisville force and wishing me luck.

"Get ready, kid. Your first call's a doozy." Fitzgerald is walking fast, leading me into the squad room. "We got a call a little while ago from Katherine Grafton at 99 Deepwoods Drive. The officer posted at the property says something strange is going on – I guess there's weird noises no one can explain, and he wants backup. Officer Roberts is already on his way over there, and I imagine the feds won't be far behind him."

Fitzgerald grabs his jacket from the back of a swivel chair. "Anything involving 99 Deepwoods Drive takes top priority, Chief's orders. That means we head over there, too. You're up to speed on the Blake Grafton abduction, right?"

"Yes, sir. Definitely. That poor kid – it's horrible."

We turn into the main corridor, Fitzgerald practically jogging.

"That's just the latest unexplainable occurrence at that house," he says. "Weird shit's been happening there for as long as anyone can remember. Some people say it's haunted – hell, a lot of people say it's haunted. Way back in the sixties there was a mass suicide in the basement, eight people dead. In 1980, it was converted to a rental property, and it seems like we've responded to incidents there every month since. Property got stolen. People heard noises, saw things. Tenants moved out, claimed the place was possessed."

"Wow, that's crazy." Not a highly astute comment, but the only thing I could muster. I remember hearing a few news reports about the mysteries surrounding the apartment building from which Blake Grafton was abducted less than a week ago, but the primary focus has remained on Blake and the investigation. The main suspect is a sex offender living half a mile away who's drawn heavy attention from police and reporters.

We push through the doors, blasted by cold air. "What happened years ago is nothing, kid," Fitzgerald says. "What's gone down there over the last year is the real scary shit. Two renters killed themselves in the building this year, one in March and the other in June. Both suicides were suspicious, especially the first one – a few of our guys thought they were murders disguised as suicides. Then, get this, a renter was drugged in September and his girlfriend was abducted for a few hours and eventually found safe. And the suspects? They told the victims their names were Mason and Gerald Blackwell, two of the people who killed themselves in the mass suicide back in sixty-five. The suspects were never found, but their descriptions matched the Blackwells perfectly."

I nod, remembering the little scraps I picked up from news reports and conversations with officers during training. The previous abduction at 99

Deepwoods Drive is familiar to me, though the details have faded, dominated by the details of the

Grafton abduction. Blake was taken sometime Monday evening. A note was found later that night warning Katherine that her son would be killed if she moved away, perhaps the precursor to a ransom note that has yet to arrive. Since then, a cop has been posted 24/7 on the site.

"Even Chief Strait's starting to think the place might be haunted," Fitzgerald continues. We're in his cruiser now, pulling out of the station. "The former landlord put the building on the market in October, and it wasn't purchased until a few weeks before Thanksgiving. Only two of the units are currently occupied, but right off the bat there's been big trouble."

I glance anxiously out the window into darkness. I thought my first week on the job would be packed with desk work and a great many hours of watching other cops protect and serve, but here I am going to 99 Deepwoods Drive, the most notorious house in town, a house that will change my life forever.

Part I: A Battle on Two Fronts

"I became insane, with long intervals of horrible sanity." ~ Edgar Allan Poe

Chapter 1

I'd die for you.

It's a phrase that has been uttered countless times, yet only occasionally is it put to the test.

Robert Overbrook had sacrificed his life for love – love of country and the freedoms it provides. He'd been memorialized and extolled as a hero at his military funeral, where his brother Nate had stood solemnly beside his flag-draped casket and thought, *He was the bravest person I've ever known.*

Now, less than a year later, Rob had already been matched by Jocelyne Marie Leclaire as the bravest person to touch Nate's life.

"Thirty-eight, thirty-nine, forty!" Joss exclaimed, reaching into the Scrabble bag to fetch new letters before grabbing a handful of popcorn.

Nate had been staring at the blue fleur-de-lis on her *I Love Montreal* T-shirt, thinking about everything his girlfriend had risked for him. Tied to a post on Shepherd's stage, death advancing from the corner of the room like a wraith, she'd told the monster of 99 Deepwoods Drive that she would die for Nate. And not even meekly, either – she'd shouted it, practically begging Shepherd to kill her and let Nate live, even after learning of her boyfriend's betrayal with Meghan. It was a thing to marvel at, an extraordinary, almost unreal memory that Nate held close every day. In the weeks and months following that stormy night, he had made love to Joss with the transcendence of those who understand that time offers no guarantees.

Nate shook himself free of his memories and met Joss's gaze. Smiling, she licked the salt and butter from her fingers. "What are you thinking about?"

Nate recorded her forty points. "Just spacing out." He didn't want to tell her for the thousandth time that he'd been thinking about that prodigious night. Although it had ultimately brought them even closer, it had also been a traumatic night, especially for Joss. The knowledge that Shepherd came for the souls of suicides had left her desperate to save Max, who'd killed himself three months ago in his South Boston apartment. Nate and Joss had tried visiting the place in October, just to look around and establish a feel for it, but Max's unit had already been occupied by a new renter, a sharp, unsympathetic old woman who'd refused to let them in. *Please, ma'am, it's really important. It'll only take a few minutes*, Joss had begged, but the witch had told her to leave or she'd call the police.

Now it was mid-December, and not a day passed that Joss didn't mention returning to Boston and breaking into the apartment. So far she hadn't brought it up today, and the last thing Nate wanted was to speak of anything that might draw the conversation to 99 Deepwoods Drive or Max Leclaire.

Nate formed a new word for a triple score and calculated his points. Across the coffee table in Anya Leclaire's "Boring Room", Joss took a sip of cherry juice from her iced glass. The divided snack tray beside the Scrabble board, once filled with popcorn, Tostitos, Pringles, carrot slices, and cashews – with two types of dip and, of course, salsa – was quickly being depleted. It had been a Saturday afternoon of fun and games that would yield to a long night of far greater entertainment, followed by an extended midnight talk about the definable things that scared them and the murky possibilities that frightened them even more. Talking made it easier. Talking helped them move forward. They couldn't tell anyone else about an ordeal that sometimes felt more like a nightmare, but they had each other.

In this new place their relationship had reached, Nate knew the love could only be felt, never described – love distilled with every kiss, burnished with every laugh, nourished with each word of kindness, and set aglow at times like paper put to fire. Nate had first seen Joss in chemistry honors class, rumors of her beauty preceding the day. Then the roller coaster had launched into motion, and they'd soared over its hills and ripped around its curves, all while Nate had watched Joss transform from an inexperienced girl to an inspiring woman who'd saved his life on more than one occasion. It hadn't always been a fun roller coaster, though. Sometimes it had been downright awful, especially during Nate's drug use, a bone-crunching coaster that thrashed you from side to side, but they'd emerged even stronger thanks to Joss.

And now, more than ever, she needed Nate. Even though she wouldn't come out and say it directly, she needed him to help save Max's soul. Somehow he had to find a way to do the impossible, a feat fit only for God. Few people would understand it. Even fewer would care. It was them against the world, just as it had always been. The old witch wouldn't keep Joss out of the apartment in which her brother had died – that much Nate understood perfectly; now it was a matter of finding a way in. If they'd been able to see Mason Blackwell, there was no reason why they couldn't see Max, too.

However, seeing and saving were as different as saying and doing.

Chapter 2

For twenty-four-year-old mother Katie Grafton, admitting that her parents had been right all along was one of the hardest truths she'd been forced to accept, a truth that would never be winged with words and released, instead doomed to fester and blacken internally like all unspoken menaces.

She often wondered where her current life had come from. So completely screwed up, it sometimes felt like the product of a bomb exploding rather than a chain of mistakes. Katie's parents had admonished her against getting serious with Travis in high school; they'd said he was a bum, a pothead, a loser who would bring her down. When her mother had described Travis as the sort of guy who would get a girl pregnant and leave her, Katie never could have imagined that she was foretelling her daughter's misery.

But that's exactly what had happened. Blake had come into the world plump and healthy a few months shy of Katie's eighteenth birthday. Now, seven years later, Travis had long ago departed the grid – the lure of drinking and gambling in Vegas had been too irresistible – and, in the world of sanity and responsibility, Katie was trying to do the best she could for Blake. It wasn't easy. She was loath to ask for assistance from her parents, who'd never been shy about expressing their shame over her pregnancy. *I can't believe it!* her father had shouted when he'd learned the news the summer before Katie's senior year in high school. *You're knocked up just like the trailer park losers across town? Where is that scumbag Travis? I'm gonna kill him!* And her mother's response had only been scarcely gentler, something to the effect of, *Why didn't you guys use protection? My God, this is a nightmare! What about college, your future...ohhh, this is bad, really bad!*

The ironic part was that Travis had used a condom. Every time. Katie hadn't learned until after the pregnancy test came back positive that the condom he'd used on the night of conception – a half-drunken night in the back seat of his Mustang behind an abandoned warehouse – had sweltered for weeks in the glove box. *I didn't know heat could break down a rubber*, he'd said, detestably elucidated.

The compromised condom stood among dozens of reasons why Katie was presently moving into a new apartment with Blake on a chilly Saturday after Thanksgiving. Her friends had spent all afternoon helping her bring the boxes and furniture up two flights of stairs and inside unit four of 99 Deepwoods Drive, which had been offered to her for a surprisingly cheap monthly rate by the landlord. Just five hundred and fifty dollars a month – Katie had no complaints.

"This place is kind of cozy," her friend Mandy Cormier said in the kitchen. "I think this is a good move for you, Katie."

"Yeah, I hope everything works out for us." Katie took a peek through the window at Blake, who was playing down on the side lawn where she'd told him to stay. Not yet a master of dexterity, he tossed a tennis ball way up high and repeatedly missed his catch attempts, instead pouncing into the leaves after his ball.

"I just hope the place isn't haunted," added Whitney Golding, Katie's best friend since high school. Latex gloves snapped over her hands, she'd been attacking a faded yellow floor stain near the door for five minutes, going after it with a steady stream of cleaning spray and scrubbing with such force that it was a wonder the sponge was still in one piece. "I think I heard somewhere that one in twenty houses in New Hampshire is haunted, or some crazy high number like that."

Whitney's boyfriend of two years, a handsome medical student named Stephen Pullman, said, "That's just a stupid rumor. This place isn't haunted – I'm getting good vibes from it already."

Katie couldn't help feeling jealous of her friends. She didn't want to be filled with envy, but sometimes the little green-eyed, green-handed monster smacked her when she least expected it, like last week when Whitney talked about how exciting her job as a TV station reporter was, or the week before when Mandy described an awesome concert. But whenever Katie found herself groped too excessively by those ugly green hands, she told herself she was lucky to have a healthy son who she loved more than anything. It didn't matter that her parents only spoke to her a few times a month, their conversations exceedingly brief, nor did it matter that Travis had abandoned his son. Katie and Blake were fighters. As long as they had each other – and a little help from friends along the way – they would turn this screwed up life into a pretty damn good one.

And they would do it right here at 99 Deepwoods Drive, their new beginning, unaware that they were moving into a house of endings.

Chapter 3

Mike Overbrook couldn't get the nightmare out of his head. It had wrenched him from sleep the last three nights, the same exact replay every time: a young boy standing in the parking lot of 99 Deepwoods Drive and looking up at the building. Nervous and alone, he didn't notice a murder of crows circling overhead…and three hooded men looming behind him.

After a light breakfast with Sue that December morning, Mike headed down to his basement office and called Dave Strait, his good friend who served as the Hollisville, NH, police chief. They spent a few minutes on small talk before Mike got down to business.

"So what's happening with Nate's old apartment?" he probed. "Anything to report over there since everyone moved out?"

Dave sighed. "I'll say, Mikey. The damn place was purchased maybe three weeks ago. They've already got someone living in your nephew's old unit."

"What? Who bought it? I never thought the landlord would sell it."

"He didn't. His son made the sale."

"His son? What are you talking about?"

"From what I gathered, the previous landlord died of a stroke around Halloween and his son inherited pretty much everything, including the house." Dave coughed noisily into the receiver. "Sorry about that – I'm always sick this time of year. Anyway, the guy's son lives in Maryland and wants nothing to do with the house. He's got some experience in real estate, and apparently he jumped at an opportunity to sell the place to a property management company in Manchester. I guess they own several apartment complexes throughout the state, most of them near colleges. They're planning to renovate the property over the next few years and rent it to college kids."

Mike's breakfast stirred in his stomach. It was happening again, another disaster to thwart at 99 Deepwoods Drive. "You've gotta be kidding me."

Chuckling, Dave said, "Wish I was, man. I met with the new landlord and told him about the building's history, including what happened to your nephew and his girlfriend, but he didn't want to hear it. He mentioned some crap about his company providing excellent security for renters. Cameras, motion lights, brand new locks in every unit – the whole nine yards."

Mike huffed. "We both know how effective that'll be."

"Yeah, I hear you on that one. I've been thinking a lot about whether something's really inside that place, or if this is all just the work of a couple psychos. In my last talk with the former landlord before his death, he told me he thought the ghosts of the people who committed suicide back in sixty-five are still in there, trapped. He asked that I warn anyone who eventually moves in, but there's only so much I can do."

Mike took a sip of coffee from his mug. "Do you think those…spirits, or whatever he was talking about, might've had something to do with the suicides earlier this year? I still can't believe Nate's and Joss's descriptions of the suspects in their incident matched the Blackwells almost to the letter."

"I don't know," Dave said. "But I still have a bad feeling about it all being connected – Keppel's suicide, Gaudreau's suicide, and the drugging of your nephew and abduction of his girlfriend. It's almost like the building itself somehow…I don't know, but the place gives me the creeps. Meanwhile, at the other end of the spectrum, I can't discount the possibility of two lunatics going around pretending to be the Blackwells. Maybe they came across the story and got obsessed, then decided they could make the house *seem* like it's haunted – sure as shit makes a lot more sense than ghosts, doesn't it?"

"Either way, you're in a tough spot as police chief. You can't exactly go door to door and warn people that the place might be haunted."

"Yeah, I can see the complaints to the selectmen already. Still, I've gotta find some way to prevent more people from moving in. I can't shake this thought that we're gonna get a call any day from someone at that place."

A thought sprang into Mike's head. Dave's hands were tied in terms of cautioning unwitting renters, but there was no reason why Mike couldn't do the job himself. The uncle of a former renter and a longtime cop, people would listen when he informed them that they were entering a dangerous situation. And in the process he would search for the boy from his most recent premonitory nightmare sequence, a boy whose life might end at 99 Deepwoods Drive if his current fate went unaltered.

The race was on again. Mike had come to realize that life is not a novel of predetermined, inescapable outcomes, but instead a manuscript of millions of potential fates outlined lightly in pencil and eager to be edited. The ultimate fate is death – that is unavoidable, unstoppable, a shadow that catches each living soul – but everything in between can be changed or improved with a little luck and an answered prayer or two, negative results averted and good fortunes seized.

God works in mysterious ways, Mike had often heard, and he considered his premonitions to be just one of His many tools. Now Mike had to use those tools to find that boy…before it was too late.

Chapter 4

Remembering the lonely nights they'd spent apart, Nate unfastened Joss's bra and guided her backward, onto the bed, capturing that moment of taut, glistening anticipation before the chaos, like a whispering wind and the scent of rain preceding the storm, rapt stillness taking over, lightning dancing in the distance.

Closer.

Close enough as to be one.

Drifts of wind and rain, an atmosphere energized, alive with glorious instability. Lightning. Thunder. Nate leaned in slowly, taking his time as he'd never done before and searching the electric blue of her eyes. Her desire was the lightning through the windows her eyes became, a razor illuminating marvels hidden deeper.

He kissed her stomach, angled higher, traversed her breasts, up to her neck now, inducing soft words of French. Clasping her hands behind the pillows, her breaths were light and infinitely pleasured. When her eyes flickered shut, those bright windowed wonders were briefly lost to a perfect arcana of desire.

Closer, closer still. Lightning, thunder, rain, a steady madness. Her lips trembled with his kiss, a shudder spiriting through her when he advanced, receded, rested upon her, their lips briefly parting.

Time moved on around them, the air charged,
Nate's gaze held in those pools of swirling
electricity, his heart claimed by anticipation of the
storm. He would leave her breathless, speechless,
and in the process find himself lifted to those levels.
They wouldn't have to remain quiet, not tonight, her
mother gone for the weekend.

He proceeded slowly, remembering the first time
they'd made love. She'd endured the pain of
inexperience, but now, three years later, they were
seamless – flawless – their harmony such that it
seemed they'd been made exclusively for each
other.

He kissed her, entwined her hands in his, faster,
faster, rain and wind and thunder, a heightening
storm. With a collective shiver, she ratcheted up to
meet his rhythm, her hands lifting, fingers sinking
into his back.

Higher, faster, wilder, the ravaging, convulsing
storm. Joss arched, returned her hands behind the
pillows, and together they arrived in that place
which had for months been lost to them.

Positions changed. Time itself changed, speeding
along now. Joss's glass of wine spilled. Nate's cell
phone went ignored. Faster, a dizzying blur. Losing
control again, a hectic, overwhelming singularity of
thought and sensation in her eyes.

When the storm reached its manic apotheosis, Joss
looked up at him deliriously, electricity surging.

Her eyes fluttered almost imperceptibly, a change in them now, windowed no longer with desire but fulfillment.

***

As Nate lingered inside her, kissing her, their hands linked, Joss whispered, "Let's break into that place tomorrow."

Exhausted, he turned onto his side, drew her against him, his hand roaming her breasts and stomach.

"I'm serious," she insisted when he said nothing, embracing his warmth, loving their closeness – the kind of closeness Mom had warned would condemn her to Hell. "Tomorrow's perfect."

His hand stilled. "Joss, I don't think that's a very good idea."

Joss wondered if she should push it. She felt lifted, weightless, as if she were floating on a cloud, his arm around her like a shield. Life could be horrible, but for this moment it was ruled not by time. It was theirs.

"We need to do this, Nate. Max might not have long," Joss insisted.

"But how can we be sure breaking in will do anything to help?"

She adjusted slightly, nestling her back against his chest so that their heads were aligned. "I know this sounds crazy, but will you do it for me? We can wait until the lady leaves, then pick the lock and get in. It'll only take a few minutes."

Sighing, he smoothed a hand across her stomach. "I guess I owe you a few favors, don't I? For everything I put you through, every insult, every lie, for almost killing you in the car crash, acting like a dick at prom, stealing your money, calling you a bitch all those times, standing there while you offered to die for me. Whatever you want me to do, just name it and I'll be there."

She rolled to face him, then whispered a line of French.

He smiled. "Translation?"

Giggling, she said, "I called you my hero."

"No, you're mine. You win the hero war."

Laughter, Joss switching to Russian, then Spanish. "You know what I just said in two languages?"

"What?"

"I want another round before bed."

Wondering if he had any energy left, Joss sat up and finished the wine bottle with a swig. Then she pulled herself atop him and prepared to revisit a place she'd often feared left for desolation.

***

As they rested in the dark after the finale, so tired that they might sleep for a day, Nate asked, "So what happened to your crucifix? I haven't seen you wear it since Max's death."

She sighed, shifted a little, cuddling more comfortably in his arms. "I like this one better." She held her small silver cross pendant, the one Nate had bought for her seventeenth birthday. "The crucifix reminds me of Mom, but this one is more special because it's my way of taking you everywhere."

Nate remembered the elaborate story she'd told about the crucifix (the whole bit describing how her grandmother had escaped the USSR and passed the family heirloom to Anya Leclaire at fifteen, followed by Anya giving it to Joss, a piece to be handed down for generations). "But didn't you tell me once that you'd never take it off?"

She yawned. "Things change. I'm not the same person I used to be. I feel like I'm stronger now, like I don't have to do what Mom tells me anymore. I'll keep the tradition alive with the crucifix, but the next person to wear it will be my daughter. From now on, I want to wear something that came from *your* heart."

He pushed aside her hair, kissed her neck. "I love you, Joss. I can't tell you how happy I am that we're back together. I missed you so much this summer."

"Yeah, me too. The love's okay, but I honestly couldn't wait to get laid again. God, it was a lonely summer."

Vintage Joss, a witty remark delivered at the most unexpected moment. She was so damn flawless, beyond beautiful from skin to soul, every freckle, every heartbeat, every kiss. How had he gone a day without her? In the calm, quiet afterglow of tonight's storm, Nate felt like the possibilities were infinite, the future theirs to seize. This was how he'd felt during junior year, when they'd made love countless mornings at Joss's house before school and sometimes arrived after the first bell, their smiles wry and regretless as they collected their tardy slips, completely spent before the day even started, staring mindlessly at the first period teachers, their heads and hearts still in the bedroom. They'd learned to master the half-dressed quickies, with skirts and shirts still on, Nate having to remind Joss one hurried morning on her way down the stairs that she was without a small though highly important component of her apparel, easy to forget since her skirt hadn't come off. It had been an incident of distracted dressing, Joss preoccupied with a call from her mother, and the jokes had come almost immediately.

Now, as then, Nate felt like he was the absolute luckiest human being on the planet...but somewhere along the way he'd taken Joss for granted. Not anymore. From now on, he was going to deliver for his girlfriend the way she'd never seen him do before, even if it meant going along with her on questionable journeys, even if it meant breaking into some old lady's apartment in Southie. So what if he got arrested – he was fortunate just to be alive, and no matter what it took, no matter how hard he had to work, he vowed to earn the title of hero in French, Spanish, Russian, and whatever new languages she planned to learn.

And when the time was right, he would ask for Jocey Marie's hand in marriage.

Chapter 5

Whitney Golding released her silvery blonde hair
from a bun and shook it free. Glancing about the
kitchen as she chewed her first bite of pepperoni
pizza, she studied the place with a disapproving
frown, the same expression received by many
unfortunate boys in high school who'd made the
mistake of asking her on a date.

Whitney was exceedingly difficult to please, and if
you committed the error of disturbing her – or, in
some cases, repulsing her – you would find yourself
dismissed from her company not by words but
facial features capable of making one feel about as
big as a nagging insect. It wasn't that Whit set out
to be a bitch – it just sort of happened, regardless of
how many times Katie warned her about the
expressiveness of those sharp hazel eyes.

"Aren't you…I don't know, kind of uncomfortable
about living all alone in this creepy house?" Whit
asked.

Seated across from Whit, Katie looked through the
bedroom and checked on Blake, who was eating
pizza in front of the television in the living room,
his very first meal in unit four. It would be a little
easier now to keep him occupied thanks to Whit and
Stephen, who'd arranged for DirecTV to set up a
dish so Blake would have his favorite TV programs
ready to greet him at his new digs.

"She's not all alone," Mandy corrected. Turning to
Katie as she poured potato chips onto her paper

plate, she said, "Didn't you say there's someone else living in the building, too?"

Katie nodded. "The landlord told me an old couple just moved into one of the apartments out front. He said this place should be full by the end of summer – it's just gonna take a little time."

Whit took a sip of Budweiser. Stephen had bought a six-pack at the liquor store after picking up the pizza from a place on Route 202 called Vincenzo's Pizzeria. "I don't know about this place," she said with her investigative reporter stare. "Tell me again why all the previous renters were asked to move out." Stephen shot a glare at his girlfriend.

"I guess the last landlord couldn't keep up with his payments and told everyone they had to go," Katie said. "The new landlord said I don't have to worry about any issues because a big company owns the place now. They're supposed to make all sorts of renovations and get the building looking good."

Whit was skeptical. "That sounds like a shady story to me – this could be worth looking into. We should ask the neighbors if this place is haunted or something. I guarantee–"

"Really, Whit?" Stephen blotted his mouth with a napkin. "Come on, don't make her nervous with all of this stuff. She's got enough to think about."

It was as if he'd glimpsed into Katie's mind and spoken her thoughts. Frankly, she didn't want to know about the house's past, and she certainly didn't want to go searching for things that would make her uneasy. Having recently been hired for a position in the admissions department of a local prep school, she was determined to make her new life successful. This was why she'd worked hard to earn her degree online, countless long nights of studying, waitressing, and caring for Blake, countless exams to prepare for, extra shifts to handle, bills to pay. And she'd done it with the help of Whit and the Golding family, no assistance from anyone in her own family beyond the one hundred dollars a month of which her parents had found her deserving, a reluctant handout to the Grafton family failure that had no doubt enabled them to sleep with clean consciences. Katie's life was a road she'd paved with bad judgment, her parents had often reminded her, and it would do her no good to have poor choices rewarded.

You made your own bed, Katie. Now it's time to lay in it.

The one hundred-dollar gifts had dried up about two years ago, and Katie often wondered why she continued to pick up the phone for her parents. They didn't care about being in Blake's life or how he was doing – it almost seemed as if the sole purpose of their calls was to confirm she was still alive. Her brother Lewis, on the other hand, could do nothing wrong. In fact, during most calls her parents spent the majority of the conversation blathering away

about how well Lewis was doing in college, a mass communications senior who was sure to have a

Pulitzer on his wall within the decade. It was beyond infuriating, beyond unfair, a reflection of life itself. But Katie didn't need her parents' support – if they didn't want to be involved with "the sinking ship" their daughter had jumped aboard, then it would be their loss, not hers.

Whit declined into a silent sulk for a few moments, occasionally narrowing her eyes at Stephen. Katie smiled at the thought of all the conversations in which her best friend had admitted she'd deprived Stephen of sex for bad behavior. *He was flirting with the waitress right in front of me, Katie, can you believe it?* Another diva beauty: *He refused to go to the bar with me because he has to study. He studies all fucking day – does he really have to do it on a Friday night?* Sometimes, when Katie was in the right mood, Whit's trivial complaints and insecurities offered comedic relief – but mostly they were just annoying.

Sitting to Katie's right at the small dinner table, Mandy was contentedly munching on her second slice of pizza, seeming to tune out her friends in favor of a hard-earned meal. She was an overweight, big-breasted, rosy-cheeked virgin with a persistent case of acne (Whit had once drunkenly referred to her as the ugly friend), but at least Mandy never complained about her image or launched into self-conscious ramblings like Whit.

"What do you think, Mands?" Whit said moodily, finishing about three-quarters of her lone slice of pizza before calling it quits and tossing a napkin onto the plate. "Don't you agree that it's creepy living here with only one other renter?"

Stephen sighed, took a long drink of beer. Whit wasn't going to let this go. Part of what made her such a great friend was her ultra-protectiveness – and she wanted to make absolutely sure this place wasn't a bad idea for Katie.

"I don't think it's scary at all," Mandy said. "And plus, the landlord said there are new locks, right?" She spoke between bites of potato chips, drawing a displeased furrow of the forehead from Whit that had once been described by Lewis as "the popular girl look", a wide-eyed expression that seemed to shout, *Ewww…Get away!*

"Yeah, and they're gonna install security cameras next month," Katie added, hoping to reassure Whit. "This place will be safer than the neighborhoods back home."

"I doubt that," Whit snapped. Stephen wisely slipped into the bedroom and resumed a project he'd been working on before dinner, well aware that one more wrong word might cause him to miss out on fun time tonight.

After dinner they all played cards with Blake. Whit lightened up once the game began. She and Blake had a surprisingly strong relationship, her fun,

carefree side brought out by a seven-year-old boy. When Whit didn't feel like she had to pretend to be something she wasn't, compete for someone's attention, or try to impress someone, she was a totally different person, a much funnier, happier person. She always joked around with Blake and made funny faces at him; she even let him play with her hair when he asked, something Katie had warned him not to do. Perhaps a future Casanova, the kid was already in love with women's hair and wasn't shy about regularly seeking Whit's permission to touch her lustrous locks. He'd shown some other obsessive tendencies over the last few years that had worried Katie about such disorders as Asperger syndrome, but the doctor had said he was just going through growing phases and seemed to display no severe social deficiencies.

"Just don't tie it in a knot, okay, bud?" Whit said in response to Blake's latest request.

Meanwhile, still not quite full after four slices of pizza and half a bag of chips, Mandy was working on a Snickers bar. When it was time for her to shuffle, she inserted the thing in her mouth and sent Whit into a spurt of laughter.

"That's my look, not yours, Mands," she said, now on her second beer.

"Don't we know it," Mandy laughed.

Still twirling Whit's hair, Blake wrinkled his nose and said, "What are you guys talking about?" His

eyes twinkled with that searching, somewhat vexed glint of a kid who knows the adults are keeping him in the dark about something. He was smart, perceptive, always trying to analyze and interpret things. Katie was excited about his development from the shy, withdrawn boy he'd once been, but there were still a few minor adjustments to be made. If she could only find some way to get him to stop reaching for Whit's hair and, as his teachers had reported, snatching other kids' pencils and stuffing them into his backpack.

Just before they finished their final card game, Whit's face grew serious. She was staring at her cell phone, eyes intense, lips thin, not even noticing that it was her turn to play a card.

"Earth to Whit," Stephen said, and she looked up with nervous immediacy and quickly tossed down a card so she could get back to her phone.

As the game came to a close, Whit kept looking down at the phone, then glancing at Katie with I-need-to-tell-you-something eyes, reminding Katie of that day junior year when Whit had admitted to getting drunk and having unprotected sex with her then boyfriend. *I'm on the pill, but what if he gave me a disease?* Whit had cried, and Katie, with a hug, had told her friend that she could get tested to make sure everything was all right (luckily, things had turned out just fine, although the boyfriend hadn't lasted much longer, too "limp" for Whit's liking).

After the game, Whit asked for a moment with Katie outside. "It's really important. You need to hear this."

Katie sighed, wondering what the urgent business was about. "All right, let's go."

They went through the living room door and stepped onto the landing of a narrow wooden staircase, Whit closing the door behind them. The air was warm out here, musty, a sharp contrast from the raw late November afternoon that had grown overcast with steely clouds.

Whit shoved her phone into Katie's hand. On the screen was an article from a local newspaper. "This is 99 Deepwoods Drive, right?"

"Yes, why? What is this?"

"Just read."

The article described the suspicious death of graduate student Blake Gaudreau, who'd died at his 99 Deepwoods Drive apartment in March of that year. The police had refused to go into much detail beyond the use of the word *suspicious* and the phrase *active investigation.*

"Oh my God," Katie murmured, chilled to her core.

"You think *that* has something to do with why everyone cleared out of here so fast?"

"I...I don't know." Katie was disturbed, not only by the story but the shared name between her son and the victim. It was a coincidence, of course, but why did it feel like something else entirely, like an omen or a warning?

She handed Whit the phone without finishing the story.

"Are you sure you want to live here? What if it really is haunted?" Whit pressed.

"It's not haunted!" Katie hadn't intended to raise her voice, but she was becoming frustrated by Whit's insistence that there was something wrong with her new home. "It's one death," Katie said, this time in a lower voice. "It doesn't mean the place is possessed, okay?"

Whit shrugged. "I just thought you should know."

"I appreciate that, but I want to stay positive. I'm sure every apartment has seen its share of deaths over the years, but they're not all haunted."

"A lot of them are."

"You watch too many of those dumb ghost hunter shows." Katie turned toward the door, but Whit held her back.

"Katie, you're my best friend. I just want to make sure you're safe here. We live an hour away and your family…well, you know they're not your

biggest fans. I just don't like the idea of you and Blake being all alone up here with no one to check in on you."

"Whit, we call each other every day. That won't change."

"I know, but I'm just really worried about this. Can you blame me?"

Katie gave her friend a hug. "We'll be just fine. You're a great friend for caring this much."

Whit pursed her lips. "Promise you'll call if anything weird happens. I'll come straight up here, no matter what."

Placing a hand over her heart, Katie said, "I promise."

They shared another hug. "Love you, girl," Whit said.

"Love you, too, girl."

Chapter 6

Half a mile past the

Welcome Bienvenue
To
New Hampshire
"Live Free or Die"

sign at the state line, Mount Monadnock loomed
into view off to the north. Rising prominently above
Cheshire County like a skyscraper commanding all
eyes that fall upon a distant city, the gray-blue
mountain would soon be powdered white with the
season's first snow. The months were hurrying
along at a deceptively quick speed, and it was
already Finals Week at the university.

Nate had completed two exams on Thursday and
another on Friday. After a day off yesterday with
Joss, he was on his way back to school to finish off
his final two exams of the semester. He sprinted
along Route 202 North, a stack of textbooks and
notes serving as his only passengers. He hadn't
gotten enough studying done (academics never took
center stage when Joss was around), but the exams
were the least of his concerns. What really made
him nervous was the anticipation of what would
happen that evening.

Stopped at the intersection of Routes 202 and 119,
where an easygoing guy named Earl was known for
making sandwiches and good conversation in his
adjacent convenience store shop, Nate felt a little

jolt of fear at the thought of what he and Joss had planned. They would travel to South Boston, wait for the witchy old lady to leave Max's former apartment, and break into the place. Then Nate would cut through the wall and hope to free Max or establish a connection with his spirit (that had been Joss's idea based on what Mason told her in September, and although Nate had found it insane, he hadn't been in a position to argue; when you owe someone dinner, you don't complain about where they choose to go).

A horn blared behind him. The light was green. Nate got his old Taurus going, but his thoughts quickly drifted from the road. He couldn't believe he would actually go through with this, but Joss remained adamant that Max was trapped in his apartment, a prisoner just as Mason had been. Nate wondered if somehow she was right. He'd seen Mason, too, just as he'd seen Shepherd, a half-bird, half-snake monster perpetuating an insoluble mystery inside a room that didn't exist. Those who would refuse to believe that Max was a trapped soul would also refuse to believe that a tiny shed could house a steep staircase leading to a room larger than the shed itself.

But Nate and Joss had witnessed the impossible. They'd been to that room and seen that awful stage, undetectable to the masses but reserved for a misfortunate few. Sometimes it didn't seem real. None of it. During those instances, now being one of them, Shepherd and Mason and the maddened birds seemed like the relics of nightmares. If they'd actually been real, surely he and Joss would be dead, but by the most miraculous of means they'd been spared. Even the raining fire of debris had failed to inflict damage to Nate's head and arms, fortunes Joss described as God's gifts.

Although Nate was still furious with God for taking his brother, he couldn't deny His work that stormy night. However, danger can only be embraced so many times before disaster eventually stabs through. Nate and Joss had been given another chance. They'd scratched and clawed their way up the slippery walls, pulled themselves out of the pit hissing with snakes, and run to safety without looking back or recounting their struggles.

So why the hell did they want to visit another pit just like the one they'd escaped? What would possess them to glance over the edge into whispering darkness, never mind expose themselves to evil's blackest depths once more?

The only answer was love – Joss's love for her brother and Nate's love for the girl who would die for him. Yet no amount of rationalization or contemplation of this noble cause did anything to allay Nate's fears. Driving down the thin, scenic road that would bring him to the university campus, he couldn't fight off thoughts that he and Joss were just like those foolish game show contestants who keep electing to stay and play rather than take the stacks of money they've amassed and head home.

It was a bold, reckless – perhaps even idiotic – decision, but love, if nothing else, can drive a man to unimaginable lengths.

***

Joss set down her Kindle, unable to concentrate for a familiar reason: thoughts about Mason Blackwell. She regularly prayed he'd made it to Heaven, although sometimes she couldn't sleep due to worries that he was burning in Hell or trapped within the walls of Nate's old apartment. These were unbearable thoughts. After everything Mason had done for her, he had to be in Heaven with his mother – he just had to be! During Joss's most defenseless moments that stormy September night, Mason had been there to save her. He'd cut her free, helped her escape from the stage in advance of death's encroaching shadow, and whisked her away to safety, his heroism exalted to the greatest possible platform of inspiration because he'd saved her life under the assumption that he and his father would be sent to Hell for his defiance. Shepherd had promised Heaven if he killed Joss – a reunion with his mother! – but Mason had rejected him, risking damnation to save a girl he barely knew.

Joss fought the tears. They came often when she thought of Mason, especially when she considered how his father had coerced him to end his life. He'd only been sixteen, just a kid, the years he should have enjoyed as a husband and father cruelly translated to insufferable years in the walls. Watching and waiting. Watching and waiting. Joss couldn't imagine it, couldn't begin to comprehend how he'd remained sane or the jealous rage he must have felt toward renters who were oblivious to the ghosts that starved for life on the other side of the wall.

But Mason hadn't been bitter, hadn't railed against humanity or allowed envy to blacken his soul. He'd saved Joss even though he knew it might cost him a chance to join his mother in Heaven. It was beyond heroic, beyond repayment. There were simply no words to describe what he'd done for her. Even after rescuing her, when they'd stood on Carl Larose's deck in the middle of the storm, he'd continued to protect her. She'd been out of her mind, corrupted by the darkness of 99 Deepwoods Drive, helpless. He could have done anything he wanted with her, but after a few parting kisses he'd told her to get away from the apartment. *Close your eyes*, he'd whispered, and when she'd lifted them his words had come from some distant place.

It'll all be better once you get out of there. I'll look after you, Joss.

Now, three months later, Joss felt the least she could do was pray for his soul each day. Filling her heart was instinctive knowledge that he'd been welcomed to Heaven, but it was impossible not to worry that he'd somehow failed to complete the trip. After all, he had taken his life voluntarily, a mortal sin, but hadn't he suffered and expiated enough? Hadn't he proven himself worthy? The more Joss worried about Mason or gave in to her fears, the more her stomach tightened and her head ached…for she knew that Mason's suffering could become Max's agony.

She attempted to read a little longer, but it was useless. Instead, she headed downstairs and fixed herself a sandwich, trying not to think of her brother and how he was probably stuck in the walls just as Mason had been. She and Nate had to get him out of there. Tonight. Max wasn't nearly as strong as Mason. His sanity would slip by the day – and then he'd blindly follow Shepherd's orders with the promise of salvation. It was a terrible deception, Joss now realized. In order to prove the souls of suicides worthy of Hell, Shepherd needed to force them into cruelty, she assumed, and what better way to do so than to promise them Heaven? Shepherd had been unsuccessful with Mason, but that was likely an isolated case. Joss imagined that most souls – people like Max – would be deceived, collected, and transported to the place of eternal suffering.

***

"Are you sure you want to do this? If we're caught, we could be talking jail time here," Nate said that evening. It was shortly after four o'clock and just about completely dark out.

Joss nodded. "We have to try. Max would do the same for me."

Nate grabbed his father's sheetrock knife from the garage and slipped it into his pocket. "Maybe you should stay home and let me go. I don't want you to get arrested – I can do this on–"

"I'm coming," she insisted, pulling on a pair of brown leather gloves. "I don't care if they arrest me. It's worth the risk."

Nate took a deep breath through his nose and blew it out slowly. They were really going to do this. Breaking into an apartment with the hope of freeing a trapped spirit – it sounded completely nuts, and for a time Nate wondered if they were losing their minds. "What's our excuse if we get caught?"

"I'll just make something up about my brother leaving a letter saying he hid something in the wall." Her hopeful smile offered the scantiest of veils for her fear. "But don't worry about that. We won't get caught. Even if someone sees us and calls the cops, we'll run away before they get there."

"I just hope our disguises work." Nate felt the facial stubble he'd allowed to develop since deciding to do this last night, wondering if this meager growth – along with a baseball cap and a pair of his father's old glasses – would be enough to prevent him from being recognized.

Joss adjusted the blonde wig she'd bought a few weeks ago on Ebay for this exact occasion. It looked real, any passersby to assume she was a born blonde. "Even if they have cameras at this place, no one will know who we are. We don't know anyone in Boston."

"Good point. But what if the old bitch doesn't go anywhere?"

"Then we'll wait until she does."

He frowned. "We could be there all night."

"Don't worry, she'll go somewhere. We only need her to leave for a few minutes." She kissed his lips, quickly and nervously. "Thanks so much for going with me, Nate. We're gonna get my brother out of there tonight, I just know it! We'll beat Shepherd to Boston!"

Nate smiled, sadness rising as he noted the anticipation lighting Joss's face. What would he tell her if they broke into Max's old apartment and nothing happened at all? How would he convince a girl who'd always relied on faith to now leave Max's fate to God?

"Do you really think cutting out a section of the wall will work?"

"What do you mean?" asked Joss, who'd let her mother know earlier that she would stay overnight at Nate's house. Meanwhile, Nate had called his mother – who was eating dinner at her new boyfriend's apartment in Auburn – and told her he would spend the night at Joss's place. That gave them an alibi for the entire night (but hopefully they wouldn't need that long for the witch to step out of her apartment).

"Even if your brother is trapped in that place, do you really think Shepherd would just let him leave because we cut open a wall?" Nate said, hoping she would reconsider. "I mean, he seemed pretty powerful, like he had control of everything in that place."

She let out a sigh, probably searching for a halfway rational answer. "Mason told me about how he was trapped in the wall for years. I'm assuming Shepherd only let him out so he could talk to me, but if we do something unexpected and cut open the wall before Shepherd comes for Max, maybe he'll be able to get out."

"But if Mason got out for a little while and couldn't get away, what makes you think Max will do it?"

"I don't know, Nate, this is a shot in the dark. If you don't want to do this, you can stay home."

Nate very much wanted to take her up on the offer. He hated talking about Shepherd and Mason, memories that brought him back to 99 Deepwoods Drive and the nightmare they'd endured. Their ordeal made him feel isolated, burdened with knowledge of truths so outrageous that the mere mention of them would make others think he was nuts. It was as if they'd been beamed aboard an alien ship for a week, experimented on, and returned to Sleepytown, USA, with traumatizing memories. *Sure, buddy*, they would say if he tried to describe Shepherd hovering above the stage. *Okay, pal, have another joint, will ya?*

Joss had mentioned PTSD a few weeks back – and she was right. It would be impossible to return to blissful ignorance now that they'd been enlightened in the darkest way imaginable.

"Let's do this," Nate finally said, even though he feared this was a surefire way to wind up in the back of a police cruiser…or worse.

But they would do it. Nate wasn't going to turn away, and he could tell by the look in his girlfriend's eyes that she was resolute as well.

Traffic on the Massachusetts Turnpike was light; in just under forty minutes they were passing Fenway Park. Joss had once bought Red Sox tickets for Nate and Rob but had never gone there herself, describing baseball games as boring unless her boyfriend was in them. Hockey was another story. They'd already been to the Garden twice for Bruins-Canadiens games, and the Bell Centre once (and the damn Habs had won all three times, enabling Joss to sing that *Olé, Olé, Olé, Olé* crap to her heart's fill).

Joss wasn't singing tonight. She sat silently, pensively, staring out the window when they entered a tunnel and cruised beneath Government Center. Nate kept telling himself to turn around. It wouldn't work, never, and it certainly wasn't worth the risk. If they got caught and Joss was arrested, her mother would kill him. Literally. She would probably hire someone to kidnap him, cut him into little bits, and set those bits on fire.

Yet Nate continued driving, turning south and passing the Rainbow Swash natural gas tank in Dorchester. Now they were only about ten minutes from Max's old apartment, where he'd swallowed his roommate's sleeping pills back in September and ended his life.

Chapter 7

After thanking her friends for their help and wishing them a safe trip home, Katie stood alone in the dirt parking lot, darkness pouring in around her, such an early sunset this time of year. According to the landlord, the lot would be paved and striped with numbered spaces over the summer, one of many planned upgrades to 99 Deepwoods Drive. For now, though, the place remained weathered and downtrodden, an old building that somehow seemed less manmade structure than living creature. There was something eerily watchful about the place, as if its highest lighted windows were eyes gazing down upon the lawn and parking lot.

What horrors had this building seen? Now Katie was thinking like paranoid Whitney Golding, who suspected a haunting in every room she entered.

Stop it, just stop, Katie urged, but still she found herself thinking about Blake Gaudreau's death as she climbed the lawn toward the outer staircase that would bring her up to unit four. Increasingly afraid, she wanted to learn how Gaudreau had died. Had someone murdered him? The building knew. It kept the secret each day, remaining as still and silent as a guard at Buckingham Palace but always watching.

What other secrets was it keeping?

Back inside the apartment, Katie helped Blake organize his things. Earlier, Stephen and his friend Barry (who hadn't stayed for pizza) had carried the furniture up the rickety staircase and lugged everything into the apartment, sometimes twisting and pushing items through the doorways if they didn't initially fit. Katie wondered how she would have done this without them. It looked like an entire moving team had helped her furnish the place, but it had all been the work of two guys, three gals, and a determined little boy.

Katie took a few proud moments to absorb everything they'd accomplished. The sofa was in place against the far living room wall; both beds were assembled abreast, dressers opposing each other in the bedroom; and all of the kitchen accessories had been placed in cabinets and drawers. Thinking back on the afternoon, Katie realized how efficiently everyone had worked, the boys focusing on heavy stuff while the girls and Blake concentrated on unpacking and organizing. It had been hard work, but in a few hours this place looked like a home. Their home.

Blake enjoyed stuffing his clothes into dresser drawers and tacking his posters to the wall. He progressed quickly, grinning, happy to finally have a little room to move around. After living in Whitney's parents' basement for four years rent-free, (the Goldings had never once complained about the imposition), the three rooms at 99 Deepwoods Drive seemed like chambers in a mansion. Best of all, it was a relief for Katie to finally have a place of her own. Things had gotten discomfiting, if not embarrassing, the day Whitney moved away from home to live with Stephen while

Katie was stuck in the basement of her best friend's house with Blake, tramping up the stairs all the time for bathroom visits, trying hard not to be a bother but of course failing. The Goldings' faces had flashed with joy when Katie announced she was moving to New Hampshire, the basement tenant finally venturing out into the world. *It might get a little lonely without you guys here with us,* Mrs. Golding had said, helping them pack. And her husband, who'd insisted on paying for the moving truck, then loaded everything with Stephen early that morning, had added, *If you need anything, don't hesitate to call.* Their kindness had brought Katie to tears. They'd opened their home to her and Blake, cooked for them, and constantly offered the love and support that should have come from her parents. But, as generous as they'd been, Katie had always felt ashamed of her situation and unhappy in their home, wondering by night what the Goldings thought of her and if they were glad their daughter hadn't turned out like her.

Now, finally, Katie didn't have to live in shame. She had her own address, her own mailbox, a brand new job. She had an apartment, a stove, a refrigerator, and even a television with hundreds of channels (the first few months of the DirecTV package had been a gift from Whit and Stephen, and the new dishes, glasses, and silverware had come from Mandy, as well as a few other items for the kitchen). Indeed, Katie had people who cared about her and Blake, and she had two keys to unit four, 99 Deepwoods Drive, her first real home.

If your family sucks, you might as well make up for it with persistence and damn good friends.

***

Several hours later, during a predawn torpor that found everyone – perhaps even the house – at rest, Blake Grafton woke with an emphatic jolt, not simply easing away from sleep but tearing violently from its grip. He looked around the dark bedroom, afraid, moonlight seeping through the blinds and casting combed shadows upon the carpet. The windows were cracked open, cold air slipping into the apartment. A gentle wind rustled the trees, stirred the silent hour. It seemed to whisper the language of the night, its inscrutable voice forming odd sounds and unknown words that all ended with the letter *Esssss.*

Blake didn't know why he was scared, especially with Mom sleeping just a few feet away. He just was. It made his arms feel cold beneath his sweatshirt. It made his heart drum a little quicker. He looked at the closed door separating the bedroom from the living room. For some reason he expected it to click open ever so slightly, just enough for someone to peek in at him. It remained closed. He watched it for a few moments, but it didn't move, not even an inch.

Growing sleepy, he was about to answer the pillow's call when he realized he needed to pee. Stuffing his feet into a pair of worn, rough slippers, he tiptoed into the kitchen, not wanting to wake

Mom. He did his business quickly, squinting against the bright bathroom light, and washed his hands. Yawning, he toweled them dry and clicked off the light.

And that's when he heard it.

Footsteps outside, on the deck. Coming closer.

Blake slinked over to the kitchen door, the blinds covering its window left partially open, just enough for him to see the deck and staircases. Everything out there was weirdly bright under the moon's watch, shadowy and spooky. Blake's heart went even faster. He waited. Dreaded.

More footsteps, louder. Where were they coming from? Not the deck. He could see all the way to the unit three entrance about thirty feet to his right, where a staircase took you back the opposite way, descending to the lawn.

Even louder footsteps. A shadow slid into view, creeping up the staircase, spilling onto the deck outside unit three like a pool of ink. Black. Totally black, so black that it couldn't be a shadow but something else, something blacker than a shadow.

But it was a shadow – it had to be.

The shadow expanded in height and width. Blake watched with wide, troubled eyes as its master appeared at the top of the stairs, stopping briefly and staring in the direction of the parking lot, his back to Blake. The man – it had to be a man because he was too tall for a lady – tilted his head and appeared to sniff the air. He was dressed in a long black robe of exceeding terror, as mysterious as the night itself. Behind him, Blake could see the head of another man poking up just above the deck. He was still on the stairs, waiting motionlessly for his friend to keep going.

Blake gulped. It was hard to swallow, as if there were a lump in his throat. He felt beads of sweat sprouting on his forehead. What were those guys doing out there? He wondered if he should wake Mom up – she might want to know about this.

A minute passed, the men holding their positions. Blake remained still as well, peering through the blinds and waiting for something to happen, in thrall to the fearsome oddity of these 3 a.m. visitors.

Do they live here?

A sudden, wrenching awareness came to Blake that there was no one else living on this side of the apartment. Mom had said so. The only other renters were an old couple in the front of the building.

So what were these men doing up here?

Before he could worry it longer, the first man took a right and followed the deck past unit three, holding the wooden railings with pale hands. He was facing Blake now, but his features were concealed by a hood. Light gasped somewhere beneath the garment

– dim, flickering light like that of a dying flashlight, escaping through the neck of the robe and pulsing weakly outward.

The man approached unit four very slowly, his friend following him at the same pace. He, too, was robed and hooded, and whitish light trickled from him as well, muted but nonetheless barbaric, revealing slick gray cheeks and a sharp hooked nose, the lips as worn as tombstones. Meanwhile, a third man climbed the stairs, almost to the top now.

Shivering, Blake shrank back from the door, hiding off to the side near the stove. He couldn't see what the men were doing from this angle, only their moonlit silhouettes, but he saw enough to realize they were standing just outside the apartment door, their white lights bobbing and seeping through the blinds into the kitchen. Blake wanted to scream but remained silent, hoping they'd go away.

A strong gust flared up, flapping the blinds of the side window behind Blake.
Just go away, he willed. *Please go!*

More lights penetrated the kitchen, strengthening, some brighter than others. There were so many silhouettes out there now that Blake couldn't count them.

A faint buzzing sound came from outside – a collective moan. More lights, the linoleum bathed in sickly white. More shadows. A face absent light pressed against the glass, and though Blake couldn't see the eyes, he knew they were searching the kitchen.

Blake crawled beneath the table next to the stove. Had he been seen?

Fingernails rapped the window…*Rat-a-Tat, Rat-a-Tat, Rat-a-Tat*. A hand jiggled the doorknob. Then quiet.

For more than a minute Blake waited beneath the table, his heart slamming so heavily that he was afraid the men would hear it from the other side. Another minute passed, Blake counting the seconds. Finally the lights receded, footsteps rising even higher, up the stairs to the third floor. Blake slipped away from the table and caught a glimpse of the last man heading up.

Now there was dull moaning directly above him, and creaking floorboards. They were inside the apartment upstairs, but no one lived there, Mom had said. They were breaking in!

He ran to wake Mom, told her what he'd seen, but by the time she got up and turned on the light, the floorboards upstairs betrayed no further signs of movement.

"Call 911," Blake urged, shaking with horror, but Mom was smiling.

"You had a bad nightmare, honey. It seemed real, but–"

"No, they were there! I saw them!" he shouted.

She pulled him close, gave him a hug, then filled a glass of water for him. Gradually he calmed down, beginning to wonder if it had all been just a nightmare. No! He knew what he'd seen. Those men were up there that very second. But why? What were they doing? Why were they doing it?

Far too afraid to close his eyes, Blake didn't sleep until moonlight was replaced by the earliest traces of sunlight, his fingers repeatedly pressed between the blinds so he could search the side lawn.

Chapter 8

Katie spent much of Sunday morning dwelling on what Blake had told her about his nightmare. She hoped it was a nightmare, but he'd been adamant even after finishing his glass of water and returning to bed, convinced that he'd seen hooded men on the deck with white lights coming from their faces and robes.

Katie unpacked the remainder of her clothes and hung them in the bedroom closet. It was a little after nine o'clock. Blake was still sleeping, probably exhausted after his scary overnight experience. Perhaps his anxiety about moving to a new place and attending a new school tomorrow had caused a vivid nightmare.

It had to have been a nightmare, she kept telling herself, possibly even an episode of sleepwalking. Blake had never sleepwalked before or experienced difficulty in differentiating dreams from reality, and Katie hoped this would be an isolated incident, a first-night anomaly.

And if he hadn't been dreaming – well, that would be even more worrisome. Why would hooded men walk up to the third floor at three in the morning? Stranger yet, why would they peer into Katie's apartment as Blake had described?

Just a nightmare, that's all. Yet she couldn't resist thoughts of Blake Gaudreau's March death and

Whitney's persistent speculations about the place being haunted.

Haunted – the word made her cringe.

Now that everything was situated in the closet, Katie organized a few of Blake's things and moved on to the living room, where she unpacked boxes of knickknacks and photos. Encased in a dusty frame with gold trim was an old photo of Katie and her parents taken during her freshman or sophomore year of high school, back when they'd assumed she would head to college and then perhaps medical school or law school. They'd identified a specific set of routes for her, and apparently receiving their love had been contingent upon her choosing one of those routes and never leaving its blacktop, a conditional love that had been rescinded with news of her pregnancy.

Feeling momentarily morose, she returned the photo to the otherwise empty box, then placed it on the top shelf in the living room closet and shut the door. She couldn't choose her parents, but she could choose to stay positive about her future and not let anyone bring her down. There was no room on these walls for people whose images would fill her with bitterness. This would be a happy place, always.

By the time Blake woke two hours later, thoughts of his nightmare had faded from Katie's mind. Blake had apparently forgotten as well, asking if she could make him eggs and pancakes, his favorite breakfast.

"Sure, buddy. Whatever you want for your first breakfast."

He grinned, then headed off to the bathroom to brush his teeth. As Katie prepared breakfast, a sense of triumph came over her. This was going to work, she realized. In a year or so, maybe they could get an even bigger apartment. She was finally back on track again, slowly gaining momentum in the right direction.

For the next few weeks things went well, even better than Katie had expected. Her new coworkers at the school were very welcoming, and the job – albeit a little boring – was far less stressful than handling multiple tables at the dinner rush. Meanwhile, Blake got settled in his new school and made friends quickly. He liked his teachers and his classes, acclimating brilliantly to a mid-season change. And he didn't have more nightmares, either, nor did he mention the one that had scared him badly that first night. Things were so good that Katie sometimes wondered if this was all too perfect, like a steadily rising balloon bound for tragic heights.

Then, just when Katie was starting to embrace the notion that life really was manageable again for the first time since senior year, there was a knock on the door one Monday evening in mid-December.

Chapter 9

Chris's checkups were always the same for Mike and Sue – fraught with worry. Each time they drove to Lakeside Medical Center in Worcester to meet with Dr. Richard Eller, Mike's stomach roiled with fear that his son's cancer would return.

A new patient was being taken to the cancer center for testing when they arrived Monday morning, a seven- or eight-year-old girl, her face like that of a puppy brought into the veterinarian's office for the first time. The little girl still had her hair, carefully braided, though perhaps not for long. Her mother walked beside her, held her delicate hand, the nurses pointing out the way, just as they'd done for Chris back in September, the cycle repeating.

Mike felt a shiver in his gut; the sight of this child heightened his apprehension. Depending on the extent of her diagnosis, she might be forced to leave behind family, friends, and the comforts of home as Chris had, sacrifices no child should have to make. Mike could only pray that she, too, would be fortunate enough to walk out of this building healthy and smiling one day.

The checkup went well, Eller asking all of the pertinent questions and running a few tests.

"Things are going nicely. I'm very happy with how he's responding," Eller told Mike and Sue at the conclusion of the appointment. "Today is a big milestone. We've reached the point where Chris can come every three weeks for his checkups now, and

soon it will be three months if there are no signs of
a recurrence."

Mike bought Chris his favorite McDonald's meal
after the checkup, chicken McNuggets, and they all
savored the bliss of favorable news. It was a nice
day, unseasonably warm for December, and they
went for a little walk after lunch, heading down to a
pond and enjoying each other's company.
Following such a terrifying ordeal, family time had
taken a new and profound meaning, every second
together a blessing. Mike had always known that
life is fragile. He'd understood that everything can
shatter with a single event, but his son's survival of
cancer had still managed to make him more
appreciative of just how short and unstable life can
be. You think you're the one in control, confidently
steering the ship, and then you realize you're not the
captain but instead a deckhand along for the
journey. And in that vulnerable, life-altering
epiphany, you cling to family and faith like a person
who can't swim clings to a life preserver.

Mike was still holding on. He wouldn't let go.
Never before had he been this thankful and
optimistic, but it was time to return the Big Guy's
favor. Mike had been offered visions by He who'd
spared his son, and now it was his turn to save
someone else's son.

Past the state line, Mike made a turn off 202 and
took in the familiar sights of Deepwoods Drive.
He'd thought he was done with this road, done with
Cheshire County until Nate's graduation, but there
it was, the house coming into view, jutting out

above the trees, an eerie giant resting upon a cursed hill.

He pulled into the bumpy parking lot, stared up at the house, remembering that stormy September night. The house seemed to be alive, glaring at him. He knew its secrets. He knew all about the mass suicide, the subsequent suicides (perhaps murders) of Jane Keppel and Blake Gaudreau, and, most recently, what had happened to Nate and Joss. This place was bad news, really bad, but perhaps the house's most frightening quality was its normal appearance. To unwitting visitors, it was just a house, a massive old house with peeling paint, crumbling shingles, and rotted exterior staircases, its worn black shutters a New England staple. There were no wrought iron fences or turrets stacked atop each other, nothing self-important or grandiose that would steal your eye from the road. How many houses were just like it, Mike wondered, possessing awful secrets in almost every room, filling entire decades with darkness? The idea of hauntings had once seemed ridiculous to him, but now it seemed possible, especially here.

And even if there wasn't a haunting at number 99, just a pair of lunatics terrorizing the place, that was reason enough for renters to get far away. Whoever – or whatever – infected this house had a purpose, a mission. Two people had already died suspiciously this year, and Joss had come very close to meeting death as well. Now, three months later, the house was being rented again and Mike knew the next target: a blond-haired boy maybe seven or eight years old.

Before getting out of his car, Mike tried to solidify what he would say. *Excuse me, but this building might be haunted and you need to leave.* No, that wouldn't work very well, nor would too much back story. The mass suicide would carry significant weight, but overemphasizing it might cause someone to focus on the length of time that had passed and the fact that the place had undergone a major renovation/addition project since Christmas Eve, 1965.

So what the hell was he going to say?

It was just after three-thirty. Clouds had bustled in ahead of the approaching darkness, blotting out the descending sun, bringing a measure of disquietude over the place. As Mike walked up the lawn toward the staircases, he glanced behind him and realized that his car was the only vehicle parked in the lot. In his urgency to warn these people about their new residence, he hadn't noticed that no one was home, or at least not anyone with a vehicle. Nonetheless, he climbed the creaking stairs and passed unit three – a sand-filled cigarette barrel from the previous owner still resting beside the door – then came to unit four. He opened the screen door and knocked on the door behind it. No one answered.

"Damn," he muttered. He should have known this was too early an hour on a weekday to expect people to be home.

He returned to his car. As he was about to open the door, a blue minivan pulled into the lot. The sliding door opened. A boy stepped out, a bulging backpack slung over his shoulder, but not any boy – the one from Mike's nightmares! Oblivious to Mike watching him about twenty feet away, the kid darted up the lawn and climbed the stairs, followed by a mid-twentyish woman wearing a red Franklin Pierce University sweatshirt. Mike shouldn't have been surprised, but he found himself shaking his head, stunned that the premonitions were accurate yet again.

"Wow." Mike felt the hairs on his arms rise. Sometimes his ability scared him immensely. People weren't supposed to possess extrasensory talents like this. Too bad his visions never indicated who would win the Super Bowl and by how many points.

The young woman, probably a babysitter but perhaps a family member, unlocked the kitchen door for the boy. Mike, filing into his car, almost hurried up there to offer a warning – but that would only scare them, some stranger showing up and rambling about the place being dangerous. No, he had to be patient and wait for the parents to arrive later.

Back in the driver's seat, Mike rolled down the window and grabbed a novel he'd brought along to pass the time. He couldn't concentrate for very long, though, his attention stolen by the big house on the hill.

THE INHABITANTS II

Katie returned home ten minutes shy of six. Blake was finishing up his homework with the babysitter when Katie stepped through the kitchen door with bags of groceries in hand. She gave him a kiss on the forehead and asked him how his day was.

"Good, Mom," he said distractedly, returning his focus to math problems at the kitchen table while Katie paid the babysitter.

"Did anything fun happen today?"

He shook his head.

"Did anything weird happen today?"

Another head shake.

"Did you make any new friends?" Katie never thought she'd be that annoying mom who bombarded her kid with questions after school, but she wanted so badly for him to remain happy with their new situation.

Letting Blake finish his homework in peace, Katie was about to start dinner when a knock on the door startled her. Blake glanced up from his notebook, looking nervous.

"Check it out, bud, our first visitor who isn't Whit!" Katie announced, wondering if one of her parents had finally come around and decided to visit her new place. She'd reminded her mother of the address during a recent phone conversation, but it seemed unlikely that either of them would just drop by without calling, especially now. Following each workday as vice president of a general construction company, her father loved a glass of scotch in the basement, where he worked on his model railroad before dinner. He cared more about those stupid little trains than his own grandson. And her mother – it would take an act of Congress to separate her from *Wheel of Fortune* as she got dinner prepared, 7:30 every night, never a minute earlier or later.

Katie opened the door to a friendly looking man in his forties. He was heavyset and muscular, with blue eyes and a prominent jawline. "Hi there, I'm Mike Overbrook," he said, pulling a wallet from his pocket and showing her a gold badge. "I'm the Chief of Police down in Elkins, Mass, and my nephew used to live in this unit."

He extended his hand. Katie shook it, anxious thoughts swimming through her. "I'm Katherine Grafton." She hesitated for a moment. "Can I help you with something?"

Glancing down, he said, "Hey there, pal. How are you?", and Katie realized Blake had crept up beside her.

"Blake, sweetie, how about you finish up your homework and let us talk for a second?"

"I'm all done."

"Okay, well…go watch TV and I'll call you in when dinner's ready. No chores tonight."

Katie knew that would get him running off with excitement. Usually this was his chore time, a dreaded nightly reunion with the vacuum cleaner. Instead, he took advantage of the fortunate visitor and hurried into the living room.

"Looks like a good kid," Mike noted.

"He is." Katie shifted uneasily. "So, is there something I can do for you? I'm kind of busy with getting dinner started."

Mike nodded. "I didn't mean to bother you, but I just need a few minutes of your time." His eyes darted to the parking lot, then returned to Katie. "There's no easy way to put this, but as an officer of the law whose job is to keep people safe, I feel obligated to inform you that this place is not safe for you and your son."

Dumbfounded, Katie could only blink for a few seconds, no words coming. Her mouth fell open, but nothing spilled out of it.

When she remained speechless, Mike continued, "There was a mass suicide in this house back in the sixties, and ever since it's had a history of suspicious events. Two renters committed suicide this year alone, one in your apartment, and my nephew and his girlfriend were also terrorized here. He moved out in September, couldn't get away fast enough, and when I found out someone had bought this place, I felt I needed to warn the renters."

Katie stepped onto the deck, closed the door behind her. "What do you mean by terrorized? What happened to your nephew?"

Mike chuckled, but it was easy to tell he found nothing funny about the situation. "For starters, his girlfriend was briefly abducted by two people going by the names of a father and son who died in the mass suicide. She wasn't hurt, thank God, but the cops never found the people responsible. Nate, my nephew, was drugged so they could kidnap his girlfriend. And there were also notes left by...whoever is doing this. They took pictures of him, wrote threatening messages warning him not to leave, and even snuck around the apartment while he was inside. There were shadows, lights randomly turning on, weird noises – whatever you can think of, it happened here. Some people in town think the place is haunted."

Katie lifted a hand to her mouth. This arrangement really was too good to be true. She felt like she was sinking, though this was nothing compared to what the night would bring next.

Chapter 10

Parked on a street adjacent to Max's old apartment building, a five-story brick structure as worn down as its neighborhood, Joss asked Nate one more time if he really wanted to do this. There was mounting reluctance in his eyes, accompanied by skepticism that stung Joss. He was doing this entirely for her, not Max, and she hoped he didn't think she was acting crazily. It was a shot in the dark, as she'd said earlier, but at least it was a shot. If they grabbed the dart and hurled it hard, maybe it would somehow find its way toward the target.

It was better than doing nothing.

Having spied on the building for almost two hours and finally watched the old witch drive off in her gray Buick, they were ready to make the leap to criminality. It was just after seven o'clock. To their left was another deteriorated apartment complex, and flanking the busy road were rows of vacant buildings and seedy establishments. CLUB XTREME – EXOTIC DANCERS, read a blue and green neon sign ahead on the left. Opposite Xtreme was a tavern, outside of which a group of men talked and smoked, hands shoved into their pockets.

Joss shook her head, just as she'd done when she used to visit Max here. She couldn't believe her brother had wanted to live in this dump, but he would have preferred a cardboard box in an alley over a home with their mother. And Joss couldn't blame him for wanting to get away…far away from Mom.

"Let's do this," Nate said, and they made their way around a corner toward the front entrance of Max's apartment.

The lobby was dim, smoky, and redolent of sorrow. This was a place where people resided out of circumstance, not choice. Two men stepped off the elevator, one of them making a wolf whistle as he passed and drawing a glare from Nate. He hated it when people made occasional remarks about her, but she didn't take exception to them, reminding Nate that there were far worse reasons why people might stare and comment. Plus, if she felt particularly insulted, she could always say *Mange d'la marde!* with an angel's smile. In one such case a guy had smiled back, completely clueless, and it was like he really had eaten shit.

"What an asshole," Nate mumbled when they took the stairs up to the fourth floor.

"I guess the blonde wig looks hot," she chuckled, hoping to mask her fear. "By the way, those stupid glasses make you look like the Zodiac Killer."

Joss was a little short of breath by the time these words were spoken, Nate smiling only faintly. It was time to get serious, but Joss's palms were sweating and she was scared, stupid humor the only thing that came to her…because what if they'd driven all the way here and nothing happened?

What if Max was beyond saving? What if she and Nate were forced to give their fingerprints later on because she'd ridden an impulse?

The main fourth floor corridor was empty, Joss aching with fear and tiredness. All of that water she'd gulped down earlier was starting to apply some uncomfortable pressure, but she leveled her focus squarely on what they'd come for, Max's face firm in her head. Quickly, quietly, they proceeded to the last door on the right, unit 420. Nate knocked on the door to make sure the witch didn't have any unexpected visitors. Silence.

"Hurry!" she whispered, and he pulled from his pocket two pieces of a bobby pin he'd broken in half. Hopefully the YouTube videos he'd watched on how to pick a lock would work.

Joss kept an eye on the elevator while Nate twisted and poked at the lock inside the silver door handle. For a few tense moments he struggled, perhaps not achieving the right angle or inserting the pieces in the right spots. But just when Joss considered trying it herself, something popped and the door slipped open.

"Come on," Nate said, grinning, and they stepped inside.

Joss was briefly overcome with sadness. Glancing about the dark apartment, lit only by a pair of lamps in the far corner of the living room, she felt something hanging in the air, a heavy, invisible cloak comprised of the misery and despair this place had seen. The rugs were new, not the matted, stained rags Max had fallen upon in his final seconds. The walls had been painted a soft blue, and the drapes were different, too, the windows now covered by a regal burgundy fabric. Yet even with its new rugs and drapes, even with the art deco paintings on the walls and the faux Tiffany lamps resting atop tables and shelves, the place would always be dark and bleak. Also hanging in the air as part of that thick, dolorous cloak were hints of words unsaid, dreams unfulfilled, conversations never to be had.

Joss was becoming nauseous, feeling lost and alone, oblivious to Nate's words.

"Babe, did you hear me?" He grabbed her arm.

"S...sorry. What'd you say?"

He had his knife out. "Which wall do you want me to cut open? I've gotta do this quick. She could come back any second."

Joss led him into Max's old bedroom, pointed to the wall his bed had once stood against. "That one."

Part II: The Slow Rot

"But in the end one needs more courage to live than to kill himself" ~ *Albert Camus*

Chapter 1

Within the walls of his South Boston apartment, Maxime Leclaire tried to remember what, specifically, had caused him to swallow his roommate's sleeping pills, shoving them into his mouth like a trick-or-treater with a bag of Skittles. A bottle of tequila had washed the pills down (apparently they weren't lying when they said Patrón made you do crazy shit).

Yet Max remained convinced that drunkenness was not to blame – he'd been drunk and miserable countless times before. When you worked as a janitor, mopping piss puddles in front of urinals and staring down shit-smeared maws all day, drunk and miserable went together like peanut butter and fucking jelly.

But even worse than Max's job had been the people in his life, he'd once felt, the people who'd poisoned him with lies and deceit and falseness. His mother, a pompous university president and religious fanatic, had constantly nattered about his "unacceptable grades" in high school, his "bad influence friends", his "distasteful music", and his "abandonment of the Lord." In hindsight, her obsession with trying to mold him into a college valedictorian priest, or some priggish likeness, had strengthened his rebellion. His grades became worse – slipping from mostly B's to lower C's – and he relished the agony on his mother's face when she reviewed the report cards. She tried to punish him, of course, grounding him and threatening to take away his possessions, but he sneaked out by night and hung with those bad influences she so passionately condemned.

During senior year, horror turned Mom's face ghostly white when Max told her that he wouldn't be applying to colleges. Even better, she was furious when he got arrested one night for causing a public disturbance with his friends. *You'll never amount to anything!* she shouted during an argument in July of 2007 (just a few months after the family had moved from Montreal to Massachusetts), and the next day Max packed his things and drove to a fresh start in Boston.

He would have driven to Hell itself to get away from Mom.

In the years since Max's father died of esophageal cancer when he was eleven, the brightest light in his life had been his sister, Jocelyne. They'd been best friends growing up and remained close even after Max moved to Boston at eighteen. Jocey had always been supportive of him, religious but not oppressively devout, her faith elevating her in Max's eyes because she was strong but not fake or pretentious.

But that had all changed in December of 2007. Knowing his mother would be at the university until after five o'clock, Max had traveled home to central Massachusetts with his roommate one Friday afternoon to pick up his remaining possessions, which he'd expected to find boxed up and stored in the basement or the attic out of sight (painful reminders of the failure who'd moved away to Boston).

An unfamiliar car was parked in the driveway that afternoon, probably Jocey's boyfriend's car. She'd spoken to Max on the phone about how much she liked this guy from her new school, and he'd told her to go slowly because the guy might be trying to use her. But what happened that day was anything but slow. As Max and his roommate climbed the stairs, they heard muffled sounds emanating from Jocey's bedroom at the end of the hall. Max assumed she and her boyfriend were watching something on TV, but when they got a little closer the sounds became sharper, indicative, definitely not the TV, Max's fists clenching.

His roommate grinned. "He's railing your sister, man," he whispered. "Are you gonna take that shit?"

Max, feeling like he'd burst with rage, wanted to kick down the door and beat the guy senseless – but he couldn't humiliate his sister. There was no stopping what was already in motion, a snowball that had probably been rolling for some time now.

Forced to take everything in with disbelieving
dread, it seemed all Max could do was listen
helplessly as Jocey made awful little sounds of
satisfaction.

But no, this couldn't be happening! Somewhere in
the furthest recesses of Max's mind, way, way back
there, he hoped this was just a joke, that she'd
somehow known he was coming and planned to set
him up. But he hadn't told her he would stop by –
this was no joke.

Her pleasure escalating, Jocey called out to a far
different god than the one whose guidance she
sought in prayer. Motionless with shock, Max was
momentarily robbed of breath, his roommate gaping
and smiling with perverse enjoyment.

But this couldn't be possible. This couldn't happen
to Jocey, who wore her Sunday dresses and sang
religious crap along with their mother and all the
other churchgoing frauds; Jocey, who hadn't taken
off her crucifix since turning fifteen; Jocey, who'd
worn a purity wristband last year as part of a church
group initiative.

Jocey…a slut? It was beyond unthinkable, as
though she'd become another person.

Max trembled with fury. In a disillusioned flash, he
remembered the little girl who'd followed him
everywhere, looked up to him, and wanted to be just
like her big brother, the red-cheeked little bundle of
winter gear he'd helped whenever she fell on the
skating rinks and couldn't get back up, the little

person he'd shared marshmallows with during campouts at Lake St. Pierre, so small and fragile and impressionable.

A weird lifting pressure coiled its way up Max's chest, heavy with realization of change and inevitability. He couldn't look out for Jocey anymore, couldn't keep her from getting hurt.

Resignedly, Max turned away from his sister's room, away from the disgusting noises, away from the past, shoving Billy Moreland down the hall toward his room.

"Wow, talk about a homecoming to remember," Billy murmured.

"Shut your mouth!"

Billy shrugged. "Relax, dude, it's no biggie. Catholic girls need action to balance out all of that...Catholic shit."

His head throbbing at the temples, Max grabbed Billy by the collar and forced him against the wall. "Would you shut the fuck up already!" he snarled.

"Okay, okay. Just chill, bro."

Max released his roommate. "Let's just pack this shit up and get out of here."

The room was hot and stuffy. Max's things were just as he'd left them, some items in boxes and the rest awaiting assignment. Even a few papers remained scattered across the floor, as if his mother hadn't stepped inside the room since he left. Max packed things quickly, angrily, throwing them into boxes. He couldn't wait to get back to Boston, but a few minutes later there was a knock on the door.

"Max, you're home!" Jocey exclaimed, hurrying over to embrace him (seemingly oblivious to the scarring auditory show they'd just put on). But, standing behind her, the boyfriend looked nervous – he knew they'd been snagged.

"I didn't even hear you come in. When did you get here?" Jocey said, noticing Billy for the first time. "Hey, I'm Joss, Max's sister." Max hated the nickname Joss, which she'd begun calling herself since living in the States. What was wrong with Jocey, the nickname everyone knew her by in Montreal?

She extended her arm. Smirking, Billy shook her hand. "Billy Moreland, Max's roomie. Nice to meet you, Joss. I hope we didn't bother you guys by showing up unannounced."

Jocey's face went a little red. She looked down, then behind her at the boyfriend, then at Max. "This is my boyfriend, Nate Overbrook."

The guy stepped forward and the nightmare was complete, Max obligated to shake the hand that had just fondled his sister. By the transitive property of unwashed hands, Max was essentially touching

Jocey's…NOOO, anything but the hand that had pleasured parts of his sister never to see the light of church. And as if the situation wasn't unbearable enough, stuck in Max's head was the image of a five- or six-year-old Jocey from a large family portrait he'd just passed in the hallway – a girl who'd endured her father's death at age eight and was now growing up way too fast.

"Good to finally meet you," Nate said, and Max could barely muster, "Yeah, hey." He was going to lose his lunch right here, a sandwich and a bag of chips on the carpet. Drawing from his deepest reserves of self-control, he somehow stopped himself from breaking the guy's nose.

Things weren't the same after that day. The experience had slashed Max with a realization that his mother and sister were both just a pair of frauds. Pathetic frauds who dutifully read their hymnals each Sunday but applied little of what they preached to real life.

But I'm the most pathetic of all, Max presently thought, reflecting on everything he'd wasted, still convinced that he might discover the elusive needle of cause that had gleamed amidst the drunken haystack of his final night. There had to be a definitive reason…*Right?* Shitty as his life had been, you could always flush the Lincoln Logs down with alcohol and move on to the next day.

Why? Why the fuck did I do it?

Max was pacing, enraged not by his death but
instead the fact that he'd died for nothing,
absolutely nothing, the ultimate waste, his life no
more significant than the brownies and bits he used
to launch down the gurgling pieholes of time and
oblivion.

Worst of all, what had his death done to Jocey?

Chapter 2

In April of 2008, Max was invited to Jocey's birthday party, a sweet sixteen at the house. He reluctantly attended, even though he knew it would be a day from Hell, wondering during the trip from Boston if he was making a terrible mistake.

Many of Jocey's friends from her new school were there, as was Nate, sitting across from Max at the dining room table and probably envisioning Jocey naked. And beside Jocey was Mom, who directed occasional glares at Max. *I'm inviting you not because I want you in my home but because Jocey wants you here*, she'd said on the phone. Thanks for calling, Mom!

Max hated that his mother viewed Jocey as a perfect little angel who could do nothing wrong, when she was actually just a better pretender than Max had been. It was so twisted that, if Max hadn't been the victim of the cycle, he would have found it funny. He was the "indolent sloth", the "apostatizing fool", the "uneducated bum", constantly compared to Jocey's unfaltering ambition and righteousness. Just because he'd stopped going to church after his father died, he was a friend of Satan, perhaps even a drinking buddy.

"Do you know how well your sister's doing? She understands what it means to be a good Christian, and God has rewarded her," his mother said when they had a private moment an hour after Jocey blew out the candles and unwrapped her gifts. Her favorite gift would probably come that night (these were the kinds of deranged thoughts Max had been having since December, certified appetite killers).

Max almost laughed, thinking back to that afternoon when his ostensibly Perfect-Christian-Sister had evinced glaring streaks of imperfection. Max had learned more about Nate during subsequent phone calls with Jocey; she said she loved him, but it was painfully obvious that he was using her. That's what jocks did – why couldn't Jocey see it? She wasn't going to marry this guy. She didn't really love him. She was more than a year younger than Nate, and how could you possibly love someone after only a few months, anyway? She'd barely known Nate four months at the time of the December Debacle.

Max shook his head. "Whatever, Mom. I don't want to fight with you."

"Neither do I," his mother shot back. "You know, Max, it's not too late for you to have a life again. I have connections – I can still get you into a good college."

"But I do have a life. I've got a job, an apartment...I met a new girl last week."

"Please, Max, you have nothing. You don't even have God to guide you now that you've abandoned Him. I'm ashamed to tell people what you're doing – I have to tell them you're away on charitable missions. Do you know how hard it is for me?"

Max bit his lip. Even though he'd endured her caustic words for years, they still had a way of burrowing deep and stinging him.

"You're so selfish," she continued. "Jocey would never put me in this position. She knows the Christian way, Max. She embraces it, and her life reflects that."

It took every bit of strength for Max to remain quiet but he did, remembering how close he and Jocey had once been. He couldn't rat her out, couldn't subject her to the wrath of Anya Leclaire. If Mom learned that Jocey had given it up at fifteen, she would probably crucify her at the church Sunday morning.

"Mom, we're not gonna have this conversation again. I'm done."

His mother scowled, eyes as sharp as barbed wire. "You won't even consider my offer about college? Don't you want a life?"

"I don't need your college friends to succeed," he snapped. "I can do it on my own. You watch."

Later, Max joined Jocey and Nate for a night out; she'd insisted that Max come along so he could get to know Nate better. At dinner, Max's view of Nate changed a little. He was reserved, polite, and – as much as Max hated to admit it – pretty funny. And Jocey really did seem to love him, looking at the guy with the moonstruck sheen of a girl who's fallen completely for someone – a sheen with which no woman had ever regarded Max.

To Jocey's credit, during a conversation far away from their mother when she was about thirteen, she'd told Max she didn't believe in saving sex for marriage. She'd said, *As long as you love someone and want to be with that person forever*, and Max had found it refreshing. Maybe this was it for her. Maybe she'd stumbled into love. But Max was unconvinced – he still thought the guy would devastate her. It was too good to be true. Nate had simply gone after the new girl from Montreal – the French-speaking novelty – and he was having some fun with her before moving on. He still might even dump her via text.

In the movie theater restroom, another two hours gone by, Max warned Nate that he would be **REALLY** sorry if he hurt Jocey.

"I'd never hurt her," Nate blurted. "Max, I love your sister. She's the best friend I've ever had." There was honesty in his eyes, something deep and defensive, as if he'd been insulted by Max's threat.

Max felt conflicted. He hoped the guy was telling the truth, but for now all he could do was wait for Jocey's depressed phone call.

A call that would come more than two years later.

Chapter 3

While Max brooded about his sister, his mother, and
the existence he'd run from, things in his new life
continued to spiral in the summer of 2008. He
couldn't muster much energy for his girlfriend;
something just wasn't clicking. It often felt forced,
even the kissing, Max wondering why he kept
trying so hard.

Inevitably, they broke up, each side agreeing that
the severing of the relationship was in the best
interest of both parties, a brief transaction nullified.
Thankfully. He met a new girl a month later, but she
was the exact opposite personality of her
predecessor, way too charged up and talky, like one
of those little dogs that yap and jump and skitter
tirelessly about, the ones that have a strange habit of
growling at much larger dogs. Tina was her name,
and she tried to rip Max's clothes off one night after
getting drunk, continually saying, "Oui, oui, my
little Frenchy." Max feigned an illness and left
without the jacket she'd yanked off but with his
virginity still intact.

Months later, around Halloween, Max met a girl he
really liked. Jennifer Locke was a college student at
Boston University majoring in veterinary medicine.
She loved animals and was a big Bruins fan, which
Max – a diehard Habs supporter – could easily get
over because she was beautiful and funny and
passionate. He loved her smile, loved her laugh,
loved the stupid jokes she always told. They got
along great, possessing many of the same interests

(outside of favorite NHL hockey team), and it wasn't long before they were in a relationship.

Weeks passed. Their bond strengthened with every moment, and Max found himself ready to move to the next level and tell her he loved her. This was it, the love little Jocey had found at fifteen. Max knew it in his heart, felt it as strongly as he'd felt anything.

But then he returned to Boston one morning after a trip to see friends in Montreal. He wasn't supposed to be back until the next night, but he couldn't go another day without seeing Jenny. Flowers in hand, he had just stepped off the elevator at her apartment building when he saw her in the hallway outside her unit…kissing another guy, some tall scumbag in a suit. They turned, spotted him. Max dropped the flowers and took the stairs, blinded by rage, leaping down to the landings. He loved this girl; she was supposed to be the one, but no, she was just a fraud like everyone else, another lying phony.

Max tore down the street, blew a red light, his hands shaking, another lesson learned, another board of the old life rotted, a new segment added to the foundation under construction – the one that would support his suicide.

Jenny Locke was his final girlfriend.

Confined in his prison within the walls, unable to sleep or eat or enjoy the pleasures of the life he'd forfeited, Max was deep in thought about Jenny's betrayal when the door to his former bedroom clicked open. He glanced through the wall, an ability to which he'd grown accustomed, but the old woman wasn't walking in, not this time. Instead, a young man and woman stepped through the door – and it didn't take long for Max to recognize them.

"Jocey!" he shouted. She wore a blonde wig but it was undoubtedly her. And there was Nate behind her, with big glasses and a baseball cap. Had they gotten back together? What were they doing here?

There were a million questions. Max jumped to his feet and banged on the wall, reminding him of his early days in captivity. He'd pounded and kicked the walls for hours in search of an escape, but he hadn't even been able to achieve a single crack in the sheetrock. Tonight was no different.

When Jocey pointed at the perpendicular wall to Max's right, Nate sliced it open with a knife and then busted out the sheetrock with his boots. Jocey stood behind him, arms crossed, anticipation lighting her eyes. They were trying to free him! They somehow knew he was trapped and had come back for him. Max shouted frenetically, but they couldn't hear him. He was on the other side, impossible to reach.

But then something happened, something Max had never experienced before. When he punched the wall in frustration, he lost his balance and fell through it without causing a hint of damage. Now he was in his old room, scrambling to his feet and racing over to his sister. He called her name and tried to hug her, but his arms passed right through and came away warm, as if he'd stuck them in front of a heater.

Recoiling, Jocey yelped in surprise.

"What is it?" Nate turned from the wall; he'd cut and kicked out a rectangular hole about four feet high and two feet wide, chunks of sheetrock forming a dusty pile on the other side.

"I...I don't know," Jocey said, her eyes darting about the room. "I just felt something cold, like *really, really* cold." Her fear had yielded to a wary excitement. "I think it worked! Max, can you hear me?" She was studying the room again, even the ceiling.

Max resumed his shouting to no avail. He felt moisture in his eyes. They'd never be able to see each other again, he feared, not after what he'd done. Worse than being dead, worse than being stuck in the wall – the worst part of all – was realizing that Jocey somehow knew what had happened to him.

Tears running down his cheeks, Max sat on the old woman's bed, listening to his sister as she toured the apartment and called his name. Finally she returned to the bedroom, where Nate hugged her and told her they didn't have long – and then they were both calling for Max, tapping uselessly at the walls. But how did they know about his imprisonment? Was it something in the Bible, maybe something Mom had told her? Max had never paid attention to all of those dumbass Bible stories, but now he wished he'd read Mom's favorite book – then maybe he would have known what his little sister knew.

"Come on, babe, let's get out of here," Nate said. "Maybe it worked and we just can't see him, you know? Maybe he went to Heaven already."

She nodded, bit her lower lip, eyes still searching. "Thanks for doing this, Nate. I love you so much." She hugged him again. Then they left the bedroom and headed for the front door in the living room.

Max followed them, screaming for them to stay. "Please don't go, Jocey! I'm here! I'm right fucking here!" He tried to grab her arm, but flesh passed through flesh yet again.

"There it is, that cold air!" She spun around and smiled. "I really think he's here! Max, where are you? Can you hear me?"

Max was standing directly in front of her now. "I'm right here, Jocey! Why can't you hear what I'm saying?" He tried to offer another guiding chill, but she didn't feel it this time.

Desperate, Max reached for a paperback novel on the coffee table, hoping to throw it against the wall and get their attention, but the thing was glued to the table, as was every other object.

"Come on," Nate said. "That lady's probably on her way back. We need to go."

Jocey scanned every wall. She looked distressed, haunted, ambivalent, wanting to stay but knowing she had to go.

Please don't leave me, Jocey! Max made a final attempt at communication. It failed, of course. IT FAILED!!!

Collapsing to his knees beside the coffee table, Max sobbed until the old lady returned home many minutes later, a few plastic bags of groceries in hand. Max pulled himself up and accidentally brushed the thin paperback off the table; it fell to the floor and bounced onto its front cover, exposing a black and white photo of some gloomy author. Max stared at the book for a few disbelieving seconds. Now that Jocey and Nate were gone, it apparently didn't matter if he could move the book – clearly whatever controlled him hadn't wanted him to interact with his sister.

As the old woman unloaded her bags and placed items in drawers and cabinets, humming happily as she went about her work, Max's anger slowly rose toward the boiling point. He could feel himself heating up like an egg in a pot of water on the stove…hotter, hotter, burning, scalding with guilt…and it was suddenly too much to bear. The water sizzling over, Max flew into such a tumultuous, inexorable storm that nothing could stop him, not even himself, taking out every ounce of pent up rage on unit 420. He shattered glassware, hurled paintings down from the walls, overturned furniture, moving from room to room like a tempest destroying everything in its path. His thoughts were of the life he'd cut short but mostly of Jocey, his endlessly devoted sister whom he'd once considered to be a slut and a fraud.

But Jocey hadn't deserved his awful judgments. She had been strong and Max had been weak. He'd allowed contempt, loneliness, and selfishness to fester in his heart until something ugly and dangerous was constructed, never confronting his problems or even acknowledging them. Now everyone was paying for his weakness.

You'll never amount to anything!

When Max finally emerged from the storm of destruction, he was amazed by the immense damage he'd done. Lamps lay smashed and forever darkened. The lucky paintings were slanted on the walls, the unlucky ones in pieces on the carpet. Fragments of colorful glass sparkled like diamonds. And amid the devastation was the old woman, lying dead at the center of the living room, probably of a heart attack.

Max hurried to her side and attempted to revive her, but she was gone. His actions had killed her.

Chapter 4

Joss was quiet on the way home, looking out the window as they headed west on the Pike. Nate didn't know what to say or how to console her. She'd agreed that their actions might have released Max, but anything short of concrete evidence wasn't good enough for her. She wanted proof that could never be provided, and Nate knew there wasn't anything more he could do. *Dammit!* He wanted so badly for her to have closure. If only there was some way she could know Max had gone to Heaven, but how could anyone know that about any loved one?

She would just have to move on, plain and simple. Nate had recently entertained ideas of a miraculous meeting between deceased brother and living sister – a transcendent paranormal experience that would set Joss's mind at ease – and now he felt like an absolute moron for having come up with such thoughts. There would be no spirit rising skyward, no glittering cloud to represent Max's ghost, no revenant resembling a person as Mason had appeared.

Nate stopped at the Framingham Plaza for a bathroom break and a very brief refueling (at the Pike's overpriced stations, you only got as much gas as you needed to reach your destination). Nate regretfully put fifteen dollars into the tank, wishing he'd fueled up back home. Five minutes later, Joss still hadn't exited the building; maybe she'd gotten a craving for something at the convenience store.

But when Nate walked inside, he found her in the atrium, staring vacantly at a tourist information board that included a lighted map of Massachusetts.

He called her name, but her eyes remained on the board, her hair tousled from being stuck under the wig. She looked uncannily beautiful, but Nate couldn't appreciate the moment, too worried about his girlfriend. For a while he watched her from a distance of maybe twenty feet. She was breathing shallowly, unblinking, making not the slightest movement as she stared fixedly at the board, oblivious to Nate's presence.

He came beside her. "Joss, what are you doing?" Still no movement, nothing.

Panicked, he touched her shoulder and she blinked once, then moved her head very, very slowly to the left. Her eyes were glazed and scary, deep with some unknowable burden. Finally she came out of it, blinking rapidly, and it was as if she'd awoken in a new place following hypnosis.

"Where are we?" Her voice was soft, surprised.

Luckily, there was no one in this section of the building, only a janitor mopping the dining area behind them, which was closed off by retractable overhead gates.

Nate touched her cheek, icy and short of color. "We're at the rest stop," he whispered. "Did you pee? You said you needed to go, remember?"

She looked confused, afraid, embarrassed. "Ah...yeah, that's right. No, I didn't go." She hurried into the bathroom, emerging a few minutes later with damp hair and a refreshed face, her eyes normal again.

"Are you feeling okay?" he said on their way out. "What was that all about?"

She shrugged. "I don't know. Since Max's death, I've been getting really lightheaded and tired sometimes. I must have, I don't know...gone into a daze or something."

"What were you thinking about? Could you even hear my voice?"

"No, it was like I fell asleep, probably just too much stress from everything we did. I got myself all worked up, so stupid. I can't believe I forced you to go to Boston with me."

He took her by the arm before she reached the car. "Hey, it wasn't stupid, okay? Don't say that. After what we went through, it was worth a shot."

She was briefly quiet, seeming tired and defeated. "I love you, Nate. Thanks so much for coming."

"I love you, too," he said, and they shared a brief yet passionate kiss, a single action carrying more weight than any words that could have been spoken.

Joss slept the rest of the way home. A few flashing
State Police cars zipped by on the eastbound side of
the Pike, and Nate couldn't help but think they were
on their way to South Boston, hurrying to the scene
of the crime. Ridiculous, yes, but he could sense
paranoia lurking.

Maybe the anxiety had been eating at Joss as well.
She'd never even been pulled over or received a
parking ticket, not a single detention in high school.
She wasn't used to breaking the rules or going out
of bounds, but ever since her brother's suicide she'd
been unpredictable. She'd even gone to Montreal
with a friend for a week in early November to take
her Aunt Laina up on an offer made over the
summer to be a lingerie model. Laina, a high profile
fashion designer in Quebec who specialized in
lingerie and ran her own company, had asked Joss
in July if she'd be interested in being on the other
side of the camera for a change. She had even
offered Joss two thousand dollars for a spread of
photos in different garments. *Thanks, but no thanks*,
had been Joss's initial response, or something
politely similar, but in November she'd said it
wasn't a big deal, returning to Massachusetts a
week later with five pieces of lingerie that had
temporarily silenced Nate's worries and questions.

But now his concerns were back. This was a
different girl, a changing girl. Nate wished he knew
how to stabilize her, suddenly fearing she might
break down. The combination of his drug addiction
in the spring, losing Max in September, learning her
boyfriend had slept with another girl, and the

haunting at 99 Deepwoods Drive had clearly affected Joss in far more deleterious ways than Nate had originally realized. He thought the latter ordeal had brought them closer and strengthened their love, when in reality it might have driven Joss to the brink of a nervous breakdown. In fact, the longer he thought about it, the more disturbed he became. Joss no longer wore her crucifix; her phone conversations with her mother were much shorter; she drank often; she spoke almost daily about saving Max's soul; and she maintained a dramatically increased sex drive.

Maybe this latest move had been a huge mistake, he worried, an attempt to bring Joss peace that could have instead thrust her into chaos. Nate felt like they were in the middle of the night woods with no compass, navigating uncharted territories. If they didn't find their way soon, he feared things might get even worse for Joss.

At least the semester was over and he could keep an eye on her. He suddenly didn't want to let her out of his sight.

Chapter 5

Less than twenty-four hours after Nate and Joss broke into the witch's apartment and cut open her bedroom wall, Mike stood on the deck outside unit four, doing his best to convince Katherine Grafton that she needed to move away from this place for her safety and that of her son.

Seeing the kid from his nightmares in person was like being soaked with ice water. Now Mike's urgency was soaring. If the Graftons didn't leave unit four soon, Blake would be stalked just as he'd been in Mike's nightmares, a boy unknowingly walking into evil's web.

Katherine looked frightened out of her wits, but that didn't necessarily mean she would leave. Mike had to ensure she realized her son was in danger.

"I encourage you to research the mass suicide online," he said. "You'll find several articles about Joseph Johansen, the defrocked priest who owned this place in the sixties. He organized a suicide cult, and it happened on Christmas Eve in the basement. Eight people died, one of them as young as sixteen."

Turning away in disgust, Katherine walked to the edge of the deck and leaned over the railing. "I can't believe this. Whit was right. She knew this place felt wrong." There was a tearful echo in her voice. "We obviously can't live here anymore, but we've put so much money into this. What are we gonna do?"

She seemed to be talking mostly to herself now, but Mike stepped in beside her. "If you need a hand in packing up your stuff and moving, I'd be glad to help. What's most important is that you leave right away. They never should have rented this place again – that only happened because the previous landlord died and left the building to his son. I'm sure this new company will refund your security deposit and first month's rent – if not, I'll have a word with them for you."

She faced him, wiping away her tears. "What did you say his name was, the priest?"

"Joseph Johansen." Mike spelled the name. "Do as much research as you need to. The two renters who committed suicide this year, although both of their deaths were suspicious, were named Blake Gaudreau and Jane Keppel. Information about them can be found online, too, but I can put you in touch with Chief Strait if you'd like. I can even have you talk to my nephew about what he went through – anything you need."

She began pacing the deck, overwhelmed, hands on her head. Mike couldn't imagine what it would be like to receive such news. "I knew there had to be some reason why the rent was so low," she murmured. "I guess I was just hoping I'd finally caught a break."

Mike's instincts told him there wasn't a husband or a boyfriend in the picture. Katherine conveyed a survivor's fortitude he'd seen in many abused women over the years, a passionate resolve to move forward and provide the best possible life for her child. But that life couldn't happen here. This place would only lead to darkness for all who inhabited it, as Nate and Joss had found out in quick fashion.

Pulling his business card from his wallet, Mike said, "I wrote my cell number on the back. If you need any further information or help, don't hesitate to call. I've got a son of my own, and I'd never, ever let him live in a place like this. It's just too dangerous."

She nodded feverishly, accepted the card with shaky hands. "Thank you so much for telling me. I...I don't know how to thank you."

"Just get out of this place as soon as possible. Tell your son they had to close down the building due to a contaminated well or something. He doesn't need to know the truth – he just needs to be far, far away from here. Meanwhile, I'll ask Chief Strait if he knows of anywhere you can stay. When Nate was searching for apartments in the area, there were a few rooms for rent available. That might work for you, at least for now. Anything is better than living here."

***

Katie studied the business card as her shocking visitor descended the stairs and headed back to his car.

Michael Overbrook
Chief of Police, Town of Elkins, MA

Katie hurried back inside. A quick internet search verified Overbrook's identity; and the Elkins Police Department's homepage featured a photo of the man who'd just come to warn her about her new apartment. She couldn't fathom it, couldn't wrap her mind around anything he'd said. For a few seconds she actually wondered if a reality television crew would knock on the door and say this was all a prank orchestrated by Whit and Mandy.

But no cameramen or sleazy hosts appeared. This was real, every word of every story. Reading about the mass suicide online, she learned that the youngest victim, sixteen-year-old Mason Blackwell, had died along with his father, a World War II soldier who'd earned several commendations and awards for valor. Friends of the family had described Mr. Blackwell as becoming depressed following the death of his wife, and he'd easily identified with Johansen's dark ramblings.

Katie closed her laptop. It was all too much. Eight people had really killed themselves in this very house more than forty years ago – and people were still dying here, chaos still ruling 99 Deepwoods Drive.

I have to get Blake out of this place! Tonight!

They would pack a few bags and stay at a motel, anywhere but here. And the landlord or his company would foot the bill; Katie was sure of that.

It couldn't be legal to not report at least the most recent crimes occurring here, especially with the suspects still at large. An urge crisped through Katie to call a lawyer – what that company had done was not only wrong but reckless.

What are we gonna do? she worried, walking into the kitchen with her hands clasped above her head. They'd need to find a new place soon. More apartment tours, more packing and unpacking, more hefting and hauling. This was a disaster, a high-speed train wreck that somehow made perfect sense considering her life had been a series of derailments since high school. She should have anticipated another setback, or at least been better prepared for one. Now she was blindsided, completely invested in her new life but suddenly thrust into a panicked exit from the place she'd thought would become her home.

Katie wanted to scream. She was so disturbed and preoccupied with Overbrook's revelation that she didn't initially notice her son was missing when she walked back into the living room to search for the landlord's phone number. It was listed somewhere on the rental agreement papers she'd been given, but where had she put them?

Finally, as she was about to leave the room after finding the paperwork in a folder, she realized Blake was no longer watching television. The TV had been shut off, something Blake hadn't done before (he could turn it on perfectly fine but never the other way around).

"Blake, we need to talk for a second," she called,
but he wasn't in the bedroom, kitchen, or bathroom,
either.

Fear seized her, a vise grip that made it hard to draw
air.

"Blake!" she shouted, her chest throbbing with a
sharp pain that quickly subsided.

She ran out onto the deck and glanced down at the
side yard. The lawn was empty, illuminated by a
security lamp recently affixed to the side wall of the
building.

"Oh God!" she whispered, momentarily frozen
before tearing through the property in a panicked
search for her son.

He wasn't in the front yard or the parking lot.
"Blake! Blake, where are you? Blake!" Katie
returned to the apartment, praying he was hiding.
But he'd never hid from her before, not once.

She flung open each closet door, every cabinet,
checked the bathroom twice, but her son was gone,
not inside or outside. Mike Overbrook's warnings

and Blake's nightmare from a few weeks ago
suddenly collided head on, and she instantly knew
he'd been taken.

Hands trembling, she dialed 911.

Chapter 6

Shortly after destroying his former apartment and causing the old lady to die of a heart attack, Max fell asleep. When he awoke, he was imprisoned within a new set of walls. The space was narrow, maybe forty feet in length, with two little recesses at each end. There was an arched window halfway up the far wall; layered with dust and cobwebs, it allowed very little sunlight to seep through but enough to define the room.

Max wondered if he was in Hell. His tantrum had resulted in a woman's death, and he hadn't even considered the overwhelming distress his destruction might cause. Just like the night of his suicide, he'd activated his impulses without regard for others, blind to the consequences. Now Jocey was left without a brother, lost and devastated...and a lady was dead. There was no way to undo his crimes, no way to go back – the only option was to figure out where he was and face the results of his impetuous actions.

Similar to the walls of his former prison, Max couldn't damage these walls or the dusty window. He could, however, see through the walls into three rooms: a kitchen, a bedroom, and a living room. Beyond the near wall of the prison was a bathroom that connected to the kitchen. In it was an attractive young woman, showering and sobbing. Face red and puffy, she just let the water hit her and cried, minutes passing and still she cried and cried, eventually collapsing to her knees and rocking back and forth, holding herself.

Max wondered what had happened. Something very serious, perhaps the loss of a loved one? He couldn't hear her sobs – couldn't hear anything on the other side – capable only of watching the woman as she toweled off and dressed. Her right shoulder bore a heart tattoo, her hips decorated with flowers. She was toned and trim but not nearly as thin as Jocey, who Mom had always encouraged to gain weight because she looked "anorexic and ungodly."

Finally the woman stopped crying, scarcely improving to a jittery, indecisive mess. It seemed she couldn't commit to anything, darting through each of the rooms and almost completing several tasks, including taking out the trash (she pulled the bags out of the bins but left them untied against the cabinet). Max, the former janitor, cringed at this occurrence. *Tie them up or they might tip and spill trash everywhere*, he thought.

After five minutes, the woman did get around to tying them up, then gathered her keys and purse from the countertop and left the place through the kitchen door. Everything was still now, a cumbersome stillness that weighed upon Max and forced him to contemplate how he'd ended up here, not only his decisions in death but also those that had marred the final years of his life.

He'd developed a predilection for alcohol following the Jenny Locke Debacle in late 2008. It seemed everything in his life had been destined to become a debacle – the December Debacle, the Jenny Locke Debacle, the Religious Mom Debacle (that had been a lifelong debacle). And Billy Moreland, a roommate who'd become a good friend in spite of his constant ball-busting, had always been ready to throw these disasters in Max's face at the bar and, worse, narrate the miserable stories to others. *Dude, did I ever tell you about the time I went to this kid's house and we heard his sister not only getting banged, but having the orgasm of her life?* And: *This kid's mom is so religious she probably tried to friend Jesus on Facebook. No, she's so religious that I bet she reads the Bible on the toilet!* A longtime favorite of Billy's: *This poor kid caught his girlfriend cheating on him. He'd brought her flowers and everything, and there she was smooching some guy outside her apartment! For Christ's sake, buy the kid a beer already. Can't you see he's down on his luck?*

Max had known he would have a hangover the next morning when the stories actually seemed funny – and the hangovers started piling up that fall and winter. Several nights a week, he and Billy would play pool and talk with women at the bar, swapping tales of their misfortunes and ribbing each other over their pathetic lives. Billy had lived in New York City until middle school, then became "a masshole", his single mother doing her best to support him and his two brothers. College had been out of the question, not with their financial standing

and Billy's average grades. He wound up working
as a trash collector, no way out of the pond –
impossible to rise above mediocrity – and he often
questioned why Max had elected to leave the oceans
of affluence in favor of a rundown apartment in
South Boston.

But being rich had come with a high price.

Sometimes, when he'd been drunk enough, Max
had actually regretted not going to college. But
then, in the lucid world, he'd realized he made the
right decision, even if he was stuck as a janitor. He
never would have been able to live as a man molded
by his mother, some God-loving, churchgoing prig
with a degree and an **I LOVE JESUS** poster in his
bedroom. Mom had pushed him so hard in that
direction that he'd been relieved to finally get away,
regardless of where he'd gone to escape. A lifetime
of penury would trump a hollow life of wealth,
worship, and fraudulence, he'd determined, religion
the greatest fraud of all. There was no such thing as
God! Why hadn't his mother and Jocey been able to
see it? If that "merciful Lord" they kept talking
about really existed, he would have ended his
father's suffering after the third, fourth, fucking
fifth month. The man was dying, God, rotting from
within, as weak as an August stream. *Keep praying,
just keep praying,* his mother had said, and Max and
Jocey had done just that, kneeling before their beds
and begging God to make Dad better. *Not like that,*
Mom said one night. *You're doing it wrong. Pray
for his soul to be saved, not his body.* Little Jocey
looked up at her, confused, a few of her front teeth

missing – to be exchanged for quarters that night but only if she prayed hard – and then she held her brother's hand and prayed for Dad's soul.

But it had all been worthless. Dad died, DIED, gone, never to take them to a Canadiens or Expos game again. Mom was a wreck, alternating between periods of inactivity and hyperactivity like a crazy person, trying out different antidepressants and cursing herself for doing so. And Jocey was smashed up so hard by depression that she pissed herself during nightmares and had to wear diapers to bed for months. She wouldn't eat, sometimes wouldn't even talk. It got so bad that Mom brought her to a specialist in Montreal, telling Max before each trip to pray for his sister's emotional recovery. Pray, pray, pray – what a farce! Max didn't need prayers or God or church, and he didn't require diapers, either. He got through it by inhaling and exhaling, one breath at a time, one second, one hour, one day, one leg in front of the other, just like Dad would have done. He forced himself to concentrate in school, forced himself to help his mother with Jocey, spending hours talking with his anemic sister and telling her stories. He was strong for her because he had to be; he was the man of the house now, and Jocey needed him to help her cope.

Eventually – his mother would later credit the specialist and God – Jocey overcame her grief, but Max knew it was the result of the kindness he'd provided, the constant shoulder for his sister to cry on, and the hand for her to hold at three a.m. after she had a nightmare. Max had wiped her embarrassed tears away during her earliest bedwetting episodes, when she was too afraid to call Mom for fear of being jerked out of bed again and called "a weak child." But Max had told her it was okay. He'd told her not to be scared.

And so Max's new life had begun at the age of eleven, a simpler existence free of prayer and God. There were no more early Sunday mornings listening to the rambling priest, no more nights wondering why God didn't save Dad. It didn't happen because there was no God, simple as that! It had taken the death of his father, but Max finally understood that God was just an idea, an illusion people liked to pray to because it helped them feel like their families would be protected from harm. It brought them comfort, made it seem like everything happened for a specific reason and that no soul went overlooked. But it wasn't true. Sometimes people just suffered and died because their bodies failed, straight forward and scientific, no God, no angels, no beings in the sky carefully plotting out every car accident and fall down the stairs to ensure that everything happened for a reason.

It was Dad's time. He's in Heaven now, watching over us. We need to be strong and lead good lives so we can see him again one day, his mother had said, and Jocey had believed her, attending church every Sunday again – diaper-free thanks to the boundless support from Max – and praying alongside Mom. But Max had refused to go back to church no matter how many times his mother slapped him across the face and punished him, taking away his video games and forcing him to stay in his room for entire days, where he developed a passion for reading (especially challenging books from famous authors, ones that taught him new words and brought him to unimaginable places). It wasn't so bad, either. Screw church!

The punishments had only gotten worse, though. Sometimes, on particularly angry Sundays, his mother had forced him to go without dinner and locked him in a clammy basement room where dusty books, old clothes, and a small, stiff bed awaited his next crime. *If you refuse to respect He who provides your food, then you can go without it!*

But each time Max was confined, Jocey tiptoed down to the basement around midnight with a sloppily made sandwich, a bag of chips, and a glass of water. Many years later, when Max refused to report Jocey's sexual relationship to Mom, it was thoughts of his sister's midnight meals that served as one of his most prominent reasons. She was his best friend, bravely delivering the food even though she knew she'd probably be shoved into the basement room as well if caught. But she kept coming with tired eyes and nourishment, every time, to make sure her brother wouldn't go to sleep hungry. During Jocey's earliest risky trips to the basement, she asked Max why he didn't just go to church. *Even if you don't believe, do it to make her happy. Please, Max, I don't want to see you locked up anymore.* But Max stood defiant. His mother wouldn't break him. He was done with church, done with God, and even though Jocey hated his decision, she seemed to respect him for making it.

One imprisoned Sunday night in January when Max was twelve, he read a novel in three hours and was on the final page when Jocey unlatched the door at midnight, carrying a tray of food as usual. They talked during his meal as they always did on Sunday nights, a sibling ritual Max looked forward to in his long hours of confinement. But that night was different. Just as Jocey was about to return to bed, there were footsteps on the basement stairs, quickly descending. Seconds later their mother was in the doorway, her haggard face twitching, eyes bulging, a storm about to unleash its wrath.

"Jocey, how could you do…?" She seemed to run out of breath, the air getting stuck in her chest. She'd been acting especially strange lately, blaming it on a new medication.

Max and Jocey exchanged fearful glances, and Max thought about the Kansas farmers he'd just read about in the novel, the ones who'd shared a look of terror when the funnel cloud descended. But on that January night it was the tornado of Anya Leclaire that came crashing in, an EF5 twister of fury. She marched over to the little closet, grabbed a metal clothes hanger, and before Max could react – still blinking in horror – the damage was being done. Mom took Jocey by the hair and led her to the bed, her face twisting with rage.

Jocey screamed. "Please, Mom, stop! You're hurting me!" She tried to run, but Mom snatched her by the sleeve of her T-shirt and tugged her backward. Jocey fell hard, screeched, briefly crawled on the cement floor toward the door, but was yanked up.

"Stay still!" Mom ordered, but Jocey tore free. A scuffle ensued, Jocey's arms flailing, and in the chaos of trying to control her nine-year-old daughter, Mom pulled Jocey's shirt over her head with an awful rip. It fell down her arms to the floor, exposing a chest as white as printing paper.

Max tried to help his sister, but Mom glowered menacingly at him, no longer their mother but a rabid animal. "She needs to take her punishment like a big girl! Raise a hand to me, and I'll send you both to reform school!"

Stunned, Max stumbled backward, pressing himself against the far wall. Seeming to realize that continued resistance was useless, Jocey went still, whimpering at the sight of her scraped elbow. She reached for her shirt, but Mom scooped her up beneath an arm.

"How dare you refuse your mother's orders, you treacherous little sinner!" Mom carried Jocey to the bed, bent her over like a life-size ragdoll, and pulled down her happy face-patterned pajama pants with no concern for her privacy, then beat her so ferociously with the hanger that she wouldn't be able to sit without pain for weeks, every detail

imprinted maddeningly in Max's mind, the knifed air and shredded skin forever to haunt him.

"This is what happens to girls who rebel against their mothers! Stop crying! This is nothing compared to the suffering of Christ!"

THWACK! *THWACK*! *THWACK*!

Max was slack-jawed – neither he nor Jocey had ever been spanked before, but this was well beyond a simple punishment. Max thought about running upstairs and calling the police, but that would only cause more trouble, he feared, enormous trouble for him and Jocey.

It was a dizzying haze from there. Mom wasn't simply hitting Jocey but reaching way back and railing the weapon with full strength, each *THWACK* accompanied by a tortured shriek that echoed off the walls and hurt Max's ears. He didn't know how long Jocey's suffering continued, but finally it was over, their mother throwing down the blood-rimmed hanger. "I never would have expected this from you, Jocey! To betray your mother like this – it's unthinkable!", and she staggered out of the room, forgetting to latch the door behind her.

Crying uncontrollably, Jocey collapsed onto her stomach on the bed. Hurrying upstairs to grab a box of medical supplies from the kitchen cabinet, Max glanced at the bowl in which Jocey had mixed

canned chicken with mayonnaise for his Sunday night sandwich. He almost cried himself.

Following her explosion, Mom had gone out the front door and left it open, dashing out into a snowstorm, hopefully never to return. *Fucking evil bitch!!!*

When Max ran back into the basement, his sister was still on her stomach, still exposed, her backside torn open. Max would never forget the glaring contrast of coloration, runnels of blood cutting through banks of pulverized skin, Jocey's back reddened with the marks of the hand that had forced her down.

"It's okay, I'm here," he said, putting a hand on her shoulder, the skin brutally cold. She was trembling, and Max knew the physical pain was worsened by the humiliation of being stripped and beaten in front of her brother. She'd only wanted to give him a meal so he wouldn't be hungry, a humane gesture met by insanity.

Jocey's cries would not relent. "I hate her!" She pulled herself up and hugged Max. "Why didn't *she* die instead of Dad?"

Max grabbed a sweater from the closet that Jocey could wear, one of Dad's old things which Mom hadn't found the strength to discard. Jocey was right about Dad – too bad it hadn't been the other way around.

Although reluctant at first, Jocey allowed Max to medicate and bandage her wounds, wincing with each dab, yelping with the worst stings. Max was enraged, his body shaking, too. He couldn't believe how badly Mom had hurt her – physically and psychologically – and in those twisted moments of hate, caught in a dark, deranged vortex, he wished his mother dead.

Doctoring complete, Max held Jocey's small shoulders and kissed her forehead, fears ravaging him that she would retrograde back to her recent turbulence of nightmares and bedwetting. She was still so fragile and Mom had broken her, uncaring, monstrous, evil – only an evil person could force such cruelties upon a little girl…and hadn't Jocey worn those very same smiley face pajama bottoms a few Christmases ago, back when Dad was alive, the photo albums perhaps to prove it? Yes, she had, Max was sure of it…but now everything was ruined, shattered, just Max and his sister left to pick it all up.

Jocey's cheeks were streaked red, eyes bloodshot and bleary, hair disheveled. She looked like the victim of a horror movie. "This is all my fault, Jocey. I shouldn't have let you bring me food. I was scared you'd get caught one day, but I didn't think she'd do…this."

"No, it's *her* fault! I never want to see her again!"

Jocey fell to her knees and just stayed there, slumped, defeated, staring at the floor, Max

shuffling behind her and wrapping his arms around her stomach, holding his sister. After a while he lifted her into the bed, where they lied beside each other, disturbed sleep eventually claiming them.

When morning came, Max's fears were confirmed, Jocey waking up soaked and scared, red-faced when Max realized what she was trying to keep from him, even apologetic, and then she was begging him to bring a change of clothes so Mom wouldn't know.

That was Max's final time in prison. The next day, Mom told him, "I'm done trying to punish you – now you're spreading your poison to Jocey, and I won't have you corrupt her! God will deliver the ultimate punishment one day if you don't accept Him into your heart again. Just you wait, you'll suffer along with your atheist cousins! Absent church is absent faith!"

Mom bought Jocey a new video game a few days later, describing it as a reward for her continued commitment to faith. And she took Max and Jocey out to their favorite restaurant in Montreal that night, apologizing for her behavior Sunday, saying she'd recently added another antidepressant to the mix and had never imagined it would cause her to become violent.

"My physician was a fool, but don't you worry, baby. I threw those meds out, every last one. Nothing like that will happen to you again, my sweet angel. Does it still hurt a lot?" she asked during the ride to the restaurant.

"Of course it still hurts a lot!" Max snapped. "It takes her ten minutes to sit down."

"Max, I wasn't talking to you. I asked Jocey if it hurts."

"It hurts bad," she said meekly. "Don't you love us anymore?"

The car fell briefly silent. Max would always remember those words; pain of the heart could far outweigh pain of the flesh.

"I'll always love you, baby, but you have to respect me even if you don't agree with my decisions," Mom finally said, glancing at Jocey in the rearview mirror. "If you hadn't brought Max that meal, I never would have needed to discipline you."

The next Sunday, Jocey slid with great agony into a pew beside Mom and listened to the priest's words about kindness and faith and family, probably afraid of the hanger that might come if she disobeyed, the charade continuing on like it always did. If Jocey hadn't already been a good God-fearing little girl, the fury of Anya Leclaire would have rounded her into form. But Max was free of church, free of the constant lectures, free of the endless recitations of the rosary – Mom had finally given up on him. He smoked his first joint two years later, counting down the years until he could get away from his mother.

There would never be another assault. Anya Leclaire would never so much as slap her children again, but she'd caused enough damage that one snowy January night in Montreal to last a lifetime.

Max was so entangled in memories that he didn't initially notice the change in his new prison. He looked up from the floor at which he'd been staring for what might have been ten minutes or two hours, completely lost in thought.

But no longer was he alone.

Twenty feet away, lying on his back, was a boy about eight years old. A boy who would transform Maxime Leclaire.

Chapter 7

Using his cell phone, Nate once again checked websites operated by Boston news stations and couldn't find anything related to their crime. He wasn't sure why he kept expecting it to be the focus of each homepage, especially considering the amount of criminal activity in the city that was infinitely more serious than what he and Joss had done last night.

But just as he was about to put his phone away, a headline halfway down one of the websites caught his eye. *South Boston Woman Found Dead*, it read. Not thinking the story had anything to do with their break-in, Nate clicked the link and was shocked to learn that the woman's address was Max's old apartment, same street, same number, same unit – 420. The witch was dead, but there would be no singing or celebrations.

Stunned, Nate quickly pored through the short article. Apparently the woman had been found dead this morning in her heavily damaged living room. There were no signs of an assault, but police weren't ruling out foul play, refusing to provide additional information until the investigation was completed.

Nate almost dropped the phone. He was sweating even though it was fairly cold in Joss's house (having lived in Russia and Quebec, Anya Leclaire often wore T-shirts and shorts around the house in the middle of winter). Thankfully it wasn't any warmer – otherwise Nate might have passed out. His skin suddenly felt like a soaked spandex shirt.

Heavily damaged living room? But Nate had only cut open a small section of one wall in the bedroom, touching nothing else. It didn't make any sense. How had the woman ended up dead? Had someone else broken in after them and ransacked the place, then killed the lady? Or was it something…else?

"Jesus," he said beneath his breath, pacing Joss's room. "We could be in deep shit."

Fresh out of the shower, Joss emerged from the adjoining bathroom with her hair wrapped in a towel. She lotioned herself liberally per usual. She pulled black stockings up to her thighs. When a thong of the same color was hiked up her legs, Nate was taken back to the days of the "art stash" – an inconspicuous box of thongs hidden among her art and photography supplies in a chest drawer, just in case Anya had gone for an inspection one day. In Joss's dresser drawer, meanwhile, a host of granny panties had gathered dust ("Catholic clothes", as she called these garments and plenty more).

Watching his girlfriend, momentarily thinking back to how cautious she'd always had to be in order to mostly avoid her mother's suspicions, Nate considered telling Joss about what he'd learned. But then he remembered her behavior at the Framingham Plaza last night. On top of everything she'd already endured over the past three months, she might not be able to handle the knowledge that they'd inadvertently caused a woman's death, not to mention the potential legal action they might face if caught. Supposing the police could connect them to the crime, they could possibly be slapped with involuntary manslaughter charges. Nate had essentially no legal knowledge outside of what he'd seen on TV shows and movies, but he assumed they could be sent to jail for this, especially if it was discovered that their actions had caused the lady to suffer a heart attack.

But they hadn't created heavy damage! What was going on? There were thoughts of Shepherd stirring in Nate's head now, but Joss interrupted them.

"You ready for dinner with the fam?" she asked. She was still in her underwear, lithe and gracefully transfixing – but there was a rigid severity to her face tonight that made fifty percent Russian seem like an easy majority. In that moment, she looked frighteningly like her mother, Nate thought.

Carefully applying makeup using the dresser mirror (a rarity), Joss added, "Don't worry. At the rate we're dying off, you probably won't have to sit through too many more of these things."

Nate chuckled uneasily. "Come on, Joss, don't say that."

Finessing eyeliner, she said, "I'm serious. They should label our family as an endangered species."

Nate had made the right call. Now definitely wasn't a good time to bring up the tragic news. God, what had they done? That poor old lady – mean as she'd been, she might have had a heart condition or something. They hadn't even thought about how she might react upon realizing her apartment had been damaged. Nate had assumed she would call the police, make a report, and let the insurance company handle it, Joss going as far as leaving a pair of hundred-dollar bills on the kitchen countertop to help pay for repairs…but now the lady was dead!

Jesus, she's gone! In the fucking morgue!

Although Nate was held in the clutch of panic, he kept his breaths steady and tried not to betray his turmoil. Having finished with her makeup, Joss slid into a long-sleeved gray dress, then pulled on a black jacket and adjusted it around the shoulders with a few shrugs. It was hardly a Christmassy outfit (usually she wore a red sweater or blouse to holiday dinners), but she clearly wasn't in a festive mood.

Nate took a seat on her bed, watching his girlfriend and worrying about her. "You look beautiful, Joss."

She smiled faintly, as though she didn't quite believe it this time, and stepped into a pair of black ankle boots. "You don't look so bad yourself." She fidgeted with her hair. "Thanks again for coming. I know there's a hundred other things you'd rather do, but after dinner we're going out to celebrate."

"Celebrate what?"

She came over to the bed where he was sitting and put a hand on his knee. "What do you think? You survived your first semester in college." Again there was a little smile lighting her face.

He stood, held her shoulders firm. "The only thing I want to celebrate is being with you."

Now he had her smiling wider and showing off gleaming examples of dental mastery. He hadn't seen that smile nearly enough since September.

 Joss kissed him, throwing her hands behind his neck. "I love you, Nate."

"I love you too, babe. No matter how hard things get, I'm always gonna be here. You know that, right?"

She nodded. Before she could respond, he added, "By the way, if there's ever anything you want to talk about, I'm all ears. Don't feel like you have to keep it inside. I went through the same thing you did – I know exactly what you're feeling."

Her eyes briefly fell. "Are you referring to Max's death or, you know, the event?"

"Both," he blurted. "I want things to be the way they were before everything went crazy. There's nothing you can't tell me. I want us to be...I don't know, fully connected again, like we know exactly what we're thinking. Sometimes I feel like we've been a little off."

Her mouth stretched into a rictus. "I take it you're not talking about the sex."

"No, definitely not. I'm talking about some of the other stuff, like last night at the rest stop."

"Oh, yeah...that." She turned away, ran a hand through her hair. "I don't know what happened, I swear." She faced him again, eyes evasive. "I got really dizzy. Then it was like I fell asleep standing up."

"That's never happened to you before, right?"

"Only one other time. Last month in Montreal, I was getting dressed in Aunt Laina's house, and I got really dizzy. Next thing I knew, I was waking up on the ground. I thought it was just overtiredness from travel, but last night it happened again."

"Do you think maybe you should see someone?"

"No, it's just stress, I'm sure of it. Getting back to school and trying to live a normal life again will help. It's been so hard worrying if Max is suffering. I can't sleep, can't even eat sometimes." Now it was Joss who paced the room. "At least I know we've done all we can, but I'm scared it won't help. I'm scared I'll fall apart, Nate. Scared to death. The wine makes it easier, but fuck, I still get so messed up sometimes, so scared about everything."

Nate broke her pacing and hugged her. "It's gonna get better, Jocey, I promise. Just stay strong, okay?" He held her cross pendant, kissed her neck, took in the scent of her perfume. "God's gonna help you get through this, just like He always has."

Nate couldn't believe what he was saying. Suddenly he wasn't so angry at God about Rob's death, as if he'd rounded a corner without realizing it. There was no further room for spiritual hostility – he needed to commit all of his energy to helping his girlfriend through a jam. She wasn't handling the pressure, crumbling slowly before his eyes, and he felt like the only person who could help her recover. He couldn't imagine losing her, not after everything they'd overcome.

They stayed there for a little while, Nate holding her shoulders and rocking her and whispering to her. It felt good to support her again, to be the person she held when she was upset. She didn't have a father or a brother anymore; he was it, the most important man in her life.

"Let's go eat dinner before you make me cry," she finally said, looking up at him with watery eyes.

An eerie sensation swept over Nate. He no longer felt like he was looking into the eyes of an adult but the sad blue eyes of a little girl. For just a second, maybe even a millisecond, her face seemed to morph into that of nine-year-old Joss Leclaire, vulnerable in the absence of her father. Now, as then, she was so fragile and desperate, so confused and adrift. She'd been betrayed, victimized by far too many lies, repeatedly insulted – and to top it all off, her world had been shaken by the cruelest realization imaginable, that her brother was likely enduring Mason's curse.

Somewhere between that moment and the first bite of dinner, Nate became aware that Joss would require an immense amount of guidance to persist through the instability that governed her life. The very ground upon which she walked was sliding out from beneath her, and Nate prayed he had what it took to build a bridge long enough to span the gaps she would have to cross in order to finally heal.

***

At the candlelit dinner table, Joss suffered through the umpteenth prayer for Max's soul delivered by her mother. Anya had worked the prayer into her typical pre-meal grace, but it had lengthened each time and was currently better than a minute long, rambling on in a glorified characterization of Max's abbreviated life. Joss feared all the prayers in the world wouldn't help her brother, not when such a powerful force as Shepherd was pursuing him.

When it was finally time to eat, Joss quietly nibbled her mother's pâté chinois and listened to the conversation. Since everyone had conflicting schedules around Christmas, her mother, Grandfather Francois, Aunt Laina, and a few other family members had decided to get together tonight. Unfortunately, Laina's children, a few years younger than Joss, hadn't been able to make it because of school. Joss wasn't close with her cousins, but she enjoyed spending time with them on holidays and hearing about how life was proceeding up on the irresistible island of Montreal, a cherished place always to be held for the city in Joss's heart because memories of her father and brother resided there. She wished there could be more memories, that she could spend another day with Dad and Max, the best things in life always gone too soon – but sometimes, if she closed her eyes and it was quiet enough, she could envision fleetingly what might have been, peaceful and warming in its abstraction, like a daydream laced with infinite impossibilities.

In customary mealtime form, Francois slowly savored his food, especially the mashed potatoes, while Laina chattered endlessly about her career as one of the most successful fashion designers in Quebec. Joss always found the opposing personalities of her mother and Laina to be comical – a conservative, Russian, Catholic university president forced to dine with a lingerie specialist from Quebec, the ultimate clash between traditional and avant-garde. The daggers they sometimes stared at each other were often sharper than the silverware on the table, but at least their mutual dislike made dinner eventful.

In addition to their temperaments and viewpoints being one hundred and eighty degrees apart, Laina and Anya were perfect antitheses of each other in several other regards, including wardrobe preference. Mom wore a stately maroon skirt suit adorned with a golden wreath pin, which accentuated an awful white turtleneck sweater that looked to Joss like a neck brace. Across the table, Laina sported an exceedingly tight red sweater dress featuring elaborate lace embroidery, no doubt one of her masterpieces. On top of creating lingerie, she also loved designing dresses for every occasion, and this one exalted her breasts to such prominence that they almost required their own seat at the table. With a body like that, Joss didn't know why her aunt hadn't gotten photographs taken of herself for the online catalogue.

There were a handful of other striking differences between the two women that jumped right out. Mom's hair was pulled into a bun; Laina's flowed sleekly down her back. Mom lacked visible jewelry other than her wedding band; Laina wore stunning ruby pendant earrings and three garish rings, one of them so extravagantly diamonded that it might be classified as a dangerous weapon if she were to hit someone with it. The dissimilarities continued from there in a long train that stretched across the continent, two women whose only connection had been Joss's father, Jean-Philippe Leclaire.

Laina continued to talk for the next several minutes, glancing at everyone and thereby keeping them imprisoned in her garrulous cell. Meanwhile, Francois pretended to listen to his excessively talkative daughter while sipping his soup and enjoying his mashed potatoes, occasionally nodding to make it seem like he was interested in what she had to say but mostly just focusing on the food. Nate took after Francois, smiling discreetly at Joss whenever a funny or awkward moment arose. She was beyond grateful that he was here with her. Now that he'd gotten clean and turned his life around, she trusted that she could lean on him and confide in him again. He gave her much-needed confidence and made her feel like she could find her way through this, so empowering to know that he believed in her – but where had her faith and self-assurance gone?

The conversation eventually shifted to Mom's career. Laina asked her how things were going at the university, and although reticent, Mom outlined some of the new programs and initiatives. To Joss, the big words spilling from her mother's mouth translated to Boring, Boring, and Very Boring. She quickly tuned out everything and turned her focus inward, wondering what the hell was wrong with her and why she kept experiencing these weird trancelike departures from reality. They were just as she'd described them to Nate, like waking sleep events. She couldn't remember what she'd been thinking while staring at that board last night – she'd just been…asleep standing up.

Unsurprisingly, a Google search of her symptoms had revealed a plethora of diseases and afflictions: brain tumor, internal bleeding, post-concussion syndrome, lesions, etc. She'd fainted and suffered a concussion back in September after learning of Max's death, but how would that cause her to have incidents in November and December but not in

October? No, it was something else, something psychological. But what? Did it have something to do with Nate? She didn't think so, especially since she'd forgiven him for sleeping with that girl.

A better bet was Max. Maybe this all surrounded the connection between Max and Mason, particularly the knowledge that Shepherd would come for her brother just as he'd come for Mason. The demon – or whatever Shepherd was – had explicitly told her that final night at 99 Deepwoods Drive that everyone who commits suicide is eventually collected and taken to Hell. But had Mason eluded the fires intended for him? Had he risen above his sin and proven himself worthy of Heaven? There was no way of knowing, just as there was no way to tell if Max would ever get to Heaven, and that lack of concrete fact was perhaps the root of her trouble. Faith wasn't helping, not this time. The odds simply seemed too slim that Mason and Max were both in Heaven.

Why, Max? Why did you have to do it? How could you be so selfish?

Joss was vaguely aware of a hand on her thigh, Nate's hand. When she glanced at him, he nodded toward Mom, who'd apparently asked her a question. Everyone was looking at her in anticipation of her answer.

She felt her face warming. "Sorry, I was kind of spacing out."

Francois chuckled. "Too much talk tends to get everyone spaced out." Joss had always loved his blunt honesty, which had become increasingly sarcastic since his second wife's death three years back. Francois had been a professional hockey player who spent three seasons scrapping and occasionally scoring for the Chicago Blackhawks, not the sort of guy who wanted to spend his dinner listening to talk about fashion trends and college curriculum. He'd much prefer discussions about Hockey Night in Canada and who this year's Cup Final favorites were.

Frowning, ignoring her father-in-law, Mom kept her eyes trained on Joss. "Tell everyone about the great work you've been doing down at the animal shelter."

"Oh, right. Yeah, the shelter. It's been a lot of fun." Joss struggled to come up with something. She hadn't visited the shelter since October, using it as an excuse to spend time with Nate or drive to her friend Kirsten's apartment and drink wine.

As she fabricated a bunch of garbage about caring for animals at the shelter, Joss felt Nate's disapproval like a draft of cold air. It made her tingle with shame; he knew she was lying, knew she would say anything so her family wouldn't worry about her. But he also knew she was floundering, desperate to stay above water, sex and alcohol her best defenses against fear and uncertainty. Still, the dark currents kept tugging relentlessly, yanking her a little deeper with each pull, a complete submersion not far off.

Chapter 8

By the time two police officers arrived at 99 Deepwoods Drive, Katie and the landlord were already sweeping through a mostly empty building, flipping on every light they could find, their flashlights cutting through the darkened rooms, winter silence broken by their hurried footsteps.

Having come to address a problem with the elderly couple's unit out front, the landlord had put his plans on hold and joined Katie in a panicked search for her son. They were about to climb the stairs to the vacant third floor apartment when blue flashing lights caught their attention.

Katie wanted to finish searching, but she knew the police would be more efficient. Reluctantly, she followed the landlord down the stairs to the lawn, where Sgt. James Fitzgerald introduced himself and another officer.

Fitzgerald, a muscular man in his forties, took charge, asking Katie when she'd last seen her son and what he'd been doing. Katie quickly recounted the events of the previous hour, Fitzgerald's eyebrows raising when she described Michael Overbrook's visit.

"Did you see Blake after Mr. Overbrook left?" the burly sergeant asked after Katie handed him Overbrook's business card.

Katie nodded, tried to think through the haze of terror. "I went inside to research the guy online, and

Blake was still watching TV. But then I went to the kitchen, and when I got back to the living room he was gone."

Fitzgerald said, "Does your son know his address and telephone number?"

Nodding again, on the edge of new tears, shivery and wobbly, Katie reached for a strand of hair with trembling fingers. "But he's never just walked off before. I always tell him to stay close."

"What about his father? Does he live here with you?"

"I haven't seen him in years. Last I heard, he was living in Vegas. He doesn't care about Blake – never has."

Fitzgerald turned to the landlord. "We'll need to search each vacant unit and any outbuildings."

"Absolutely," the landlord said. "Whatever you need from me, just name it."

A sudden thought almost floored Katie. "Those people Overbrook talked about, the ones who terrorized his nephew – they must have done this! They took my son, officer!"

Fitzgerald lifted a hand. "We're going to find him, Ms. Grafton. Right now, the best thing you can do is return to your apartment and wait by the phone. Blake might call and tell us where he is, or maybe a call will come from a neighbor who's found him. Does Blake know the landline number?"

Katie nodded, then scrambled up the stairs to unit four, where seconds of watching both the landline phone and her cell phone turned into torturous minutes. She felt like she would pass out, terrified tears raging when Fitzgerald knocked on the door twenty minutes later. His grim face obviated the need for explanations, and Katie burst into hysteria before he'd uttered a single word.

"We cleared the entire building, every room and stairwell, even the attic and shed," Fitzgerald reported, the landlord solemn behind him. "The tenants in unit nine allowed us to search their apartment, too, but there was no sign of Blake anywhere."

Katie collapsed to her knees, feeling as if the third floor had come crashing down upon her. Blake had been watching television one minute, safe and happy, but now he was vanished.

Though Katie wanted to respond to Fitzgerald, the words wouldn't materialize. She was ensnared in a web of memories surrounding Overbrook's warnings. Someone had abducted his nephew's girlfriend from this very unit only three months ago!

"I called Mike Overbrook but didn't get a response," Fitzgerald continued. "Meanwhile, the State Police and more people from our department are on their way. We're gonna search the entire neighborhood until we bring him home."

Katie managed to stand on unsteady legs, tottering nauseously to the table and slumping into a chair. "Please, you have to save my son! Just stop talking and save my son!"

"We'll find him, ma'am. Absolutely," Fitzgerald assured, but a hint of uncertainty had crept into his eyes.

Fitzgerald spoke into his radio, then to Katie. "Is there someone we can call for you? A family member, maybe a friend?"

"Yes, my friend Whitney Golding. I'll call her – you find Blake!"

Katie spent the next several minutes lost in a desperate fog that made everything seem distorted and dreamlike. Sentences came to her in fragments, as if she'd just risen to consciousness following an operation. Her ears rang. Searching through the windows, her eyes darted frantically across the shadow-stricken lawn but failed to locate her son. Outside it was cold and hostile, the woods like portals to some unreachable place.

A part of Katie remained in disbelief, unable to admit that her son was missing, Blake, the little boy who made her life worth living.

"My God, this is bad, real bad. He's definitely not anywhere in the building," the landlord said many minutes later.

Katie and the landlord were at the end of a curving corridor which funneled beneath the heart of the building from the shed. They pointed their flashlights at a utility sink and a workbench affixed to the far wall, shadows dipping and swaying, none of the lights in this part of the basement working. A second tour through the building had proven just as futile as the first.

"NOOO!!!" Katie cried. "There must be somewhere else we can check, a crawlspace or something. Anything!"

The landlord shook his head. "I'm afraid not, at least not that I'm aware of." His words sounded so soft and distant that he might as well have been speaking to her from another room. "I pray a neighbor found him and will call any second."

Katie leaned against the wall and sobbed. Nausea burned in her stomach, climbing steadily higher, and she just made it to the utility sink in time to unload her last meal. Then, as if she'd boarded a time machine, she was back in unit four, speaking to Sgt. Fitzgerald again.

"Are you sure Blake doesn't have any friends in the neighborhood?" he asked.

"Yes, positive. And he would never leave without telling me."

When Fitzgerald finally ran out of questions, he said, "The State Police are going door to door. Because of this place's history, we've already got a missing person report on the NCIC. We're tracking Overbrook as well."

"Please find my son," Katie urged, near voiceless from shouting for Blake. "Bring him home, I'm begging you."

Whitney arrived at nine o'clock, almost three hours after the agonizing ordeal began. The searchers and their dogs still hadn't found Blake, and now there was a reporter on the back lawn, her breaths escaping in plumes of steam as she described the situation to the camera – another abduction at 99 Deepwoods Drive, this time a child.

Katie stood on the back deck, numb to the icy air, exhausted after searching the surrounding woods for an hour with the landlord and a neighbor who knew the area well from hunting. The temperature had dropped to twenty degrees, according to the last cop who'd tried to coax Katie inside. One of his colleagues from the State Police was reviewing a map of Hollisville in the kitchen; another cop spoke to someone on his cell phone.

To Katie, the scene was infuriating because these people weren't out there trying to find her son. What good would looking at a map do? It sure as hell wouldn't bring warmth to Blake on such a cold night. Katie wanted to shout at them, wanted to drive them out and demand they search the neighborhood again. The helplessness was eviscerating, tearing her open from the inside.

Katie brightened but only weakly at the sight of Whit climbing the stairs, running toward her, and now they were hugging, her best friend in her arms, Katie telling herself that Whit would know what to do. She'd known this place was bad all along.

"Oh my God, Katie, I can't believe–" Whit closed a hand over her mouth, stanched the tears. She glanced behind her, where Katie's parents were bustling up the stairs to the deck, Dad wearing a flannel pajama shirt beneath a parka. Apparently Whit had alerted them to the disaster, a well-meaning but foolish move. They would offer nothing but distractions during a time when everyone needed to stay squarely focused on finding Blake.

Mom had been crying. She embraced Katie tightly, and for a moment Katie thought she would vomit again. Her parents had hardly shown any interest in Blake over the years, viewing him not as their grandson but instead as the product of a mistake that never should have been made. No matter how many times Katie had tried to get them to see Blake as the engine that ran her life, they'd always insinuated that he was an anchor holding her in place. But here they were tonight. Now that Blake was missing, they'd found him worthy of their time.

As expected, it didn't take long for her parents to introduce distractions. In the kitchen, her father interrupted a conversation between two cops. "Have you guys investigated all of the criminals who live around here? Why didn't I see any police activity on the street driving in?"

Sgt. Fitzgerald pulled Dad aside. "Mr. Grafton, we're doing everything in our power. We're conducting interviews and following up on leads, but you need to give these guys some space to do their jobs."

"Interviews? That's just not good enough!" Mom snapped. "Our grandson's been abducted, and you're standing around interviewing people? He could be miles away by now."

"And what about this Overbrook guy?" Dad pressed, Katie having given him the truncated version of the nightmare. "He should be your top suspect."

"Chief Strait's in contact with him – apparently they're good friends," Fitzgerald said. "Overbrook should be here within the hour to join the search. He's a police chief in Massachusetts, you know."

Dad wasn't satisfied. "He should have been here an hour ago if he knows so goddamn much about what's going on. I swear–"

"Dad!" Katie shouted. "Stop bothering the police – you're wasting their time."

Whit brought Katie's parents mugs of coffee. "Let's all just calm down. We need to stop arguing and come up with a plan."

Katie willed the phone to ring. Almost as suffocating as the fear was the guilt, every second tormenting because she knew Blake's disappearance was her fault. She should have paid better attention to him, her little boy, the best thing that had ever happened to her. How could she have let this happen?

Ten minutes clicked by. Twenty. Half an hour. Still no calls. Katie's parents scowled at passing officers. It would be an exhausting night, Katie's first ever night without Blake and, far worse, Blake's first night without his mother. No bedtime tuck-in, no nightly prayers, no closing of the closet doors – Katie felt like a piece of her soul had been ripped out. It was hard to breathe, hard to think, her head beginning to throb. Her neck ached, too, hurting whenever she glanced to the left. Life as she had known it was shattered; now there was nothing but debris and no conceivable way to put everything back together without Blake here.

Although Whit wanted to make a plan, Katie knew the only thing she could do for now was bury her head in her hands and pray.

Chapter 9

Mike spent an hour after dinner Monday night playing video games with Sue and Chris, grateful for a break from the pressures he'd been feeling from various sources. But even his family game time wasn't free of interruptions. His cell phone buzzed twice in his pocket, though whoever was calling would have to wait until the conclusion of Mario Party.

When Mike descended into his basement office just after nine o'clock, his phone vibrated again. The sight of Dave Strait's name on the screen rifled cold fear into his gut. Having alerted Dave in advance about his plans to warn Katherine Grafton, Mike wasn't expecting a follow-up call, unless…

"Jesus, no!" Mike shouted upon learning of Blake's disappearance. "Whoever's doing this knew Katherine was gonna leave. They must have heard our conversation – I bet they've got the place bugged."

"And the timing couldn't be worse for you, Mikey. The state troopers – hell, even some of our guys – were talking about you like a suspect. I did some damage control, but you need to get over here ASAP and clear things up."

"Absolutely, I'm on my way." Mike slammed his fist against the desk. "I knew this would happen – I can't believe they let people move back in there!"

"You did everything you could to warn them. You were the only guy to stick his neck out there for those people. I feel terrible – I should have done more. I should have watched that place more closely."

Mike cannoned up the stairs and quickly explained to Sue that there was an emergency situation in Hollisville that Dave had asked for his assistance in solving.

"A little boy might have been abducted from Nate's old apartment, and Dave wants me there to explain to the troopers what they might be up against."

Sue nodded understandingly. "How old is the boy?"

"Seven."

She gasped. "Oh my God, go help them. I hope it wasn't the people who took Joss."

"We can only hope not."

On his way to New Hampshire, Mike resisted the urge to admit that his appearance at 99 Deepwoods Drive had caused the abductors to strike early. Judging solely by the timing of his nightmares, there still should have been at least a few days before Blake was taken. But what if Mike's surprise visit had forced the abductors to speed up their plan out of fear that Katherine Grafton would move out?

When Mike arrived at Nate's old building for the second time that night, about a dozen officers,

including Dave, were surrounding a red sedan.
Mike pulled on a beanie hat and a pair of gloves,
then stepped out of his car and joined the fray.
Eyeing him mistrustfully, a few of the officers
appeared ready to escort him from the premises, but
Dave quickly introduced him.

"Folks, this is Police Chief Michael Overbrook, of
Elkins PD. As I explained earlier, his nephew's
girlfriend was abducted from this building in
September. He came here tonight to warn Ms.
Grafton about the threat that exists, and clearly" –
he pointed to a piece of paper taped to the driver's
window of the car – "it's an extremely viable
threat."

A thick-necked, beefy cop emerged from the circle
and extended his hand. "Sgt. James Fitzgerald,
Hollisville PD. Nice to meet you, Chief."

After Mike shook Fitzgerald's hand, the sergeant
broke into an explanation of recent developments.
"We just found this warning taped to Ms. Grafton's
car. Whoever took her son, they don't want her
going anywhere."

Dave shined his flashlight on the 8.5 by 11 sheet of
copy paper so Mike could read the handwriting,
which had been produced by a red marker. Mike
instantly recognized the penmanship.

Ms. Grafton,

Do not move out of unit four. If you leave,

your son will die.

"Jesus Christ, Nate found notes warning him to stay as well. Same red pen, same exact handwriting. I can tell you without a doubt we're looking at the same suspects who took Joss, the guys who said their names were Gerald and Mason Blackwell."

"We've got the threats he's referring to in evidence," Dave said.

The State Police officers began to murmur amongst themselves, some of them writing notes. A trooper of Asian descent introduced himself as Lt. Ellis Wouk, of the State Police Missing Persons' Unit. "Chances are good these individuals are still in the area. There's clearly a reason why they want Ms. Grafton to stay."

"Or maybe they just enjoy seeing how people react after they take their loved ones," Dave said. "Couple sickos. They let Joss go unharmed – let's pray for a similar outcome tonight."

"Chief Overbrook, would you mind making a quick statement about your visit tonight?" Wouk asked. "I'd like to see if we can get a more detailed timeline and narrow down the exact time when Blake was taken."

"Sure. Whatever you need me to do, I'm on it."

"Meanwhile," Wouk said, turning to Dave, "I want to see those threats you have in evidence right away. We'll need to have a graphologist confirm the handwriting is the same."

As Mike listened to other investigators, he found himself repeatedly looking back at the house, a place he'd hoped to never see again. Uncannily, 99 Deepwoods Drive seemed to blink back at him through illuminated windows, an ominous structure conveying a silent message: Welcome home, Mike.

At half past eleven, a few minutes after the local news van rolled off into the night, Dave asked Mike for a few minutes inside his unmarked cruiser. The heat was on full blast, a thermos of coffee in the cup holder.

Dave sighed in frustration. "This is unbelievable, Mikey. I can't imagine what that poor lady's going through. This fucking house'll be the death of me."

"We'll find these guys," Mike said, pulling off his hat. "They've proven to be reckless. Sooner or later they'll make a mistake."

Dave shook his head. "Not if they…" His words trailed off.

"Not if they what?" Mike pressed.

"Never mind, it's ridiculous. It just can't be. Impossible."

"Come on, Dave, tell me what you're thinking."

"What if our suspect is the house itself?" he blurted. "Or something in it?"

There was a moment's silence as each man considered a possibility they'd discussed before.

"Almost every renter of unit four since 1981 has called the police reporting something extremely bizarre," Dave said at last. "Some came right out and said the place was haunted; others were less direct but still suggested something was off with the place. And the previous landlord told me the people from the mass suicide are still in there, but that's not even the weirdest part." A sip of coffee. "Turns out that landlord was Frank Albert, the lone survivor of the mass suicide. I found out he inherited the house from Johansen back in the sixties, which is well beyond suspicious considering they were both part of a *suicide* cult. I've been doing my research, Mikey, and this place doesn't add up. For business transactions, Albert listed his name as Alvin, even setting up separate bank accounts, but the residential records don't lie."

Looking up at the house, Mike found himself grasping for explanations. "Maybe these suspects have been at it for decades, but now they're no longer satisfied with scaring people. Maybe they want to hurt people now. The landlord, Albert, could have been part of it, maybe even the architect. Think about it – guy feels guilty for backing out of the suicide, goes a little nuts, thinks the house really is haunted, and decides to make his own haunting by terrorizing his renters."

"Yeah, I definitely need to do a lot more digging on Albert and his family. Meanwhile, would you mind asking Nate and Joss to come up here and speak to the state troopers about what they experienced? Maybe they can help a sketch artist draw images of these guys."

"I tried calling Nate tonight but didn't reach him – I think he's at dinner with Joss's family. First thing tomorrow I'll call him back."

***

Nate got a call from Mike just before seven Tuesday morning. He rolled onto his side in bed and stretched, then reached for his cell phone on the nightstand.

Yawning, he said, "Hey, Uncle Mike."

"Hi, Nate. I left a few texts and voicemails for you last night. Did you get them?"

"No, my phone died. What's going on?"

Nate wished he could have a few more hours of sleep. It had been a long night of trying to deter Joss from driving to a bar to celebrate with him the completion of his first college semester. He'd wound up playing games with her as she slowly got drunk on wine, an activity that had started as an anomaly in September and was quickly becoming a habit. She'd taken a liking to drinking at night and sleeping in late, often forgetting her early morning exercises. Even worse, she'd returned from her Montreal lingerie modeling trip with a fake I.D. – a license belonging to some woman vaguely resembling Joss named Caroline L'Ecuyer – and she urged Nate to take her to bars every weekend. It seemed that nothing short of an intervention would work, and that would go about as well as trying to navigate a raging sea in a raft. The pill popper chastising the wino – a real smart move that would be.

"You're not gonna believe this, but it's happened again," Mike said. "A woman moved into your old apartment a few weeks back, and her son was abducted last night."

"Holy shit!" Nate jolted out of bed. "I thought they closed that place down."

"They did, but it was purchased last month by some company. Anyway, the abductor taped a message to the woman's car warning her not to leave. The guy threatened her son's life, just like he threatened to tell Joss about your situation, same red ink and penmanship."

"She needs to get out of there right now! She can't stay – Shepherd will kill her!" The words had come out on their own, Nate wishing he could pull them back.

"Shepherd? Who the hell is that?"

"Forget it. You wouldn't believe it. No one would."

Mike grunted in disagreement. "Try me."

"Later. We should really talk about it in person."

***

On his way back to New Hampshire that afternoon, Mike thought of the fatal Hollow Road accident, the one he'd seen in his nightmares ten years ago but hadn't been able to prevent. A mother and her son had been killed, and now it was a new mother-son combination that haunted his visions, a new pair caught in death's crosshairs. According to what Mike had seen in his nightmares, Blake Grafton must have wandered down to the parking lot last evening, whereupon the hooded suspects had taken him. There'd been three of them in his nightmares, as well as birds circling overhead. Mike wasn't sure what the birds signified; there was still so much to learn in order for him to help the Graftons.

Northbound traffic on Route 202 was light, affording Mike a little extra time before he was supposed to meet Nate at the Hollisville PD. While stopped for a quick lunch in a McDonald's parking lot, a curious thought snuck up on him. If Blake had been taken last evening, why had Mike's recurring nightmare woken him again overnight? Assuming the event he'd been given a chance to thwart had already transpired, there seemed to be no need for ongoing nightmares…unless this was only the beginning.

Mike bit into his cheeseburger, then dipped a few fries into a puddle of ketchup on the wrapper and gobbled them up. Sue would kill him for this (he was supposed to be dieting with her), but some of his greatest ideas had come to him during fast food excursions. He'd spent a career eating whatever was convenient, though not even McDonald's could deliver the magic this time.

The thoughts and fears whirled around his head like windblown flakes in a nor'easter, elusive and enigmatic particles he couldn't manage to grasp and process without more information from Nate. He couldn't believe 99 Deepwoods Drive was dictating his life again; he would have to go into work for hours this weekend to catch up on the paperwork he couldn't get to this afternoon.

"Place needs to be demolished," he murmured, shoving the last of the fries into his mouth and slurping down his Pepsi, so engrossed by the Blake Grafton abduction that the meal seemed to have eaten itself.

He pulled back onto the road, then headed north toward Hollisville. He was glad Nate had agreed to meet him and speak to the State Police about his ordeal, but he remained puzzled by Joss's refusal to cooperate. At Mike's request, Nate had asked his girlfriend if she would make a statement as well, but the kid had called back and said Joss didn't want to speak to anyone about 99 Deepwoods Drive. Nate had also said she'd been acting really strange of late.

Damn it, Joss. The investigators need all the information they can get. Your interview could help bring this kid home.

Mike remembered the night of the storm. Nate had gone into the shed (Mike was almost positive he'd busted the door down, but when he'd gotten down to the lawn himself, the door had been shut and locked). Nate had emerged less than a minute later, completely distraught; and Joss had been up on the third floor deck, staring out at the parking lot.

The questions were stacking up. What had happened to Joss during that brief disappearance at Nate's apartment following her abduction? What had she seen? Most importantly, how had it traumatized her to the point that she was declining to help the police?

And who was Shepherd?

Mike couldn't wait to finally learn the truth from Nate.

Chapter 10

Max warily studied the boy, afraid to get too close, observing each inhalation with mild trepidation, waiting for something to happen. A minute later, feeling only slightly less nervous, Max took a few steps in the boy's direction. He was lying on his back. His dirty blond, curly hair and milky skin seemed real enough, but what if he was actually a deleterious creature disguised as a boy?

How had he gotten here, anyway?

Max came beside the boy, whose suddenly hitching breaths and trembling arms suggested the beginnings of a seizure. Max grabbed his right arm. "Hey, kid, are you okay?"

When the boy failed to respond, Max tapped his shoulder, eliciting a series of shivery moans.

"Hey, kid!" Max shouted, touching his forehead, and the boy's blue eyes shot open, wide and scared, reminding Max of all the times he'd hid under his sister's bed and spooked her. It had been fun when she'd chased him and hit him with pillows, but Max had stopped scaring her after their father's death, when sleep itself had terrified poor Jocey enough to scream herself out of nightmares and find her diapers soaked.

An odd sense came over Max that this seven- or eight-year-old boy would need his support just as Jocey had when she was that age.

"It's all right. I'm not going to hurt you," Max said as the boy got to his feet and scrambled back to the far wall, where he huddled in a pitiful little ball below the cloudy window.

"Wh…who are you? Where's my mom?" the boy squeaked. Max hated that he was scared. He had to find a way to calm him down.

"I'm Max Leclaire," he said, crouching to make himself appear less imposing. "I'll try to help you find your mom, okay? Tell me where you're from."

"M…Massachusetts. Where am I?"

Max came a little closer. "That's a good question. I'm not really sure, but I'm glad I'm not alone. I know this is really scary, but we're gonna get through it, okay?"

The boy nodded, verging on tears.

"Would you mind if I sit next to you?" Max said. "I just want to talk for a while so we can get to know each other."

Something shifted in the kid's eyes, and his mistrust seemed to soften a little. "Okay."

Smiling, Max walked to the far wall and took a seat beside his new cellmate, using the wall as a backrest. He extended his hand. "What's your name?"

Shaking his hand limply, the boy said, "I'm Blake. Blake Grafton."

"How old are you?"

"Seven." Blake sat against the wall as well.

"How did you get in here?"

"I…I don't know. I just moved to a new apartment with my mom. I was watching TV. I fell asleep and woke up here."

"Where's your apartment?"

Blake began to cry. "New Hampshire," he said with an explosion of tears. "I can't remember what town. I just want to go home. Please take me home."

Max pulled the boy into a hug. "It'll be okay, pal. I'll find a way to get you to your mom." He remembered the times he'd wiped Jocey's tears away and comforted her. "We'll find a way out of here. We just need to stick together."

The boy cried in his arms for a long time, finally composing himself enough to glance about the prison.

"Can you see through the walls?" Max asked, wondering if the kid shared his ability.

Blake shook his head, wrinkles of confusion on his face. Very interesting, Max left to question why he was allowed to see through the walls but not Blake.

Was there something he was supposed to see, something meant only for his eyes? So much for not believing in a greater power and the afterlife.

Max looked through the walls into the three rooms, carefully searching for clues as to his location. There were framed pictures on the opposite bedroom and living room walls, but they were too far away for him to see the faces in detail. There were two beds in the middle room; to the left, in the living room, was a television, a sofa, and a desk with a laptop and printer; and to the right, the kitchen boasted all of the expected appliances, the stove and refrigerator yellowed with age.

A door opened. Max peered into the kitchen, where the young woman from before – the one who'd sobbed in the shower – stepped inside and set her purse on the countertop. She looked exhausted, eyes ringed from sleep deprivation. A thought came to Max that she was Blake's mother, that these three rooms were his new apartment. Blake's disappearance would certainly explain her devastation.

Max turned to Blake. "Can you tell me what your mom looks like, pal?"

Blake proceeded to describe the woman on the other side: light brown hair, green eyes, pretty tall (although the latter detail was to be expected of any description provided by a seven-year-old).

"Does she have any tattoos?"

He nodded. "A heart. On her shoulder. It's red."

Confirmed, this was his mother. The heart had indeed been red, and Max had also noted tattoos on the woman's hips, though he now felt little pangs of guilt for violating her privacy. This whole thing was so messed up. He should have been dead, in the dirt, done. There should have been eternal nothingness – no Jocey, no Nate, no seven-year-old kid stuck in a wall with him.

Max decided not to send Blake into a panic by informing him that his mother was just a few feet beyond the wall, her face buried in her hands. Instead he hunted for a spot in the wall through which he might gain entry to Blake's apartment. If he'd been able to do it back in Boston, then maybe he could manage it here as well.

"What are you doing?" Blake asked when Max began pressing his hands searchingly against the walls.

"Just trying to see if we can get through the walls. I did it before but not here. Help me out – maybe there's a gateway."

Max finally did find a gateway, but he didn't simply pass through it like before. He was violently yanked through the wall, as if someone had taken hold of his arm and pulled him from the other side, the force so intense that he stumbled into the bed Blake's mother was sitting on. But she didn't notice him there. She didn't even move, unaware that he'd just slammed into her bed.

Max got to his feet. "Hey, lady, your kid's on the other side! He's trapped in there!"

Her head remained stuffed into her hands. She was crying. Max could hear her now that he was on the living side of the wall. "Where are you, baby?" she said, her words muffled.

"Lady, Blake's right there!" Max shouted. He tried to grab her shoulder, but his hand passed through and experienced fleeting warmth, just like the night he'd tried to communicate with Jocey.

Startled, the woman quickly stood, probably disturbed by the same icy draft Jocey had felt upon coming into contact with the dead. This was the formula, the same thing wherever he went. Warm = alive; cold = dead; dead = invisible. Pretty fucking simple.

Yet Max didn't want to absorb this new reality because dead would eventually equal forgotten.

"Shit!" Spinning around in panicked observation of his new surroundings, Max tried to think of something he could do, feeling just as helpless as he had when trying to alert Jocey to his presence.

A message. He could write a message. But when he dashed into the living room and found a pen, his hand passed through it, as if he'd tried to grab a gust of wind. Again he was being denied an opportunity to communicate with the living world. It was all a game, he realized. Someone was screwing with him.

Or maybe not someone but something. Mom's Almighty God.

Max took a deep breath, looked around, suddenly terrified. Was this indeed Hell? Was this the punishment he would endure for taking his life? He thought of the demons his mother had often warned him and Jocey about, creatures that inhabited a world of fire and sometimes rose up to lurk the shadows in search of human souls to corrupt. While reading *The Divine Comedy* one day a few years back following a high, Max had thought of Mom at least once a page.

But now it was Max who felt like he was navigating the circles of Hell, and he had no idea how to find his way out. He feared it would always be this way, an eternal relegation to the sidelines, where he would be forced to watch the game of life drag on until the sun finally burnt itself out.

No! There had to be a way out. He just needed to stumble across it.

Deciding that further attempts at communication with Blake's mother were useless, Max stepped back through the gateway wall, marveling at his ability to penetrate solid structures, a man without molecules or composition.

A dead man.

Back inside the dusty space within the walls, Max discovered that Blake was gone. He searched each alcove, found a stack of old notebooks and papers, but couldn't locate the boy. The window was intact; he hadn't gone out that way. Had he somehow passed through the wall just now and returned to his mother? Max glanced into the apartment – no sign of the kid.

"Blake!" he shouted. No answer. "Blake, where are you?"

Max grimaced, looking up at the ceiling and shaking his head at Mom's God, or Jocey's God, or whatever God had put him in this brutal place. He threw his hands out in resignation. "You got me! I give up! Why don't you cut the shit already?" He shifted his rant into his first language, and now the French expletives were spilling out.

However, no amount of curses would permit his release. Shepherd, a trusted transporter of suicidal souls to Hell, had a specific mission for Maxime Philippe Leclaire. A trade would be negotiated, but first the pieces had to be primed for the transaction.

Part III: The Monster of 99 Deepwoods Drive

"The shepherd always tries to persuade the sheep
that their interests and his own are the same." ~
Stendhal

Chapter 1

Saturday, December 18

I'm sitting in the passenger seat of Sgt. James
Fitzgerald's cruiser, eager to reach 99 Deepwoods
Drive but also nervous. Very nervous. I'm about to
meet a woman whose son was abducted on
Monday, a woman who's going through Hell, alone
on her island of anguish. The community is shaken
by Blake's kidnapping, everyone terrified about the
possibility of another abduction. And I can't protect
anyone. It's only my first night, a rookie cop feeling
very small, entrusted to keep the community safe
yet enslaved to the cold truth that sometimes the
police don't get there in time. Sometimes they don't
find the bad guys.

Sometimes they don't bring kids home.

As Fitzgerald accelerates to sixty on Route 202, the
early flakes of an approaching nor'easter brush
against the windshield. Most of the houses and
businesses out this way are dark, a few still glowing
with Christmas lights. It's a few minutes before
midnight. The majority of residents are tucked into

bed, their doors locked, many of those doors left unlocked this time last week.

Nervousness builds. I tell myself to keep it together. I've had countless hours of courses, training, and testing that have prepared me for the real thing, and I can't mess it up, not tonight, not on this call.

We eventually turn onto Deepwoods Drive, a narrow road that twists in S-curves through the woods. Most of the houses are on one side of the road, including address 99, which we come to about halfway down. The snow is starting to pick up as we pull into the parking lot, where two Hollisville cruisers and several other vehicles are parked. The building looms tall to our left, perched atop a hill like an eerie fortress. There's a bright light up there – a motion sensor light on the second floor deck, outlining the falling snow. Officer Roberts, who I met the other day, and another officer are speaking to a woman on the deck, most likely Katherine Grafton.

We step out of the car, into the strengthening storm. "You ready, kid?" Fitzgerald asks.

"Yes, sir." My stomach heavy, I take another look up at the ominous building, suddenly filled with inexplicable dread. It's weird being here and knowing this is the place where Blake Grafton was abducted. This is the house where the mass suicide happened back in the sixties. This year alone, two more people died in there.

This is it, 99 Deepwoods Drive.

I tell myself to relax – everything's gonna be fine, especially with three other cops here. The FBI field agent in charge of the investigation will be here soon as well. I'll just let him and the others take the lead.

What I don't know is that they aren't in control here. Only the house holds control.

Chapter 2

Nate had been under the impression that he would
be asked to elaborate on the statement he'd made
back in September. He was expecting maybe a
handful of cops at most, not an entire conference
room filled with investigators eager to hear what he
had to say. Earlier, Mike had instructed him to give
the same recollection of events he'd offered in
September (Mike and Chief Dave Strait wanted to
hear the new details in private).

"Thanks for meeting with us, Mr. Overbrook," said
Lt. Ellis Wouk, of the State Police Missing Persons
Unit, who, according to Mike, would lead the
investigation of Blake Grafton's abduction until an
FBI field agent was assigned to the case later that
day.

"No problem." Nate gulped, trying not to look as
nervous as he felt. Considering what he and Joss
had done Sunday night, he couldn't help but think
of himself as a defendant in a courtroom. This
wasn't a good time to be around a bunch of cops.
How did wanted criminals and people with warrants
out for their arrests manage to appear halfway
normal, he wondered. The guilt and paranoia were
unbearable.

Wouk motioned for Nate to sit at the head of a
rectangular table, where a bottle of water was
waiting for him. Oh, no. If water had been provided,
it was a good bet they planned to keep him here at
the Hollisville police station for a while. Nate

reluctantly took a seat in an uncomfortable cushioned metal chair, Wouk sitting to his immediate right. There were eight others seated around the table, and a dozen or so more were pressed against the walls, everyone in possession of either a recording device or a notebook. To Nate's left was a chubby, ponytailed man with a laptop and electronic drawing tablet.

Wouk addressed the group. "This is Nathan Overbrook, the previous renter of unit four who left after he was drugged and his girlfriend was briefly abducted in September. I've provided each of you with copies of the police reports, which include statements made by Nathan and his girlfriend, Jocelyne Leclaire. Nathan is prepared to answer your questions, and we also have Mr. Wilhelmsen here" – he pointed to the ponytailed guy – "to create a facial composite of the suspect going by Gerald Blackwell."

The first question came from a woman seated on the left side of the table. She looked stern and demanding, her face a microcosmic snapshot of the overall group. "When did you become aware that the names these individuals used were the same names of the father and son who committed suicide in 1965?"

"I didn't find out until later, when my uncle and I were talking to Chief Strait that night."

"And you'd never seen either of them before that Sunday?" she continued.

"Never. Joss did, though. She'd had at least three separate conversations with Mason. He always came up to her when I wasn't around."

The questions continued for half an hour and beyond. Nate wished he could tell these cops what had really happened, but the fact remained that none of them would believe him. They'd think he and Joss were drug addicts who'd been on one hell of a high, which wouldn't be too much of a stretch in light of Nate's painkiller addiction last spring.

Though Mike had assured Nate that no one would ask about the photographs taken of him and Meghan, he nevertheless steeled himself for such a question. According to Mike, the photos would only be reviewed by high-level investigators and a graphologist to determine if the handwriting matched that on the note left for Katherine Grafton. Still, Nate's stomach churned with expectation that the awful photos would be distributed any second.

Minutes and questions passed, Nate spared from humiliation. There were some strange questions, many about Joss and some about the landlord – who'd apparently been part of the suicide cult and backed out! – but at least there weren't any inquiries about the photos.

Later, after almost everyone had left the room, Wouk asked Nate if Joss would come in for an interview as well. "Considering that she had interactions with the individual claiming to be Mason Blackwell, it would be extremely helpful if we could speak with her." Wouk flipped through the pages of his report. "I'm afraid she didn't get into much detail in her statement that night."

Nate crossed his arms. "I'll be sure to ask her, but she really wants to keep what happened in the past."

The sketch artist session endured with surprising length, a process replete with digital erasures and corrections. At last Nate was looking at the face of the man who'd drugged him on the lawn, every facial aspect rendered perfectly.

The face of Shepherd, meanwhile, remained as obscure as midnight.

Finally free, Nate met Mike outside the station. It was almost dark out, the shortest day of the year rapidly approaching.

"How'd it go?" his uncle said.

"Good. Glad it's over."

"You didn't tell them anything about…you know?"

"No, nothing new. They know as much as you do."

"Perfect. You ready to head over to Dave Strait's place? He can't wait to talk to you, but I want to hear it first. Everything."

Nate nodded. "Right. Everything."

In the passenger seat of Mike's car, before they headed south to Winchendon, Nate tried to identify a good place to begin recounting the horrors. They were so outrageous that there seemed to be no way to ease Mike into the icy waters of the supernatural. The best thing to do, he realized, was to just take the plunge.

"My old apartment is haunted," he said.

As expected, Mike looked at him askance, though not quite as incredulously as Nate had anticipated. "Haunted by what?"

Nate shook his head. He couldn't believe he was telling his uncle about this. He and Joss had agreed it was best to keep everything to themselves, but circumstances had changed. A boy's life was on the line. "We think it's a demon. It calls itself Shepherd."

"You've *seen* this thing?"

"Yeah – and it was almost the last thing we saw. It had Joss tied to a post in a room that doesn't exist. We were in another dimension, I swear to God."

Mike was staring at him in disbelief, his eyes wide and apprehensive. "What do you mean, doesn't exist?"

Nate felt like his words had been involved in a wreck, crashing into each other and preventing any of them from proceeding. "It's…it's hard to explain. I went into the shed, but there wasn't a sink at the end like usual. There was a stairwell that led up to a room. Shepherd was in there – he had Joss tied to a post. Mason snuck in and saved her life!"

"Mason?"

"Yeah, talk to Joss about this. She'll confirm everything. That wasn't just some guy pretending to be Mason. It was really him, a ghost. I know this sounds insane, but please believe me. There's no one we can talk to about this."

Mike turned the key in the ignition, bringing the car to life. "Tell you what, kid, if you finish your story and don't leave out any detail, I promise to believe you no matter what."

"Really? Why? Aren't you gonna say there must be some other explanation?"

Mike shook his head. "Sometimes there are no rational explanations. When you're done with your story, I've got a secret of my own I need to share with you."

Chapter 3

Before continuing on to Dave's house in
Winchendon, Mike pulled into a gas station and
parked the car. He was about to unleash a mind-
blowing revelation, certainly not something he
wanted to toss out there while focused on the road.
Nate deserved his full attention, especially now that
the kid had described every memory of what really
happened on his final night at 99 Deepwoods Drive.

Mike took a deep breath. He didn't even know
where to start. After so many years of keeping his
premonitions to himself, it seemed wrong that Nate
should find out before Sue. He would have to tell
her tonight, first thing when he got home, even
before dinner made it to the table. That's what he
should have done a long time ago, yet it had always
been easier to keep his family and friends shielded
from his ability.

Removing his glasses, Mike said, "Nate, what I'm
about to tell you here is pretty wild. You probably
won't believe it, but it's true."

Nate chuckled. "After I told you about the ghosts
and demons in my old apartment, you're worried *I*
won't believe something?"

"That's part of what inspired me to tell you. I know
it wasn't easy for you to tell the truth about that
place, but I believe you, every word. And now you
need to hear what I have to say." He cleared his
throat, glanced out the window. "The thing is…I
have this crazy gift. Well, sometimes it's more of a

curse than a gift. Anyway, I can see things before they happen."

There. It was out of his mouth, a prisoner freed from a dark chamber, squinting against the sun. The release of this nearly half-century old secret was somewhat cathartic, like lifting a tremendous weight from his shoulders. Now that the burden had been removed, Mike couldn't believe he'd carried it around all these years.

Nate blinked in shock, the same way Mike had probably looked when Nate told him he'd busted through the shed door back in September, only to spin around and find it fully repaired and locked. "You can see the future?" Nate said.

"Only in my nightmares," Mike clarified. "It's not like I walk around all day with these visions. They come when I'm asleep, recurring nightmares that warn me about something that's gonna take place. It's only happened to me five times, including now, but the premonitions are always correct."

Nate went to say something but stopped abruptly, as if he'd answered his own question or come up with a better one. Finally, he said, "What kind of things have you seen?"

Mike sighed, bracing himself for the bad memories. "I was seven years old the first time it happened. I kept having nightmares about my dad dying in a fiery airplane crash, and sure enough, about two weeks later his little prop plane slammed into a house just after takeoff."

Nate's mouth dropped. "No way!"

"Yes, sir. I'm sure you've heard a million times about how your grandfather was a great pilot. He absolutely loved planes – loved flying them, loved fixing them, loved everything about them."

"How'd the crash happen? All anyone's told me is a mechanical failure. Is there anything more to that?"

Mike shook his head. "Not that I'm aware of. Dad was training a guy to fly when it happened. The thing just went out of control; investigators later guessed it was the engine, although they couldn't be sure. The damn thing was wrecked beyond belief – some of it just disintegrated."

"And you saw the crash in your nightmares two weeks before it happened?"

Mike glanced out the window at Route 202, where vehicles were ripping along a straightaway between the center of Winchendon and Templeton. "I'll never forget when Mom told us he'd been in a crash. She didn't even need to say any more – I knew he was dead right away because of my nightmares. No one could survive the disaster I'd seen."

"That must have really messed you up."

"It did. Absolutely. I couldn't sleep well again for maybe five years, but luckily I didn't have another recurring nightmare until adulthood. It happened ten years ago. You know that bad wreck on Hollow

Road I told you about a few times, the head-on crash where the mother and son were killed?"

"Yeah, you said their dog died, too, right?"

Mike nodded, pleased that his story had been important enough for Nate to remember it.

"How many times did you see that crash before it happened?" Nate said.

"At least ten times, all of them showing a woman and child whose faces were somewhat blurry. Somehow I knew the ages, too. Information flashes out there real quick in these nightmares – sometimes it's addresses, photos, names; other times it's streets or vehicles. It can take a while to figure out what things mean, but that time I wasn't able to put anything together."

"What were the other times you had these nightmares?"

"Well, as you might imagine, I was pretty torn up after the Hollow Road ordeal. My inability to stop these things after seeing them haunted me, but I was finally able to use my premonitions five years ago. Locked up a real bad guy because of them."

Nate's eyes widened. "Really? Someone's in jail because of your visions?"

Mike felt proud, like a former pitcher telling his grandkids about the time he struck out a Hall of

Fame slugger on three pitches. "You bet your ass. He'll be in prison for a long time, kid."

Nate took a sip of water, his green eyes ablaze with interest. "What'd you get him on?"

"Distribution of child pornography. I put all the visions together in time, thank Christ, and we busted the evil fuck."

"How'd you do that? I mean, it's not like you could tell a judge you had visions of him committing crimes."

Mike smiled, remembering how it had all gone down. Five years seemed like five days. "Based on my knowledge of what was in his basement, I knew a simple police search of the place would be more than enough for an arrest. The problem was getting the police inside his house."

Mike didn't want to get into the whole story, but Nate's eyes begged him to continue.

"Let's just say there was an anonymous call from a payphone reporting a crime at his address. The police didn't find evidence of that crime, of course, but they saw what the caller wanted them to see in the basement. When the guy got home from work, he was arrested for possession of child pornography, and the charges stacked up from there. He tried to fight it in court by saying it was an illegal search, but the 911 call gave the cops justification to enter the house. Court battle went on for a while, but in the end he found himself behind bars."

Mike was tired of talking about himself. "Anyway, the past isn't important now. The reason I'm telling you all of this is because I've had two different nightmare patterns involving your old apartment, one in September and one now."

"Really? What were they about?"

"I saw Joss walking through a wall in September. She was wearing a dress, and her eyes were really dark. Sometimes a few men went through the wall with her. That's why I left the hospital that Sunday night when your mom said she couldn't find you or Joss. Whatever was happening, I knew it was much deeper than anyone realized."

Nate's face had gone white. "So you knew something bad would happen to Joss?"

"Yes, that's why I tried to get you to move out. Then Chris was diagnosed with leukemia, and the visions stopped altogether. To be honest, I was so worried about Chris that I completely forgot the nightmares. I don't think I slept long enough to even have more nightmares."

Nate nodded solemnly. "I'm so glad we're away from there."

"You and me both – but I just started having new nightmares about a boy being watched from the parking lot of your apartment. I drove up there last night to warn whoever moved into unit four, and sure enough, I saw the boy from my nightmares. A few hours later I got a call from Dave Strait saying the kid was missing."

"Jesus. I can't believe it's happening again."

"At least I know what we're up against now. You've gotta tell Dave the same thing, okay? Tell him everything you've seen – you can trust him." Mike put the car into drive. "It's important that the four of us – you, me, Joss, and Dave – keep this to ourselves. Outsiders will never believe it. They'll just assume it's someone pretending to be Mason and Gerald Blackwell, but we know the real deal."

Nate lowered his head and rubbed his temples. "How are we supposed to stop Shepherd though? He might have already killed that kid."

"No," Mike said confidently. "If I'm still getting the nightmares, it's not too late. I just need more information."

Chapter 4

Katie leaned heavily on her friends and family over the next two days. Whitney slept on the sofa and served as Katie's second shadow during that time, preparing meals and cleaning the apartment, even keeping the media at bay.

Whit's presence was a blessing for Katie, who didn't know what to do or where to go, overcome by desperation and exhaustion after a day of searching and another sleepless night. The threatening message had changed everything. Now she knew her child was in the possession of a monster – a revelation that had brought her to her knees, every muscle in her body straining with helpless rage.

Her parents arrived Wednesday morning with thousands of missing person posters featuring Blake's information, as well as a color photo in the upper right corner that made Katie sob. With the help of Whit, Mandy, Stephen, and a host of volunteers from an area church, Katie and her parents distributed the posters throughout Hollisville that afternoon.

Also taking part in the effort and, more importantly, providing an empathetic voice of guidance was a middle-aged woman named Sheila Frost, of Nashua, whose then twelve-year-old son had been kidnapped more than a decade earlier. A smart, resourceful boy, her child had managed to escape his abductor's house and flag down a passing car – a result Katie prayed for continually, seeking God's assistance in ending the nightmare her life had become. And with Sheila at her side, Katie felt a few hopeful streaks of light shimmer through the darkness; despite the ominous statistics, Sheila's son was living proof that abducted didn't mean dead.

As the sun began to fall beyond the trees Wednesday evening, Katie slipped into inevitable sleep while reclined in the passenger seat of Whit's car. The first thing she glimpsed upon lifting her eyelids was the building from which her son had disappeared Monday night. Shingles crumbling, paint peeling, wood rotting, it symbolized what Katie would become if Blake was gone forever – broken.

Whit squeezed her hand. "Ready to go inside?"

Katie stayed where she was, feeling nauseous again. The energy required to open the door and walk up the lawn seemed beyond her limits. She glanced up at the house again. Its roof bathed in orange by dying sunlight, the place suddenly seemed menacing, a hellish, monstrous building set ablaze by a winter sunset.

Katie thought of what Mike Overbrook had told her about the suicides and his nephew's ordeal, then remembered Blake's nightmare for the zillionth time…the hooded men slowly climbing the staircase, waiting outside the door, peering in. Blake had tried to warn her. He hadn't experienced a nightmare; it had all been real!

And now he was gone.

Once again Whit took her hand. "Let's get you something to eat."

Katie tore her gaze free of the building, then looked back at it warily.

"This place," Katie whispered. "This place is cursed, Whit, just like you said."

Whit shook her head. Katie had told her about everything yesterday, and Whit had confirmed Mike Overbrook's claims online. But strangely enough, she'd abandoned her haunted house assertions in pursuit of a logical explanation: people who exploited the house's past and played upon people's fears.

"It's not the house," Whit insisted. "It's psychos who want everyone to think the house is haunted. They're gonna catch these guys, Katie. They must live around here – they want you to stay, so that obviously means they're after something." She lifted Katie's hand and squeezed. "They're gonna come back here, and when they do the police will be ready."

Katie found herself nodding, wanting desperately to believe it. The police had been so helpful. Everyone had been helpful – her friends, her parents, Sheila Frost, the searchers, and the people from the church. Katie hadn't needed to worry about keeping up the apartment since Blake's abduction, her meals cooked, her clothes washed, her groceries purchased. Her boss at the school had told her to take as long as she needed. A fund was being set up to assist her. A candlelight vigil was scheduled for tonight.

But in spite of everyone's generosity, a part of Katie wanted to be left alone at the bottom of this pit of darkness, where unspeakable fears assaulted her relentlessly, each one somehow more disgusting than its predecessor. This was where she belonged, she felt, the only place suitable for a woman who'd let someone take her son. She'd done everything wrong *again*, and this was her punishment, darkness her new home.

Just as Katie began to embrace the darkness, accepting her place in its guilt-ridden abyss, Whit pulled her from the depths with a warm smile on a cold day. The smile chased out some of the worst thoughts, replacing them with dimly encouraging hopes that constituted the greatest solace Katie had experienced since Blake's abduction.

Above all else, Whit's smile reminded Katie that she wasn't alone.

"Come on, let's get you some dinner. I'll make whatever you want," Whit said, and Katie managed to haul herself out of the car and head up the lawn with her best friend.

In the coming days, Whit's friendship would prove invaluable in response to the unthinkable.

Chapter 5

Joss sipped her pinot noir straight from the bottle, wondering how long the stash of alcohol she'd purchased in Montreal a month ago would last (a collection she kept hidden in the back of her closet). She couldn't believe she'd gone through three bottles in less than a week, plus a bottle of whiskey, her former distaste for alcohol a distant memory.

She let out a long sigh and closed her eyes, slipping neck deep into the hot tub. It was so peaceful out here all alone on an early Wednesday afternoon, little on her mind beyond the wine and the warm, bubbling water. Sometimes she fell asleep in the tub, her mother assuming she was volunteering at the animal shelter or tutoring area high school students in French and Spanish (another lie she'd made up to cover for her drinking). Occasionally she worried about a possible addiction, but she always dismissed the thought quickly. She could stop if she wanted to, but why stop? The wine helped take the edge off reality. She would get her act together when the second semester began, she told herself – just a few more weeks of chillaxing in the hot tub. After everything she'd endured in the last year from Hell, she deserved a little down time to drink and do whatever she wanted. It was only fair that she be allowed to heal in her own way.

Footsteps thudded along the back walkway, quickly approaching. Joss opened her eyes and spotted Nate jogging up to the pavilion. He was scowling, apparently still angry from their fight last night. He'd tried to convince her yesterday to drive to

New Hampshire and speak to a bunch of cops about the night Mason abducted her, but she'd told him she wasn't interested. When he'd forced the issue, she'd said the cops could go screw themselves, sending Nate into a tirade about a boy who'd been abducted from unit four. He'd yelled at her about not helping the cops, and Joss had told him she didn't care. They were out of that place – whatever happened from now on wasn't their problem. Plus, even if she did help, no one could combat Shepherd, not without the help of Mason. If a boy really had been taken by Shepherd, there was nothing she or Nate or anyone else could do to bring him home.

Nate pulled a plastic chair up to the hot tub and took a seat. "I'm sorry about last night," he said. "I was pretty harsh."

"No worries," she muttered, bringing the bottle to her lips and savoring the rich flavor. She wished he would just go – he was damaging the peace and solitude.

He nodded at the bottle. "Looks like you're drinking even earlier these days."

"Yeah, looks like it." She closed her eyes, tried to relax.

"Joss, you're really starting to worry me." She heard him stand. "The drinking and the–"

Her eyes shot open. "*You're* gonna criticize *me* for drinking? Seriously?"

He blew out a frustrated breath. "Joss, don't you see what you're doing here? It's the same thing I did, just a different drug."

When she insulted him in French, he said, "Please don't start with the foreign language shit. I'm not in the mood."

"Well, maybe you should find your orientation slut. I bet she doesn't annoy you." The words had come out of their own accord, Joss instantly regretting them. "Sorry, Nate."

He returned to the chair, stunned by the low blow, stripped of words. He stared into the water, lost in what might have been regret, confusion, anger, or a combination of the three. "I thought we'd agreed that was in the past," he finally said, meeting her eyes again. "Is that what this is all about? Are you still pissed at me for that?"

"No, it's just" – she decided on a sip of wine first – "I just don't like it when you tell me how to live. You don't have a leg to stand on after everything you did to me, Nate. Don't you think I've suffered enough? Just because I like to get drunk sometimes doesn't mean I'm an alcoholic."

"But you get drunk every other day. All you want to do is sit around and drink."

"At least I don't steal people's money to get high."

He shoved the chair back so forcefully that it fell over. "Stop being childish! It's pathetic!"

"Is that why you came over? To call me a pathetic alcoholic?"

"No, I…" He looked hurt, a look Joss enjoyed for some reason. "I just want you back, Joss. You're changing – can't you see it?"

"I think *you're* changing."

"Whatever. You know that's not true."

"*Whatever*," she mocked.

He glared at her, deep and searing. "Just get dressed," he said flatly. "Uncle Mike will be here in ten minutes, and I'm guessing you don't want to talk to him naked in a hot tub."

"What are you talking about?"

He nodded emphatically, perhaps even antagonistically. "You heard me. You might not talk to the police, but you're gonna answer my uncle's questions. Like I said last night, I told him everything and he believes it all. Aren't you happy we can talk to someone else about this? We can finally get it off our chests."

Joss slapped the water with both palms, spraying chains of bejeweled droplets over the edge. "I'm not saying anything to him!" she shouted. "I told you, I don't want to talk to anyone about that!"

"Oh, you're gonna talk – and you're also gonna stop drinking all the time. If you don't, I'll tell your mom exactly what you've been doing all semester, Miss Lingerie Model."

Joss felt tears forming. "You wouldn't."

He grabbed her robe from its hook on the near wall, picked up the chair, and laid the robe over the back of it. "Believe me, I will. I'll tell her everything. I'd rather do that than watch you turn into an alcoholic like my dad."

She wiped the tears away. "Why are you doing this to me? Why can't you just leave me alone? I don't want to talk to anyone!"

He came around the tub to where she was sitting, knelt down beside her. "What's the big deal? You don't ever have to go there again – you're safe, Joss. Uncle Mike just wants to find out what happened so he can give as much information as possible to the police chief. He's in on this, too. They're doing their own investigation of the haunting, or whatever it is. That's the only way they're gonna find this kid. Don't you want to do everything you can to help?"

She waved a hand, fighting an urge to splash him. "Why does your uncle care so much? Doesn't he have to worry about his own town?"

"Yeah, but he's freaking out about this kid now that he knows what's really going on. He knows the cops won't believe it, and he feels like him and Dave Strait are the only ones who can stop Shepherd."

She took his hand, shivering at the icy grip. "Okay, I'll talk to him, but I don't think there's anything I can say that will help. This is it, though – I'm not driving all over the place and giving interviews."

He massaged her shoulders. "This is it, I promise. Thanks for reconsidering – I know this isn't easy."

"Well, it's not like you gave me much of a choice. Mom would murder me if she found out about the lingerie. Seriously, you can never tell her."

"I know, but I wanted you to see how serious I am about this. I can't even imagine what that kid's mother is going through right now. I mean, her son – he's trapped somewhere in that house, probably on the same stage where you were tied up."

Joss shuddered at the memories, not wanting to find herself a prisoner to the past yet again. The whole point of coming out here was to experience a few simple pleasures that would ease her mind, but Nate and his uncle kept insisting on dredging up the past and disturbing stones better left untouched. How was a scab supposed to heal if they incessantly picked at it? Just leave the past alone already!

Dripping and cold, Joss pulled on her pink fleece robe, slipped into her sandals, and returned to the house with Nate.

Upstairs, in her bedroom, he said, "I'm sorry about everything I said last night and today. I've been so worried about you, and I don't know what to do sometimes."

She kissed his lips, a fleeting joy. "I'm sorry too. I know I haven't made this easy, but I'm not gonna turn into an alcy. You don't have anything to worry about."

"What about your trances?"

She huffed. "That's just stress, like I said. If you and your uncle would just leave the past where it belongs, maybe I wouldn't be so stressed."

Joss knew this last statement was ridiculous. She was indeed a prisoner to her past, and it had nothing to do with Nate or his Uncle Mike. She remained helplessly shackled by her brother and Mason Blackwell, the mystery of their fates continuing to weigh heavily upon her. Because they'd committed suicide – MORTAL SIN – her faith just wasn't enough to ameliorate her unremitting dread. She'd even tried searching the internet for a respectable religious official who had asserted that people who commit suicide can still reach Heaven, but the only person she'd been able to find was a quack priest who'd started his own religion and now spent each Sunday cybercasting sermons from a makeshift church in his basement.

Nate looked concerned. "Promise you'll let me know if you need help. Don't shut me out, babe."

"I promise," she said, wondering if she'd long ago crossed the threshold of needing help.

Chapter 6

Mike was impressed upon pulling into the driveway and staring up at Jocelyne's house, a three-story colonial in the town's most affluent neighborhood. It was a stout, self-important house, not merely a residence but a statement to all whose eyes fell upon it, with a prominent white-railed front balcony over a four-columned portico, large picture windows, and a three-bay garage bedecked with a golden weather vane. Boasting maroon shutters against a gray stone siding, the place seemed to be the perfect blend of traditional and contemporary designs, a home that might be described by realtors as handsomely unique or charmingly exquisite.

Parking his car behind Nate's Taurus, Mike stepped out and scanned the property. The still snowless front lawn had been cut short and cleared of leaves. A few naked trees bordering the driveway had been stripped of threatening branches, splintered knots identifying where the amputations had been made. Closer to the house, the gardens had been trimmed back and readied for winter, no doubt in a fussily prescribed manner. A university president in Worcester, Joss's mother was wealthy enough to afford a landscaping team to keep the place in a constant state of perfection, Nate said. Judging by the house and its accessories, including a black wrought iron fence surrounding the entire property, Anya Leclaire was a great deal wealthier than Nate had initially indicated.

Mike rang the bell and was let in by Nate. "Joss is showering. She'll be down soon."

"No problem. I'm not going into work until three."

"Any news on Blake Grafton?"

Mike shook his head. "The cops are out there interviewing people, but now that I know what's really going on, I'm pretty sure they won't turn up anything. The only way to find Blake is to get back to that room in the shed – trouble is, it's not always there."

Joss hurried down the stairs. Delicately pretty, yet somehow a little different today – paler? – she wore gray sweatpants and a navy blue fleece pullover that read **TROIS-RIVIERES** across the chest. Still wet, her golden brown hair was combed straight down her back. She carried a scent of perfume, something light and airy that reminded Mike of springtime.

"Hi, Mr. Overbrook," she said with a big smile. "Would you like something to eat or drink?"

"No thanks, Joss, I'm all set. It's good to see you. I'm glad things are going better for you two kids."

Joss smiled uncomfortably. Even with the pullover and baggy pants, she still looked incredibly thin. "I can make coffee if you're an afternoon coffee person like my mom," she said. "Or maybe tea, although you don't really seem like a tea sort of guy."

"I guess I'll have some water," Mike said, just to be polite. He wasn't thirsty, but he remembered Nate's stories about his girlfriend's exceeding generosity.

Apparently he'd sometimes been forced to take her purse away to prevent her from paying for meals. She was a sweet kid, not one of those beautiful yet caustic women who ended up divorced by thirty-five. Mike hoped it would last between them.

Returning shortly with a glass of ice water for Mike and a Gatorade for Nate, Joss led them into a large parlor off the foyer she referred to as "The Boring Room." The furniture was first-class stuff, as lavish a collection as Mike had ever seen. A burnished piano dominated the far wall, which was actually a floor-to-ceiling window looking out on the front lawn. Dozens of faces smiled from gold-framed photos on the other walls, Mike recognizing a few of them as younger versions of Joss. She still had the same contagious smile, which hadn't lost its childhood vigor, although her face had become more tired and serious in recent months.

One photo in particular struck Mike hard and made him hurt for Joss. She was about five or six, held and kissed by her father, the joy on their faces pure, nonpareil. They were on a boat, the railing to their left, the ocean beyond, Joss's light hair windswept and tousled, her tiny hand on her father's shoulder, a captured moment of perfect happiness, profound but endangered, neither of them knowing then that there wouldn't be many more father-daughter memories to follow.

Mike's eyes were repeatedly drawn to that photo. It made his stomach clench, made him want Nate to always keep Joss safe because Mr. Leclaire would never walk her down the aisle, would never hold his grandchildren, would never kiss his little girl again.

Joss slid into a rocking chair, resting her pink-socked feet on the coffee table. Nate took the rocker beside her, while Mike, across from them, set his water on a coaster and eased into a comfortable leather sofa easily worth a thousand bucks. If this was the parlor, Mike could only imagine what the entertainment room looked like. This was luxury at its finest, but Joss would trade all of it for another day with her father and brother.

"Joss, I want to thank you for agreeing to talk to me about this," Mike said. "I completely understand why you don't want to speak to anyone."

Nodding, she brought a hand to her hair and began fidgeting with it. Her fingernails were bright red, neatly manicured. Her complexion was unblemished. Her hair shined in the sea of sunlight filling the room. She was ostensibly flawless, but Nate had alluded to an inner turmoil that concerned him. Apparently she'd been drinking a lot and acting strangely, most likely the result of what she'd endured at 99 Deepwoods Drive. But how could someone *not* change after such a scarring night? Mike himself felt changed by what Nate had told him, still unable to process the maddening truth. How many thousands of paranormal investigators had toured allegedly haunted places around the world in search of ghostly evidence, only to come away with a few echoes from old pipes? But on a stormy September night in southwestern New Hampshire, Nate and Joss had seen the unthinkable.

Now their lives would be dramatically different, each day filled with dark memories. And fears.

"I want to make this as quick as I can," Mike said. "When you're thinking about your answers, just remember that no one will ever force you to go to that place again. You're safe. Whatever you say here will stay with four people – myself, Chief Strait, you, and Nate. The State Police aren't gonna be involved with this. Dave and I are gonna run our own investigation and go directly to the source to find Blake – no red tape, no nonsense."

Nate took his girlfriend's hand. "See, babe? We're keeping it small."

Her face softened a little. "Okay. What do you want to know?"

Mike pulled his notebook and pen out of a coat pocket. "Tell me as much as you can remember from the day you were abducted. Feel free to take as much time as you need. There's no pressure."

Her eyes fell to the floor as memories took hold. "I left Nate's apartment because he wasn't feeling well and took a nap. My car wouldn't start, though." She was still looking down, apparently more comfortable that way. "Mason came out of the shed. I told him about my car, and he asked to look at it. He eventually brought out a battery charger and fixed it. I wanted to repay him, so I offered to make him lunch in his apartment, unit seven."

She finally met his eyes. "After lunch he showed me the picture of Nate having sex with that girl." Nate shifted uneasily in his chair. "I was so devastated that it made me sick. I wasn't thinking straight. I just…I don't know what came over me, I snapped. It was like I was a different person. I started kissing him – it was crazy."

"Kissing *Mason*? You could kiss him?"

She nodded impatiently, as if she'd been asked to confirm some rudimentary detail. "It was like I wanted to ease the pain, or get back at Nate. I don't know. Anyway, I only kissed him for a few seconds. That's when Shepherd came up behind me. He said something, I can't remember what, but I knew he and Mason were working together. I was so scared – I thought they would kill me."

"Could you see Shepherd's face at that point?"

"No, he had a hood on. It's all kind of blurry from there, but I remember waking up in the dark. It was the shed, but I didn't know it at the time."

Mike was writing furiously in his notebook. As Joss described how she'd been tied up, brought out to her car, and eventually driven through the neighborhood, Mike kept writing and writing, five pages quickly turning into ten. By the time she finished recounting the exchange between her and Mason in the car, Mike had consumed half of the notebook, writing in increasingly large and tired font.

"So Mason didn't want to hurt you? This was all Shepherd's idea?"

"Yeah, Shepherd controls them all."

"Them – who's them? The ghosts?"

She nodded. "All of the people who committed suicide at that place in the sixties. Mason, his father, the crazy religious guy."

"Johansen."

Her eyes widened. "Yeah, I take it Nate told you about most of this."

"He has, but you're doing great, Joss. Without you, I never would have known about all of those things Mason said."

Her eyes glinted with moisture. "He was such a good kid. What happened to him was horrible. Horrible!"

Mike's urgency built as he heard the rest. They had to find Blake before Shepherd followed through with his intentions, every passing minute further reducing the boy's chances of survival.

But how would they combat something beyond understanding?

After Joss concluded with a memory of how Mason had disappeared from the third floor deck, Mike was left speechless. All he could do was write and shake his head.

"So you experienced Mason vanishing twice?" he finally said, glancing again at the photo of Joss and her father on the boat.

She nodded. "Pretty crazy, isn't it? I–" She stopped, bit her lip. There was a weird intensity in her eyes, a combination of sadness and fear. But there was something more, deep and inscrutable. And dark.

She blinked, her eyes going eerily vacant. Then, just as quickly, they returned to normal, their color actually seeming to brighten. "Are you sure you don't want a sandwich, Mr. Overbrook? I'll make whatever you want." Then she said something in French, speaking in a markedly different tone that verged on cheerful.

Mike declined the sandwich offer, surprised by this sudden change in her personality. He'd witnessed profound vagaries like it only a few times before, once while interviewing a patient at a psychiatric facility. Nate had good reason to be concerned about her, Mike decided. There was something buried deep, inaccessible – but what?

Joss stood, smiling at Mike. "I'm feeling a little tired. Thanks for coming. It was so nice to see you again." Then a line of Russian, her accent hardening.

Nate noticed her oddness as well. "Joss, are you okay?"

"I'm fine, just tired." She took a few steps toward the foyer. Glancing back at Mike, she said, "Did I answer all of your questions?"

He nodded. "Yes, thanks again, Joss. I really appreciate it. You can rest easy now – I promise not to bother you again about this."

"I'm happy to help. Good luck finding that little girl. I hate to think what she's going through in that place."

She turned and left the room, leaving Nate and Mike to exchange disturbed glances.
"What the hell was that?" Mike whispered. "Good luck finding that little *girl*?"

Nate took a deep breath. "You see what I mean? She's seriously screwed up," he said after closing the parlor doors. "She drank a lot this afternoon, and she's been having these weird trances, too."

"Trances?"

"Yeah, I saw one of them in person Sunday night. It was really scary. She was just…totally spaced out, like in another world. I couldn't even get her attention by touching her. Then she came out of it and said she felt like she'd been sleeping while awake."

"Really? Jesus, Nate, she should see someone about this."

"Yeah, but good luck trying to get her to do that. You'd have to put her in a straitjacket and drag her in there."

Mike understood his nephew's dilemma. No one could force Joss to do anything, at least not yet, and Nate risked driving her away by obsessing over her mental health.

"Keep me posted on this," Mike said. "If she does anything too crazy, I'd tell her mother and let her take the lead on it."

Nate shook his head, looking helpless. "I'm pretty sure what happened at the apartment caused her to be like this, not her brother's suicide. That place messed us up so bad. Of all the apartments out there, why did I have to choose *that* one?"

Mike hugged his nephew. "Sometimes things are out of our hands, kid," he said, a message pulsing with deep personal resonance. It was a truth that had been ingrained in Mike following Chris's cancer diagnosis, a reality that had previously given him difficulties but now rested peaceably in his heart because he'd finally accepted that many things in life were beyond his control.

Yet each day he continued to fight, just as his son did, scrapping and battling in an effort to make the best out of what they could control. The situation with Blake Grafton was no different. Much of it was beyond Mike's control, but he would squeeze every drop of productivity from the tools he possessed.

Still, the odds were slim. He and Dave Strait were perhaps guaranteed to fail.

But they would try. It was all they could do, the rest of it in God's hands.

Chapter 7

Blake awoke on a small bed in a dimly lit room, not
the first room where he'd met Max but another one.
It was a perfect square, the walls painted a soft
yellow and floorboards stained dark brown. There
was a damp, unpleasant smell reminiscent of the
early years living in the Goldings' basement, before
Mr. Golding paneled and carpeted it.

Blake called out to Max. No response. He came to
the door in the right corner of the room and tried the
handle. Locked.

Scared to the point of shaking, his heart pumping so
hard that it hurt his chest, Blake gazed up at the
high ceiling, where dozens of wooden beams
bridged over each other like highway flyover ramps
in the heart of a city. Some were horizontal, others
slanted at angles from the ceiling to the walls; a few
were vertical, connecting to the levels immediately
above and below them. Beyond the confused
woodwork, way up high, something black crawled
like a giant spider, its scuttling shadow on the
ceiling, its movements bringing scratchy little *tick,
tick, ticks.*

Before he could study the black thing further,
flapping arose from beneath the tiny bed and
grabbed his attention. A bat flew out, sweeping its
way upward and disappearing within the beams.

Blake staggered backward, bumped into the wall
opposite the bed just as the door clicked open. An
old man stepped in, strangely silent. He was thin

and pale, with wild gray hair that strung out in puffs and curls. His chestnut eyes gleamed with predatory intensity, and his arms dangled limply as if they'd been stuffed with straw.

"Good evening, boy!" he exclaimed with a forced jollity that made Blake even more afraid. He scrambled to the foot of the bed, away from the man, who put his hands above his head. "Calm yourself now. There's no need for fear, child."

"W…who are you?" Blake stammered.

The man took a few steps closer. Dressed entirely in black – shirt, jacket, pants, belt, boots – he seemed to Blake like a walking, talking shadow. "My name is Joseph Johansen. I used to live in this house." He smiled, trying to appear friendly, but his wolfish eyes betrayed him.

"What do you want?" Blake felt the tears about to fall, his voice shaking.

Smiling again, Johansen said, "I'm here to let you know the shepherd is coming! You're supposed to be excited – the *shepherd* is coming, boy!" He marched over to Blake, stopping just a few feet away. "The Lord is my shepherd. I shall not want. He makes me lie down in green pastures. He leads me beside still waters. He restores my *soul*!"

Blake stared in wide-eyed horror as Johansen extended his arms outward and upward, gesticulating emphatically to an invisible audience. "He leads me in paths of righteousness for His name's sake! Even though I walk through the valley of the shadow of death, I will fear no evil!"

Crying, Blake ran to the door. Still locked, the man having snapped it shut behind him.

Blake tugged at it. Tugged and tugged and tugged. No use. He was trapped in here.

Behind him, the old man's tone had plummeted to a saturnine rut. "Turn to me and be gracious to me, for I am lonely and afflicted. The troubles of my heart are enlarged. Bring me out of my distresses."

Blake kept his back to Johansen, hoping he would disappear. *Just go! Leave me alone!*

"Who is the man who fears the Lord?" Johansen called, progressing on a rant that lasted several minutes.

Blake heard little of it, covering his ears and squeezing his eyes shut. He thought of Mom, who would surely find him. Soon. Hopefully soon. But where was she? Why couldn't she get to him?

When Blake finally uncovered his ears, silence filled the room. He whirled around, expecting to see Johansen raging on but instead finding an empty room. The door was still locked. Above him, there was nothing but dusty wooden beams and the lofty fluttering of the bat which had flown out from under the bed.

A low moaning wind rose up on the other side of the door. Somewhere in the distance, an organ began to play; it sounded like the big pipe organ at Blake's old church. His body went cold. He slid down the wall into a squat, a million thoughts racing through him. He screamed for his mother – screamed for what felt like an hour – but no one came, not Mom, not Max, not even the crazy old man.

Finally someone did come. The door creaked open, a robed visitor stepping in, making not a sound as he walked. His face was covered by a veiled hood, but Blake somehow knew what lurked behind it wasn't human, a face even more hideous than those he'd seen on the deck that first night.

"Do you want to see your mother again?" the monster asked in a raspy voice.

Blake nodded furiously.

"Then you must do exactly what I say, understood? This is my house now, and all who inhabit it must follow my rules. I am Shepherd."

Impossibly, the bat descended from the rafters with the placid ease of a domesticated bird, landing on the intruder's shoulder, its wings twitching.

Chapter 8

On Wednesday night, Mike called Dave Strait from his office at the Elkins Police Department. The paperwork seemed to be expanding by the minute, as did the number of new emails, but convincing Dave to believe Nate and Joss was far more important. Yet how could Mike expect Dave to accept their claims if a tiny part of his own heart continued to search for another explanation?

"I don't know, Mikey – let's pray this is all just the drugs at work," Dave said after hearing Mike's descriptions of his interview with Joss.

Shockingly, even after the former landlord had warned Dave that the place was haunted, even after Nate had confirmed it, Dave had still tried to ascribe everything Nate saw to the drug he was injected with by Gerald Blackwell. And Joss, he now assumed, was likely injected with the same hallucinatory drug. Oddly, though, it had seemed like Dave was ready to embrace the idea of a haunting on Monday if pushed strongly enough in that direction, but now that the truth was at his doorstep, demanding to be acknowledged, boasting repeated corroborations, he was searching his way past it, perhaps too afraid to look at it straight on.

"I can see why you're doubtful because they were drugged," Mike said, "but would they really hallucinate the exact same thing?"

Dave chuckled nervously. "Who knows, maybe there was no hallucination at all. Maybe they were just dazed from the drugs and the suspects messed with them. They could have used lights, fog, mirrors, backdrops, whatever – it wouldn't be the strangest thing that's happened in that place."

"What they saw was no trick!" Mike shouted, exasperated, his voice quickly moderating. "Come on, Dave, what's it gonna take for you to believe? This Shepherd thing – it's likely responsible for the Gaudreau and Keppel deaths, plus the other unexplainable stuff you've been tracking there over the years, and now Blake. The answer to everything is right in front of you – Albert gave it to you straight, just like Nate and Joss."

Dave was silent for a while, absorptive. "If this is really happening, then God help us," he finally said. "We should meet up and compare notes – we need to go over every report we've got on 99 Deepwoods Drive."

***

Katie awoke to fleeting music, but not the normal radio tunes blaring from the alarm clock. It was far too early for that, still dark outside, moonlight filtering through the blinds and throwing shadows about the room. It was 3:44. Outside, a cold wind was braying, naked tree branches shifting in its thrall.

The music resumed, organ music, each note crisp and resonant. It sounded like it was emanating from directly above her, but that must have been an auditory illusion. There was no way music could come from the third floor because no one was currently living upstairs–

The men! Blake saw them!

Katie sat up and switched on the bedside lamp. For a while she listened to the rambling song, something low and melancholy, the precise origin of the music indeterminate. The walls seemed to thrum, alive at an unspeakable hour, a few of Blake's posters rustling ever so slightly.

Suddenly the music died, replaced by her son's voice. It was faint but unmistakable, rising up from the bowels of the house. "Mom, help me! Mom!"

Katie tore out of bed and shoved into her boots in the kitchen. She couldn't hear Blake as well in here, his words reduced to muffled sounds. Running back into the bedroom, she heard her son with even greater clarity than before.

"Mom, where are you? Help me!"

Katie pressed her ear against the wall – Blake now sounded like he was on the other side, trapped in unit three.

"Blake, where are you?" she shouted. "Can you hear me? Yell if you can hear me, baby!"

Silence.

Katie repeatedly slapped the wall. "Blake, can you hear me? Tell Mommy where you are! I'm right here, sweetie, just let me know where to find you!"

The door to the living room clicked open. Squinting, Whit shuffled in wearing her robe and slippers. "What's going on?" she mumbled.

"It's Blake! He's here! He's calling for help!" Katie exclaimed, but her son's voice hadn't returned.

Whit blinked in disbelief. "What? When?"

"Just now!" Katie pointed to the wall. "I think he's in the next unit."

"Are you sure it wasn't a nightmare?"

"Of course I'm sure!" Katie was on her way to the door, desperate to get to the parking lot. Since Monday night, the Hollisville PD had posted an officer in the lot at all times.

"Where are you going?" Whit demanded, but Katie was already through the door, onto the deck, Whit's words trailing her down the stairs.

The cop exited his car before Katie even reached the parking lot. "Is there a problem, Ms. Grafton?"

Katie sprinted through an explanation, Whitney arriving beside her, shivering.

The officer barked a request for backup into his radio. As if warning them to stay away, a vicious gust sprang on them, knocking Whit off balance.

But Katie took no notice of it, her eyes fixed on 99 Deepwoods Drive.

***

Mike drove to Hollisville, New Hampshire, early Thursday morning. He hadn't told Sue what he and Dave Strait were involved in, only that he was helping with the Blake Grafton investigation. At breakfast, he'd said things were slow in Elkins and that he would have some extra time to assist Dave's department with the case, a story that had been mostly true. Elkins was quiet with crime but busy with paperwork; and Mike really was working with Dave to find Blake Grafton. He hadn't lied to his wife, not outright – he'd simply omitted a few important and terrifying details. Sue didn't need to know about everything, he'd decided after much brooding, especially not now, when she was finally starting to unwind from the upheaval of Chris's battle with cancer. Mike had kept several disturbing things he'd encountered on the job from her in the past – this was no different, just another dark corner that didn't need to be illuminated for her.

But then there was the matter of the premonitory nightmares. He still hadn't gotten around to telling Sue about those, not even after revealing his secret to Nate, the greens of guilt flourishing in his heart.

Soon. Real soon.

Dave's office at the station was cluttered, stacks of paperwork and files on the desk towering over framed family photographs like skyscrapers dwarfing small buildings. Additional documents covered two chairs and a circular table in the near corner, all of them pertaining to 99 Deepwoods Drive.

"I tried to assemble everything in chronological order," Dave said, sipping coffee from a thermos and regarding his office with a daunted look. "There's so much stuff on this place, you'll probably be here reading it till noon. Too bad our department lost the reports on the mass suicide, but you already know about that from online articles."

Mike bit into a blueberry doughnut he'd grabbed from a box in the kitchen. "Yeah, I could tell you anything you want to know about the mass suicide, but right now I'm concerned about what's happened in the years since."

Dave plucked a manila folder from the table and handed it to Mike. "This is the first suspicious incident report I could get my hands on. I spent an hour in storage rifling through old records."

Mike reviewed the documents in the folder: a police report from 1981 and a few yellowed pages of typewritten notes. The report described a theft called in by Don Kelly from his 99 Deepwoods Drive apartment (unit four, of course). According to Kelly, the individual(s) stole food, clothing, and small items like notebooks, pens, and candles. The responding officer had marked two asterisks beside the line, *Suspects did not steal any money or valuables,* a fact that was heavily emphasized in the subsequent notes prepared via typewriter. According to these notes, a brief follow-up investigation of the incident revealed nothing, and Kelly moved out of unit four only two weeks later, citing additional thefts and strange noises in the night.

"Whoever took Blake Grafton, I think you're right about them being responsible for crimes at that place for decades," Dave said.

"Yeah, but why? And why are the crimes becoming worse now? There has to be a reason for the timing."

Mike moved on to the next file. By the time he completed his journey through Eddie Pascale's month-plus tenure in unit four – which allegedly culminated with items from the man's refrigerator flying across the kitchen – he knew it was time to revisit the subject of a haunting.

"Dave, how can you not be convinced about this with so much evidence? Items inexplicably flying across the kitchen? What more do you need?"

Dave smoothed a hand over his shaved head. "I guess I'm just in denial, Mikey, afraid that if we admit this is really happening, it's like admitting defeat. I mean, how do we beat this?"

"I don't know, but we better do it fast before someone else goes missing. For almost thirty years there've been reports of bizarre stuff in that place, but never any suicides, murders, or abductions. Now, all of a sudden, you've had two suspicious deaths and two abductions in less than a year."

Dave rubbed his chin. "And you really think it's all this…Shepherd thing and a bunch of people who died back in sixty-five?"

"Nate and Joss think Shepherd comes for the souls of people who kill themselves, but it has to be more than that. Why would this thing wait until now?"

Mike quickly scanned through another file, stopping when he read the arrest report for Richard Judd. In December of 1981, he was arrested for breaking into unit four (then rented by his ex-wife, Martha Tillman). Upon entry, responding officers found him cowering in the bathroom and ranting about the place being haunted.

"Jesus, Dave, have you read about this Judd guy? Says here he told the cops a ghost locked him in the bathroom and took his gun – then the ghost said it was there to protect Judd's ex and daughter." Mike read on. "Holy shit, Judd also claimed the shower turned on by itself and the lights were turned off once he went into the bathroom to check it out." He read word for word from the report. "R. Judd was adamant about the place being haunted, maintaining that a ghost was inside the bathroom with him. A recommendation was made to the Cheshire County District Attorney's Office to arrange for a psychological evaluation prior to the suspect's dangerousness hearing–"

"Okay, you can stop now – I read it already." Dave sighed in frustration. "Why does this goddamn building have to be in my town?" His eyes roamed the hoards of files, then leveled on Mike again. "So what do you want to do, get a priest to bless the damn place? Order a bunch of crucifixes to hang from the walls?"

"Let's start by heading over there and getting a look at the shed. I want to see it for myself."

Dave froze. "You want to go back there? But the place has already been examined countless times, and the feds – they'll shut us down." Knots of tension were tightening beneath his skin, giving rise to a thin sheen of sweat across his forehead.

Shrugging, Mike said, "In my opinion, that's the best thing we can do for Blake right now. After learning what we did from Nate and Joss, we'd be remiss if we didn't at least check it out. And don't worry about the feds. My cousin ranks pretty high at the Bureau – I'll give him a call."

Dave mulled it over. Finally, he said, "Okay, but let's do it quickly. And if we find nothing, lunch is on you."

Chapter 9

Nate received a call from Joss early Thursday afternoon. She was frantic, speaking too fast for him to understand. When she finally slowed her pace to a comprehensible level, Nate realized she'd learned about the old woman's death in South Boston.

"I confirmed the address – it's her, the lady who lived in Max's apartment," she said in a distressed voice that approached a shout. "She must've had a heart attack after seeing the damage, *our* damage! We killed her, Nate!" A storm of French ensued, Nate making out a few words he'd picked up over the years but not much.

"Joss, calm down, just calm down." Nate proceeded to feign ignorance, asking where she'd heard about the woman's death.

Joss said she'd read an article online, which meant she hadn't discovered any additional facts beyond the revelation that the woman was dead. Since Nate had first learned of her death, he'd searched often for internet updates. So far, the police hadn't released any information about suspects or even provided the woman's name to the media, but that didn't mean they weren't tracking leads.

Nate told Joss he would stop at her house so they could talk about it. He'd been hoping to keep this from her – now she would have another burden dropped on her already sagging shoulders. Nate imagined her on the other end, a bottle of wine in her free hand as she wasted more time drinking in her hot tub.

"Dammit!" he shouted after ending the call, again wondering how he'd been stupid enough to go to Boston with her. Even if the police couldn't identify them, there would be no escaping the handcuffs of guilt.

**

Following her phone conversation with Nate, Joss grabbed a bottle of Absolut vodka from her hidden box of alcohol in the closet (the stash she'd purchased in Montreal). This was no time for wine; only the strong stuff could blunt her current horrors.

She peeled off her clothes as if afire, threw on her robe, and hurried outside to the hot tub. The wind-chilled air bit her face, but soon she was submerged up to her neck in welcoming water.

We killed her. It's our fault.

The first pop of vodka was like a shot of acid, burning her throat and shredding its way downward. She coughed, feeling lightheaded, then returned to the well, this time downing considerably less liquid fire. Yet the more she thought about the old lady's death, the greater her desire for drunkenness became. She needed to get away from it, to check out for a while. It didn't matter how she left her guilt behind; she would swallow the first drink or pill that promised an instant vacation.

By the time Nate arrived, Joss's surroundings were somewhat blurry and dreamlike. She heard her boyfriend shouting but couldn't see him, the water feeling so gelatinous that she might as well have been bathing in Jell-O. She'd fallen asleep for a few minutes, Nate's voice having drawn her out of it. Squinting against the bright back lawn, she searched the disquieting haziness and steadied her gaze on an approaching shadow.

"Joss, are you okay?" His voice sounded distant and distorted. Slowly, his facial features began to take shape, like the letters on an eye chart gradually being brought into focus.

"I'm fine," she said, feeling nauseous. Now the details of the back yard were achieving clarity behind Nate: the covered pool; the walkway; the shrubs; the trellis, with its fancy arch, beneath which Mom went ambling in the mornings, tea in hand.

"You're drunk again," Nate muttered. "Joss, you've gotta stop this. You're gonna end up poisoning yourself."

Joss skimmed a hand across the water, which suddenly felt cold. She began speaking in a French-Russian combination, though not intentionally. She had indeed checked out, but it would do nothing to mitigate her problems; they would wait patiently for her return, as would the gnawing guilt.

***

Nate couldn't believe Joss was already drunk. The bottle of Absolut resting in the hot tub cup holder was mostly full, but at her size it wouldn't have taken much to achieve intoxication.

Sighing, Nate stared up at the sky, as if God would offer His advice. Splashing and laughing like a child in a bubble bath, Joss looked gorgeous and pathetic, Nate remembering the September afternoon he'd carried his drunken girlfriend away from this very hot tub.

Three months later, he would have to do it again.

"Come on, Joss, let's get you to bed."

She offered token resistance but quickly gave in. Nate helped her out of the tub and eased her into a robe, then carried her inside and upstairs to her room. Shivering, she hugged herself on the end of her bed as Nate gathered a pair of towels from the closet.

"Joss, this is no good at all," he said, sliding off her robe and toweling her dry. He tried to wrap the other towel around her hair like she always did, but it wouldn't stay. She swept it up and began whipping his shoulders, laughing wildly in the throes of inebriation.

Nate yanked the towel away from her. "Stop, Joss! This isn't funny! Do you realize how serious your drinking problem is?"

She nodded vacantly before falling back on the bed and resuming her laughter. When Nate returned with a sweatshirt and pajama pants, her eyes were closed and she appeared to be sleeping.

"What now?" she said when Nate touched her shoulder.

"I got some clothes for you. Put them on so you stay warm."

"No." She snapped her eyes shut.

"Fine. Have it your way." Nate tossed the clothes on her legs. He felt like a babysitter, or an orderly trying to care for a mentally ill young woman at a psychiatric hospital. For a moment he thought of Jean-Philippe Leclaire, her father, and what he might think if he could see his daughter now.

Her stubbornness fading, Joss tugged on the clothes Nate had selected and slid beneath the covers, her red-painted toes peeking out from the disarrayed sheets until Nate straightened them.

Joss's eyes were dazed and frighteningly remote. "Love you, Nate," she whispered.

"I love you too." He couldn't bring himself to scold her further. Instead, he lied next to her in bed.

In less than a minute, Joss was breathing shallowly in the earliest stage of sleep. Nate decided to stay with her out of fear that she might choke on her own vomit...or some other disaster. He wanted to continue the Christmas shopping he'd been doing when she called, but Joss's safety had seized the moment. She was in such a worrisome state, a burgeoning alcoholic with a flare for the occasional trance. Great. Just what he needed. Maybe this was his payback, a sort of karmic justice for the stress, sadness, and anger he'd caused Joss while addicted to painkillers.

Would she need to visit a rehab center just as he had? Nate could only hope it wouldn't come to that, but the time for serious consideration of an intervention had arrived.

Nate feared the results.

Chapter 10

Mike followed Dave's unmarked cruiser to 99 Deepwoods Drive. Katherine Grafton's car, a marked Hollisville cruiser, and a van were the only three vehicles in the parking lot – no feds, no reporters. Apparently the initial media storm was over, the vultures bringing their recorders and cameras back to their nests for a period of slumber before the next feeding frenzy began. Meanwhile, the FBI field agent and the other investigators were out conducting interviews and following leads, allowing Mike and Dave a thin window.

Dave spoke briefly to the officer keeping watch from his cruiser, who handed him a set of keys. "You want me to go with you, Chief?" he said, eyeing Mike suspiciously. It must have been weird for him to see Dave working with some cop from another town, perhaps even a little insulting.

"You stay here in case Katherine needs you," Dave said. He nodded at her car. "I take it she hasn't left yet today."

"No, sir, but Roberts told me she asked him to check out the place overnight. She was frantic, I guess, said she heard Blake screaming for her. Roberts called for backup but they didn't find anything – most likely just a nightmare, they assumed."

Mike and Dave exchanged alarmed glances. "I want that report right away," Dave said.

"Will do, sir."

On their way across the lawn to the shed, Mike said, "Looks like Shepherd might be keeping Blake in the same place where he took Joss." Mike felt a strong urge to explain his premonitory nightmares, but he held back, not wanting to become overwhelming.

Dave was silent, his face pinched with words unsaid. Standing before the shed, he opened the padlock securing a rusty latch. The latch keened loudly when he pulled it forward, the door itself offering an eerie groan at first movement. The interior was dark and musty, smelling of sawdust, and for a moment Mike thought he heard something scurrying in the depths of blackness, something of moderate size.

Dave found a dropdown string and tugged it, filling the shed with flickering, sickly fluorescent light from overhead lamps. The left side wall bristled with nails supporting an array of tools. Running parallel to the far wall was a chain-link fence, behind which stood the furnace, a hot water tank, the electrical distribution board, and other vital equipment. This was the heart of the house in more ways than one, the main hub where the lifeblood originated before channeling outward through wires and pipes. If they were to find anything of significance, this was the place for such a discovery.

Reluctantly, Mike closed the door behind them, eliminating the sunlight except for a circle that passed through the door's thin window. He remembered Nate ignoring his warnings and coming in here that stormy September night, the door locking behind him. Mike hadn't been able to force it open despite repeated attempts, and now he knew why –which summoned fears that he and Dave would find themselves locked in today.

"This place is creepy," Dave muttered, slowly pressing forward into a small empty room to the right of the fence. The shed had already been cleared multiple times by investigators, but Mike nonetheless expected to locate something that had been missed. A trapdoor maybe, or a secret panel in the walls.

After examining the vacant back room, they proceeded to the left part of the shed, where the infamous tunnel curved in a gently downsloping path that had once connected to the basement. Since the main structure had been built on a hillside, its foundation was slightly higher in elevation than the base of the adjoining shed, a series of extensive construction projects having amalgamated the two. Old walls had come down and new ones had gone up, probably when it was determined that the building would serve renters and an enhanced network of utilities would be required.

But had the workers who'd undertaken these projects known about what happened here in 1965, they might have sprinted for the parking lot long before the passageway to the basement was complete.

Because the overhead lights didn't illuminate the tunnel, Dave pulled out his flashlight and showed the way ahead with its bright bouncing beam. As expected, the passageway terminated with a workbench and a foul-smelling utility sink, as if an animal had climbed into the basin and hadn't been able to scratch its way out.

"Christ, that sink smells disgusting," Dave said, covering his nose and mouth, but Mike was less focused on the odor than a noise. It sounded like footsteps on the other side of the concrete wall behind the workbench.

Mike tapped the wall. It was damp and cracked in places but solid, certainly not a movable wall.

"This wall wasn't here the night Nate went through," Mike said. "And the basement wasn't on the other side, either – it was a staircase."

As Dave analyzed the wall, gliding the light along each crack and chip in the concrete, Mike spun around and listened for a new noise. It had sounded like a hollow exhalation, drifting in from the darkness beyond the curve of the passageway where they'd come from.

"There's something weird about this wall," Dave said.

Mike turned to face him, but the noise came even louder behind them, blooming into an echoing whisper. Mike whirled around to find something briefly there, a tall shadow somehow visible about ten feet away in the darkness, swaying, watching, black amidst black. Then it was gone.

"Dave, shine the light down there!" he shouted, but by the time his friend illuminated the tunnel, there was nothing but concrete walls and a low ceiling.

"What is it?"

"I'm not sure. I thought I saw something. Did you hear those noises?"

"No, what noises?"

"I don't know. They sounded like whispers. It's almost like…never mind."

After a few moments of anxious waiting, Dave returned his focus to the upper left portion of the wall. "You see all these little lines?" he said, indicating a spider web of cracks in the concrete like those of a smashed windshield.

Mike tested the wall, half-expecting his hand to ram through it, into a secret room. But the wall held firm, tendriled with cracks and dents.

"I'd like to hit it with a sledgehammer – we might just find a staircase on the other side," Mike said.

Instead, they left with the same questions they'd carried into the shed, unaware that a single wall had separated them from Blake Grafton, a wall dividing dimensions.

THE INHABITANTS II

Part IV: Welcome to Hell

"Abandon all hope, ye who enter here." ~ Dante Alighieri

Chapter 1

Max spent another lonely night in his prison. It wasn't like he had a choice in the matter. He could no longer pass through the walls or even see through them, a captive in a hopeless tomb. He felt like Fortunato from "The Cask of Amontillado", except there would be no promise of eventual death at the hands of starvation. He would be trapped in this place forever, he feared. No food, no water, no sleep, no entertainment beyond the creations of his mind. No interactions, no connections, no aspirations, only isolation. This wasn't eternal burning but perhaps its psychological equivalent, one day after another of watching the sunlight come and go beyond the unbreakable window.

Max wondered what Jocey was doing. In the drunken haze during which he'd taken his life, he hadn't thought of his sister, not even a flicker of consideration to light the darkness of impulse. He'd only seen Jocey a few times in the months preceding his death, and on each occasion they'd argued fiercely.

"Get over yourself already!" she'd shouted one August day at his South Boston apartment. She'd brought him a sandwich, just like old times, hoping to reconnect with her brother. "You need to find your faith, Max. Get off your ass and make something of your life. Go to college – *do* something. Look at yourself, you're a janitor. What would Dad think?"

"Oh, come off it already. You sound like Mom."

"Fuck you! I'd rather be crazy than empty like you."

"Since when did you become such a bitch, anyway? It's not like your life's all that great. When's the last time you even talked to Nate?"

She flinched, Max feeling a pang of regret. "Nate and I will get back together," she declared with a pointed finger. "I just need time to rebuild my trust, and he needs time to move past his brother's death. Oh, that's right, you wouldn't know because you weren't even at the funeral!"

"So? I never met the guy."

"Nice, real nice, Max. Did you ever think that maybe I wanted you there? This isn't just some random guy–"

"Save it. I know how much you love Nate, blah, blah, blah. But for all that love, he sure did ditch your ass pretty quick."

She began to cry, and Max was consumed by guilt. He remembered the December Debacle and how little he'd thought of his sister that afternoon – memories that made him feel cold and contemptuous. Jocey loved Nate, and they'd been together for more than two years after that December day, separating only recently following the death of his brother.

"Jocey, I'm sorry," he said, trying to hug her.

She pulled away and faced the living room window. "I just want you to be happy, Max. Whether you accept God or not, I want us to be close again. Your drinking has to stop. Don't you know that's only gonna bring you down, just like what happened to Nate?"

"I know, but–"

She spun around. "What do you want me to do, Max, congratulate you on all of…this?" She briefly regarded the room, throwing her hands up in disapprobation. "This whole thing fucking sucks!"

She was right. It sucked. Everything sucked. But Max didn't want to stop drinking, and he certainly didn't have an interest in returning to Mom's house to try that life again, the one that had driven him out here in the first place. It was easier to just stay where he was and keep his little clunker of a life dragging along.

You'll never amount to anything!

Jocey sat on the threadbare couch, the one Billy Moreland had just banged his girlfriend on last night. Max had walked in on it, his habit of stumbling upon people's private moments continuing.

"You always had my back when we were kids," Jocey said. "Whenever I needed help, you were there – like after Dad died and I was a wreck." She glanced down, deep in memory. "I couldn't even get through a night, and you always told me stories and waited for me to fall asleep again." She looked up at him, searching for a way in, a path to inspiration.

Max sat beside her. "Yeah, those were some long nights. I remember helping you up whenever you fell on the rinks, too. You couldn't skate to save your life."

She smiled. "Yeah, I was terrible at that. But even when your friends were there and you wanted to be cool, you still helped me." She took his hand. "How about we become the Leclaire sibling team again? We could get an apartment in Worcester. I've got some money saved from the photography studio, and you could get a job in–"

"Jocey, Jocey, slow down. I'm not moving to Worcester with you."

She looked deflated. "Why not? It could work."

Music jolted Max free of his memories. Organ music, so deep and vibratory that it shook the walls. It sounded like a pipe organ, its tune solemn and familiar, and by the time the song transitioned from its ominous opening and began a steady rise to chaos, the notes were considerably softer…fading, fading, and finally gone. Silence.

"Toccata and Fugue, in D minor," a voice called from the far alcove. "Do you like it, Maxime?" A man in a black robe stepped out, his face hidden by a hooded veil, the robe dragging behind him, rustling across dusty floorboards.

"Who the hell are you?"

Distantly, the music came again, seeping through walls and joists and floors in relentless pursuit of a listener. If Max closed his eyes, he could be an uncomfortable eight-year-old kid again, back in church, sitting in his stupid suit beside little Jocey, restless and itchy, bookended by Mom and Dad.

The hooded creep approached slowly, watching Max with his head slightly tilted. On and on the organ played, the music shifting to a merry yet eerie set of chords tailor-made for carousels. A sudden tinkling flourish spirited through the walls, higher, happier, crazier…in his mind's eye, Max could see the carousel horses going faster and faster…and the man had come to a stop about fifteen feet away. When he clapped his gloved hands, the music abruptly died.

"Welcome to Hell, Maxime," he said in a gravelly voice. "If you want to leave this place, you'll need to do exactly as I say. I am Shepherd, and this is my house."

Chapter 2

Blake nibbled at the stale, saltless spaghetti that had been delivered to him in a small bowl an hour ago. Absent sauce and meat, the meal looked like a cluster of slimy yellow worms twisted together. Gross. He didn't dare complain, though, not after the hooded man had warned him that he would only be taken back to Mom if he followed the rules.

He brought another forkful of insipid worms to his mouth, took a small bite, and washed it down with rust-tinged water. His belly felt sick. He rubbed it in vain, hoping he wouldn't throw up – that might make the hooded man mad. He'd told Blake to put a smile on his face, promising to return him to Mom if he obeyed every instruction.

After finally giving up on his bland dinner, Blake set the bowl down on the bed and studied the room. It was the same one he'd initially found himself trapped in, the small bed nestled into the back corner and the network of wooden beams looming overhead. There was nothing crawling up there this time; no bats swooping out from under the bed, either. Still, the lack of visible threats in the room did nothing to reduce Blake's aching apprehension. His stomach was nauseous with dread, an instinctive, portentous feeling that filled him with dark certainty beyond his understanding and imagination.

Beyond his youthful years.

Beyond his worst nightmares, where he fell from infinite heights and was chased by menacing creatures.

The old man entered the room some time later, quietly closing the door behind him. Blake couldn't remember his name, something that began with a J. His hair was even more unruly than before, frizzed and staticky. He wore a blue wool sweater and gray pants. Smiling, he tried to appear friendly but failed, his smile sending a jolt of fear into Blake's heart. He knew the man was planning a bad thing. Very bad.

Nodding at the bowl, the old man said, "How did you like Ms. Keppel's spaghetti?" He was apparently referring to the frail old woman who'd given Blake the food and water. She'd said nothing to him, offering a wistful smile before locking the door behind her.

"It was good," Blake mumbled, looking down. He hoped the man would go away, but instead he came a little closer to the bed where Blake was sitting.

"You didn't eat very much," he noted. "Was there something wrong with your dinner?"

"No, it was good," Blake hastened, afraid to anger him. "I'm not very hungry."

The man sighed, gazed up at the complex woodwork. There were no windows in the room, but it must have been at the edge of the building, for a shrieking gust buffeted the walls and ushered in a cold draft. The wind sounded alive, like an enraged monster waiting for Blake outside; only in the winter did it sound like that.

"Tell me, boy," the man said after a while, "have you studied the Bible in church?"

Blake shook his head. Frowning, the man advanced a few steps. He ran a hand through his wild hair. "Do you and your mother attend church regularly?"

"Only on Christmas and Easter," he said quietly, fixing his eyes on the man's shiny black shoes, the laces impossibly thin.

The man's frown deepened. "No wonder you didn't understand what I said before. You haven't been properly introduced to faith." He nodded as if graced with sudden enlightenment. "Are you even familiar with the suffering of Jesus?"

Blake's tears welled, the minimal contents of his stomach churning on a sea of nauseous fear. He stood and hurried past the man to the far wall near the door. It would be locked, of course, but he tried it anyway.

Locked. Always locked.

The man sat in the spot Blake had just occupied on the bed. "Fear not, child!" he declared. "I am the first and the last, and the living one. I died, and behold I am alive forevermore, and I have the keys of Death and Hades!"

Blake sank to the floor, pulling himself into a little
ball and crying. When he finally looked up, the man
was smiling at him from the bed. "This is no time
for tears – this is an exciting time. Soon you'll be
back with your mother, but just think of the lessons
you can learn about your Lord in the meantime.
Aren't you excited, boy?"

Blake sniffled. It required every bit of strength to
hold back more tears. He eyed the man, overcome
by fear. Immense fear, too much to handle.

Bile rose steadily, shooting upward, forcing Blake
to hunch over, his meager dinner spilling onto the
dusty wooden floor.

He looked up when it was over, terrified. But the
old man did not scold him or strike him. Kneeling
beside Blake and placing a hand upon his shoulder,
he chuckled at some enigmatic humor.

"Fear not, for I have redeemed you. I have called
you by name; you are mine," he said in a soft,
convicted voice. "When you pass through the
waters, I will be with you. And through the rivers,
they shall not overwhelm you. When you walk
through fire, you shall not be burned – and the
flame shall not consume you."

Though Blake had no idea what was being said to
him, the stench of vomit assaulting his nose, he
found himself a little less afraid.

"Come on," the old man urged. "Let's get you back to Max. I think you two could use some more time together."

***

Katie wished everyone would just go home and leave her to miserable solitude inside the apartment. Their endless platitudes were becoming suffocating, especially the ones about having faith and never giving up. If Katie heard one more person pledge to pray for the Grafton family, she might run screaming from the building.

Most bothersome of everyone were Katie's parents. She'd originally embraced their help, but now their presence was barely tolerable. It was Thursday evening, three nights since Blake's abduction, and Katie's reactions were changing quickly and dramatically. The sight of her parents suddenly made her angry. They hadn't cared enough to help her move into this place last month or even visit the apartment in the following weeks, but now that Blake was missing they were apparently ready to assume the role of loving grandparents.

"The Facebook page is set up, and I'm almost finished with the website," her mother said. She faced the stove, adding milk to a pot of mashed potatoes. Across the kitchen, beside the sink, Katie's father was preparing a bowl of salad on the countertop.

"Thanks for everything," Katie said blandly, staring at the small kitchen table and wondering yet again if she was slowly losing her mind. But she knew she'd heard Blake calling for her – it hadn't been a trick of exhaustion and desperation.

He was there. So close. It wasn't a dream, and I'm not losing it! He was in the house!

Sitting opposite Katie, Whit reached across the table and took her hand. She said nothing, just smiled, the greatest comfort Katie could ask for. Long-winded declarations of support, it turned out, were half as soothing as a well-timed smile from a friend.

Still tending to the potatoes, her mother continued her report of tasks accomplished. "I uploaded a few photos to the website, and tomorrow I'll add a bunch more. By the way, Katie, don't forget about that interview you have tomorrow."

"Interview?" Katie searched her memory. Nothing.

Her mother turned from the stove. "The *Boston Globe* reporter, remember?"

"Oh…right. That," Katie nodded.

"It's at noon. Whit, make sure she remembers, okay? This is really important."

"Yes, very important," her father added, choosing four plates from the cabinet for dinner. "Katie, now that the police have given you the green light to publicly discuss the message from the abductor, this article should be the most informative one yet. The reporter said he wants to focus on the history of this place, especially the fact that the last renter's girlfriend was abducted, too. The article will reach a wide audience – maybe someone will remember something. It's way better than just talking with the local news people."

"The abductor must be someone who lives in the neighborhood. Must be," her mother said. It was a belief she'd mentioned at least a dozen times, yet she always sounded as if she were bringing up a new point.

Katie was loath to speak to another reporter. She'd talked to so many journalists and cops over the last three days that each face had blended into the next one, the questions like a fusillade of darts being tossed at her from all angles. Regardless of whether it originated from an honest desire to help bring Blake home or a morbid fascination with the abduction of a child, everyone was taking an interest in the investigation. The parking lot had been filled over the previous two days with news vans representing almost every station between Manchester and Springfield. Finally things had lightened up today, but now Katie would have to start again with the media tomorrow. Just the idea made her feel daunted. Another reporter with questions – another story to be spun however its writer saw fit. But did these people really care about Blake coming home, or did they just want to upstage the next guy?

Katie's parents dictated the dinner conversation, recapping everything they'd done as though someone had demanded a status report. Meanwhile, the only sounds that came from Whit's end of the table were the clinking of silverware and the occasional assenting mumble.

Although Katie said nothing, her parents more than made up for it with optimistic chatter. They kept saying things like, *It's only a matter of time before they find him* and, *This guy's gonna make a mistake, and the cops will be there when he does.* Dad was in the middle of praising the police department for placing a unit in the parking lot around the clock, when a series of thumps came from directly overhead, strong enough to rattle the kitchen light's frosted glass cover.

They all looked up, then at each other.

"What the hell is that?" Whit said, dropping a spoonful of mashed potatoes to the plate.

A soft creaking of floorboards indicated movement. Someone was walking around upstairs!

Dad frowned. "No one's living up there, right?"

Katie shook her head, remembering Blake's nightmare from his first night in the apartment.

"We should get the officer," Mom said, and the four of them stood, forgetting dinner.

Chapter 3

In spite of Joss's hangover Thursday night, Nate hoped to have a productive conversation with his girlfriend. He'd wound up spending the entire afternoon and evening with her, watching sadly as she puked into a bowl he'd brought in anticipation of such emergencies.

It was almost nine o'clock. Having washed her face and brushed her teeth, Joss slogged out of the bathroom with the edges of her hair damp and dark. The rest of her hair fell down her back in a disheveled mane. Her eyes were red. Her face was pale. She looked terrible and yet strangely exquisite; she could be covered in mud and still look gorgeous (Laina hadn't given her that lingerie modeling gig out of the kindness of her heart).

"You feel any better?" Nate said.

She shook her head weakly, then pulled off her clothes and fetched new ones from her dresser. "I feel like my head's gonna explode," she said, throwing on a Montreal Expos T-shirt and a pair of pink shorts. Nate had turned up the thermostat a few hours ago, and now the room felt like an oven.

"Don't worry about your mom. I told her you caught a bug, so she didn't cook anything for dinner. She said she'll be in her office for a few hours to catch up on work."

Joss sighed in relief. "Thanks, Nate. I owe you big time. If she knew about this, I'd be so screwed."

Sitting on her bed, she shielded her face with a hand as if bothered by the dim lamplight. "God, this is awful. I feel like I got hit by a car...no, a bus."

Nate eased onto the bed beside her. Settling a hand on her thigh, he said, "You've gotta stop drinking, babe. Between the trances and the alcohol, you're really scaring me. I know I'm the last person to talk, but take it from an addict who's got an addict for a father – this is a bad road you're going down."

She looked at him apologetically, perhaps even sheepishly. She took his hand. "I'm *so* sorry, Nate. I don't know what's wrong with me. Will you take the box away? I know I'll drink again if it's here – I don't trust myself."

"What box?"

She sought the warmth of the covers, assuming a supine position and tilting the pillows upward so she could speak to him. "It's in the back of the closet, behind my shoes. I've got all the alcohol in there."

Nate had been under the impression that she was asking her friends to buy alcohol for her, or using that newly acquired fake I.D. What the hell was this box all about? He walked to the closet, reached behind her massive collection of footwear, and found a big cardboard box, its flaps hanging open. Inside were four bottles of wine, another bottle of Absolut vodka, and an assortment of other alcoholic beverages.

Stunned, Nate pulled out one of the wine bottles and examined it. Clos du Bois chardonnay. "Joss, where'd you get all of this?"

"Montreal. Since you can buy it legally up there, I figured I might as well load up." She coughed, and for a moment Nate worried she'd vomit again.

"I'm glad you told me about this. Are there any other boxes?"

"No, just that one."

"And you bought all of that alcohol yourself?"

"No, they gave it to me for free after an orgy at this strip club on Saint Catherine Street." She smiled faintly, her eyes closing.

"Always a wiseass, even with a hangover."

Nate crossed the room and dispensed water into a plastic cup from her Poland Spring cooler. There were a few others in the house, their three-gallon bottles refreshed as needed by the maid.

Nate set the cup on her nightstand. "You should drink some water."

"Maybe later. I might get sick again if I drink that."

"Fair enough." He knelt beside the bed and stroked her hair. She smiled, this time sighing in content.

After a while, Nate decided to bring up what had been eating at him all afternoon. "You know, that lady didn't die because of anything we did."

Her eyes shot open. "Can we not talk about that?"

"Just close your eyes and listen. You don't have to say a word, but I need to get this off my chest. That lady...the article I read said there was major damage in her living room. Clearly something else happened, because what we did in the bedroom was hardly major damage. And we didn't touch a thing in the living room."

She sat up. "Regardless of what happened later, the police will be looking for us. That poor lady is *dead*."

"It's horrible, I know, but there's nothing we can do to change it – we can only move forward. I think our disguises were good enough that no one will be able to identify us."

There was a moment's silence as she nodded in agreement. "You're probably right. They would have arrested us by now, or at least questioned us. But I still feel like shit. What if you broke the lock or something and allowed someone to get in? In that neighborhood, there's probably gangbangers all over the place."

"Gangbangers?"

"Yeah, what would you call them?"

He held her cold hand. "How about gangsters? At any rate, I don't think someone broke in after us. It's something else – I've got a really weird feeling about this. We'll talk more tomorrow, but I want you to know there's nothing for you to feel guilty about. Whatever went down, it's not our fault."

A sad smile played across her lips. "I seriously don't know what I'd do without you, Nate."

He leaned in for a kiss. "I'm gonna take off. Rest up, beautiful. You'll feel better in the morning."

Joss pointed at the box of alcohol. "Take my stash with you. If Mom asks you what's in there, just say Christmas gifts or something. She'll believe anything."

"How much are you paying me to keep your secret?"

"You'll find out tomorrow night. I'll even pay interest."

"Damn bootlegger. I'm surprised customs didn't catch you with all that alcohol."

"Well, if you ever need to smuggle anything over the border, I'm your girl. But next time I go, I'm hiding the Laura Secord chocolates from you."

"Yeah, I get a little carried away with those things, don't I?"

"You eat them like popcorn."

A sudden thought of his father grounded Nate with fear. "Seriously, though, you've gotta stop drinking. Giving me the box is a good first step, but you need to follow through on this and stay clean."

She brought a hand to her heart. "I promise, Nate. No more drinking for me. From now on, I'm dealing with my problems head on."

There was insincerity in her words, Nate wondering if she was pretending just as he had in the spring. He wanted to keep the conversation going, but Joss lied back and closed her eyes.

He could only pray she would keep her promise.

Chapter 4

Max was staring at the wall, lost in a mindless stupor incited by unremitting boredom, when he suddenly became aware of movement. It was like waking after a long sleep, except Max didn't feel rested but panicked and disoriented.

A few moments passed before he could register what was going on, but finally everything clicked in and he was able to remember the name of the boy standing before the window.

"Blake, what are you doing here? Where'd you go?" Max ran to the end of the prison and hugged him.

"He thinks I should spend time with you," Blake said in a small voice.

Again Max wondered if the boy was dead – why else would he be here? The hooded creep had called this place Hell, but how could a kid be in Hell?

"Have you seen a guy with a hood over his face?" Max asked.

The boy nodded feverishly. "He said I have to do what he says if I want to see Mom again."

"He was wearing a black robe, right? And he had a really raspy voice?"

"Uh-huh."

Max crossed his arms. "He threatened me, too."

"He's bad, real bad," Blake said, turning quickly toward the window as if he'd heard something. His eyes were wide with fear, the same fear that wrapped around Max like a suffocating plastic sheet.

Max took the boy's hand. The front of his sweatshirt was stained with brown splotches that looked like vomit. He smelled vaguely of a recent hurl, Max trying not to gag. He'd always been sensitive to foul smells, but why hadn't death done away with the olfactory system? If he was going to be stuck in the walls for eternity, couldn't he at least be spared the offense of every rancid odor that seeped into his prison?

"We can't wait for him to come back," Max said. "Whatever he told us is a lie. He's using us, and we need to find our own way out of here."

Blake shot him a worried look. "But how will we do that?"

Max's eyes fell upon the window. "Come on, I have an idea."

***

The four of them – Katie, her parents, and Whit – hurried down the staircase and across the lawn to the parking lot, where they found the officer assigned to the building in his cruiser, busily entering information into the laptop. It was another cold night, heat pouring out of the car when the driver's window came down.

Katie's father explained the situation, which hardly seemed to alarm the officer. Stepping out of his car, he spoke without urgency into the radio and checked his keychain. He'd probably heard about Katie's false alarm, but this time her parents and Whitney could verify everything. Someone was definitely up there, thumping around the darkness of unit five, which was supposed to be empty along with the majority of the building.

"You folks can head back to your apartment," the officer said. "I'll check the third floor and see who's up there. This place has been all over the news – brings a lot of unwanted attention."

"I'm going with you," Katie said, starting toward the apartment.

"No, let me handle this. Protocol," he said apologetically.

Katie wanted to run up to unit five, but she stopped herself, watching as the officer climbed the stairs, wondering what the camera footage would show. The police had set up exterior surveillance cameras to catch any suspicious activities around the building, but it seemed like nothing suspicious ever happened outside…only within those walls where so many had perished.

While the officer investigated unit five, his every movement betrayed by the creaking of floorboards,

Katie listened carefully with her parents and Whit in the kitchen. They alternated between looking at each other and the ceiling, their faces aglow with apprehension. Katie braced herself for a gunshot, or the officer's shouts, but all she heard were footsteps and groaning wood.

When the waiting became too agonizing, Katie made her way to the kitchen door, but Whit leaped up and held her arm. "Just stay here. Let him do his job."

The officer soon began moving more quickly and confidently, striding from room to room now that his initial sweep was likely complete. With no other sounds supplied by a windless December night, his footfalls were amplified substantially.

"There's something wrong with this place," Katie blurted, again remembering Michael Overbrook's words.

"Do you think it's possible the abductor is living somewhere in the apartment?" her mother suggested. "I mean, who knows how many secret rooms this place has. Maybe the cops missed one."

Katie shuddered to think of her son confined in some crawlspace or hidden room. All that searching, and what if Blake had never left the building?

"There's no way," her father said. "The feds went through this place countless times –they would have found someone hiding out here."

"Unless there's another tunnel or something," Whit said. "I've read a lot about what happened here in the sixties, and maybe there's more to this place than anyone knows. That Johansen guy was completely insane – there's no telling what he did before they all killed themselves."

Katie and her parents silently contemplated the possibility. They'd all read about Joseph Johansen, in addition to dozens of other internet stories involving 99 Deepwoods Drive. But there wasn't anything online about the abduction here in September. The victim's name had been sealed by the police, who'd said they could only reveal information about the crime, not the individuals involved. It wouldn't be too hard for Katie and her family to work around the privacy barriers, though, especially since Katie had been visited by Michael Overbrook, the uncle of the previous renter. Now it was just a matter of getting in touch with the guy and learning who his nephew's girlfriend was.

But so far Dad's calls to Overbrook had gone unanswered. According to the Hollisville PD and the FBI, he'd provided each agency with a statement and was cooperating fully, but no one ever got into much detail about him, constantly referring inquiries to Chief Strait.

The officer rapped on the kitchen door five minutes later. "All clear up there," he said. "Another officer just got here – we'll go through the rest of the place and check the surveillance footage."

"You didn't find anything suspicious?" Katie's father demanded.

"No, sir. The place is empty, but it might have been kids. All kinds of rumors have been going around about this place – maybe someone took a dare."

"Just check the cameras already," Katie urged.

They returned to the dinner table after the officer left, but now the food was cold and no one felt like eating. Instead, they cleared the dishes and speculated about who they'd heard roaming apartment five. It didn't take long for the subject of Blake's nightmare to emerge...the one that hadn't been a nightmare at all.

Chapter 5

Mike experienced a major shift in his nightmare sequence during the early hours of Friday morning. Gone was the image of the helpless boy standing in the parking lot, replaced by a scene featuring that same boy trapped in a gray, murky room. He was talking to a young man around twenty with blue eyes and wavy dark blond hair. The man's skin was pale. His clothes were stained and torn, holes lining his black jeans.

Then Mike saw something else. Immediately before returning from the depths of sleep and reaching the surface of consciousness, a vision flashed into his head that would prove crucial to the investigation.

At the station later that morning, after catching up on a seemingly endless line of emails, Mike debated whether he should get in touch with Katherine Grafton's father. The guy had left three voicemail messages in the last two days seeking information about what Nate endured, but Mike didn't know how to respond. The truth would cause him and Nate to seem insane, but lying might make Grafton determined to question Joss in person. She and Nate were entitled to a little peace and privacy after such a traumatic event; most important, they deserved time to heal. The last thing they needed was a new person demanding that they answer questions about the night they'd almost died.

For these reasons, Mike had reluctantly avoided Katherine's father. He would never believe the real story – no one would, evidenced by the reactions of

Dave Strait. Even Mike himself wouldn't have believed it unless two people very close to him had described exactly what happened at 99 Deepwoods Drive. There really was evil in that place. Everyone assumed Blake's abductor lived somewhere nearby, but the true criminal resided in the house itself.

Mike knew he didn't have time for calls and questions, anyway. He had to figure out what this latest information in his nightmares meant and how it fit into the equation. That was the best way for him to help the Grafton family, not answering questions that would ultimately form a futile circle.

Yet he found himself dialing the number Mr. Grafton had provided, which began with an area code for western Massachusetts. The call was answered after the first ring.

"Hello?" Grafton's tone was impatient. Having likely been contacted by dozens of reporters, he probably assumed Mike was another member of the media looking for a quote.

"Hi, Mr. Grafton?"

"Yeah, what?"

"This is Mike Overbrook, returning your calls."

Grafton's voice immediately moderated, losing its hostile bite and acquiring a friendly, let's-start-over quality. "Thanks for getting back to me – I didn't recognize your number. Anyway, I wanted to learn more about what happened to your nephew and his girlfriend at this place. Whatever went down, it was bad enough for you to drive up here Monday and warn my daughter."

Mike felt a pang of guilt for keeping the truth from Grafton, but it had to be this way. Introducing new people to the mix would only complicate matters.

"It's a hell of a lot to swallow," Mike said, then described the haunting in such a diluted way that it focused solely on a pair of psychos who stalked and abducted renters from unit four.

"What about the two previous suicides in the building this year? My daughter said you mentioned those on Monday – do you think the same guys were involved?"

Mike didn't want to venture much deeper. "It's likely. I've explained all of this to the police up there, and they'll do everything they can to bring Blake home."

Grafton changed the subject. "What about your nephew? Where's he living now? It'd be great if Katie could speak to him and his girlfriend."

"I can't make any promises, but I'll ask if they're up for a meeting. They both feel terrible about what happened to Blake, but unfortunately there's nothing they haven't already told the police."

With this many lies stacked up, Mike wondered if he was qualified to be the White House press secretary. Before he ended the conversation, he told

Grafton to be careful at his daughter's apartment. "You never know when those guys will come back," he warned. "They're unpredictable. Make sure you don't leave Katherine alone there, especially since it's obvious they want her to stay for some reason."

"Yeah, the cops are here twenty-four seven, but that doesn't make me feel any better. Just last night we were eating dinner and heard someone walking around upstairs."

"Really?"

"Yeah, it was unmistakable. The cop checked it out and found nothing, but I'm telling you, someone was up there. Katie even heard Blake calling to her the other night."

"What? Where?"

"She said it sounded like he was in the next apartment over. She could hear him clearly through the walls, but the cops just chalked it up to exhaustion. My wife has this theory that the abductors are keeping Blake somewhere in the building. The cops don't believe it, of course – said they've checked every inch of the place. Tell me, what do you think of that closed-off tunnel that used to lead to the basement? Do you think there could be other tunnels?"

"At that place, anything is possible."

Mike had pulled out a notebook and begun scribbling, suddenly pleased about his decision to call Grafton. Combined with his latest visions, this information would give him and Dave a fresh scent to track through the nethermost chambers of 99 Deepwoods Drive.

Chapter 6

Joss woke early Friday morning feeling markedly better than the previous night. Her head still ached dully, but she forced herself through her morning exercise routine (half an hour on the treadmill, followed by light stretching and crunches). She showered, cooked breakfast, made coffee, and prepared two plates. When her mother entered the kitchen at seven, Joss was humming as she spread jelly across slices of toast.

"Morning, Mom," she said cheerfully. For the first time in weeks, she didn't feel like dragging herself back to bed.

"Good morning, angel," her mother said. "You made breakfast – what a nice surprise!"

Seated opposite her mother at the dining room table, Joss quietly ate her breakfast and thought about how lucky she was to have such a great boyfriend. Nate had overachieved since September, doing everything he could to take care of her and make her feel safe. She hadn't been the ideal girlfriend, though, drinking regularly and nagging him to accompany her to Boston. Now she felt like an idiot for forcing him to break into the old lady's apartment, an act that had caused her to experience tremendous guilt yesterday upon hearing about the woman's death. There had been thoughts of Max, thoughts of Shepherd, but she'd kept telling herself not to go there, that it would only make things worse.

Joss's mother barely looked up during breakfast, her focus alternating between the food and her cell phone, which buzzed every minute with an incoming text or email from someone at the school. She was always so busy, caring more about the job than her own daughter. Thankfully, she'd all but discontinued her anti-Nate campaign; now she did her best to avoid him and no longer badgered Joss about finding someone who was "more deserving of her love." Sometimes she frowned when Joss spoke of Nate, or rolled her eyes with resigned disapproval, but the energy had slowly leaked from her once fervid resistance effort. Soon there would be no fuel left to run on – no moral lectures, no castigations about sexual sins, no warnings of God's imminent wrath, no threats of Hell. Until then, Joss would endure the occasional blistering comment; frankly, she didn't care if her mother thought she was a sinful slut. She didn't need Anya's permission to live, and she no longer sought respect from a woman who'd hurt her in countless ways. Of course, she was obliged to tolerate her mother because of the childhood meals she'd prepared, the clothes she'd bought for her, the roof she'd put over her head, and the opportunities she'd afforded her. But now Joss was a young woman, not a dependent kid, and both she and her mother understood that if things went south she could easily move into a place with Nate and leave the wealth and luxury behind, just as Max had.

As Joss continued eating in silence, she remembered vividly many of the times Mom had injured her, usually with the strength of words. No matter how hardened she'd become, being called a whore and a sinner had always stung, the wounds pulsing long after the initial jabs. Joss had wanted so desperately for her mother to approve of her relationship with Nate, but nothing had convinced Anya to see him as anyone other than a guy who was using her daughter.

Much earlier in Joss's life, however, had been the absolute worst experience with Mom. The beating in the basement. Joss would forever carry the scars from that night; Nate had once asked how she'd gotten them, forcing her to lie about sitting on a radiator. She hadn't wanted to relive the suffering then, nor did she wish to describe it to him now or ever. Regardless of how much money she made in her life or how high she climbed, she would always remember how it felt to be stripped down and made to feel worthless. She would always know how it felt to have nothing, not even her dignity.

Joss stopped eating, set her fork on the plate. She was hungry for the remaining eggs, but her eyes were drawn helplessly into a glare. Anya Leclaire, meanwhile, gazed down at her phone as she'd done for much of the meal, oblivious to her daughter's hateful glower.

Joss's face twitched. Her thoughts vanished. Her hand drifted across the plate, found the knife, gripped its handle. She smiled, blinked once, and now she was wearing a short, tattered black dress, her torso partially exposed through ribbons of fabric.

Her eyes widened, full of malice. Slowly, calmly, she rounded the table and stood directly behind her mother, holding the knife above Anya's head, remembering the night her mother had beaten her without mercy. This time Joss wanted to hurt Mom, make her suffer, inflict the same agony she'd known as a little girl bent naked and helpless over a bed.

Still smiling, Joss thrust the knife downward, into the back of her mother's skull, pushed it deeper, past the resistance, deeper still, laughing at the ear-splitting, soul-seizing shriek.

She blinked again…and realized she was standing behind her mother, gripping the knife from her breakfast plate so tightly that it hurt her hand. Mom didn't even notice her there, still fixed on her phone.

Joss returned to her seat and set the knife on the plate, wondering what she'd just fallen victim to, a strange pressure lingering in her forehead. It was as though she'd momentarily sleepwalked and awakened behind Mom's chair, a knife in hand.

Without finishing her breakfast, she brought her plate to the kitchen and scraped the remaining food into the trash. Had it happened to her again, another trance? She couldn't remember anything.

Panicking, she splashed cold water against her face. Her mother was still in the dining room, nibbling on strawberries, her phone finally given a rest. Now she was reading a familiar pamphlet, one that made the rounds of the house this time each year: HOLY LAND TRIP – 10 BREATHTAKING DAYS OF BIBLICAL DISCOVERY, it read. (*Jocey, are you sure you don't want to join our group this summer?* Mom always asked. *Don't you want to see Nazareth, Jesus's boyhood home, and Capernaum, and the Chapel of the Primacy?*)

(*No thanks, Mom. It sounds amazing, but I'm gonna be really busy at work – and getting laid – this summer. Those ten days sure will be breathtaking, though!*)

Feeling suffocated, Joss hurried outside. She desperately needed some fresh air – anything to distract her tenuous mind from its own deficiencies. It was exceedingly frightening and debilitating to no longer be in control, a danger to herself and anyone around her.

"It's getting worse, much worse," she mumbled, fighting off fears that she was going insane.

***

Nate finished up his Christmas shopping at the mall on Friday morning. The major gifts had already been purchased – including tickets to an upcoming Carrie Underwood concert for Joss – and now all that remained was the small stuff.

He bought an Applebee's gift card for Uncle Mike and Aunt Sue, an Amazon.com gift card for Chris, and a few mystery novels for Joss's mother (she got annoyed by gifts every year, mentioning all that crap about Christmas not being for gifts and blah, blah, blah). Joss, on the other hand, loved the gifting experience, delighting Nate and his family each Christmas with baked desserts and handmade gifts, usually her photographs encased in carefully decorated frames. Her youthful enjoyment of the holidays was unrivaled, even though she rarely received Christmas gifts from her mother, who instead gave her two hundred dollars to purchase food for the less fortunate.

But this year had been different. There hadn't been any brownies or cookies from Jocey this month – and no gifts had been placed early beneath the massive tree at her house (every year Anya paid someone to deliver and erect the tree, although Joss always insisted on decorating it). Yet this season the big tree stood mostly unadorned in the foyer, boasting only a handful of items that Anya or Joss had gotten around to hanging.

On his way out of the mall, Nate made a mental checklist to ensure he didn't forget anyone. He was passing the movie theater when he received a call. "Hey, Uncle Mike. What's up?"

"Hey, Nate. I just spoke with Katherine Grafton's father. He's wondering if you and Joss might consider talking to Katherine sometime about what you experienced there."

"I don't know if that's such a good idea."

"You wouldn't have to tell the truth about the…you know…the whole Shepherd thing. But maybe it would do some good for Joss to talk with someone about what she went through. Only if she's up for it, of course."

"I'll talk to her, but I don't think she'll do it."

"How is she anyway?"

"Not good. She got drunk again yesterday – it seems like she's falling apart right in front of me."

"Unfortunately, it's gonna reach a point where you have to make a tough decision. You may not want to tell her mother about this, but you've gotta do what's right for Joss."

"Yeah, but her mom is nuts. She's part of the problem, not the solution."

"Nate, if your girl is sinking and you don't use every option available to you, you'll regret it. Maybe give it a little more time, but be careful about this."

"At least she gave me her box of alcohol last night. She bought a ton of wine and other stuff in Montreal, so maybe giving up that box was the first step."

"I don't know, Nate, it might have just been a front. There'll always be a guy willing to take her money and buy whatever she wants at the package store. Remember how sneaky you were during your addiction? Joss could have the same problem with alcohol. Who knows, she might have even started drinking after you guys separated over the summer."

Nate reached his Ford and fired it up, setting the heater on high. He hadn't even considered the possibility that Joss might have been drinking since the summer. "God, this could be worse than I thought," he admitted.

"She needs to get a handle on this right away. I've seen alcoholism ruin too many lives – just look at your dad. I'm glad he's gotten himself back on the wagon these last few months, but when someone has a drinking problem, there's always the fear that they're gonna fall off. Don't let Joss reach that point – tell her this is the end of the line. She's gotta stop."

Nate's father had gotten himself cleaned up since the fall and was now working as a superintendent at a general construction company. Nate was proud of his dad for attending the AA meetings and getting his life back on the rails, but like Uncle Mike had said, the fear of a relapse would always lurk in the back of Nate's mind.

After finishing his conversation with Mike, Nate called Joss and asked if he could come over her house.

"Of course. Would you like me to make you a sandwich? I'm stopping at the grocery store right now."

"Yeah, I'll have a sandwich, I guess. I'll be there in twenty minutes."

"Great! I can't wait to see you!" Her tone was so exuberant that he could envision her smiling on the other end, a striking picture limned in his head, that smile so frequently lighting his life. "Love you, Nate."

"I love you too, Jocey Marie."

Chapter 7

Max lifted Blake up and helped him balance on his shoulders. The boy scarcely weighed fifty pounds, an easy load to manage for an extended period.

"What if I fall?" Blake quavered.

Max held his legs firmly. "Don't worry, pal, I got you. Just see if you can jar the top loose."

They were facing the tall arched window at the far end of the room, spectral in its admittance of hazy orange light indicative of another sunset. Or maybe the light came from the furnace of Hell, slithering through the window and threatening to burn them. It was impossible to see anything outside clearly, even after they'd dusted off the lower portion of the opaque window. Only vague images took shape in the world beyond, a few of which were obviously trees, their limbs jutting outward as gray-black shadows amidst the orange gloom.

The window extended almost to the ceiling. Blake tapped it gently at first with the butt end of a flashlight they'd found in the near alcove, then with increasing vigor. Once he realized Max wasn't going to let him fall, he began to pound the window with all of his seven-year-old might. "It won't break."

"That's okay. Keep trying."

A voice startled them. Blake swayed, but Max maintained a firm hold and eased him to the ground.

Behind them was a thin, gray-haired man in his sixties or seventies. His face seemed to have petrified into a scowl, his hair a springing mess, deep lines cutting angry paths across his forehead. He wore a black robe and clerical collar, but Max knew he wasn't here to help. This was just another segment of the freakish plan they'd been forced to endure.

"Father Joe!" Blake exclaimed with a nervous smile.

Max was confused. Who was this guy? Had he been trapped just like them?

"There's no sense in trying to escape. Shepherd will only let you out if you do exactly what he wants," the man said, looking longingly up at the window.

"What does he want from a kid?" Max demanded.

Father Joe, as he was apparently called, offered a smile meant to placate. "I'm not sure what his plan is for us. He's not usually clear on that until it's time for action, but such is life."

"He told me this place is Hell." Max got in the old man's face. "What was that supposed to mean?"

Joe waved a hand. "Oh, that's just Shepherd being dramatic. He wants all of his sheep to be obedient. He helps those who respect his orders."

"Screw that! We're getting out of here!"

Wincing, Joe said, "Watch your language, would you?"

Max held up both middle fingers, then took Blake by the hand. "You actually expect me to believe this Shepherd wants to help us? How stupid do you think I am?"

"Now, Maxime–"

"Don't call me that! It's Max, you piece of…" Max switched to French so he could freely swear in front of Blake.

The old man extended his hand. "Clearly we've gotten off on the wrong foot. My name is Joseph Johansen."

Keeping his arm down, Max squeezed Blake's hand. "What do you want from us?"

Johansen grimaced, probably realizing it would be far more difficult to sneak his bullshit past Max than it had been with Blake. "It's not what *I* want – it's what *Shepherd* wants," he finally said. "You two would be wise to obey his commands, because you're not going anywhere until you do."

Max and Blake glanced at each other, exchanging tacit fears. Blake's eyes were huge with dread. "Why do we have to stay here, Father Joe?" he said.

Johansen made a phony little smile, the same patronizing smile Mom had forced whenever Max or Jocey had asked about why they needed to attend church events all the time. *Because it's God's will,* she'd always said, and Max was stunned when those exact four words passed Johansen's lips.

"We're not interested in your shit," Max heard himself say, the words having come out unchecked.

Johansen's brown eyes ignited like pools of gasoline introduced to a spark. "How *dare* you blaspheme the Lord!"

Max tore away from Blake and challenged the old man again, their heads just inches apart. "You have some nerve calling me out – look what you've done! Taking a little kid from his mom–"

"I didn't take him – Shepherd did! I'm just a messenger!" Johansen shouted. Stinking spit flew out of his mouth and landed on Max's cheek.

Stepping back, Max wiped his face. "Don't kid yourself. You're just as bad as he is. Everyone who's helping him is evil."

"You act as if I have a choice. There's no questioning God's will!"

"You always have a choice."

The old man laughed at him, exposing teeth that were almost school bus yellow. "How ironic it is to hear that from you, Maxime."

A deluge of sobs made Max spin around. Blake. Tears ran down his cheeks.

Max pulled him into a hug. "It's okay, pal. We're gonna find a way out. You're staying with me, and Joe's gonna help us escape, okay?"

The boy nodded, wiping his tears away. Behind them, Johansen was silent, most likely glaring at Max and hating him the way Mom had hated him after he'd renounced God.

Max glanced over his shoulder. "If you're such a man of God, then tell Shepherd to do the right thing," he said in a soft, pleading voice. "Let this kid go. Do what you want to me, but please don't hurt Blake and his family." He pointed to the wall. "You know what I'm talking about, don't you?"

Johansen averted his eyes to the floor. "I'm afraid we all must make sacrifices in the name of the Lord. The sooner you accept that, the sooner you'll reach His kingdom."

"Well, if you listen to everything Shepherd says, how come you're not in Heaven?" Max pressed.

The old man was briefly silent. He shook his head disapprovingly at Max. "Your faithlessness will be your doom, boy."

Chapter 8

Fresh off his phone discussions with Katherine Grafton's father and Nate, Mike called Dave's cell phone.

"Can I buzz you back in an hour, Mikey? I'm getting ready to head over to the press conference."

"What's that about?"

"The feds are planning to announce a suspect. The guy's a sex offender who recently moved to town from New York – failed to register when he got here."

"When was he arrested?"

"The Staties picked him up this morning. I'd be shocked if he had anything to do with Blake's abduction, but he's still in some deep shit for failing to register."

Mike and Dave decided to talk again after the conference. A suspect would indeed be presented to the public, but 99 Deepwoods Drive, they both knew, was infected with an infinitely deeper darkness.

***

Just as Katie was about to call the *Boston Globe* reporter to reschedule their interview, her cell phone started humming on the kitchen counter.

"Hello?"

"Hi, Katherine?" The man had a high, squeaky voice.

"Yes, speaking."

"Hi, Katherine. Peter Dobyns, from the *Boston Globe*. I hate to do this, but can we push the interview back? They just announced–"

"The press conference, right?"

"That's right."

"I was just about to call you. I can't believe there's a sex offender living so close – they say his house is only five minutes from here."

"I heard the police are in the process of searching his house."

Katie's hands were shaking. "Something tells me this isn't the right guy, though. It's just not adding up."

A momentary silence, then: "Your family is in my prayers, Katherine. Tell you what, how about we meet right after the conference? I'll ask the police if we can use a spare room at the station."

"That sounds good. Thanks..." She wanted to finish with his name, but she couldn't remember it.

She set the phone down and wandered into the bedroom, taking a few moments to squeeze Blake's teddy bear, Ralphy, the scent of her little boy infused in its patchy fur. She held the bear against her chest, just as she'd done before bed each night since her son's abduction. But Ralphy hadn't kept the nightmares away; not a night had been free of their torments, and with limited sleep Katie felt even more depleted and hopeless. She couldn't stand to think of what Blake might be enduring, the endless, nausea-inducing fears routinely catching her in the sides and tearing jagged lines of pain. Her world had become a living hell on Earth filled with panic attacks and floods of tears. Her son was gone. His bed was empty. Life was shattered.

Chapter 9

Nate made it to Joss's house a few minutes past noon. The first snowflakes of the season had begun drifting down from steely clouds, instantly dissolving on contact. A clipper was expected to spread an inch of powder across the region by sundown, a hint of winter ahead of what was projected to be a more powerful storm tomorrow night. Having never been a snow lover, it didn't matter to Nate if the white stuff stayed away until February.

The house was dark and cold. Joss had sent Nate a text a little while ago saying she would be home in ten minutes. In the foyer, Nate stared at Anya Leclaire's prized crucifix of gold, his eyes then lifting to the meagerly ornamented Christmas tree. Upon closer examination, he realized that the only ornaments hanging from the boughs were part of Anya's religious collection, the same brightly colored balls Nate had seen in conspicuous locations on trees since his first Christmas with Joss. One of them depicted a nativity scene of Mary, Joseph, and baby Jesus in the manger. Another featured a golden cross and a message that read, GOD BLESS SUNDAY SCHOOL TEACHERS. A green, blue, and white ball said, TEACHING GOD'S WORD MAKES AN ETERNAL DIFFERENCE. There were also religious figurines, small wooden crosses, and other trinkets to praise the Lord, but none of Joss's favorite ornaments – many of which were from Montreal – had been unpacked yet. Even with scarves of gold tinsel wrapping their way up the tree, this was a far cry from the usual Leclaire setup.

There were no lights, no gifts beneath the tree, not even the colorful star at the top.

The front door clicked open. Wearing a black trench coat and her dark blue Montreal Canadiens beanie hat, Joss set down her grocery bags and kissed Nate, her cheeks flushed mildly by December's windblown caress.

"You hungry?" she said. "I'll have whatever you're having."

"Well, in that case, I hope you're a cannibal." His wink earned him a slap on the shoulder.

"Sicko."

"You set yourself up for that one."

They laughed, kissed some more, but then Nate made the mistake of asking, "So, what's with the tree this year? There's only a few ornaments on it."

She sighed, glancing up at the tree with irritation. Usually she forced Nate to spend hours decorating it on the day after Thanksgiving, a ritual he'd grown to love. He'd been looking forward to pulling out the ornaments for another season, drinking eggnog with his girlfriend as they transformed the tree into a dazzling memory. He wanted so desperately to see that childlike excitement light her eyes again.

But all she could offer for now was an annoyed scowl. "It's good enough as it is, I guess."

Nate closed his arms around her stomach and kissed her neck. "How about we spend an hour on it today?"

She shook her head. "That's okay. It's really not a big deal."

She tried to pull away, but Nate held her firm. "Come on, just one hour. You love Christmas – what's going on?"

***

Joss wrenched herself free and retreated to the kitchen, Nate following closely behind her, questioning her. She didn't want to talk about Christmas celebrations, not after everything she'd been through with Mason. He'd killed himself on Christmas Eve, forfeiting the gift of life because of his father's demands, subjecting himself to decades of imprisonment that perhaps remained ongoing.

No, Joss hadn't been feeling particularly festive. But if she described her troubles to Nate, he might say she was too attached to Mason. She didn't want to be told to move on and focus on the future, not when a ghost from her past was the only reason she drew breath.

She washed her hands beneath warm water. "I'm just not that into the whole decoration thing anymore. It takes so long."

"Bull," Nate said. "Something else is going on. Weren't you the one who always told me about the importance of not having secrets? What's really happening?"

"It's nothing, really. I'll decorate the tree with you, okay? Why does everything have to be so intense with you?"

"Because you're changing and it's really scaring me."

"What are you talking about?" Yet she knew exactly what he was talking about, and it made her feel as if she'd been backed into a corner. She was angrily grabbing items from the refrigerator and slamming them against the countertop.

Exasperated, Nate went through the list. "The drinking, the trances, taking off the crucifix you've worn since you were fifteen, lying to your mom all the time, going to Montreal to model lingerie when you had no interest in that before. I don't know what to do, Joss. I can't help you if I don't know what's wrong."

She fought back the tears. "Are you actually gonna come at me with all of this stuff? Really? After everything *you've* put me through, you're gonna yell at me for changing?" Suddenly pulsing with waves of anger, she felt like throwing something at him.

He shook his head. "That's the problem, isn't it? You can't get over what I did to you. There. It's out there." A miserable smile. "You said you forgave me, but you never really did."

"I do forgive you, but you need to let me get through this in my own way. You broke me, Nate, and you don't get to fix me!"

"How are you gonna fix yourself, getting drunk all the time?"

She'd forgotten about the lunch ingredients. She and Nate were opposing each other like two boxers, each combatant bracing for the next attack.

"I'm done with the drinking." She pointed at him. "That's why I told you about the box. You don't know how to let things go. Can you just give me a fucking break already?"

"Fine! But that's exactly what my dad said all the time, and he sounded pretty damn convincing."

Her anger softening a little, she advanced a few steps. "I'm not an alcoholic. I would never hurt you like that."

He took her hand. "I love you, Joss. I know things can't be like they were, but I still think the future can be good. We just both need to work at it. We can't hide from this – we have to face it head on, and I promise we'll get through it together."

She hugged him. "I love you, too," she managed, tears emerging.

They remained locked in a tense embrace, rocking gently back and forth. "About that lunch," she finally said, and they broke into uneasy laughter.

***

After Joss made him a sandwich for lunch, as they unpacked ornaments from boxes, Nate mentioned an idea he'd been reluctant to bring up before.

"Let's drive up to Montreal," he said.

Her eyebrows lifted. "Why would we do that?"

"I think getting away will be good for us."

She hung a creepy gingerbread man from a low bough. "We could go between Christmas and New Year's, I guess. Maybe Aunt Laina will let us stay at her place again." After positioning the ornament just right, she turned to face him. "But what's with the sudden urge to go up there?"

"I just think a change of scenery will help give us some peace," he said, reaching into the nearest box and grabbing two ornaments.

She smiled, looking genuinely happy. "I'd really like that. There's so many places I'd love to take you."

"Then call Laina. Let's make a plan."

Though Nate wasn't expecting her to call right away, Joss returned an angel ornament to its box and pulled her cell phone from a jeans pocket. Nate grinned, relieved to have finally found something that might help her healing process (that is, assuming he could keep her away from the booze).

Chapter 10

The press conference inside the Hollisville Police Department was packed, a throng of reporters and camera crews filling the small room to capacity. The crowd even spilled out the door, where a frustrated young journalist – probably the local newspaper's kid straight out of college – tried to push through the insanity.

He carried a thin notebook, and a camera bag was slung over his shoulder. His press credentials hung from a lanyard around his neck, the words too small at this distance to indicate his employer. He wore glasses that offered an unassumingly sexy charm, like a rural version of Clark Kent (he probably didn't possess superhuman powers, though – too bad).

Whitney Golding watched him carefully from a bench in the lobby. She was in the middle of composing a phone email to her boss, who expected her to get back to her own reporting duties soon. But how could she leave Katie now? Blake was her gravity, and without him she would just float around aimlessly.

Please allow me one more day. I'll take on extra weekend coverage, Whitney wrote, becoming increasingly angered with each word. But the business world didn't care about Katie. Corporate America never rested, a ceaseless machine that sucked you in, used you up, and spat you out, then proceeded to slowly drain the youth from another bright-faced college grad.

Whitney sent her email and stepped outside the station into a freezing afternoon. She lit a cigarette, ran in place for a few moments to get the blood flowing. Katie and her parents were still in the privacy of a side room, watching the conference on a television monitor along with police personnel, Katie's grandparents (who'd made the trip from California to be with her), and that annoying Sheila Frost lady, who'd constantly shared her advice and stories with Katie over the last three days. Whit thought the woman was a kooky attention seeker, but if she comforted Katie then she was worth having around.

When the conference had crept close to thirty minutes, the same information about the pervert being repeated, Whit had excused herself from the side room.

"Fucking conference might never end," she muttered, blowing out a long puff.

It was frigid out here, even for December in New Hampshire, the dagger wind flinging down from Mount Monadnock and slicing across the little towns below. Shivering, Whit took in the minimal sights of downtown Hollisville. Not much to see. There were a few municipal buildings and a tiny Town Common to the right, a library straight ahead, and a brick church with a white steeple at the bottom of a hill to the left. Everything was aged and in rough shape. Even the Common had been neglected, branches, leaves, and litter scattered across the grass. Whit didn't like it up here. She didn't like the town. She didn't like Katie's apartment building. She didn't even care for the people.

"Hi there," a voice called.

Whit jumped. She turned to her right and found a teenage boy smiling nervously at her. He seemed very familiar, although Whit couldn't pinpoint where she'd seen him before. He was handsome, with grayish blue eyes and a strong jawline. He held a plain white envelope in his right hand.

Whit dropped her cigarette and stamped it out. "You scared me, kid."

His smile widened. "Sorry about that. I have something for you – it's really important."

He handed her the envelope. Reluctantly accepting it by the edge and eyeing it suspiciously, Whit said, "What is it? If you're handing out church fliers or something, I'm not interested."

He shook his head. "No, it's nothing like that. I'm here to tell you Blake is alive, but there's only one way to rescue him."

Whit felt like her mouth had been sewn shut. She went to speak but nothing came out. "What did you say?" she finally managed.

He pointed at the envelope. "Show that to Katie. She'll know who to call. Whatever you do, don't tell the police about this. They'll mess everything up."

Before Whit could respond, he jogged down the sidewalk and disappeared around the police station, leaving her with the wrinkled envelope which felt like a block of ice in her hands. She considered running inside and flagging down the nearest officer, but her instincts told her to let Katie see the envelope first.

By the time Whit rounded the station, the kid was long gone.

Part V: The Snake Pit

*"Now the serpent was more crafty than any other
beast of the field that the Lord God had made."* ~
The Holy Bible: Genesis

Chapter 1

When Sgt. Fitzgerald and I reach the back entrance
of unit four, Officer Patterson (the officer initially
posted in the lot) steps onto the deck to explain the
situation.

"It's incredible, Sarge – I've never seen anything
like it. Every time they tap on the walls, someone
taps back from the other side." His eyes are like
moons, glittering with shock.

"Which wall is it coming from?" Fitzgerald says.

"Only the ones bordering unit three. If they tap
once, they get one tap in return. Two taps gets two
from the other side – it's been happening the last
five minutes, but there's no one in unit three, sir."

Scowling in disbelief, Fitzgerald swipes his boots
against the doormat and enters unit four, Patterson
and I trailing closely behind him. Katherine Grafton
and her parents are standing with Officer Roberts in
the kitchen, their faces lighted with hope and
shadowed with terror.

Fitzgerald asks for a recap from Katherine,
beginning when she made the initial call. Everyone

else glances fearfully at the walls and ceiling, as if poisonous snakes might lash out from any corner.

"Okay, let's see what this is all about," Fitzgerald says after Katherine's panicked account.

The sergeant knocks twice on the wall above the kitchen sink. A few seconds pass, and then it happens – two faint but unmistakable knocks from the other side!

I recoil slightly, my hand on my weapon. Luckily, no one seems to notice my apprehension, too focused on the wall.

Fitzgerald knocks three times; moments later, all three are reciprocated.

"What do you think, Sarge?" Patterson says, careful not to speculate about the potential that Blake Grafton is the source of the noises. "We already checked units three and five. Both of them are empty."

"And it's only coming from the walls on this side of the unit?" Fitzgerald confirms.

Katherine nods. "Yes, only this side. It takes a few seconds for a response, but it always comes."

After a quick discussion with Katherine, Fitzgerald barks out instructions. "Roberts, Patterson, I want you to stand at opposite ends of unit three. Zach, you wait here in the kitchen, and I'll stand outside the living room entrance. Let's see if we can pinpoint where the sounds are coming from." He nods at Katherine. "Ms. Grafton is gonna knock three times on the bedroom wall. Once we clear this level, we'll work our way up and down from here."

Everyone exchanges nervous glances before taking their respective positions. Soon I'm standing alone in the kitchen, watching Katherine and her parents in the bedroom as they prepare for the next attempt at communication. Finally Katherine raps her knuckles against the wall, then recedes to the middle of the room and stands guardedly between her parents.

Five seconds pass. Ten, twenty, half a minute.

Just when I expect silence to endure, three knocks come from the other side, more protracted than before. Not *knock, knock, knock* but *Knock. Knock...Knock.* They sound like they're originating directly in front of Katherine, which would place the location in the middle of unit three.

Patterson's voice comes over the radio. "I heard it to my left. I'm heading over. Zach, can you tell Katherine to knock again?"

I relay the information, then step back into the kitchen. Katherine responds with three more knocks that are rapidly returned with a trio from the other side.

"I think it's coming from *inside* the wall," Patterson says. "Have her do it again."

THE INHABITANTS II

Three knocks from Katherine, but this time the response stems from the wall opposite the kitchen, followed by three additional knocks beyond the bedroom. Heavy thuds boom from above – footfalls that rattle the light fixtures. Voices light up the radio, interspersed with crackling static. Patterson and Roberts are in a panic. Fitzgerald demands to know what's going on, says something about footsteps coming up the front stairs.

Katherine huddles with her family. They're all looking at me from the bedroom as if I know what to do, but I'm so scared I can barely think straight. This place really is–

The lights click out, submerging the apartment in blackness. I fumble for my flashlight, tug it free, and when I finally switch it on I'm surrounded by strangers in the kitchen, dozens of faces staring blankly at me but only for a few seconds before vanishing.

Held in momentary paralysis, I wonder if what I just saw was real. No, it can't be! It *cannot* be real!

Wind rushes against the house. My hands are shaking. My whole body seems to clench, and I'm instantly aware that something evil is watching us. It's a sickly intuitive feeling I've never experienced before, an incontrovertible knowledge of imminent danger.

Organ music rings out from above. The faces return, surrounding me, each one misty, disembodied. I

shine my shaking light upon them, taking in one
pair of vacant eyes after another.

I pull my weapon, but by the time I have it directed
in front of me, the inhabitants are gone, replaced by
shadows leaping across the walls, fading, fading,
fading, black to gray to nonexistent.

Fitzgerald races into the kitchen from the other end
of the apartment, the beam of his flashlight
temporarily blinding me. Neither of us realizes that
the madness has only just begun.

Chapter 2

Katie held the envelope for a few moments of ambivalence, wondering if she should open it.

"Maybe we should just let the cops handle it," she said.

Whit shook her head. "But he told me not to. I don't know what to do – this is all so screwed up. It really seemed like he wanted to help."

They were in Katie's car, parked behind the police station where the officers stored their vehicles. Chief Strait had been more than gracious to Katie and her family, constantly accommodating them; it seemed senseless to exclude him now, but that was specifically what Whit had been told to do.

Slowly, hesitantly, Katie opened the envelope and took hold of its contents: several yellowing notebook pages folded into thirds. There was a lightly smoky scent to them, but also a hint of something sweet like candy. Whoever had enclosed the papers had also attempted to smooth out the crinkles, but the little creases were impossible to eradicate. Still, Katie was able to read the spindly handwriting that skipped every other line.

His name is Shepherd. He visits me within the walls, but only when he wants something from me. Last time, he asked me to bring a little girl, Lizzie Tillman, into the wall, but I refused. I could never bring Lizzie here. This is a place for the dead, not the living. I will never bring anyone in here, no matter what he threatens me with...

"What's it say?" Whit demanded.

"Just hold on. Let me finish."

Katie continued reading, dropping the pages to her lap in horror when she read about three "ghosts" that had allegedly loomed over Lizzie Tillman's bed for several nights. Their faces were described as "glowing with a pale light", a close resemblance to the descriptions Blake had provided of the men he'd seen the first night in their new home. Blake had said they'd peered into the apartment before heading upstairs to unit five.

"Oh my God!" Katie cried when she flipped to the last page and read the signature. Although written in cursive, it was still perfectly legible: Mason Blackwell. Below his name was a message written in blue, which was odd considering the remainder of the writing had been done in black ink.

Call Mike Overbrook. Tell him you can only get to Shepherd's realm if someone has recently been taken through the wall.

"These people are insane. They're torturing you," Whit said after reading most of the literature. "You need to tell the cops about this, Katie. They can probably get fingerprints off these papers."

Katie shook her head. Suddenly it all came together – Blake's encounter, the history of 99 Deepwoods Drive, the unexplainable noises, Blake's cries for help, every story and report, including the ones outlined in these pages – and Katie knew something beyond rational explanations had taken her son, a force Whit had perhaps detected during her initial visit to the apartment.

Katie pulled out her phone, eager to call Mike Overbrook. Though Whit kept urging her to bring in the authorities, the fact remained that the investigators hadn't made any progress as of yet, searching the building top to bottom but failing to find her son.

Something in Katie's gut told her there were far more places to search at 99 Deepwoods Drive…but no easy way to get to them.

Chapter 3

Mike was preparing his monthly report for the selectmen when his cell phone buzzed in his pocket. He expected a call from Dave, but a strange number lit up the screen.

"Hi, this is Chief Mike Overbrook."

"Hi, Mr. Overbrook. It's Katherine Grafton – I need your help. I just got an envelope with papers…well, actually my friend Whit got the envelope. There were papers inside describing things that happened in my apartment. They're signed by Mason Blackwell."

Mike stood. "How did your friend get this envelope?"

"Someone gave it to her while I was at the conference. He was young, like a high school kid, I guess. Anyway, when I saw the name Mason Blackwell, I didn't know what to think. At the bottom of the last page, it says to call you."

"Call me? For what?"

"It says, *Call Mike Overbrook. Tell him you can only get to Shepherd's realm if someone has recently been taken through the wall.*"

A cluster of thoughts spilled into Mike's head. Had Mason actually written this message, or had it been contrived by Shepherd as a trap?

"You're not alone in the apartment, right?" Mike asked.

"No, why?"

"Just make sure you're never alone in there. Always stay with someone. I'll be there in a few hours with Dave Strait. And one more important thing – have you mentioned this to any other cops?"

"No. The kid who gave Whit the envelope said the cops would only mess things up."

"He's probably right. Would you mind keeping this between us for now? If more people get in the way, everything will become confusing. We don't need a media circus – this has to be a controlled, focused investigation."

Later that afternoon, Mike and Dave met Katherine and her friend Whitney Golding in unit four. It was weird being back inside the place, especially now that Mike knew about everything that had happened here. He couldn't help but feel like they were all in the house's crosshairs.

Mike and Dave arranged the pages on the kitchen table and carefully read each one, noting the difference in ink color between the lengthy accounts and the message written on the bottom of the last page. "It's not only a different color, but the ink is much fresher," Dave observed. "Look, the black ink is faded from time, but the blue is so recent it's practically still wet."

During a phone conversation before arriving at 99 Deepwoods Drive, Mike and Dave had agreed to not mention anything about a haunting. They were here to look at the documents; there would be plenty of time for additional discussion in private.

"If this guy had something to do with Blake's abduction, why would he give us a message saying to call you? It makes no sense," Katherine said.

Dave glanced at Mike, hoping he might provide an explanation. Perhaps prayers would serve as better weapons than pistols, an idea that made Mike want to run from the house and never return. He couldn't leave the battle for anyone else, though. Because of his nightmares and the knowledge he'd gained from Nate and Joss, he was in the best position to save Blake.

"Chief Strait and his officers will keep you safe here while we figure this out," was all Mike could manage for the moment.

Meanwhile, Dave pulled an old yearbook from his duty bag. He'd borrowed the 1965 volume of *The Arrow* from someone at Hollisville High School, probably one of those ancient teachers who outlived many students.

"Have a look at this, Ms. Golding." Dave flipped through the dusty yearbook and pointed to one of the tiny black and white photographs. "Does he look like the individual who gave you the envelope?"

Whitney gasped. "Jesus, that's him! But it can't be
– he's dead!"

Katherine looked at the yearbook as well. "Maybe
it's his grandson," she suggested. Looking at Dave,
she said, "Have you checked into the entire
Blackwell family? What if they have relatives
around here?"

Dave shook his head. "There's no one we're aware
of. His father committed suicide with him in 1965
when the kid was sixteen, and his mother died of a
blood disease a year earlier. The family moved here
from Virginia, I believe – no other family in the
area. Mason didn't have any kids, either, at least
none we know of."

Mike could hardly believe it. Mason Blackwell was
now attempting to assist Katherine from the other
side of the grave, just as he'd assisted Joss. All of
this was *really happening*.

Mike looked around the kitchen and through the
window, a frigid gust swaying naked tree limbs in
the side yard. Shadows had spread across the lawn.
The whole property seemed to be alive with dark,
forbidding energy.

"What are we gonna do?" Katherine asked. "Should
I call my parents and have them come back up here?
They needed to go home for a few hours to get
some things in order."

Dave shook his head. "That won't be necessary. I'll
ask the officer outside to patrol the place on foot."

"I can stay over," Whitney said. "I don't have to work until tomorrow, and I'd hate to leave you alone." She took Katherine's hand and smiled weakly. They were both justifiably afraid, perhaps guessing in the right direction, but they would be terrified if they knew what was really going on.

Although Mike wanted to reveal the truth of 99 Deepwoods Drive, nothing but panic would result from it. If they were going to find Blake, Katherine needed to be focused, not looking over her shoulder every two seconds in anticipation of the Devil behind her.

Later, Mike and Dave emerged from the police station with a wishful strategy. They'd spent half an hour discussing and arguing over the documents that had been given to Katherine. Now all they needed was a chance to get to "Shepherd's realm", a challenge that had nearly cost Nate his life.

Mike checked his watch. It was just after four o'clock. The sun had recently departed the cold December sky, leaving in its wake slashes of orange across the horizon and suffusions of pink along the jagged edges of approaching clouds. The storm was slowly drawing closer, a world of white soon to dominate the region. But an even greater storm – a prodigious monstrosity – would be unleashed at 99 Deepwoods Drive, a place of constant upheaval. A place of sorrow and tears. A place of prisoners trapped in Shepherd's pestilent darkness.

Mike stared off to the northwest, where Mount Monadnock was a slumbering shadow backlit by the colors of twilight. He didn't want to go home. He wished he could stay here and continue investigating, but regardless of the emergency situation he was assisting with in New Hampshire, the demands of his job couldn't be pushed back to next week. It would be a long night of catch-up at the station. Meanwhile, many miles north of Elkins, Blake Grafton would spend another night in confinement, a boy on the wrong side of the walls, just as Joss had been in September, the curse continuing relentlessly onward.

It'll be over soon enough, Mike told himself. *This damn house will finally be out of our lives for good.*

He could only pray Blake would be alive and unharmed when the storm cleared.

Chapter 4

After a somewhat awkward dinner with Joss and her
mother, Nate watched a movie with his girlfriend
and then helped her bake Christmas cookies shaped
like stars and trees, each one topped with green or
red sprinkles. They talked and kissed and laughed.
They tossed cookie bits toward each other's mouths
with NBA style and pickup league accuracy. They
told stupid jokes, enjoying the night and staying
away from anything too serious. Whenever an
unfavorable topic of conversation threatened to pop
into the mix, one of them would quickly change the
subject and reestablish the light, easygoing mood.

Looking into Joss's eyes and losing himself in the
magnetism of her smile, Nate wanted to remain in
that moment forever, a safe place where nothing
was haunted, nobody was dead, and the police
weren't looking for them. The kitchen was rich with
the scent of baked treats, the house warm and cozy,
the Christmas tree lights splashing in from the
foyer.

Lying beside her in bed that night, Nate thought
back to their first Christmas together, memories he
conveyed to Joss, who'd been his new best friend
that year, the girl from Montreal he'd fallen
completely for. "Sophomore year feels like
yesterday, doesn't it?"

She smiled, running a hand across his cheek. "I
remember the first time I saw you. Such a sexy boy
sitting there in science class."

"That's exactly how I felt about you."

"Really? You thought I was a sexy boy?"

Their laughter was pure, fluid, proceeded by inevitable talk of recent events. Joss's eyes were searching and expressive, but there was also a peace to them Nate hadn't seen in weeks. He wondered if divesting herself of the box had allowed the healing process to speed up. There was still a long way to go, however, and Nate knew he would need to play a vital role in her recovery.

Nate woke just after three a.m. following a rare pleasant dream. He and Joss had been reclining on lounge chairs on a deserted island, glasses of lemonade in hand as they watched sailboats drift by on sparkling Caribbean waters. There'd been no one around for miles, only Nate and Jocey Marie.

Smiling, still wrapped snugly in the vestiges of his dream, Nate turned onto his side and let the room trickle into clarity. Joss's bedside lamp was on, but her half of the bed was vacant, the blankets pushed back. Nate blinked in confusion, slowly departing from the paradise island of sleep and perceiving the room with heightening dread. Perhaps his apprehension was a subconscious response to the metronomic creaking noises that were just now registering in his ears.

Creak, Creak, Creak, Creak, Creak. They came from behind Nate, over and over and over.

Nate was seized by fear. He didn't want to roll over, afraid of what he'd see when he did.

Slowly, reluctantly, he flipped to his other side and beheld the terrors he'd somehow known were awaiting him. Sitting in a rocking chair she'd dragged in from the guest room, Joss was easing back and forth, a huge knife in one hand and an unpeeled apple in the other. She was staring at him with that empty, chilling look in her eyes, the one he'd seen at the Framingham Plaza. Her face shined softly like the porcelain countenance of a doll, her hair pulled tightly back. She wore one of the pieces of lingerie Laina had given her in Montreal – a white, long-sleeved fishnet chemise, a red thong exposed below.

Nate exploded out of bed and took the knife from her, and it was then he realized how badly she was bleeding. The apple wasn't unpeeled, after all; the entire thing was soaked in blood.

Still stuck in her trance – or whatever the hell these things were – Joss didn't move or even blink as Nate pried the apple from her slick hand and identified the injury. Her left index finger bore a fairly deep gash, blood still escaping the wound and trickling down to areas of the finger and palm where earlier streams of blood had dried and crusted. There was also blood on her left thigh, thin distributaries of red trailing down her leg.

"Joss, what the fuck?" Nate shouted, grabbing her by the shoulders and finally bringing that awful creaking to a silence.

No response, but her head tilted a little as if to acknowledge a change in her surroundings.

"Joss, wake up!" He repeatedly snapped his finger. Still no response, nothing, her lost eyes gleaming.

"Joss, come on, wake up!" Her mouth slowly dropped, eyes dilating slightly. Her breathing intensified, whistling hoarsely.

Panicking, wondering if he should call for an ambulance, Nate carried her to the bed, where she lied quiescently for a few moments, eyes closed. Her breaths were calmer now but still strained. A seizure? No, she wasn't convulsing, but what was it?

After wrapping a cloth tightly around her bloody finger, Nate squeezed her hand and kissed her forehead, speaking softly in an attempt to coax her mind out of its prison cell. Finally her eyes lifted – the shifting, frightened eyes of a child awakening in an unfamiliar place. A single word escaped her lips: "Max."

"Joss, we need to get you to the hospital. You cut your finger."

She was looking up at him, still dazed. She said something else about Max in French, then descended into a maddening one-sided French conversation, at times giggling as if someone had told her a joke. Because she was distracted by her own manic words, she allowed Nate to pull her up into a sitting position and hold her. He was gripped by a fear worse than any he'd ever known, a fear that he was losing Jocey, helpless to save her from whatever malady was gradually taking control.

When he mentioned the hospital again, she finally turned to English and addressed him.

"It has to be true, Nate! It just has to be!"

"What are you talking about? What has to be true?"

"It's Max, I saw him – he's trapped!" She looked down, suddenly aware of her injury. "Mon Dieu!" More French followed.

"Joss, look at me!"

Tears of realization welled in her eyes. "It happened again, didn't it?" she said in a voice barely exceeding a whisper.

He nodded at her hand. "You cut yourself with a knife. You had an apple, and you were just rocking back and forth in the chair. It really freaked me out."

"Fuck, it's deep," she said after unwrapping the cloth.

"Keep that wrapped around your finger," Nate instructed. It was bizarre for him to see how seamlessly she transitioned from these trance-fugue episodes to normality. He should have insisted that she see a psychiatrist before, but now it had reached a point where professional treatment was unavoidable.

After helping her dress, Nate said, "Once they stitch you up at the hospital, you should have an MRI so they can find out what's causing these trances. You're hurting yourself now, and they have to stop."

"It must be from the concussion when I fainted."

He shook his head. "I don't think so. That was three months ago, and you're getting worse every day. You could have killed yourself."

The door swung open, a squinting Anya Leclaire stepping inside. She wore a flannel robe and only one of her red slippers, her mind still foggy from deep medicated sleep. "What's going on, Jocey? I heard voices. Are you okay?"

"Everything's fine, Mom. Just go back to bed," Joss snapped.

Finally Anya noticed Nate. "What are you still doing here, Nathan? I thought you'd left!"

"Joss was peeling an apple and cut herself. Don't worry, I'll take her to the hospital."

"The *hospital?*" She gasped at the bloodstained cloth. "You cut yourself, Jocey? How bad is it?"

Joss pushed past her. "I'll be fine, just a few stitches."

Anya wouldn't be denied so easily, though. She followed them down the stairs, firing a new question at Joss with every step.

"Fine, you can come to the hospital," Joss eventually conceded. "Just try not to get in the way."

Twenty minutes later, they were entering the sparsely populated emergency room waiting area at Lakeside Medical Center in Worcester. As Anya helped Joss obtain the requisite paperwork, Nate stood off to the side, consumed by dread, listening to the distant cries of a baby in the ER. He kept fearing Joss would lose it again, and he was actually glad her mother was here, just in case she had another meltdown. The first trance had been frightening enough, but this was in an entirely different stratosphere. She'd cut herself open and hadn't even realized it. That meant she was either suffering from a serious brain injury, or...

The house. Is Shepherd still–? No, impossible!

When Joss and her mother disappeared through the doors leading to the emergency room, Nate collapsed into a plastic chair facing the reception windows. He stared at the floor, thinking back to his girlfriend's worst episode yet and wondering if he could have done anything differently. For some reason he felt responsible for what had happened. It wasn't a remotely rational thought, but guilt nonetheless burrowed its way inside him. Maybe he should have given her more space. Maybe he should have noticed signs of an imminent disaster. There were a million maybes, each one delivering a sting of guilt.

Anya emerged from the ER twenty minutes later. She looked exhausted, the dark rings beneath her eyes accentuated in the bright room. Her hair had been pulled into a loose ponytail, a few strands dangling before her face. Pushing them aside, she slid into the chair next to Nate.

"Tell me what happened," she said quietly, seeming only a little less daunting than usual.

Nate swallowed hard. There would be no more sleep for him this morning, not with Jocey Marie, the girl who commanded his heart, in complete turmoil. To ensure that Joss received the best care possible, Nate knew he would have to team up with a woman he'd previously tried hard to avoid (a woman who hated him for everything he'd done to her daughter).

But it was time to man up, he realized. No more pretending. No more wishing everything was good. After a deep breath, Nate proceeded to tell Anya Leclaire about Joss's calamity.

Chapter 5

Johansen returned a while later with a white plastic bag stuffed with so many things that the strained handles were on the verge of snapping. Having given up on finding an escape, Blake had fallen asleep beside Max, who was staring at the window when he heard Johansen's soft footsteps.

Max sat up quickly, ready to protect the boy if needed.

"I've brought some things for you and Blake," the old man said, nodding at his bag.

Max stood. "How did you die, anyway?"

The man nodded contemplatively. "I took my life to be with God. One day I'll reach His kingdom, but I must be patient."

"You thought suicide would bring you to Heaven? I don't remember reading that in the Bible." Max pointed at Blake. "And what's he doing here with us? Is *he* dead, too?"

Johansen ignored the question, solemnly unloading the contents of his bag: a chess board and pieces, cookies and crackers, bottles of juice and water, plastic cups, a flashlight, and several other things.

"What is this, a fucking campout?" Max spoke softly, not wanting to wake the boy.

"Such offensive language," Johansen muttered. When he finished arranging the chess pieces on the foldable plastic board, he looked up at Max with an expression of moronic glee. "Shepherd informed me that you'll be asked to do something soon. If you obey him, you could be released to Heaven immediately. Isn't that wonderful?"

Heaven. At least now the idea of it was real for Max, though he knew it held no place for him. Shepherd and Johansen were lying; this really was Hell, a place of endless deception. Blake had to be dead as well, although he still retained hunger, thirst, and the functions of digestion, all of which Max had lost following his final breath.

But what did they want with Blake? The question remained, and there was nothing Max could do to force an answer. He briefly considered choking Johansen, or breaking his fingers until he revealed pertinent information, but with death came an absence of physical pain. There were no scrapes or cuts or stings, no reminders that you existed beyond the thoughts in your head and the repeating sights captured by your eyes. The clock was frozen. Time was irrelevant. It could have been a Tuesday, or maybe a Sunday, but it didn't matter. Morning or afternoon – who cares? Max imagined an endless road, perfectly level, stretching on for infinity, its surroundings unchanging. Its start was its end, as was every inch of pavement in between, and those compelled to travel it could only carry on one mile at a time with the flickering hope that it might finally yield to something new. Anything new.

"There is no Heaven for us," Max finally said.

Johansen tilted his head, as if he hadn't heard him right. "What would cause you to say such a thing?"

"Just cut the shit! I don't want to hear it, okay?"

Soft pattering noises came from the floor behind them, where Blake had stirred from sleep. He called out to Max.

"I'm right here, pal," he said, relief spreading across the boy's face when Max spun around.

"Father Joe!" Now Blake was smiling. "When can we leave?"

"Very soon, I hope," Johansen said, running a hand through his untamed hair. "Shepherd will make the announcement any day now. If you two follow his commands, you'll get to go home to your mommy."

Max glared at him. He wanted to punch the guy but managed to grit his teeth and restrain himself. Of all the individuals he could have encountered in death, why did it have to be the elderly male version of Mom? It seemed that Hell's offerings were not eternal flames but cruel ironies.

"I can go home soon?" Blake's eyes expanded. "When? I want to see Mom!"

Johansen held up a cautioning hand. "Perhaps a few days, depending on when the order comes."

Max shook his head at Johansen, a silent warning
not to build the kid's hopes for nothing.

"I should be going," the old man said. "Max, I think
it would be a good idea for you to teach Blake
chess. It's such a wonderful game and a great way
to pass the hours."

Johansen stepped into the near alcove, just out of
sight. Max followed him, watching as he passed
through the wall and disappeared. When Max tried
it himself, he was denied release from his prison,
doomed to spend an indefinite period in
confinement. He wondered what he would
eventually be asked to do – undoubtedly something
awful.

Max and Blake spent the next hour munching on
cookies and crackers, drinking juice and water, and
playing chess. The food and drink still tasted good
and went down easily, and Max figured that maybe
he could work up a leak for old time's sake (what
he'd give to piss all over these walls). But strangely,
he never filled up as Blake's introduction to chess
continued. Long after the boy had turned his
attention from the snacks, Max was still absently
eating.

*He must be alive. Otherwise he would still be
eating, too.*

Blake was a fast learner, very smart for his age. He
quickly realized how the pieces functioned and the
basic concepts of the game. Max had learned chess
from his grandfather, although he hadn't played in

many years, his last game an online tournament match.

"This is fun," Blake remarked after their third game. Soon the kid would be better than Jocey, who'd always protected her knights at all costs and left her other pieces vulnerable. She used to get more upset after losing a knight than a queen, perhaps likening it to the killing of a real horse. Then, around age ten, she completely lost interest in chess, describing it as too long and boring.

When they were finally done with chess, Blake asked Max when he thought they'd get to go home.

"I don't know, pal, but I'm not going anywhere without you, okay?" Max ruffled Blake's hair.

"I won't go without you, either." He spoke bravely, almost defiantly. "I'm glad you're here with me, Max."

"Me too, kid." They were sitting next to each other against the far wall, just below the window. Max wrapped an arm around Blake's tiny shoulders, remembering the awful nights he and Jocey had spent together after Dad's death.

A stiff wind rattled the walls. They both glanced to the left, listening as an organ's melodies slipped through ancient crevices. Overhead, floorboards creaked beneath the weight of someone's movements.

Blake shivered. "It's so cold in here."

Max offered his sweatshirt to the boy. "Here, take this."

When Blake pulled the sweatshirt on, it looked like he was wearing a blanket. "Thanks, Max."

"No problem, man. It's cold as…as an igloo in here."

As the wind escalated and the organ drifted into its next song, Max and Blake got to talking again, a conversation that would continue until Blake fell asleep. It was all they could do to pass the time and keep their fears at bay while blackness slithered inside, the flashlight's beam shined upon every corner at Blake's request.

Neither of them noticed the faces occasionally peering out from each alcove, faces hatefully aglow with dim white light.

Chapter 6

Joss's mother was convinced that stress had caused her unexplainable trances. The doctor had said the tests revealed nothing wrong with her brain. No tumors, no lesions, no little gremlins biting on the wires. Joss felt fine, tired but fine, and now she just wanted to go home.

"Nice to meet you, Jocelyne," said Dr. Carrie Proulx, a highly recommended psychiatrist who'd been working in the Lakeside system for over a decade. They'd initially been told that Proulx had a packed schedule, but then Mom had pulled some people aside and, sure enough, here Joss was in Proulx's office.

Shaking the doctor's hand, Joss sensed her face reddening at the thought of seeing a shrink. She felt pathetic and weak, but above all else she felt afraid. If there was nothing physically wrong with her, then what was going on?

Proulx, a thin woman with graying blonde hair, sat behind her desk and leaned back in her chair, conveying the same air of relaxation she'd hoped to create with the arrangement of the office. Soft lamplight illuminated the corners, and the rest of the room was lit the natural way thanks to a pair of rectangular windows overlooking the lake.

"Don't think of this as anything other than a conversation," Proulx said, smiling at Joss like she probably smiled at all of her patients, the kind of people who heard voices in their heads and found themselves reduced to shivering bundles at the sight of strangers or open spaces or even children – and Joss was apparently one of those people. "We're just two ladies having a chat, okay?" Proulx carried on. "Nothing said here will leave this room."

Nodding, Joss took a reluctant seat on the edge of the brown leather sofa, her hands clasped. Suddenly aware of how tense she looked, she forced herself back and flattened her palms across her jeans. Thank God Proulx had asked her mother to remain in the waiting room – she would have only made Joss more stressed.

"Would you like to tell me about what you've been experiencing?" the doctor said, removing her glasses and setting them on the desk. She was about sixty years old, with soft, kind eyes that for some reason made Joss very uncomfortable. It wasn't just Proulx's eyes, though. Just being in this office and realizing that the woman seated before her might think she was mentally imbalanced was an insult to Joss's pride.

Worse than anything, the way Proulx talked – perpetually striving to soothe – stirred up memories.

Too many memories.

Joss remembered her old shrink in Montreal, who'd told her she didn't have to be embarrassed about bedwetting, the shame of an eight-year-old girl roaring back. There'd been toys and coloring books meant to reassure, Joss constantly reminded that it wasn't her fault, words bereft of remedies. She'd

hated waking up soaked and tearful and scared,
everything wrong, wrong, WRONG, trying to hide
it from Mom and Max, Dad gone, his study empty,
where Joss sometimes crept in and sat in his big
swivel chair, legs dangling, fingers curled around
the locket he'd given her on their last Christmas
morning, eyes sliding over the things he'd left
behind…and it was always so lonely in that house
without him there. The sight and scent of his brown
leather briefcase, leaning patiently against the back
wall, made it seem like he would walk through the
door any second, Joss to be scooped up in her
father's arms, life returning to normal. But instead
the desk clock ticked on and on, and the door never
opened, Joss forced each time to drag herself out of
her father's study, tears springing, the locket to find
its place in the corner of her jewelry box.

Joss suddenly broke into conversation, speaking
only to avoid the memories, an image from an old
photograph lingering in her mind – the one of a
father and his daughter in Montreal, a photo
confined to the darkness of a heart-shaped locket in
a quiet corner. Occasionally Joss wore the piece,
wanting always to keep her father close, but its
yearning weight was usually too much for her to
manage.

Joss told Proulx about her trances, the worst of
which had happened overnight, her stitched and
bandaged left index finger serving as a constant
reminder of her crisis. If not for Nate, it could have
been much worse.

"Can you remember how you felt immediately before these events?" Proulx asked.

"No, it's like I just fall asleep."

"Do you remember waking up last night and getting the apple and knife? Or changing clothes?"

Joss nodded. "I was really hungry. I remember grabbing the apple from the kitchen, and then I got dizzy. It was a blur from there. I don't remember changing at all."

Proulx scribbled something across her notepad. Joss could only imagine how her behavior had been interpreted. By the time the session was over, a pair of guards would probably be waiting to escort her to the nearest padded room.

"And these events started last month?"

"Yes, last month. I've only had four of them, but they've gotten worse each time."

Proulx sipped coffee from her mug. "Give me an idea of what the last six months have been like. Have you experienced any major changes that have caused an increase in stress?"

Joss felt like laughing and crying at the same time. How would she even begin to answer that one?

"My brother committed suicide in September." She spoke impassively, as if she were mentioning the suicide of a distant acquaintance.

Proulx nodded sympathetically. "I'm very sorry for your loss. Were you and your brother close?"

Shrugging, Joss said, "Not lately. He moved to Boston, and we didn't see each other much."

"Still, that must have been really hard for you. The loss of a sibling can be particularly traumatic."

As Proulx kept asking questions designed to ferret out the source of the trances, Joss's focus shifted to memories of what she'd seen at the conclusion of her latest event. It had been like a dream, except far more vivid. Max had been trapped in a dark place – but not his old apartment. Joss knew she had to save him soon, very soon, or it would be too late. She also knew she was getting closer to finding him, a thought that made no rational sense but somehow seemed infallible, as if Joss were being magnetically pulled in the direction of her brother by some innate sibling connection.

When their session was finally over, Joss expected Proulx to hand her a card and advise her to return in a week. Instead, the doctor said, "Jocelyne, due to the nature of these events, I think it would be in your best interest to spend a few days at McAllister Hospital on the north end of the campus."

"*What?*"

Before Joss could begin her protest, Proulx added, "The staff will be able to give you a diagnostic evaluation in a safe environment. After what happened last night with the knife, I think you'd agree that it's not safe for you to be alone right now."

Joss squeezed back the tears. "You want me to go to a mental hospital?"

Proulx frowned. "You'll get the very best services at McAllister, and I could be part of your team if you'd like."

Proulx's attention was stolen by her pager. "Excuse me, but I need to take care of something real quick. Would you mind waiting outside for a few minutes? We need to come up with a strategy that will keep you safe and help begin your recovery."

"Okay, sure, fine." Joss hurried back to the waiting room, her mother absorbed in a text message per usual. She had yet another conference on Monday night, where she would undoubtedly speak about fellowship and solidarity, the audience to nod in dutiful unison.

"How'd it go, angel?" Mom whispered.

Joss led her out of the room toward the bank of elevators. "She said to come back tomorrow for another session."

"But what if it happens again today?"

Joss hastened to the elevators and pushed the down arrow button, nervously glancing back at the door in anticipation of Proulx coming through.

"I'll be fine, Mom. You and Nate can look after me. I promise I won't leave the house, okay?"

The elevator dinged. They stepped inside the empty car, Joss repeatedly tapping the DOOR CLOSE button. At last the doors slowly came together and they were descending. Thank God.

The elevator hummed drearily. An advertisement on the wall read, *At Lakeside Medical Center, we're here to keep you healthy*, followed by a list of the hospital's services. The advertisement featured a smiling elderly couple whose faces brought Joss to tears. Max would never be a grandparent. He'd never fall in love or make another birthday wish or stare up at the stars.

Turning away from her mother and drying her eyes, Joss suddenly felt like she couldn't breathe.

"Are you sure it's fair to put Nate in this position?" Mom asked. "He shouldn't be expected to monitor you all day, and I have commitments this afternoon. Jocey, are you hearing what I'm saying?"

Her head beginning to pulse, Joss ignored her mother's question. When the elevator doors slid open, she rushed through the lobby and waited for Mom outside the revolving door, thankful for a snowy, refreshingly blustery morning, the ground dressed in white, the flakes coming down large and hectic. Joss wished she could teleport home and avoid one of her worst childhood haunts – vehicular interrogation from Anya Leclaire. (*Jocey, I only want what's best for you…*)

In the heated car, as Mom pulled out of the parking lot, she glanced over at Joss as if she might say something. Instead, she sighed and stared ahead at the slippery road, probably weighing the risks of burdening her daughter with more questions. A few miles later, however, she couldn't resist her urges.

"Perhaps it would be good for you to speak with Father Conrad about what you've been going through."

Combined with the incessant scrape of the windshield wipers, the suggestion brought Joss's fists to a squeeze. Too bad she'd sent Nate home earlier – then she could have driven with him.

"Save it," Joss said, watching buildings and cars flash by, everything gray and white, clenched in winter's grip.

Joss pulled her cell phone from her pocket and began a text message to Nate, then immediately deleted the message, reluctant to contact her boyfriend and explain everything she'd experienced. She just wanted to be left alone, at least for now.

"Embracing God will help you through this time of uncertainty," Mom pressed, speaking with the same piousness that had failed to work on Max several years earlier.

Disregarding her mother, looking out the window again, Joss decided to play a one-person alphabet game, the only way she could keep from yanking open the door and leaping out. It would be a long ride home, but she wouldn't let Mom infuriate her. She would simply seal her mouth and wait for the trip to be over.

She'd managed it before, many times.

Chapter 7

Nate was immensely relieved when Anya Leclaire called a little after six o'clock and told him the tests had indicated no physical problems responsible for Joss's trances. She would see a psychiatrist later that morning, and a course of action would be developed.

"Can I talk to her?"

"Later. She's resting right now."

"When can I see her again?"

"Probably this afternoon...if she's up for it. I really think she should take a day to rest, Nathan."

"I agree, but you have to watch her at all times. You can't let her out of your sight – it could happen again."

"Yes, I'm well aware of that. I pray the psychiatrist will recommend an inpatient stay. That would be the best thing for her right now."

"Yeah, I guess it would be. She definitely needs professional help, but what if she's afraid to stay in the hospital? What if it makes her worse?"

Nate took a deep breath, remembering the day he met Joss sophomore year. She'd been so happy then, so light of spirit and free, but now she was badly damaged...and Nate felt mostly responsible for her deterioration.

"Whatever happens, I want to be there for her," Nate said. "Will you have her call me as soon as there's a decision?"

Anya sighed. "I imagine she'll call you the moment she wakes."

Nate tried to return to sleep, but he wound up just lying in bed for a few hours and worrying about Joss. He was wide awake, staring at the ceiling, listening to the wintry morning quiet, when Uncle Mike called just before nine o'clock.

"Hey, kid, I've got big news about the Grafton investigation. How soon can you make it to my place?"

"I don't know, forty-five minutes, maybe more with the snow. Why? What's going on?"

"It's about Mason Blackwell. This could be a huge break."

"What do you mean?"

Mike quickly described the situation, finishing his explanation with, "I need you to take a look at something right away."

Snow had started drifting from dark predawn skies when Nate returned home from the hospital. Now there were about two inches spread neatly across the lawn, precursors to the main event tonight. After pulling on his winter gear, Nate shoveled a sloppy path to his car, then grabbed a snow brush and cleared the front and back windshields. His mind wasn't focused on snow and ice, though – he couldn't believe what Mike had just told him.

Even though the precipitation had all but stopped, the roads were still a slushy mess. Spinouts had accumulated along with the snow, expanding Nate's trip into an hour-long adventure. When he finally reached Mike's house, his uncle was waiting for him in the garage, his snowblower caked with powder. The driveway was clear and salted, as were the front and back walkways. Mike usually went above and beyond by removing snow from his neighbors' driveways, but this morning he was consumed by the Grafton case and its connections to what Nate and Joss went through.

"I feel like we've got most of the information," Mike said, leading Nate into the house. "Now it's just a matter of figuring out how to use it."

The house smelled like coffee and eggs. Passing through the kitchen, Nate saw a stack of dishes resting in the sink, along with glasses and silverware. On his way up the short but hilly driveway a few minutes earlier, Nate had seen Aunt Sue and Chris building a snowman on the front lawn. If not for this dire situation, Mike surely would have been out there with his family.

But 99 Deepwoods Drive commanded him. Again.

They went downstairs into Mike's basement office, which was exceedingly warm thanks to a space heater. Mike pulled off his coat and set it on a rack, then guided Nate to a table in the far corner. "Check these out," he said, pointing to a handful of papers spread across the table – photocopies of the original documents.

Nate read for a while. With every sentence he grew increasingly tense. When he eventually came to the signature and the message written below it, he said, "I'm pretty sure this is legit. Jesus, Mason came back! There's no way anyone else could have known all of this. The only reason I got to Shepherd's realm was because Joss was taken first, so the part about someone needing to be taken through the wall must be right."

Mike nodded. "Whitney Golding said she's positive it was Mason. Dave Strait showed her a yearbook photo of the kid, and she was convinced."

Nate's neck muscles tightened. He felt a bristling fear in his chest. The thoughts spilling into his mind suddenly made the heated basement seem very cold. "So what are you and Chief Strait gonna do about this?"

Mike explained what had come to him during his latest visions, and by the time he finished, Nate was left frightened to the point of speechlessness. But he wasn't terrified for Mike or Dave Strait or even Blake Grafton, not when his uncle had seen in nightmares a young man named Max whose appearance closely resembled that of Joss's brother.

Worst of all, in last night's dream Max had been hugging Blake Grafton, both of them trapped in the walls with Joss!

Chapter 8

Katie was staring at the Christmas gifts she'd bought for Blake when Peter Dobyns, the reporter for the *Boston Globe*, called at ten-thirty Saturday morning. Katie's parents, Whit, and the ultra-supportive Sheila Frost were in the kitchen preparing breakfast and completing other chores (someone had just started up the vacuum).

Katie closed the living room door to shut out the noise. When she realized Dobyns was on the other end, she found herself apologizing repeatedly for forgetting the meeting they'd arranged yesterday after the press conference.

"There's no reason for you to apologize, Ms. Grafton. I can't imagine what you're going through," Dobyns said. "Would it be possible for us to meet today?"

"Sure, whatever time works for you."

"How about two o'clock at the police station?"

"You can come to the apartment if you'd like. I don't mind."

"Okay, I'll plan on meeting you there."

Katie sighed. "I'm sure you know the unit number."

When the conversation ended, Katie wished she were still talking to the reporter. He'd provided a brief but needed distraction from her agony, each gift before her like a stab to the heart. She remembered the excitement she'd felt upon envisioning her son tearing off the wrapping paper and eyeing for the first time his new toys. She'd even saved up enough to buy the video gaming system that had topped Blake's list.

But now the gifts brought only pain to Katie during a time that should have been filled with joy. For some reason she'd decided to retrieve them from bags on the top shelf of the living room closet and spread them across the room. Whit had offered to return them to the closet, but Katie had insisted on looking them over, a bad decision. Just moments after setting down the phone, she was sobbing uncontrollably, surrounded by happy children smiling from the boxes of Blake's gifts. The boy on the back of the Lego dinosaur set box even looked like Blake, but *that* little boy was probably home with his parents right now, not alone and afraid, not trapped somewhere horrible, not suffering.

Katie slammed a palm against the wall, tugged her hair, wanting to break something, wanting to break everything! The mornings were the worst. Every morning, in the foggy lands between sleep and wake, her son was home, safe in bed…but then realization leveled her anew, unfurling another day of tears.

The door clicked open. A hand came down on Katie's shoulder. Whit knelt beside her, said nothing, just wrapped an arm around her and held on tight, patient as Katie cried for so long that her chest and neck hurt when the tears finally ceased.

Katie turned to Whit, grateful for her strength. Slender of build, her friend might as well have been a tower of steel. Katie hugged her, shunting aside a new train of tears. "Thanks for being here," was all she could manage, and they embraced for a long while.

"I have to go to work after breakfast, but I promise I'll be back tonight," Whit said when they finally separated.

Katie nodded understandingly. She knew she couldn't ask Whit to stay; if she didn't get back to work, she might be fired.

I have to be strong. When Blake comes home, he'll need me to be strong.

Mom hollered from the kitchen that breakfast was ready.

"Go get washed up. I'll take care of these," Whit said, lifting the Lego box.

"No, I need to do this," Katie urged, and together they returned the gifts to the closet. With Blake gone, there was no need to hide them way up on the highest shelf. Instead, they would sit lonely atop a few boxes, waiting for their future owner to come home so he could unwrap them on Christmas morning.

Yet there was a distinct possibility that they might never be wrapped in the first place, the packs of colorful bows and rolls of wrapping paper tucked away in the back of the closet, the holidays put on hold. Christmas was only a week away now, but Katie's countdown ornament, the one she and Blake so eagerly flipped each year, beginning at 25 and winding quickly down, remained on DAY 12.

Day 12. It was like time had stopped the second Blake was taken, twelve days till Christmas.

Before shutting the closet door, Katie deliberately positioned the boy on the backside of the Lego box so he was facing the wall.

Peter Dobyns familiarized himself with the kitchen in respectful silence, taking everything in with the solemnity of a funeral guest. But his eyes conveyed something even heavier, a deep sadness that had likely been elicited by the realization that he was stepping into an apartment from which a little boy had been abducted. A little boy who might not be coming home.

"Make yourself comfortable," Katie said tiredly, motioning for him to sit at the table. "Would you like anything to eat or drink?"

Dobyns set his recorder and notebook on the table. He removed his coat and draped it around a chair. "Thanks, but I'm all set."

Katie sat across from the reporter at the table. She didn't mind having him here, if for no other reason than to create a diversion from her assailing fears. Sheila Frost, who was currently making calls about the investigation in the living room, usually took turns with Whit in distracting Katie, but it was helpful to have a new face in the apartment.

"So what can I tell you?" Katie searched Dobyns's pale blue eyes. He wasn't a handsome man, but there was a rugged intensity about him that compensated for it. His face was thick with stubble, and his hair looked like it had gone down a roller coaster. His laminated press credentials hung from a navy blue lanyard around his neck, revealing a photo of Peter Dobyns about ten years younger and forty pounds lighter.

Dobyns readied his recorder. "Thanks again for speaking to me, Ms. Grafton. First, I wanted to confirm that the landlord didn't mention anything to you about the previous crimes and incidents at this place when you were considering moving in."

"That's right. I didn't realize there'd been suicides here until my friend found a story about one of them online. And the landlord didn't say a thing about the abduction in September."

"Have you questioned him about why he didn't tell you anything? The last renter moved out of this unit after his girlfriend was abducted, quite possibly by the same individuals who abducted your son. Are you upset about not being notified of a potential threat?"

Katie felt the pangs of annoyance creeping in. She had no interest in answering questions about the landlord. "I haven't spoken to him about that. All of my energy has gone toward looking for my son."

"What can you tell me about the message from Blake's abductor?"

Katie remembered the helpless dread she'd experienced after first reading the message. "It was pretty straightforward. It said my son will die if I move out."

Dobyns waited a moment, as if expecting her to elaborate. "There's been a great deal of speculation about why the abductor wants you to remain in your apartment. Do you think it's because this individual, or individuals, is familiar with the neighborhood, particularly this building?"

Katie shrugged. "I guess. Like you said, whoever did this, chances are good it's the same people who abducted the last renter's girlfriend. I have no idea why they target this unit, but it obviously has something to do with the mass suicide. Why else would they have said their names are Gerald and Mason Blackwell?"

Dobyns took a moment to write notes. When he looked up again, his expression had grown noticeably darker. "I'm guessing you've learned quite a bit about what happened that night in 1965."

Katie sighed. "Yes, and I think the monsters who took my son were involved in it somehow. Either that, or their family members were involved in it – parents, grandparents, who knows? It's almost like they want people to think the place is haunted or something."

Dobyns nodded. "By using the names Gerald and Mason Blackwell, it does appear as if they have a fixation with projecting the image of a haunting. However, with yesterday's press conference, the police seem to have shifted their attention from the possibility of two suspects to that of a single suspect – Douglas McDermott, the sex offender who was recently arrested."

"It's not him." Katie thought about the contents of the envelope that had been given to Whit, each detail flashing through her mind.

"But he doesn't have a credible alibi for Monday night," Dobyns said, wanting like everyone else to have a solid suspect.

Katie knew it wasn't McDermott. An unregistered sex offender who'd recently moved to town was the easy answer, but whoever was really responsible for Blake's disappearance hadn't just moved to Hollisville.

"There's no way it's him," Katie insisted. "He offered to take a polygraph test and even said the police could have samples of his handwriting so they could match it to the message I got from the abductor. Plus, he hadn't even moved here yet when the last tenant's girlfriend was taken. By the way, everything about McDermott is off the record, okay?"

"Absolutely. On a totally separate note, what's your response to the increasingly prevalent claims that this building" – he looked about the room for added emphasis – "might actually be haunted by the spirits of those who committed suicide back in the sixties?"

Katie had no idea how to respond. Caught off guard by the question, she searched for an answer but couldn't come up with anything, partly because she was starting to take the idea of a haunting very seriously herself. She'd kept dismissing it and making rationalizations, but the notion had a bothersome tendency to write itself back into the equation, challenging her to accept a supernatural explanation, especially after yesterday. It was like something straight out of the movies – and her son was stuck in the middle of the madness.

Perhaps mistaking her silence for disapproval, Dobyns said, "I only mentioned it because of the rumors. A lot of folks in town are talking about it, but there's a growing number of people who think there might be something…paranormal going on."

"It's a fair question. There's no denying the things that have happened here."

Katie absently grabbed the salt shaker and began fidgeting with it. She felt constricted, as if someone had wrapped her in a roll of tape. For a few seconds, she thought she heard an organ come to life in the distance.

It didn't surprise her moments later when she became convinced that someone – or something – was watching them. It was a feeling that several

other individuals would soon share in that very
room.

Chapter 9

For Peter Dobyns, journalism had recently slipped from a rewarding occupation to a means of making money. He was a talented writer and reporter, but the act of delivering the news had waned in excitement over the last few years. Even the high-profile court cases failed to amp Peter up the way they once had. His true passion was paranormal research, an activity that took up most of his free time. When he wasn't working, Peter was touring allegedly haunted places throughout New England and organizing events for the paranormal exploration society he'd established last year with his wife.

Fascinated by the idea of the supernatural lurking within seemingly harmless buildings, Peter had eagerly pitched to his editor a trip to Hollisville, New Hampshire, explaining that he could write a series of articles on the Blake Grafton abduction. What he hadn't revealed to anyone other than his wife was the intended dual purpose of his trip, the second phase of which he was currently beginning.

After taking a few glances at the parking lot, where a cop was in his cruiser, paying no attention to the building, Peter hurried down the lawn to the shed. Assuming the door would be locked, he was stunned when he managed to pull it open and stare into the dark interior. With a gentle outward draft, the darkness itself seemed to be whispering to him.

Peter blinked in surprise, wondering if he should go inside. He hadn't actually expected the door to open. Then it hit him – of course he should go inside! There was no way he'd forgive himself if he passed up an opportunity like this.

Acting quickly for fear that the cop would spot him, Peter located a string that turned on an overhead bank of lights. They sluggishly buzzed to life as though they hadn't been activated in a decade, dim and dusty like the lights inside a handful of Cold War-era bunkers Peter had toured in northwestern Massachusetts.

Excited, he closed the door behind him, reached into his canvas bag, and removed his camcorder. But where was his flashlight, the one he always kept in the side pouch? Had he forgotten to return it after replacing the batteries?

There was a moment of crisp fear, Peter searching the darkness ahead, uncharacteristically hesitant. The lights didn't project into what appeared to be a tunnel, only the ranks of blackness to embrace him in there. But he had to do this – it might be his only chance.

Afraid someone would hear him, he spoke softly during his self-guided tour of the shed, his voice hollow and unnatural, each word unleashed with the expectation that something would happen.

"This is live footage from a shed attached to 99 Deepwoods Drive in Hollisville, New Hampshire, where several potential paranormal events have taken place since the eighties." Now he was following the curving corridor into darkness, requiring the night vision mode on his camcorder. "There was a mass suicide in this building back in 1965, long before it was converted to a rental property. But perhaps some of those souls are still haunting the place, terrorizing current renters. Seven-year-old Blake Grafton was the latest person to be abducted from the building, but 99 Deepwoods Drive has had a long history of misfortune. This year alone, two renters have committed suicide in the building, although some believe their deaths were made to look like suicides."

He took slow steps, advancing cautiously.

Wow! This was so much more exhilarating than the abandoned psychiatric hospitals and defunct Catholic schools and desolate mills – dark, cold, frightening buildings inhabited only by critters and squatters. But this place was different, Peter sensed, heavy with a far greater burden. He'd spent hours researching number 99, and the other members of his paranormal society would be thrilled to see the footage he was capturing.

He continued his narration, proceeding steadily forward and constantly checking the green world of night vision. The walls seemed to be closing in on him. The air was becoming thicker. And there was a smell, too, something pungent and perhaps decomposing.

Suddenly filled with an unexplainable, consuming dread, Peter stopped speaking and considered turning around. But what paranormal investigator deserving of any respect would run from a home with a dark history? No, he would force himself to keep going further into darkness, deeper into the unknown.

At first Peter hadn't been sure if the walls were creeping in on him, but a few minutes later he was certain the passageway had narrowed. Extending his arms outward, he could lay his palms flat against both walls, which he hadn't been able to manage just a few seconds ago. Space was indeed being reduced, and for just a moment Peter thought he heard someone crying in the distance.

Arms tingling, he pulled an EVP recorder from his bag and stood motionlessly for a while, listening carefully. Nothing. He was alone with his thoughts…for now.

But just as he was about to retrieve another piece of equipment, a series of thumps flared up a short distance ahead, originating high and slowly descending, like footfalls on a staircase.

A lump tightened in Peter's throat, his body stiffening, steeling itself for…

The cries came again, unmistakable, high-pitched bleats like those of a wounded animal.

Heavier thumping. Closer.

Now the ululations rang in the walls, reverberating in Peter's ears. He'd never experienced anything like this before, not even during his overnight stays at some of the most infamous haunted houses and hotels in New England.

With shaking hands he directed the camcorder straight ahead…and noticed a shadow advancing quickly, cascading toward him like a midnight tide, a jagged sheen of black amidst the green. Intuition told Peter, backpedaling, that even the slightest contact with this searching blackness would be fatal.

His heart sticking in the terrified clutch of his chest, Peter was so engrossed by the onrushing shadow that he wasn't aware of the dim white lights looming behind him. But even if he'd whirled around that very second, there would be no escaping 99 Deepwoods Drive.

This time Peter had ventured into the wrong building.

***

Max fell asleep after his chess games with Blake. Had he known what he'd find upon waking, he never would have closed his eyes.

The moaning wind disrupted his sleep, buffeting the far window with icy assaults. Despite its opacity, sunlight penetrated the window and revealed a new inhabitant in their dusty prison. Lying on his back beside a still sleeping Blake, the man was about thirty-five or forty. He wore a heavy coat, and from his neck hung an identification card, Max hurrying over to read it:

The Boston Globe
Peter M. Dobyns

The first thought crossing Max's mind was that of a suicide, but maybe this man had been abducted like Blake. Whatever Shepherd was planning, Max sensed it would happen very soon.

Movement behind him. Max spun around and discovered Joseph Johansen watching him intently from the near alcove, his arms crossed. "It's time, Maxime. Are you ready to see your father in Heaven?"

"Fuck you, asshole! What do you know about my father?"

Johansen recoiled. "Language, Maxime, language!"

"Screw you!" Although his voice was nowhere near a whisper, it was low enough to preserve Blake's sleep.

Taking a few reluctant steps closer, Johansen said, "Shepherd has told me all about your father. If you obey this one command, you'll see him again. Isn't that wonderful?"

Max allowed himself a moment's optimism. To see Dad again would be…impossible. He'd never be allowed to see his father again – they were simply using him for something.

"What does he want?" Max said.

Johansen smiled faintly, nodding at the man apparently named Peter Dobyns. "End his life."

"*What?*" Max couldn't hold back a burst of incredulous laughter. "You're saying I'll get to Heaven if I *kill* this guy?"

Johansen scowled in the man's direction. "He's a sinner, Maxime. A sinner deserving of death. End his life, and you'll see your father again."

Max glanced at Blake, who rolled onto his side. "What about the kid? What happens to him?"

"He'll be assigned his own task. I'm afraid Shepherd makes the rules – I just convey them."

"Bullshit! You guys are trying to fuck us over. I'm not killing anyone."

"Oh, yes you will!" Johansen snarled. "If you don't kill that man, only bad things will happen to you and Blake."

"Leave him out of this. Please. He's just a little kid."

Johansen turned away from Max. "How many times must I tell you that I don't make the rules around here? Shepherd has given you a choice – now you must decide what to do, Maxime."

Max watched his sleeping cellmates, the boy he'd promised to protect and the man he'd been asked to kill. On the other side of the wall, sitting at her desk, was Blake's mother, just a few feet from her son but absent the knowledge and the means to save him – and how darkly impeccable it was that Max could see her again, today, at this moment. The irony of their prison was immense, but the evil controlling it was prodigious, a voracious force in constant preparation of its next move. Chess – they'd been given chess pieces here, yes, Max could see it all now, just like the moves in a game…a game with an opponent that couldn't be stopped or even slowed, always one step ahead.

Now the next move was upon Max, its consequences as mysterious as those who'd devised his torments.

Chapter 10

Nate was still trying to accept the possibility – more accurately, the likelihood – that Max's soul was trapped inside 99 Deepwoods Drive, when Anya Leclaire called around one o'clock.

"Jocey wants to see you," Anya said, sounding weary. "She's extremely resistant to the idea of psychiatric help."

"Where is she now?"

"In her room, resting. I'm just outside the door."

"I'm on my way. Don't let her out of your sight until I get there."

Nate's speed was well in excess of the limit. He tried to think of what he'd tell Joss, but it seemed like there was nothing left to say, no further reassurances to offer or promises to make. He wasn't a psychiatrist. He wasn't a bodyguard. And he most certainly couldn't protect his girlfriend like he'd once told her, couldn't watch her twenty-four-seven to ensure she didn't hurt herself. A thought that she'd eventually follow Max's suicidal path made him press the brake and dip below the speed limit for the first time.

Max – was he really stuck inside 99 Deepwoods Drive as Mike's visions had suggested, held prisoner along with Blake Grafton?

Anya actually seemed relieved to see Nate when he arrived, taking his arm and leading him up the massive staircase. "I never thought I'd say this, Nathan, but I'm glad you're here for her."

Nate stared straight down the hall, eyeing the last door on the left that separated him from his girlfriend. "Whatever she needs me to do, I'm on it."

Anya's eyes were so heavy with exhaustion that they looked like they might force themselves closed. After opening the door and confirming Joss was still in bed, she nodded to Nate. "I'm going to see if I can sleep for a few hours. Can you stay that long?"

"Sure, no problem. I'll stay as long as she wants." Anya smiled tepidly, Nate recognizing the tiny bond they'd developed.

When Nate slipped into the room, Joss rolled onto her side, facing him. "Hey."

Nate came beside the bed and kissed her forehead. "Hey, beautiful. How are you feeling?"

The weakest of smiles stole across her chapped lips. "Only slightly less insane. But I need to tell you something, and you have to believe me." She propped herself up, sitting against the pillows. She looked both apprehensive and excited, girlish yet stunningly adult, her eyes aflame with some new revelation. "A few minutes ago I got a flashback of what happened right before one of my trances, the one at the plaza on the Mass Pike. I *saw* someone, Nate."

"Who?"

Her eyes glazed with cold fear. "The old lady from Max's apartment. She was on the floor, dead. It was so vivid, so real. Then there was this bright light, and I can't remember anything after that."

Nate held her hand. "So you just remembered all of this now?"

She nodded repeatedly. "I know I've been acting crazy. I can't tell you how pathetic I feel that you and Mom have to babysit me. The stupid shrink wanted to lock me up."

"She did?"

She hugged Nate, tears exploding. "Please tell me you don't think I'm nuts."

Nate patted her back, stroked her hair. He wished for a return to better days, remembering how easy life had been when there was nothing between him and Joss, no deaths, no lies, and no tears. Joss hadn't been haunted and broken back then, just a girl who loved her boyfriend and wanted to spend as much time as she possibly could with him. Movies on the weekends; endless texts and calls; Scrabble games; dinners at King Street Pizza (the site of their first date); sex before school and, consequently, tardy slips; pretending to be Olympic divers off the board and into her pool, then kissing in the hot tub, their closeness indescribable – but now that life seemed so unimaginably distant, like looking back on Earth from space.

Nate held her hands, careful with the bandaged finger, wanting badly for her to know he didn't blame her for anything. "Joss, what you've been through these last few months is insane. It's been too much for you to handle, but that would be true for anyone. You just need time to heal."

Sheltering herself once more in his embrace, she said, "Why do I feel like most people would get through this better than me? Why am I so screwed up?"

"You're not screwed up, Joss. You're just broken, like Humpty Dumpty. You need to be put together again."

Her tears shifted from sorrow to laughter. She sniffled, wiping her cheeks dry. "Shitty analogy, guy."

He held his hands up. "Hey, it was the best I could come up with on the spot."

She stared in the direction of the dresser. "I just wish I could remember what I saw before the other trances."

Nate had a sudden memory himself. "Remember a few months ago when you said you saw your dad in the woods that day we went for a walk?"

Her eyes flickered, the light of memory pouring in. "Yeah, that was really freaky."

"When you saw the old lady, was it kind of like that? Did it seem like she was in the plaza with you, or was it a vision of somewhere else?"

"She was in her apartment, I think. That day in the woods was totally different, like nothing I've ever experienced. It was like my dad was right there with me." A touch of French, Joss shaking her head as if to rid herself of the memory.

Nate thought of Mike's visions. Was Joss suddenly developing an extrasensory ability as well? This was all getting too complicated and entangled…Mason, Shepherd, Blake Grafton, Max, 99 Deepwoods Drive, Mike's visions, Joss's trances, the old lady who'd died at her South Boston apartment…and Nate couldn't resist the urge to assume everything was interconnected.

He kicked off his shoes and eased into the bed, caressing Joss's wounded hand, so small and slender. He kissed her lips. "Whatever's happening, we're gonna figure it out together."

Smiling, she spoke another line of French. Nate didn't need to understand a single word to know how grateful she was for his support.

Nate talked with Joss for over an hour in bed, the conversation rambling. They were lying on their sides and holding each other as they'd done countless times before, but today was different.

Colder. She looked at him searchingly, as if trying to decipher his thoughts. She didn't trust herself to be alone for even a few minutes, and Nate couldn't imagine how terrifying that was for her.

They finally slipped into a light sleep, but Joss was barely out twenty minutes when she jolted up in bed, startling Nate.

"What is it? What's wrong?"

She stared straight ahead, eyes wide. Another trance. Slowly she turned to him, blinked rapidly, then came out of it.

Nate held her shoulders. "Joss, what happened? Are you okay?"

Her expression was a portrait of stark, primal fear, her face wan. "I just saw Max again! He's in your old apartment, trapped in the walls!"

Part VI: Decades Below the Surface

*"I do not fear death. I had been dead for billions
and billions of years before I was born, and had not
suffered the slightest inconvenience from it."* ~
Mark Twain

Chapter 1

Joss was dismayed by Nate's initial reaction to what
she'd told him. He wasn't distressed or even
disturbed, his face stony and impassive, a
momentarily blank slate that should have been
colored with emotion. Then there was a flash of
worry in his eyes – but it had nothing to do with
Max; he was worried about *her*.

"You think I'm crazy, don't you?" Joss said. She
tore out of bed, suddenly wanting to be alone.

Nate remained nestled within the warmth of the
blankets. "It's not that, I just…I don't get it. How
did you come to this all of a sudden?" Now his face
revealed a blossoming dread, and for a moment Joss
thought there might be something withheld behind
it, some hidden knowledge that had rendered him
fearful in light of the information she'd relayed.

Perhaps what she'd initially perceived as an absence
of emotion on his behalf was actually shock. "Nate,
is there something you're not telling me?"

He shook his head, but she sensed he was lying. He'd never been a good liar.

"Tell me what's going on! Why did I just see my brother trapped in that place? Do you know something about Max?"

***

Nate couldn't believe what Joss was saying. Somehow she'd acquired Mike's ability, or some related talent. Regardless of how it was happening, they'd both experienced visions of Max Leclaire trapped in the walls of 99 Deepwoods Drive.

Panicked, incapable of keeping the truth from Joss any longer, Nate told her about his uncle's infallible visions, including the latest one.

A broad smile spread across Joss's face, her eyes glittering with an optimism Nate hadn't seen in months. "So Max really is there. Jesus, of all the places he could be…Shepherd, it has to be Shepherd. He wants to lure us back there. I think *he's* causing the trances!"

"Yeah, Shepherd probably knows Max is the key to getting us to go back." It was a thought that had dogged Nate all afternoon. "He's obviously pissed we got away, and now–"

"He wants to finish the job." She quickly corrected herself. "*It* wants to finish the job."

They were both silent for a moment. Then, simultaneously, they suggested divergent plans.

"We need to go there," Joss blurted, just as Nate was saying, "We can never go back."

A period of tacit opposition ensued, the heated room suddenly seeming chilly. Nate was unnerved by the conviction Joss exuded; she wouldn't be denied, he assumed, and now he regretted telling her about Mike's visions.

"We can't go back," he maintained, matching the intensity of her stare. "Joss, we barely got out the first time. If not for Mason, you would have been killed. And I still can't believe the landlord and I got out."

"Would you go if it was Rob?"

Nate was stunned by the question. "I…well, that's…" The words just ended, a stream gone dry. He'd been beaten. Game, set, match. No matter what he said, he knew in his heart that he would go back if the roles were reversed.

So how could he ask Joss to stay?

"Let's call Uncle Mike," he finally said, hoping to buy some time. "Whatever we do, we need him and Chief Strait with us this time."

Nate pulled out his cell phone. He could only hope his uncle and Strait would come up with a surefire plan, yet he knew there were no guarantees when it came to his old apartment. The place was a black hole, plain and simple, constantly drawing in and snuffing out new victims. They'd managed to escape back in September, but Nate feared that a second venture into darkness would result in disaster, two more names carved into the sepulcher that was 99 Deepwoods Drive.

Chapter 2

Carefully trailing Sheila Frost along the shoveled path winding through a few inches of snow on the back lawn, Katie barely noticed Peter Dobyns's blue sedan in the parking lot. If not for a laminated paper left atop the dashboard that read, VEHICLE BELONGS TO A MEDIA REPRESENTATIVE – PLEASE DO NOT TOW, followed by Dobyns's information, Katie would have walked right past the car.

"What's Peter still doing here?" she said, stopping.

Sheila spun around. "Who's Peter?"

Katie peered inside Dobyns's car. "That reporter from the *Globe* who just interviewed me. He must have left half an hour ago, maybe longer. Why's his car still here?"

Sheila began to shiver, and Katie felt guilty for keeping her out here. "Maybe he's interviewing someone else, like a cop or something. Or he could be taking pictures out front."

"Go get your car started – you're freezing," Katie said. "I'll be there in just a second."

As Sheila headed for her car, Katie crossed the lot to the Hollisville Police cruiser parked near the dumpster. The officer stepped out when he saw her approach. She'd seen him before, perhaps on the night of Blake's abduction. She couldn't be sure, though; the last week had been a blur of faces and information, everything blending together.

"Hi, Ms. Grafton. Can I help you with something?" The cop was young and pudgy, probably not even twenty-five.

Katie pointed to the reporter's car. "Have you seen Mr. Dobyns?"

He shook his head. "I didn't see him leave your apartment."

The wind poured in from the snow-dusted woods, nipping Katie's cheeks and nose. It was a gray afternoon, new clouds vaulting in ahead of tonight's nor'easter. It would be a bad one, according to the latest forecasts, a persistent storm expected to bring about a foot to the region by tomorrow night. Glancing up at the clouds, Katie felt something beyond the wind freeze through her coat and hat. A fear that something terrible had happened to Peter.

"Would you mind looking around for him?" Katie said. "He's not in my apartment and he's not in his car, so where did he go?"

The officer nodded. "I'll check it out. Thanks for the heads up, Ms. Grafton."

Katie watched him jog around the front of the building. Her fear that Peter Dobyns had met with calamity continued to escalate.

Quit being paranoid, she thought, forcing herself in the direction of Sheila's car. *He probably took some pictures and went out front for a smoke.*

But Peter Dobyns hadn't gone for a smoke. He hadn't jaunted down Deepwoods Drive for some frigid exercise, either. Instead, he'd done a little ghost hunting and wound up finding the roles reversed.

Chapter 3

Just as Nate was about to call Uncle Mike, a few knocks sounded against Joss's bedroom door. Nate blew out a sigh of frustration. He wished Anya Leclaire would sleep all day and leave them alone.

But when he opened the door, the person standing on the other side was not Joss's mother. Nate gasped. For a moment he couldn't draw breath.

"Hi, Nate," the intruder said. "You look like you've seen a ghost." He forced a nervous smile. "Sorry, I couldn't resist."

Nate stared at him. This couldn't be happening. Was it really him? Yes. Yes, it had to be.

Their visitor extended his hand. "I'm Mason Blackwell."

Nate kept his arm down, his body frozen because his brain didn't know how to react, firing mixed signals of consternation, hate, gratitude, and even hope. Before he could manage to find the words that wouldn't come, Joss appeared at his side. "Oh my God! Mason!"

She burst through the doorway and leaped into his arms.

"How can you be here?" Joss said. "Did you make it to Heaven? Did you see your mom?"

Mason set her down, and they all filed into her room. "My mother and I are together again–" Mason began.

"What are you doing here?" Nate interrupted.

Mason turned to him. "I was sent here with a message for your uncle."

"What kind of message?" Nate locked onto Mason's pale blue eyes. He wore a gray T-shirt, sunglasses hanging from the V-neck, looking as though he were ready for a date with a girl he'd met at the local teen center.

"Tell your uncle that he and Dave Strait have to go into the shed today. I'll try my best to help them, but it won't be easy. I don't have much time."

Joss took Mason's hand. "Do you know if my brother Max is trapped in there?"

Mason nodded. "He is, Joss, but you can't go back. Let Nate's uncle and Dave Strait handle it. I don't think Shepherd has an interest in taking them – he wants you and Nate because you guys got away. You'll always be unfinished business to him."

"He's right," Nate added. "We can't go back, Joss. Listen to him."

Joss began to cry, Mason squeezing her hand. "It's gonna be okay," he assured. "Your brother will be saved, just like me."

"You promise?"

Mason embraced her once more. "Max has helped that boy, Blake Grafton, just like I helped people when I was trapped. For that he'll be saved when it's all over. You just need to have faith."

"I'll give you guys a few minutes alone," Nate said, understanding that he should allow them at least that much. If not for Mason, Joss would have been killed.

"Call your uncle," Mason instructed. "Tell him he and Dave need to go there right now. The window is open because a guy just crossed over. His name's Peter Dobyns – he and Blake are in big trouble, but they can still be saved."

"And Max, too," Joss said.

Mason nodded. "Max has already saved himself. He'll be out of there soon, Joss, and you'll see him again one day. Right now he just wants to stay and protect Blake."

She smiled triumphantly, and Nate told himself to leave them alone. Stepping into the hallway, he called Mike and told him about Mason's visit.

"Jesus Christ, he's there with you now?"

"Yup. He's talking with Joss right now."

There was a momentary pause, rustling on the other end. "Are you sure you should let her be alone with him? I mean, my God, Nate, he's dead!"

"Yeah, but he really cares about her. He saved her life, so I figured I owe them a few minutes. This whole thing just blows my mind – I feel like I'm in another world."

"And he said we need to go there today?" Mike confirmed.

"Yeah, like right this minute. Mason said the window is open because someone passed through into Shepherd's world. A guy named Peter Dobyns."

More rustling from Mike's end. He was probably recording everything Nate said in anticipation of a meeting with Dave.

"Do you really want to do this?" Nate asked. "Think about Aunt Sue and Chris. What if something happens to you and Dave?"

"Nothing's gonna happen to us," Mike assured.

"But the only reason Joss made it out was Mason. He said he'd try to help you guys, but he might not be able to. I don't know, the whole thing is crazy and I hate the idea of you guys going in alone."

"Me too," Mike admitted. "But what kind of cops would we be if we didn't take this chance? A long time ago, Dave and I both took the oath, kid, and we have to honor it every day."

"Maybe you should bring a priest or something. Or the FBI, a SWAT team, anything."

"Nah, the feds only know how to do one thing really well – waste time. We'll get in, get the kid, and get the hell out."

"If only it was that easy when I went in."

A brief silence. At last Mike said, "Well, I guess there's no more time for talking. I'll get on the line with Dave right away."

"And I'll keep Joss away from there. She found out her brother's trapped – saw it in a vision just like you. Mason confirmed it."

"She has visions, too?"

"She sees the visions in her trances, not nightmares. I'll tell you more about it later." Nate searched for his next words, but he found nothing beyond: "Good luck, Uncle Mike. I love you."

"I love you, too, kid."

"Be safe, okay? If things get too nuts, you have to leave."

"Will do. I'll call you when it's done."

Nate pocketed the phone, tears in his eyes. He was terrified for his uncle, who would begin the same perilous journey Nate had taken back in September, a voyage not through the confines of a tiny shed but the tunnels of Hell. Guns wouldn't help; in fact, no assistance could be provided by manmade tools. It was all up to God, and with that truth came the mitigation of Nate's fears. If he and Joss and the landlord had gotten out alive, if Mason could come back and speak to them, then Mike and Dave could infiltrate Shepherd's realm and bring Blake Grafton home. Another miracle could happen.

But what if no more miracles were to occur at 99 Deepwoods Drive? What if Shepherd was even stronger now?

Nate found himself dropping to his knees and praying, less a conscious decision than an impulse. It was the only way he could help his uncle, but soon the questioning, fearful darkness returned. He thought of all those nights he'd prayed for his brother, begging God to keep him safe in Iraq, only to come home from school one afternoon and learn that Rob had been killed by a roadside bomb.

But although Nate had endured his brother's death, he'd also seen family and friends kept constantly safe…and so he continued to pray amidst the towering fear. God might not have answered all of his prayers, but He'd answered enough to restore Nate's faith.

Chapter 4

"Tell me what Heaven's like," Joss said. She was sitting on the edge of the bed with Mason, staring into his eyes and thanking God for saving him.

Shaking his head, Mason said, "It's beyond anything you could imagine, but you won't be there for a long time. You've still got your whole life ahead. Don't waste it worrying about things out of your control – just have faith that everything will work out."

She nodded, feeling a twinge of guilt. There'd been something pointedly reproachful in his words, as if he'd seen how she spent the last few months agonizing over his and Max's fates.

She leaned against his shoulder. "I can't believe you're here. I wanted so bad for you to be okay."

He stroked her hair. "It means a lot to know how much you care about me, but you need to move on with Nate." He looked to the ceiling. "I'm fine up there with my mom. You don't have to worry about me anymore."

"Speaking of your mom, I've kept the earrings safe."

Joss hurried to her jewelry box. In the bottom drawer, tucked away in the corner, was the black box Mason had given her in September. She returned to the bed and handed it to him, their hands remaining linked for a few extra seconds, Joss awestruck by their bond. It was like coming face to face with her spirit guide, someone she knew would always look after her.

"I want you to have them," Mason said, proffering the box to her.

"What? But–"

"I know this sounds crazy, but my mom already has them. Things are…different there – you'll see. For now, whenever you wear these, remember that you're not alone."

She kissed him on the cheek. "I love you. I'm so glad you're safe."

"I love you, too, Joss."

"What's wrong with me?" she blurted, pointing to her head. "The trances – is it Shepherd?"

His expression horrified her, but only for a moment, the absolute dread quickly cloaked by a hopeful smile as he passed the box to her. "You're strong, Joss. You can beat anything."

They hugged, Joss afraid that if she blinked he would be gone. A part of her wanted Mason to stay forever, but she knew it wasn't possible. He had to move on, and she needed to move forward and let him go. Plus, there were far more important things for him to accomplish. Blake Grafton required his assistance, just as Joss had needed him back in September.

It was time for them to say goodbye. At least in this life.

Chapter 5

Mike arrived at the Hollisville Police Department just before five o'clock that evening. He hadn't wanted to frighten Sue by describing the perils he would likely face inside 99 Deepwoods Drive. He'd simply told his wife that he was helping Dave with a break in the Grafton case.

In hindsight, Mike regretted not affording Sue a chance to talk him out of it, but his mind had already been made up. Regardless of the immense risks, a boy's life was in danger. Blake was no different than Chris, no different than any kid, an innocent little person at the mercy of evil.

Behind the police station, bathed in orange light in the small employee parking lot, Dave Strait was standing beside his pickup truck and loading his weapons. A Glock 19 was already tucked into his shoulder holster, and a Sig Sauer 9mm rested on the opened tailgate, its magazine detached. In Dave's hands, always at the ready, was his police issue Glock 22.

"Hey, old buddy," Dave said when Mike pulled up and lowered the window. "You ready to rock and roll?"

"You bet. Let's pray for a little luck." Mike had brought along his own weapons, more out of habit than anything. He knew it was extremely unlikely that Shepherd could be shot and wounded, yet it still felt more assuring to enter a potential battle loaded.

In addition to his Glocks, Mike also carried a hunting knife in a leather sheath, a flashlight, his police baton, and a Zippo windproof lighter, as well as a handful of other items that might be useful. You couldn't exactly make an online search for tools needed in a paranormal realm, so they'd have to do the best they could with what they had.

Mike parked his car and walked over to Dave's truck, squishing through piles of slush left by the plow. Having finished his weapons preparations, Dave was now adjusting the straps of a headlamp, cursing with each minor snag. He was dressed entirely in black, looking like a commando with combat goggles set atop his head. Mike suddenly felt underprepared – perhaps he should have brought his bulletproof vest and an AR-15.

"You're going full assault mode tonight, huh?" Mike remarked.

Dave blew out a heavy breath and slammed a fist into his palm. Now he resembled a football player in the locker room before a big game. "I'm holding nothing back, Mikey. This place has been a blight on Hollisville for way too long. Time to end this shit tonight."

***

Peter Dobyns awoke in a panicked, breathless haze.

He felt like he'd run a marathon while sleeping, his sides aching and throat burning. It took him several seconds to realize he was lying in an unfamiliar bed, surrounded by unfamiliar walls. The room was dimly illuminated by a pair of candlelit wall sconces whose supports featured elaborately welded dragons. The ceiling was a maze of beams and trusses, which creaked lightly under some invisible weight.

Suddenly Peter remembered everything. He'd gone into the shed of 99 Deepwoods Drive. He'd boldly pressed further, hoping to record footage for his paranormal society. Now his equipment was gone. He had nothing to reveal the many presences in the room, though high-tech equipment wasn't required to determine that the place was inhabited.

The door flung open, but no one entered the room, shadows swaying in the hallway beyond. White noise filled Peter's ears, building louder and louder, a roar of static occasionally interspersed with high-pitched whines. At the most distant reaches of the auditory scale, barely detectable, was another discordant sound. What was it? Peter listened closely but couldn't make it out. He was frozen on the bed, unable to catch his breath, mesmerized by the sounds and those shadows in the hallway.

They would come for him soon, no longer shadows but…

***

When Mike and Dave arrived at 99 Deepwoods Drive in Dave's pickup truck, the headlights shattered the building's darkness, shining upon the corrupted walls and flashing against windows to another world. The storm was knocking at New Hampshire's door, the sky leaden with clouds that would soon unleash more snow.

Something told Mike not to step out of the vehicle, that a calamity would instantly strike if he did. But without further hesitation he opened the door and hauled himself out, staring up at the big house on the hill. There was a Hollisville PD cruiser parked about fifty feet to their right, Dave leading Mike to it. They'd decided to check in with the officer monitoring the property but discuss nothing of their plans. It had been desirable to keep everything covert before, but now secrecy was of the utmost importance. They only had a small window, according to what Mason had told Nate, and they had to get inside before the window closed.

"Evening, Patterson," Dave said when the cruiser's window came down. "Mike and I need to take some additional photos to make sure we have everything documented. What's this I hear about someone going missing here earlier?" Dave was testing the information Mike had relayed to him from Mason.

The young officer nodded anxiously. "That's all been cleared up, Chief. We couldn't account for a reporter from the *Globe* earlier. He was interviewing Ms. Grafton, and she got worried because he left her unit but his vehicle was still here. I made a quick search of the building, but the vehicle was gone by the time I got back to the parking lot."

"What's his name?" Dave said.

"Peter Dobyns, sir."

Mike and Dave exchanged worried glances.
According to Mason, Dobyns hadn't gone
anywhere. So where was his vehicle?

At Dave's request, Patterson unlocked the shed for
them, their flashlights daggering the night.

"Thanks, kid. We should be finished in an hour or
so."

The officer headed back to his car, leaving Mike
and Dave to themselves, wondering with cold fear if
they would really access another realm – a window
in the walls.

After Mike shut the door behind them, Dave pulled
the headlamp from his duty bag and secured it
around his head. Then came the goggles, and even
with apprehension churning in his gut, Mike
managed a smile at his friend's image.

"Are the goggles really necessary?"

Dave zipped his bag and threw it over his shoulder,
then retrieved the Sig from its holster. "You can
never be too careful, right? Who knows what this
thing'll throw at us. Come on, let's do this."

They bumped fists. Before heading for the
passageway, Mike said a quick prayer that was
interrupted by a distant scream. It echoed

throughout the structure, its origin well beyond the interior of the shed they'd previously known.

They glanced at each other, momentarily immobile, their fears conspiring. "Let's get in there before it's too late," Mike said.

Chapter 6

Joss was crying on the end of her bed, knees pulled up to her chin, when Nate returned to her room.

"He said Max will be saved, too." She rubbed her eyes. "I pray he's right."

Nate sat beside her on the bed and wrapped an arm around her shoulders. He didn't know what to say. There seemed to be nothing to say, not after this most recent supernatural interference in their lives.

"Mason looked pretty good," Nate remarked at last, instantly regretting his words. It would have been better to remain quiet than to offer such a useless comment.

Joss laughed weakly. "It's not like he's changed much the last forty years."

Nate ran a hand through his hair. "True. But he's got better style now than before, right? Did you see the shades he had on his shirt? Kid's looking sharp."

They both laughed. It felt good to keep it light, especially since Nate knew his uncle and Dave Strait were on their way to 99 Deepwoods Drive. Moreover, it had been confirmed that Max was trapped in the building along with Blake.

But neither Nate nor Joss could do anything to protect their loved ones. All they could do was wait and pray.

Joss's smile vanished. She turned to Nate. "We
need to go there. Right now."

"We can't. Mason said–"

"I don't care what he said, Nate. We need to be
there. Your uncle and my brother are in there."

Nate shook his head. "No way, not a chance. I'm
not taking you anywhere near there, not after my
uncle's last vision was of *you* trapped in there, too."

Her eyes searing with frustration, she said, "Maybe
his vision was wrong. What if he needs our help?
What if he gets trapped and Mason can't save him?
If he dies and we did nothing–"

"He's not gonna die," Nate blurted, but he was
already taking into consideration what she'd said.
What if things didn't go well for Mike and Dave?
What if they went horribly wrong? Who would be
there to help them?

Nate expelled a long sigh, Joss flattening a hand
across his thigh. "You know I'm right, Nate. We
can't let them go alone."

He stood. "Don't you remember what Mason said
about Shepherd wanting to lure us back?"

Her eyes seemed to darken slightly. "If you don't
hear from your uncle by midnight, we go there."

He nodded in reluctant agreement. "I guess we'd be the last line of defense at that point. Let's hope it doesn't get that far."

She took his hand. "We can do more than hope. Let's pray."

Nate felt a surge of relief. She'd turned a corner, finally, and Nate knew who he had to thank for that.

***

His headlamp lighting the way, Dave led Mike through the passageway until they came to the staircase. *The* staircase!

They stopped, incredulous and fear-riddled. Each time they'd previously investigated this place – each time any officer had investigated the shed – this passageway had always terminated with a workbench and a utility sink affixed to a wall. But now that wall was gone, replaced by a staircase ascending to a platform and then jutting to the right.

Dave cautiously lowered a boot onto the first dust-caked step, jolting his foot away as if the step were a bear trap. He glanced back, illuminating the curving corridor. "How can we be sure this thing is structurally sound? What if we fall through?"

Mike, flashlight firm in his hand, Blake Grafton's image firm in his head, took the lead, hurrying up the first few steps to the platform and looking back at Dave. "This is exactly what Nate described," he whispered. "Follow me. We're getting close, but there might not be much time."

The staircase brought them past several doors inset awkwardly in the walls like windows, each marked by a gold number. There were no landings from which they could be accessed, a collection of phantom entrances to another world. Shepherd's world. The door labeled *1* was across from *2*; *3* faced *4*, and so forth. Even if they'd leaped up and tried to open one of the doors, none of them featured handles or knobs, and so they continued on, their lights casting eerie rising shadows on the walls.

At the top of the stairs, just beyond doors *9* and *10*, they followed a short hallway boasting two opposing arched doors. Made of oak and carved with elaborate symbols, they spirited thoughts into Mike's head of medieval churches and castles. Unlike the other doors, these included thin rusted handles.

"Which door?" Mike whispered. He checked his cell phone, hoping to call Nate for some quick advice…but as he'd assumed, there was no service available.

"Let's try this one first." Dave's words were urgent and smothered, barely escaping the constraints of fear welling in his throat. Sweat had developed on his forehead, certainly not a product of the short climb up the stairs.

A metallic sound rang out from somewhere below, causing them both to jump.

"Cover me," Mike said, pushing open the heavy door and stepping into an icy room where light was in thin supply. Gun pointed ahead, he instructed multiple occupants to freeze.

"This is the police! Don't move!" he shouted, passing rows of seated individuals en route to the head of the room, where a sixtyish man, surrounded by burning candles, read from a Bible.

"Police! Stay where you are!" Dave barked as Mike approached the man encircled by candles.

But no one responded to their orders or even acknowledged them. The leader sat with his legs crossed, his eyes deep and extreme. The shadowy congregants, seated in rows of wooden benches, stared not at Mike and Dave but their leader.

Their *leader*.

Johansen!

Mike had seen several online photos of Joseph Johansen, the defrocked priest who'd once called 99 Deepwoods Drive home. "Oh my God," he murmured, his chest aching sharply. "It can't be."

"What's wrong with these freaking people?" Dave said, his eyes darting from row to row. He tried to access the first row but was stopped cold by a floor-to-ceiling sheet of glass. In the dim, candlelit gloom, the glass was nearly invisible, but now Mike noticed that it spanned the entire room, blocking them from the gatherers.

"It's useless – we can't get in," Mike said. "But I know what's going on."

Johansen abruptly stood and addressed his followers. Mike's knowledge of 99 Deepwoods Drive taking over, he realized they were witnessing an event that had occurred in this building way back in 1965, the very first illusion that would be thrown at them by Shepherd. The bastard was starting off with a curveball.

"Gentlemen, our time has finally come – and how fitting that we should make the ultimate sacrifice on this holy night!" Johansen bellowed, his words clear in spite of the partition. He spread his arms outward and gazed up to the ceiling. "Four days after Lazarus died, Jesus came to Bethany and told his sisters, 'I am the resurrection and the life. Whoever believes in me, though he die, yet shall he live, and everyone who lives and believes in me shall never die.'"

"It's him, Joseph Johansen. None of this is real," Mike said, and Dave took an overwhelmed step back.

"It can't be, he's…" Dave's mouth fell open, his arms dropping to his sides. He looked down at his gun with blossoming panic, understanding how ineffective their weapons would be.

Johansen stepped over the candles and approached his followers, and as he did so, Mike's eyes wandered to the ceiling, where he spotted blue and yellow lights projecting downward from small circular openings. At the front of the room, unnoticed until now, Mike observed red horizontal laser lights beaming out and intersecting with the vertical light vectors. They'd previously been blocked from view by Johansen, who was now shaking the hand of every person in attendance. This was holography at its most advanced, terrifying level, a skill among many that had been mastered by Shepherd.

"Je-sus Christ," Dave said, watching raptly as the madness continued. With a sprinkle of evil's magic, they were seeing precisely what had happened on Christmas Eve of 1965.

Now focusing on the fourth row of supporters, Johansen shook the hand of a teenage boy who Mike immediately pegged as Mason Blackwell. He looked frightened out of his mind, eyes wide and face white.

Johansen clutched the boy's hand. "Do not fear, young Mason. Remember, he who believes in God, he who *sacrifices* himself to God, will live forever!"

A deafening bang. Shattering, showering glass. Mike's ears rang for a few painful seconds before he realized what had happened, the holographic show reduced to a chaotic scene of pulsing blue eruptions like camera flashes. No more Johansen. No more supporters. No more wall of glass, the partition now a glittering sea of jewel bits. Even the furniture and the candles were gone, all of it a grand illusion of light created by a prodigious force of darkness.

Dave gripped his gun with both hands, wincing at the flashes like a dog during a thunderstorm. "I couldn't stand it anymore, Mikey. I had to shoot. Did I fuck up?"

Mike shook his head. "Nah, let's just get out of here. Maybe Blake's in the room across the hall."

They hurried out of the room where deceptions had ruled, ready to enter the next one, where more tricks were waiting.

Chapter 7

Whit returned to the apartment around six o'clock,
Katie's parents arriving almost an hour later.
Everyone helped prepare dinner, a benefit Katie had
greatly appreciated since Blake was taken. It was a
struggle to keep herself sane, never mind maintain
the apartment and cook meals. Everything seemed
pointless in the absence of her son, especially
household chores, but her parents, Whit, and Sheila
Frost had been immeasurably helpful over the last
five days.

Less than a week. Katie couldn't believe it, feeling
like months had passed since she'd last seen Blake.
Her face spoke to a greater passage of time as well
– her eyes remote and sunken, skin pale, hair
unkempt – the woman she'd been a week ago
having faded to a broken, spiritless shell. Whenever
she imagined Blake at the mercy of evil, her fists
clenched and her head throbbed. On more than a
few occasions, sharp with anguish, she'd wondered
how she would continue living if she learned of
Blake's death. Breathing would simply be too much
to ask.

Facing the stove, Katie's mother added sauce to a
skillet of noodles. Her father had recently joined
them in the kitchen after making calls in the living
room, frustrated by his failure to turn up useful
information. The trail had gone as cold as the dark
December evening beyond the kitchen window. No
one could provide any new leads, nothing to point
them in the direction of her son.

Sighing, Dad slumped into a chair opposite Katie at the table. She'd only been half-listening to her parents' conversation, staring out the kitchen window and focusing on a trio of enormous shadows sprawled halfway up the hill on the side lawn. They belonged to three individuals standing on the second floor deck, just outside her apartment, their shadows created by the motion sensor light and projected onto the lawn, where the ambit of light extended almost to the woods.

"I'm gonna get some air," Katie said, gathering her hat and gloves. She assumed the shadows indicated three investigators on the deck intending to speak to her, possibly from the State Police, whose officers had returned to the apartment that morning for yet another observation of the building. A knock on the kitchen door would come any second.

But when Katie pulled open the door and stepped out into the cold, there was no one on the deck. She leaned over the railing and searched the snow-glistened lawn. No activity. The parking lot was dark, and none of the vehicles out there were running. Katie listened closely, taking in a foreboding winter silence interrupted only by voices inside her apartment and a light, sibilant wind that stirred the trees.

Acting on a sudden impulse, she hurried down to the parking lot. She wasn't sure what she expected to find, still perplexed by the shadows.

Three shadows. Standing just outside the door. A haunting memory wrapped its cold arms around

Katie and held her tight, not letting go, suffocating her. She remembered Blake waking her on their very first night at the apartment. Her son had been panicked after seeing three hooded men peer into the kitchen. Next, Katie remembered what she'd read in the documents given to Whit outside the police station, the final page signed by Mason Blackwell. There'd been a description of three ghosts watching a young girl.

Three hooded men. Three shadows. Three ghosts. Further, Blake's frantic descriptions and those provided in "Mason's" pages had involved a pale light illuminating the intruders' faces. And then there was the note left on Katie's car threatening her to stay. Again a powerful sensation overcame her, an intuition that Blake was somewhere inside the building. She stared up at the massive structure, so tall and ominous – and for a moment she was convinced *it* was the enemy.

Or something in it.

"What the hell is going on?" she murmured, walking aimlessly past the police cruiser in the parking lot and following a path to the front of the building, where the officer stood near the staircase and smoked.

"Good evening, Ms. Grafton," he greeted. The orange glow of his cigarette looked like the lambent eye of a nightmare creature. "Can I help you with something?"

"No, thanks, I'm fine."

Katie wished he would go away. If everyone would leave her alone for a few minutes to think, then maybe she'd figure out what was going on. She sensed that she was close, so close to unraveling the enigma and exposing the monster who'd taken her son. The police were trying their best, but the responsibility was hers to bring Blake home. She was his mother – she was supposed to protect him. She was supposed to always keep him safe and happy, but he was gone, a prisoner, scared and alone and hurting. Katie could bring him back, though. She could end the suffering and the sleepless nights.

She just needed to think!

The officer dropped his cigarette to the sidewalk and crushed it out. For a moment Katie hated him. Hated that he was out here smoking when her son was missing. Hated that he wasn't looking for Blake. Hated his failure and that of his entire department to find her child.

Perhaps her eyes betrayed her revulsion, for the young cop nodded at her and headed back to his cruiser. Finally she was alone, free to gather her thoughts, no longer feeling stifled.

She shivered. It was cold but not as oppressive as previous nights. The sky was blanketed by swollen clouds laced with tinges of orange, the nor'easter only a few hours away. Arms folded across her chest, Katie stared at the threatening sky before turning her attention to the building again. The front railing was illuminated by flashing green and red

Christmas lights, as well as white icicle lights. They belonged to the elderly couple who rented unit nine, a reserved pair who'd made themselves unusually scarce since Blake's abduction. Katie had often seen them sitting together on a rocking bench outside their apartment, sipping coffee and gazing out at Deepwoods Drive and, beyond the woods to the south, Lake Monomonac at the state line. They'd always waved when Katie unlocked her mailbox at the head of the parking lot.

But Katie hadn't spotted them on that bench since Monday evening, and she couldn't recall them participating in the search for Blake. They hadn't visited Katie's apartment to express their support, either, nor had they come up to her in the parking lot to offer the popular *We're praying for you and your son* line.

Katie continued to watch the blinking Christmas lights. An urge came over her to head up to unit nine and question the couple, but it quickly passed. They were just shy and scared, she told herself. They'd probably been unnerved by the heavy police response and were too reluctant to involve themselves in Katie's turmoil, perhaps afraid to upset her or provide an unwanted distraction. Yet her instincts kept nagging her, insisting that the couple knew more than they'd told the cops. Something wasn't right with them, but what was it? And how would she convince anyone else that they were at least a little dubious.

Taking a few steps back toward her apartment, Katie realized that not only had she failed to see the couple on their bench since Monday, but she hadn't seen them at all. The police had said they'd been accommodating, but Katie found herself full of new questions. Had they seen something they hadn't reported? Had they been threatened by the abductors?

Katie decided after all to visit unit nine in search of some answers. Not tomorrow. Not later that night. Right now. If needed, she would turn the entire building upside down, but one way or another her son was coming home.

Chapter 8

Max finally ceased his frenzied attempt to escape. He'd been punching and kicking the walls for what felt like an hour, repeatedly assaulting the drywall but feeling no pain.

When he'd refused to kill Peter Dobyns, instead engaging him in conversation, three hooded men had appeared behind them and dragged Peter and Blake, kicking and flailing, through the side wall. Max had been helpless to stop it, denied by invisible walls that had prevented him from moving even a few feet in any direction. Now those walls were gone, the prison boasting its usual dimensions. Max was alone, defeated, brooding in the middle of the room. He could no longer see through the wall, either, deprived of his ability as punishment for disobeying Shepherd.

Wracked by guilt, Max couldn't shake the image of Blake crying and screaming for help. What was happening to him now? Max had said he would protect him and bring him back to his mother, but he'd failed. Again. He'd failed Blake Grafton just as he'd failed Jocey, just as he'd failed everyone, his entire pathetic life a rotten, fetid failure.

"FUCK!!!" he screamed, shattering the solitary silence. Then he was up again, pounding the walls in desperate futility, his curses alternating between French and English.

His mind kept wandering back to Dobyns, who'd trembled with terror. In their brief, panicked discussion, Max had learned the guy was a ghost hunter who ran a paranormal society. He was also a reporter for the *Boston Globe* who'd come to 99 Deepwoods Drive in Hollisville, New Hampshire, to interview Katherine Grafton. Blake had jumped at the mention of his mother, but the hooded men had rushed in then, grabbing Blake and Peter.

Now they were gone, replaced by isolation and hopeless repetition. Max kept slamming the walls, kicking them with the very sneakers he'd worn in his dying moments. He should have given up after five or ten more minutes, but he continued railing against his confines out of sheer stubbornness as sunlight slowly drained from the prison. If he couldn't sleep and eat, if he couldn't experience companionship, then he would keep rebelling…and as he did so he remembered everything that had led him here, all of the horrible decisions and asinine thoughts. He remembered his childhood with Jocey and how they'd always been there for each other. She was still there for him, searching for a way to help even after his death. But what was he doing for her? What was he doing for Blake? Nothing. Nothing!

Enraged, he assaulted the walls with even greater force, taking running leaps and launching his shoulders into the drywall, each time recalling the Sunday nights Jocey had delivered food to him. She'd suffered for him, but to what end? Her suffering had led to *this*!

Another leaping launch, then another, and another. Finally, on what might have been the hundredth leap, he crashed through the side wall opposite Blake Grafton's apartment and stumbled onto a staircase. He rolled downward, somersaulting, his head knocking against wooden treads, until he reached the bottom and glanced up, still feeling no pain.

Everything was washed in gray, shadowy light. He had no idea where to go, but at least he was free of the four tormenting walls.

Upstairs, a scream rang out, and the grayness seemed to temporarily shimmer as the scream echoed.

Blake Grafton's scream.

***

Katie was about to head up to unit nine when her father's voice called from the parking lot.

"Katie, what are you doing over here? Your mother sent me out to find you – dinner's almost ready."

Katie quickly explained the strangeness surrounding the old couple who called unit nine home. Surprisingly, Dad supported her decision to question them.

"Dinner can wait," he said, and together they climbed the stairs up to the front deck. Perhaps it shouldn't have come as such a surprise to Katie that her father had agreed to join her. To him, everyone in town was a source of at least some suspicion, especially people living in the neighborhood. Still, Katie had assumed he would want to leave the questioning to the police.

They followed the deck past the entrances to units six through eight, past the rocking bench from which the couple had often waved to Katie. They were splashed by the Christmas lights as they came to unit nine at the end of the deck, where another staircase led up to the largest unit in the building, unit ten.

Dad knocked on the door. "Anyone home?"

No response, although Katie could have sworn she saw the white lace curtains tremble beyond the front window. Unit nine was dark and quiet. They listened for a few moments but heard nothing.

"Maybe they're out to dinner," Katie said.

Dad shook his head. "Or maybe they're dodging us. What kind of car do they drive?"

Katie searched her memory, but she couldn't remember seeing them drive anywhere. "I'm not sure. Every time I've seen them, they've been sitting on that bench."

"It does seem odd that they've kept their distance. I've never seen them myself."

Katie frowned, mostly out of self-directed disappointment. The last thing she wanted was to make her father paranoid about the old couple in unit nine. "We should get back inside. They're obviously not here."

"Wait a second," Dad said, pointing. "That curtain just moved. Someone's in there."

"Really? I thought I saw it move before, but I wasn't positive."

Nodding emphatically, Dad said, "I'm a hundred percent sure." He rapped on the door again, this time with greater force.

Still no answer, although the curtains fluttered again, unmistakable movement. Inside the apartment, a foot past the window, Katie thought she saw someone recede into the deeper darkness, a twisted shadow face.

A shudder went down her spine. Something was very wrong, she could feel it.

"They might have grandchildren home alone or something," Katie suggested, though she knew in her heart that no child inhabited unit nine.

Dad peered through the window, hands serving as blinders, trying to see past the curtains. A bout of wind caused him to zip up his coat. "Who's in there?" he shouted.

Silence. The curtains were still. Behind them, the Christmas lights pulsed green and red. Another gust chilled their cheeks. A van whispered past the house, heading slowly toward Route 202. To drivers traveling by, this was a normal house on a quiet road, but Katie sensed evil lurking inside, ruling the darkness and infecting all who tried to penetrate its cold, black realm. Within these walls countless secrets were protected, including that of Blake's disappearance.

Just when Dad seemed ready to leave, the front door nudged open a few inches, as if inviting them inside. They exchanged glances before staring at the partially opened door.

"Let's go in," Katie urged.

Dad looked worried. He leaned out over the railing and checked the parking lot, then searched the other way toward the woods. There was no one around, no vehicles on Deepwoods Drive, just them, the wind, and the blinking Christmas lights.

"Stay behind me," Dad said, pushing open the door. "Is anyone in here? Please, we just want to talk. My grandson was kidnapped from this building Monday night. We're desperate for answers – if you've seen something, please tell us."

The apartment remained quiet. Katie's throat tightened as they went inside, her stomach heavy. Dad clicked a light switch in the entryway, illuminating a small dining room with a circular table and two chairs. To their left was the kitchen, separated from the dining room by a breakfast bar, green digital numbers indicated by the stove and microwave clocks. The place smelled of incense, a thin smoky veil hanging in the air as though someone had just blown out a bunch of birthday candles.

"Please don't call the cops. We're just here to talk," Dad announced, forging deeper into the apartment and following a narrow hallway past dark rooms on both sides. He flipped light switches as he went, familiarizing himself with the layout of the place just as Katie was doing.

"Blake?" she heard herself say. Her son was somewhere in this building, she kept telling herself. She knew he was alive – she could feel it infallibly in her heart.

Dad began searching the individual rooms, starting with the living room at the back of the apartment, which was meagerly furnished with a sofa, a rocking chair, a coffee table, and a pair of virtually empty bookshelves. A rectangular Persian carpet rested beneath the table, predominantly red, with little cream-colored diamonds – but the remainder of the room was bare hardwood.

"Weird room," Dad muttered. At first Katie didn't understand, but her father pointed out the oddities. "No TV, no family photos on the walls, hardly any books on the shelves. It doesn't even look like anyone lives here."

A fair assessment. The walls were undecorated, boasting expansive spaces of pale blue. There was no television, no computer, no DVD player, no electronic devices whatsoever.

Dad walked to the bookshelves and surveyed their contents. "A Bible, a dictionary, an encyclopedia…let's see, what the hell is this?" He held up a maroon leather-bound book layered with dust. He opened the front cover. "Another encyclopedia. This is weird, Katie. Let's check out the other rooms."

They came to a pair of bedrooms, each with a crisply made bed. The closets were essentially bare. The clocks on the nightstands told the wrong times. The bathroom connecting to the larger bedroom was even more suspicious. No toilet paper on the roll, no toothpaste near the sink, only a thin, yellowing bar of soap and a pair of tweezers in the medicine cabinet. Moreover, the shower was devoid of shampoos and conditioners; another bar of soap – this one a little larger – rested on the recessed shelf.

"This is bullshit! No one lives in this place!" Dad exclaimed. "Someone wants us to *think* there's an old couple living here. Don't touch anything else – this could all be evidence."

Katie was focused on a far more worrisome realization. "Dad, if there's no one here, then who did the cops talk to? And who moved the curtains tonight?"

Dad's eyes darted. "Maybe it was just the wind," he said, but they both knew that wasn't true. The curtains had moved during windless stretches but had remained still during its frigid bursts.

Someone had definitely been in here.

"Let's keep looking," Katie said. "Maybe we'll find something important, anything that could lead us to Blake."

Dad pulled out his cell phone. "I'll call your mother and tell her not to worry. This could take a while."

Katie stared at her father, dumbfounded. She couldn't believe this was the same man who'd ignored Blake for much of his life. But why had it taken a tragedy for Mom and Dad to finally come around?

Relieved that her father was with her, Katie felt tears pooling. "Thanks for everything," she said. "I don't know what I'd do without you guys."

He gave her a hesitantly awkward hug. They hadn't hugged very much since high school, but in his arms she felt safe. "We're gonna find him, Katie. No matter what it takes, we'll bring him home."

Chapter 9

Despite assuming their guns would be useless
against Shepherd, Mike and Dave nonetheless
opened the other arched door and stormed inside,
ready to fire.

They found themselves in an ornate antechamber
that opened to two rooms of darkness. The
antechamber itself was lit by a massive chandelier
suspended from a gilt-domed ceiling. The floor was
a brilliant blue marble intersected with strips of
gold, their boots squeaking upon the polished
surface like sneakers on a basketball court.

"What the hell is this place?" Dave muttered as they
pressed carefully forward.

Mike studied the two gaping rooms. It was
impossible to determine their sizes because of the
darkness that swallowed them, one room ahead to
their left, doorless and slightly angled, and the other
to their right. Oddly, the light spilling from the
chandelier failed to penetrate even an inch into
those rooms, dying out like a flame introduced to
water.

Dave came to a pair of granite columns flanking a
wall that separated the two rooms. Or maybe there
weren't two rooms but instead one large room with
two entrances from the antechamber. Mike felt as
though he'd entered a crypt. The air was dead,
nothing to circulate the warm cloak of stagnation
that caused Mike to perspire, like standing in a

parking garage without ventilation. He concentrated on breathing slowly through his nose.

"Nate didn't mention anything about a room like this," Mike said, beaming his flashlight into the dark room to their left. He thought he glimpsed movement about ten feet in, but he couldn't be sure. "Dave, shine your headlamp in there."

Together they lit the way further, revealing a white linoleum floor...and nothing else. They proceeded slowly, sweeping the room with their lights but failing to discover anything to interrupt the sea of white. At the terminus of the joint glows provided by Mike's flashlight and Dave's headlamp, there were no walls to outline the end of the room, just a floor of interminable parchment.

Dave looked over his shoulder and gasped.

Turning, Mike's reaction mirrored that of his friend. Though they'd walked fifty or sixty feet into the room, the antechamber stood immediately before them, as if they'd made no progress at all.

A flummoxed smile crept across Mike's lips. "This is all part of Shepherd's game."

Dread slinked into his stomach. What if they couldn't find their way out of this place? He thought of Sue and Chris, his temples throbbing, but he quickly reined himself in. If they managed to keep themselves together and navigate the maze, they'd be fine.

It was with these positive thoughts that Mike led Dave back to the antechamber. "We'll eventually find the right room. I don't care if we have to search all night."

Dave wasn't looking at him, his gaze fixed on the room they'd just left. Then Mike heard it. Hollow, echoing footsteps in the blackness. Approaching slowly. Louder. Closer.

They stood abreast, guns ready. Closer, closer, silence.

A fleeting shadow, somehow visible within the darkness, moved swiftly to the left. Simultaneous movement in the other room. Now there were multiple sets of footsteps, shadows flitting chaotically, but none emerged from the darkness.

"Should I fire again and stop it?" Dave said.

"No, hold your fire."

"I don't like this, Mikey. Don't like it at all, man."

Mike held his weapon and the flashlight steady, both of little assistance. "Just ride it out, buddy."

Voices joined the madness, rising above the hollow footsteps. Mike immediately recognized them as Nate's and Joss's voices.

"This place is creepy," Joss said, her voice echoing from the blackness of the left room. "Do you get scared living here alone?"

"Not really. I'm probably the biggest creep in this entire building," Nate replied.

"You are a creep."

Another conversation flared up, the voices unfamiliar to Mike.

"But you're not invisible. I can see you," a young girl's voice called out.

"Oh, but I am," countered a male voice, perhaps the voice of a teenager. "I'm visible only to you because you're...special. If you eat some of that soup, I'll show you one of my invisible tricks, okay?"

Gunfire. Shrill ringing. Eventual silence, stillness.

"I'm sorry, Mikey, but it's the only way to stop this shit." Dave's face had gone a little green.

"At least you won't have to explain yourself to Internal Affairs," Mike said, trying not to let the dizzying nightmare overwhelm him as well. "Come on, let's get the hell out of here. There's gotta be another way."

***

Without thinking, Max offered a prayer for Blake's protection. Had he thought about it for too long, he might have given in to the seemingly insuperable darkness around him, broken only by a pale gray light that rolled in from no determinate source. Had he spent more time brooding and weltering in self-pity, he might have begun to assume that only forces of darkness could find him in this place.

Yet his heart had reacted before the encumbrances could reach it. Instinct had taken over, allowing him to access the faith that still existed somewhere far below the surface, so far down that he couldn't detect its presence. But it was there, imbued not by his mother or Jocey or the priests who'd talked his childhood Sundays away. Somehow it was just there, intrinsic and profound. A powerful stimulus.

Guided by a simple prayer and the faith that light could penetrate the darkness, Max scrambled up the creaking staircase and followed Blake's screams.

But the screams suddenly ceased. Max had come to the highest floor, no more stairs to climb. There stood a pair of arched doors as options, one to his left and the other to his right. When silence prevailed, he chose the left door and stepped inside, finding Blake blindfolded and bound to a massive column twenty feet ahead.

To the boy's right was Joseph Johansen, and behind him, looming menacingly over his tiny shoulders, was a monstrosity whose image caused Max to straighten with horror. This was the embodiment of darkness, its wings blacker than the depths of night, gleaming razors of anthracite sharpened with all the malevolence humanity had ever known. The thing shrieked with a thousand agonies, glowered with the hatred of the world, moved with the swiftness of impending death. It encircled the boy, hovered above him, and spread its wings fully, each lash and sweep like a tarp flapping in the wind.

Blake whimpered weakly. Max couldn't imagine his fear. Even *he* could hardly withstand the terror that crashed against him without mercy, let alone a seven-year-old boy.

"Max, you should have listened. You should have obeyed, fool!" Johansen chastised, shaking his head.

Max felt the rage rise up like bile, filling his throat until there was nowhere for it to go. He exploded forward, seeing nothing but shapes and colors, feeling nothing but the rage flowing out. When he finally realized what was happening, he was sitting atop Johansen and pinning his chest to the floor.

"What are you doing?" the old man groaned, his words so strained they were almost whispers.

"Don't move," Max warned, shoving a finger in Johansen's face.

Max returned to his feet, not sure what to do next but overcome by such tremendous adrenaline that he lunged headfirst at the monster…and passed right through it as he'd often done with the walls. His chin slammed against the floor, a collision that would have broken something if he'd still been alive. But in death there was no pain, only futility.

Laughter. Behind him. The raven's eyes cored through him, the snake's tongue flicking frenetically. "Back to your cage you'll go, Maxime."

Max blinked, and in that millisecond he was transported. Four walls surrounded him again. At the far end of the room, a familiar window admitted gray light. He was back in his prison, despondent but not defeated.

He would try again. As long as he could move, he would keep trying. A little boy was relying on him for survival, counting on him to succeed. In a house of darkness, Max was the only light that could guide Blake back to his mother.

Chapter 10

The discussion on unit nine was like a wildfire that couldn't be contained, burning its way through the hours and – just when it seemed ready to die out – taking a surprising course and burning some more.

Mom and Whit were alarmed by what they were being told – an apartment unit lacking some of the most basic living necessities. Perhaps the old people were ascetics who relished a life of self-denial, Mom suggested, but with a wave Dad dismissed her idea. Denying oneself TV and internet was one thing, but going without food was quite another, he explained.

"There was nothing in the refrigerator or the cabinets," Katie added. "Not even any drinks."

"Maybe they have two homes or something. They might have left for a winter home in Florida," Whit said.

Katie and her father shared skeptical glances. "Even so, there'd be some kind of food left in the cabinets," Dad insisted. "They wouldn't throw everything out, right down to the soups and cereals. And another thing – why are their Christmas lights on if they aren't there? Someone wants us to think people are living there."

Mom took a seat on the sofa. Katie and Dad were standing by the living room door, Whit seated at the computer swivel chair, the hood of her sweatshirt pulled tightly over her head.

"Do we know these people's names?" Mom said.

Katie shook her head, a new circuit of terror having developed since their departure from unit nine. "I left a message for the landlord. Hopefully he'll call me back soon – this could be a big break. I mean, who the hell are these people and what's going on in their apartment? The abductor could have been using it all along to hide Blake."

The conversation eventually wound its way back to the unexplainable movements of the curtains.

"I can't believe you two broke in there," Mom said, looking chidingly at Dad. "There's a police officer in the parking lot, for God's sake. You could have been arrested."

"Well, technically we didn't break in," Dad corrected. "The door opened on its own, and we just slipped in to see if anyone was there. We announced our presence, but no one answered."

"This place…everything about it freaks me out," Whit said.

There was a tense silence, Katie's fear seeming to build by the second. Her feeling that Blake was being held somewhere in the apartment returned with a pronounced vigor, challenging her to make yet another sweep of the building.

"I think we should tell the cop about this," Dad said.

Mom held up a hand. "But didn't they already search the whole building? If they didn't think anything was suspicious then, I doubt they'd want to return."

"But they have to!" Katie shouted. "I want to know where those people are and why they've disappeared just days after my son's abduction!"

"Damn right," Dad said, his eyes sharp with desperation.

The helplessness was the worst part, the feeling of complete impotence in the wake of the most wrenching theft imaginable. Katie felt like a piece of her heart had been wrested away, and there was nothing she could do to retrieve it. She still couldn't believe they'd scoured an old couple's apartment – probably an innocuous pair of retirees who moved back and forth from Florida like Whit said.

It suddenly seemed pathetic to Katie. They were so desperate and powerless, so entirely devoid of options, that they'd made unit nine priority one. And what the hell were Mike Overbrook and Chief Strait doing to bring Blake home? Had they made any progress with the newly received leads?

"I'm sure there's a perfectly logical explanation," Mom maintained. "Maybe they're in the process of moving. If there was anything suspicious about them, don't you think the police would have discovered it by now?"

Katie's urgency evaporated, replaced by the anchor of defeat in her gut. Another night would yield to another day – another day without Blake. Soon it would be a new week, then a new year, the chances of Blake's return dwindling further with each passing hour. Katie knew the math. She'd seen the reports, heard the rumors, watched the television programs, participated in the interviews, Blake's face flashed across screens throughout the country because the nature of his abduction chilled and compelled. Reality was not beyond Katie. There was no bubble of insulation provided by family and friends, no defense against each fear riding in on cold December winds, no way to make the thoughts and terrors stop. All she had left were faith and intuition.

And her instincts were still summoning her to unit nine. From the outside it was a normal residence, where Christmas lights blinked from the railing and curtains rustled gently without drawing notice. But inside, where the paucity of everyday supplies brought suspicion to each room, Katie knew a secret was waiting to be found.

Part VII: Inside the Maze

"When I despair, I remember that all through history the way of truth and love has always won. There have been tyrants and murderers, and for a time they can seem invincible – but in the end they always fall." ~ Mahatma Gandhi.

Chapter 1

I must be in shock because Sgt. Fitzgerald's words don't register, a storm of senseless noise erupting from his lips. He reaches for my shoulder, his movements seeming to happen in slow motion. He shakes me a little, and now I'm back from some faraway place, returned to the building of horrors where I'd seen…I still don't even know what it was. Faces. Ghoulish, vacuous, staring faces, each pair of hollow eyes locked on mine.

"What happened, kid? What the hell is going on?" Fitzgerald demands.

"I…I don't know. Something was in here with us. People."

Thankfully I'd had the sense to return my gun to the belt. My hands are twitchy, legs wobbly, heart racing. I feel light in the head and heavy in the stomach, dinner having turned into a rock that weighs me down. I'm sweating, too. It feels like the heat has been cranked all the way up.

"What do you mean, *people?*" Fitzgerald looks exasperated, afraid. He orders Katherine Grafton and her family out of the apartment, then barks something into his radio.

"Sir, I swear to God, there was something…not of this world in here with us," I tell Fitzgerald once the others are gone.

It's even hotter in the apartment now, way too hot. I feel like I'm about to hyperventilate. I burst through the kitchen door, out of the dreaded apartment and onto the deck. Fresh, cold, snowy air. I suck it in with strained gasps, as if I've been held underwater.

A hand on my shoulder. Fitzgerald's hand. "It's all right, kid. We're out of there."

Fitzgerald recoils when I turn to face him. I assume it's the look of terror in my eyes that startled him, but then I realize he's staring beyond me.

Staring at something on the lawn.

Chapter 2

When Nate didn't receive a call from Uncle Mike by nine o'clock, he was afraid. An hour later, his fear blossomed into physical discomfort. Just before eleven, his stomach soured with the nauseous panic he'd endured in September when Joss disappeared. Except this time he knew exactly what was happening. Mike and Chief Strait had gone into 99 Deepwoods Drive in search of Blake Grafton – and Shepherd hadn't let them out.

Joss couldn't keep her hands steady, and she winced with each glance at the clock. A while back she'd opened her jewelry box and retrieved her heart-shaped locket, such a rare sight around her neck, usually appearing only on her father's birthday and Christmas. Pacing, she'd held it in a closed fist, then returned it to the box.

Now she was staring into her phone, her face hard with dread.

"Something's definitely wrong," Nate said. "He would have called by now." He took a deep breath and tried to calm down, but nothing helpful came to mind, not a single spark of optimism. Mike simply wouldn't have gone this long without calling.

Joss pocketed the phone, pulled on her coat. "Let's go. They're obviously in trouble – we should be there."

"No, let's just wait." Nate stood in front of her bedroom door, unsure of what to do. He couldn't call the cops. Mike and Dave *were* the cops.

Joss gathered her Montreal Canadiens beanie hat and a pair of black leather gloves. "Wait for what? It's almost eleven. We need to go, Nate. Now!"

There was a brave determination to her voice, but it couldn't mask the fear glinting in her eyes. She'd nearly died in that place, and now she was demanding to go back.

Nate crossed his arms. His body was knotted and achy with tension, and it seemed like he needed to take a leak every twenty minutes. "If we go, you have to promise to stay in the car. I'll go in alone, got it?"

"Nate, that's shit and you know it. We both have people we love in there – we go together."

Joss's words alone were seemingly powerful enough to push him out of the way. Nate knew he would never be able to keep her here. He prayed Mike would call, but his prayers thus far had gone unanswered. Had God fallen asleep in front of the television? Had He read a few chapters of a book and dozed off?

"What about your mom?" Nate said, one final attempt to keep Joss home. "What if she wakes up and we're gone? She'll freak out."

Anya had gone to bed half an hour ago, thanking
Nate again for taking care of Joss. If only she knew
what they were contemplating now that she'd
retired for the night.

Joss waved a hand, pocketed her gloves. "She won't
know a thing. Once she takes her sleeping pills, an
earthquake wouldn't wake her."

"Joss, please don't put yourself in danger. Stay
here, I'm begging you. I'll call as soon as I get there
and figure out what's going on."

Her expression twisted, eyes darkening. "Nate, if
you go, I go. Quit wasting time."

"But–"

"Your uncle's trapped in there, my brother's
trapped in there, that little boy's trapped in there –
what the hell are we waiting for?"

Nate pulled her in and kissed her. He didn't want to
argue with her anymore, not if there was nothing he
could say to convince her to stay home. She'd never
forgive him if he didn't take her.

Wide-eyed, Joss broke away for a stunned moment,
then leaned in and surpassed the passion of his
spontaneity. Her breath was scented of Starburst,
the taste of cherry fresh upon her tongue, little
colored wrappers scattered about the desk,
reminding Nate of the first time they'd kissed.
Holding her, closing his eyes, absorbing the
blessing of her love, he remembered with perfect

clarity the fifteen-year-old girl from Montreal he'd met sophomore year. The girl he'd been born to meet, her blue eyes so refulgent it was a wonder he hadn't drowned in them. God, he loved her more than anything. He would die for her, just as she'd die for him – and he suddenly knew he couldn't take her to New Hampshire, couldn't bring her back to the place that had almost killed her, couldn't let her face Shepherd again. Never. Not for Mike, not for Max, not for Blake Grafton, not for anyone. He'd sooner break up with her than drive her to a potential grave.

Joss ran a hand down his cheek, searched his eyes. "We can do this," she whispered.

"Let's go," he said, watching her eyes fill with relief and then fear, a sickening combination. Her mouth opened, but there were no words. Instead she hugged him with a strength seemingly beyond her capability.

Had she known what Nate was planning, her reaction would not have been to embrace him but to slap him.

Chapter 3

Blake squeezed his eyes shut when the blindfold was removed. If he couldn't see it, maybe everything would just go away. He thought of Mom and Max. They would find him. One of them would save him from this place.

He screamed for them. Again. Over and over, his throat dry and hurting. There were no more tears left. He'd cried to the point of sickness, and now his nose and eyes were almost as sore as his throat. His head pulsated, reminding him of his toy drum set. Their voices made his head hurt worse. He just wanted to go home.

In his mind, he was back at Whitney Golding's house, watching a movie with Mom. They were eating popcorn, laughing...

But he couldn't move, his arms and legs tied, the ropes pressing painfully against him. All he could do was scream for Mom and Max. *Scream until your voice shatters*, one of the men had said. They called him *Boy*. Boy, Boy, Boy, Boy. Father Joe was one of them. He'd lied. He didn't want to protect Blake. He wanted to hurt him.

***

Peter Dobyns had never imagined a fear this absolute. He'd spent countless hours researching the paranormal, conducting hundreds of interviews, and reviewing endless recordings – so why hadn't he realized fear could be this incapacitating?

He couldn't think straight, could barely even breathe. The fear was too strong, too overwhelming, a venomous fear that had all but paralyzed him. He was tied to a column, but even if he'd been free, his legs had been drained of power. Useless. He'd once heard newsroom gossip pertaining to a homicide victim the police had allegedly described as being absent fight *and* flight – but Peter hadn't believed such an absence to be possible. Now he knew. Holy shit, he knew! The purest fear will immobilize its prey as swiftly as a spider injecting an insect with venom and wrapping it in delicate gossamers.

Roped from shoulders to ankles to the thick column, Peter was suddenly filled with relentless thoughts of spiders and webs, of snakes and pits, of demons and sufferers, his eyes glued to the proceedings before him. Death would be tonight's ritual, and he would soon be among the dead, as well as the little boy tied to the other column, a boy he'd instantly recognized as Blake Grafton. He'd been here all along, trapped in his own building while the cops futilely searched the region.

Peter wondered how much he and Blake would suffer, a fear that had recently made him sick. Now the bile was rising again, his breaths escaping in strained, wheezy bursts. He looked up to the domed ceiling and prayed, first for life and then, if survival was impossible, for a swift death.

***

Max repeated the same process that had resulted in his earlier escape. It took a little longer than before to bust up the wall, but once again he smashed through and plunged down the gray-shadowed stairwell. This time, however, there was a pair of men at the top. One of them had a headlamp on, its bluish light cutting mistily through the grayness.

Max called to them out of instinct, then realized they wouldn't be able to hear him. But both men turned in his direction! A flashlight beam swept down the stairs and tumbled into his eyes. Gasping, the men pointed guns at him.

"Who the hell are you?" the taller man demanded, trying to sound tough but failing to mask his inner turmoil.

Max was surprised to hear a spurt of laughter escape him. "You can put the guns away. I'm already dead."

Chapter 4

His visions having revealed Max Leclaire's name, Mike immediately recognized Joss's brother.

Dave took a few backward steps as Max climbed the stairs. His clothes were torn and stained, just as they'd appeared in Mike's nightmares, all of it coming sharply back to him.

"Don't get too close," Dave warned.

"It's all right," Mike assured. "This is Jocelyne's brother, Max Leclaire."

Dave looked as if someone had told him that one plus one equals three. "What are you talking about? What the hell is this, Mikey?"

Reaching the top of the stairs, Max eyed them suspiciously, squinting into the path of Dave's headlamp. "How do you know me?"

"Long story," Mike said, holstering his gun.

In spite of his visions, in spite of everything Nate and Joss had reported, Mike couldn't believe this was real.

"What is this place, Max? What's going on here?" Mike was glad the words had formed themselves because, at the moment, all he could do was stare in transcendent awe. It was like being set adrift in space, nothing to ground him, every cord of rationality snapped.

Dave took a few slight steps forward. "We're looking for a seven-year-old boy, Blake Grafton. Have you seen him?"

Max's eyes widened. "You know that Blake is here?" His excitement quickly faded, yielding to a worried expression. He spoke with the same French Canadian accent as his sister (saying *dat*, not *that*), their eyes the same penetrating cut of blue. "You need to send more guys, way more guys," Max continued. "Shepherd has Blake!"

"Where are they?" Dave said.

Max shrugged. "Could be anywhere. Shepherd is always changing things."

"We'll just have to keep looking then, but it's only us," Mike said. "If we leave to get more people, the window might close."

Max muttered something in French, then said, "What if you guys get trapped here?"

Mike beamed his light down the stairs. "Too late to worry about that now. Come on – there's no more time to waste talking."

"That's for damn sure," came a gruff voice behind them.

Mike and Dave whirled around and spotted a face they'd both seen often...in newspapers and online, as well as on every newscast for the last four days...the face of the eldest suspect in the Blake Grafton abduction. A man who'd told Nate his name was Gerald Blackwell. He stood outside the arched door to the right of the staircase, his face glistening with sweat.

Mike raised his weapon. "Are you Gerald Blackwell...*the* Gerald Blackwell?"

The man nodded coldly, and for a moment Mike felt dizzy, like he might pass out, the air in his windpipe seeming to stick. This was all too much, way too much, decades of police work failing to prepare them for it. No wonder Joss had taken to getting drunk. No wonder she hadn't wanted to participate in any interviews. She and Nate had survived Hell, and now it was Blake who'd been dragged to its infernal corners.

"I can help you," Blackwell said. "I once believed Shepherd was on our side, but now I know he's working for the Devil."

***

Katie slept for a few hours – a biological shutdown. She woke at eleven-thirty after another nightmare, angry that the others had let her sleep so long.

"You should have gotten me up!" she shouted at no one in particular, dragging herself into the kitchen, where she washed her face and cracked open a beer.

It went down smoothly, feeling good on her sore throat.

"You hungry?" Whit said, emerging from the bathroom. In the distance, Katie heard her parents talking in the living room, the door mostly shut.

"Nah, the beer's fine," Katie said, slumping past her friend into the bedroom, wanting to numb herself to everything. If only there was some way to stop feeling. Without Blake, she didn't want to feel anything, didn't even want to leave her bed.

She took a few swigs and stared out the window, setting the beer on her nightstand. Whit watched worriedly from the foot of the bed. She was on the verge of words when two heavy knocks came from the other side of the bedroom wall.

Whit jumped. "What the hell?"

"You heard that, right? There were knocks. I'm not crazy, tell me there were knocks!"

"Yeah, definitely."

Two more knocks. The lights buzzed and flickered.

"Oh my God!" Katie gasped. "It must be Blake!"

Whit rapped her knuckles twice against the wall in the approximate spot where the knocks had originated. Within seconds two subsequent knocks came from the other side.

"Mom! Dad!" Katie shouted. "Get in here!"

Soon Dad was rushing out to the parking lot to find the officer. That very moment, at the police station, Officer Zachary King was preparing for his maiden law enforcement shift.

THE INHABITANTS II

Chapter 5

The four of them – Mike, Dave, Max Leclaire, and Gerald Blackwell – walked for what seemed like an hour, two living souls and two departed spirits exploring the parallel plane of 99 Deepwoods Drive. The dark plane. Like day and night, darkness and light split time commanding the big house on the hill…but the dark had undoubtedly gained an advantage in the last year, systematically extinguishing light sources and expanding its insidious reign.

In an exhaustive search, the four unlikely teammates passed through countless empty rooms, navigated hallways and staircases crisscrossing like traffic grids, and followed occasional screams that brought them nowhere, a gentle wind pursuing them from one room to the next and chilling their necks. Mike felt like a mouse skittering about a massive maze. He would have feared that Max and Gerald were intentionally leading them astray, except they weren't the leaders. The ghosts dutifully followed Mike and Dave through Shepherd's realm, making sporadic comments but mostly remaining silent.

"Fuck!" Dave shouted. They'd entered another empty room, a neatly made bed at its center. Dave turned to Max and Gerald. "What do you guys think we should do? You're the ones trapped in this goddamn place."

Max shrugged. Gerald frowned. Clearly the dead wouldn't be much help, as powerless as Mike and Dave. Shepherd suddenly seemed untouchable, far too strong to combat. How would they ever rescue Blake? How would they even get themselves out?

"We're just running around in circles," Mike said. "There's gotta be something we're missing. A hidden passageway or something."

"We'll eventually find that bastard," Gerald Blackwell said. "There's only so many rooms in this place. Shepherd may be strong, but he's not God."

Another ten minutes of tireless searching. Twenty, thirty, forty. The rooms and corridors were all starting to look the same now, everything twisting and bouncing with shadows produced by Dave's headlamp and Mike's flashlight, floorboards groaning wearily beneath them. It was like the rooms themselves were following them, repeating interminably every time they turned a corner. Nothing made sense. There were no windows, no way to see outside or find their bearings. They might have been ten stories above ground or twenty feet in the dirt.

The wind shrieked, buffeting them with enough force to knock them off balance.

"The wind belongs to Shepherd!" Gerald shouted. "He commands it, just like the bats. He sees what we're doing, and he doesn't like it."

"Either that, or he's taunting us," Max said. "He's the fucking Devil, I swear." Then came a French tirade.

Dave's headlamp, meanwhile, steadily dimmed. He pulled a pack of batteries from his bag but dropped one of them upon ripping the pack open. It rolled a strangely long distance down the hallway, then rolled some more. Alive. Dave rushed after it, but the thing sped up, spinning and skidding its way to the far wall, where a perpendicular hallway led to more enigmatic rooms in either direction.

The four of them chased down the battery, Dave arriving first. Now the thing was bumping against the wall, over and over and over.

"What the hell?" Dave murmured, and then the battery levitated, rising swiftly to about three feet.

They all jumped back, afraid the possessed battery would switch directions and fly at them. But it remained focused on the wall, crashing twice against it with heavy, echoing thuds, an action quickly repeated.

A few seconds passed. Then there were two knocks from the other side, soft but unmistakable.

A cold wind blistered down the hallway, tearing out scraps of wallpaper in its screaming wrath. But it couldn't stop the battery's progress. The thing was still suspended, still insisting at the wall. They stared at it patiently, beseechingly, waiting and praying for it to do something further. A battery – was that their only hope? A damn battery? The thought guided a sliver of humor to Mike, but soon the battery was at it again, ramming the wall with its strongest assault yet. *A literal A & B*, he thought.

A minute later there was another knock from beyond the wall. Mike was instantly filled with hope. They were being assisted…somehow.

But who was on the other side? And how would they get through? And supposing they did manage to find a way through, how would anyone locate Blake?

Chapter 6

Joss couldn't stop her legs from shaking. Sitting in the passenger seat of Nate's car, she kept squeezing her knees together like an anxious student before a big test. Except she wasn't about to take a test – she was ready to return to the place where she'd nearly died.

She took a deep breath. "I can do this. Please, Lord, give me the strength to do this. I beg of You, bless me with the strength."

Why was Nate taking so long? Just when Joss had thought he was ready to go, he'd said he needed to head back inside to piss. But that had been five minutes ago. Where was he?

Finally he returned to the heated car in the garage. "Ready, Jocey?"

She smiled through her terror, relieved that he'd actually agreed to bring her. She'd feared he would tell her mother about what she planned to do, but apparently he'd awakened to the desperation of the night. Max was in that house, undeniable, and if there was a chance Joss could help get him out, she had to take it. She would do anything for him, even if it meant risking her life. They would be forever connected by their childhood joys and struggles, and Joss would always feel indebted to her brother. It was Max who'd spent so many sleepless nights soothing her after Dad's death; Max who'd helped her up when she fell down; Max who'd always been her protector; Max who'd gathered a change of pajamas each night she wet herself. He'd wiped her tears away and held her whenever she needed a friend. He'd made her feel like she could overcome the worst times, chasing away her stubborn fears. When she'd been beaten and bloodied and mortified in the basement that stormy January night, Max had pulled her up and tended to her wounds. When she'd been afraid of Mom, her trust dissolved, Max had somehow gotten her through it. When she'd been lost with no idea how to return to normalcy, Max had guided her out of the wilderness.

And now he needed her. Tonight, finally, it was her turn to help him. She'd tried desperately to assist her brother during his final months, but he'd refused. Now everything was different, a new chance offered in the most unimaginable way. If she could contribute even slightly to his release from 99 Deepwoods Drive – if she could pave one inch of the road that would lead him to Heaven – then it would all be worth it.

"Thanks again for taking me, Nate. I know how hard this is for you, but we're gonna get through it, just like we always do."

He kissed her, his eyes heavy, burdened. It looked like he'd cry. "Close your eyes," he whispered.

"What? Why? Let's go."

He shook his head. "We should pray first. Come on, it'll only take a second."

He reached for her hand, took hold of it, and began to pray. It soothed her to hear him embracing God again. She would have given anything for this moment during his days of addiction.

But suddenly his prayer went silent…and something latched around Joss's wrist. She shot her eyes open and found herself handcuffed, the other end closing around the steering wheel with a metallic click that brought panicked tears of betrayal. That's why he'd gone back inside – to find the handcuffs she'd been given for her birthday last year by a friend. The girl had laughingly said they'd be a fun sex toy, but now Nate was using them to keep her here so he could go to New Hampshire alone!

"No," she whispered, so shocked that she couldn't find her voice. "Please, Nate."

He held her shoulder. "It's for your safety, Joss. I'm so sorry, but I can't bring you to that place again."

Tears streamed down Joss's cheeks. "How could you do this? I trusted you."

Nate looked away. "I'm gonna leave you here in the garage so you'll be warm, okay? I'll take your car to New Hampshire and get back here as soon as I can."

"Fuck you!" she screamed, jerking against the cuffs, her wrist sparkling with pain. "I fucking *trusted* you!"

"I know, Jocey, but please just look at it from my perspective. What if I took you to that place and you were killed? How would I live with myself?"

"So you think it's fair to chain me up while *you* go? What if *you're* killed? What if this is the last time I ever see you?" The tears exploded. Joss tugged at the cuffs with all her strength, her arm straining. It wouldn't work, though, nothing would.

"Stop, just stop!" Nate shouted. "You'll hurt yourself!"

"I don't care! I swear to God, I'll break my fucking wrist if you leave me! I swear on my father's soul! You can't leave me! You can't, you can't, please don't leave me!"

The next few seconds were a haze of screams, Joss brought back to the night her mother had assaulted her relentlessly. As she continued to strain and wail and lose herself in the throes of desperation, she remembered the night of the beating as if it had happened last week. Remembered the helplessness. Remembered being held down, her back crushed into the bed. Remembered the fiery pain. She hadn't been able to fight back or escape, forced to stay there and endure, the taste of blood caught in her throat, crying, fearing Mom would kill her, that it wouldn't stop until she died. She'd begged as she begged now, but Mom hadn't cared. Over and over she'd suffered, each strike reverberating in her soul.

Another memory rushed to the forefront, this one far more recent. She remembered being tied to the post on Shepherd's stage, dazed and terrified, the rope coiled so tightly that it hurt her chest and arms. Shepherd had asked if she would die for Nate, leisurely taunting his powerless victim. She'd been at the mercy of evil, exposed to whatever torment it chose…but no more! Never again would she be held against her will! Never again would she be helpless!

She tore out of the red mist of memory with a violent surge, slamming her free arm against the passenger window. "I'll break it! I'll fucking break it, Nate!"

His face clenched with panic, eyes bulging. Finally he relented. Retrieved the key from his pocket. Released her.

"What's wrong with you?" Joss's words prevailed through her sobs. Her heart clouted furiously.

"What kind of person would I be if I took you there?" Nate spoke in soft tones of resignation, the cuffs in hand.

"What kind of person would *I* be if I let you go alone? We *both* have people there – both of us!" She slapped the door in exasperation. "If we both go, Mason will protect us. Somehow he'll protect us. We'll save them, all of them."

Nate held up a hand, then reached to touch her face. She pulled away. She didn't want him to touch her, didn't even want him to look at her.

"Mason said it himself. Shepherd is trying to lure us back there," Nate said. "What if Mason can't help? What if we go in and can't get out again?"

"So what's the alternative?" she shot back. "Go to bed and forget about everyone in there? Really? Is that actually what you want to do?"

"No, of course not. I want to go, but–"

"Just not with me, right? You want to go alone and solve everything yourself."

"I want to protect you!" His voice broke with desperation. "It's just too huge a risk to let you go. I can't, I just can't. I'm sorry if you hate me, but I can't."

Nate's love for her was burning bright, flashing in his eyes like flames raining down in the night. Something shuddered in Joss's chest. It lifted her, brought her to a place where Nate had so often taken her. She remembered seeing that fire in his eyes the first time they'd made love. She'd been so scared – had even asked him to stop after being partially undressed – but he'd told her he loved her and would always be there for her. It had been a surreal, transcendent moment of trust, Joss standing half-dressed and afraid in her boyfriend's arms, a fifteen-year-old girl ravaged by an explosive conflict between her emotions and everything her mother had taught her, each lesson a warning. (*There is only one way, Jocey, the Lord's way. You mustn't sin, sin, sin…*) Holding her firm, Nate had not only made promises that day but had exuded his love with such intensity that it blazed in his eyes, just as it did now.

As infuriated as Joss was, she had to admit that Nate had only acted in her best interests. To return to 99 Deepwoods Drive was indeed a huge risk, a risk of death and even worse things, inconceivably disgusting things. Nate knew it, and so did Joss. Beneath her desperate impulses to save her brother's soul, beneath her brave front, beneath everything she'd said and done, she knew at her core that a return trip would lead them right into the trap Shepherd had set for them.

An excellent trap.

A deadly trap.

A trap that would fail! God would protect her as He'd done in September. God would save her and Max. Evil was no match for faith.

"We can't go, neither of us," she said after a while, but like Nate had done, Joss was operating with an ulterior agenda.

Regardless of the risks, she had to at least try to save her brother. They were the Leclaire siblings, their bond unbreakable. As far back as memory could take her, Max had always been there – and now she would be there for him. Even if she failed, she owed Max the dignity of an attempt. If she left him alone in that place without so much as driving there in an effort to reach him, she would never be able to forgive herself–

~ 423 ~

An itch beneath her clothes, memories incited.

In the shadows of her mind, fluttering, flitting, were thoughts of a tattered black dress – memories briefly creeping at her, then gone.

***

Joss's hurried walk disturbed Nate. She'd said she wanted to go back inside the house, but why was she striding the other way, toward the side door of the garage?

By the time Nate jogged after her and left the garage himself, he could only watch helplessly while Joss climbed into her Audi in the semicircular entryway. The engine sprang to life, the headlights flashing on. Nate sprinted to the car but it accelerated around the loop, screeching to a rolling stop and then tearing out onto the street.

Enraged and terrified, the first flakes of the nor'easter coming down on him, Nate gnashed his teeth. She'd deceived him and left him, just as he'd tried to do to her a few minutes ago, and now the exact scenario he'd desperately hoped to avoid was about to transpire.

Joss was on her way to 99 Deepwoods Drive.

Back inside his car, Nate slammed the steering wheel. He should have known she'd do this.

"Dammit, Joss!"

He jerked the gear into reverse. It was time to shatter the speed limit.

Chapter 7

"Why are you doing this to us?" Peter tried to shout, but the words were nothing more than gurgling gibberish. He was sobbing, the warm, bitter taste of iron flooding his mouth.

The old man, Johansen – Joseph Johansen, the ex-priest who'd committed suicide! – had been instructed to hit Peter in the face with a crowbar. The strike had come without delay, smashing his front teeth and shredding his lips. Peter's vision was blurry with stinging tears, his mouth a sloshing sea of blood and remnants of teeth. He'd finally stopped choking and coughing, but each whistling breath brought forth swells of agony. He felt like he was slowly taking on liquid, soon to drown in a pool of his own blood, yet his greatest injury was the realization that he would never see his wife again.

Johansen stood before him, looking wistful, perhaps even regretful. Or maybe, through his obfuscated vision, Peter had wishfully assigned those qualities to the gleaming eyes of malevolence.

"It's what must be done," Johansen said. "I must follow each order to reach Heaven. I hope you'll forgive me – I've waited so long to be received by the Lord."

Even through his surging pain, Peter managed to draw upon his recollections and establish the truths of this excruciating madness. Johansen was a dead man – dead for more than forty-five years! Peter had seen his photo online, had read about him in countless articles. Impossibly, he was a prisoner here as well, desperate to finally be free.

This building wasn't simply a haunted house. No, not even close. This was Hell on Earth, a place of endless suffering.

"Kill him, Joseph," ordered the rasping voice. "Claim your place in God's kingdom."

Johansen produced a large knife. Stepped forward. Held it loosely to Peter's throat. "Forgive me," he whispered.

"No!" Peter begged. "Please, I have three kids!" he somehow managed, though half of it sounded like another language, a bubbling language spoken underwater. Actually, he didn't have any children, but with death just a slash away, it had been the most compelling thing that sprang to mind.

"Please forgive me, sir." Staring at Peter with wild, tormented eyes, Johansen squeezed Peter's shaking hand in an icy grip. The knife came against his throat with greater force.

Moisture glistened in Johansen's eyes. "Forgive me," he said one final time, but Peter had already made his departure, rising peacefully before the blood spurted, ascending above Blake Grafton's echoing screams.

There was a moment of unconsciousness. Then Peter awoke in a world of light.

Chapter 8

Nate raced north as fast as he dared to go, at times exceeding the speed limit by thirty miles per hour. Lights and buildings flew past, the snowflakes at first drifting like ludic fluffs of pollen, then, closer to the state line, driving downward with conviction, the pavement slickening. Whenever Nate came to a straightaway, he reduced other northbound vehicles to fading headlights in the rearview mirror. Operating at such speeds in the storm-dark made him feel like he was flying, especially when the speedometer tickled eighty on a fifty MPH stretch of Route 202.

But no matter how fast he drove, he couldn't catch up to Joss's Audi. Had he already passed it, maybe? He'd tried to look at each vehicle as he went by, but some of them had been too slow and clustered for observation. Joss wouldn't be driving slowly, though. She was a better driver than Nate, far more confident and relaxed in all situations. A gnawing thought told him she'd torn up these roads at even higher speeds than he was using.

He made it to Hollisville in record time, dreading what he'd find upon pulling into the parking lot of his old apartment. He prayed that Joss's car wouldn't be there, that she'd had a brief period of rational thinking and avoided the godforsaken building.

Unlikely.

On Deepwoods Drive, sinuous and dangerous in winter months, the lanes were tracked with snow. Halfway down the road, the apartment came into view, Nate's headlights glinting off the windows and casting shadows on the walls. Someone had strung Christmas lights from the front deck, but only at this place could they look less festive than ominous.

Nate turned right into the parking lot, bracing himself as he scanned a row of vehicles, the crunch of snow groaning beneath his tires. At first there was relief – the Audi wasn't here. But then he stepped out of his car, came around to the front of the building, and felt his heart plummet. Joss's car was parked discreetly, just off the road beyond a pair of large snow-covered bushes flanking the front porch. From Nate's position, he could only see a tiny portion of the car, including the rear license plate.

But where was Joss?

Nate hurried back to the parking lot. A Hollisville Police cruiser stood dark and empty. A few vehicles down was a black Ford F-250 Nate recognized from his visit to Dave Strait's house. A handful of other vehicles occupied the lot, but none of them belonged to Mike, who'd probably gotten a ride here in Dave's truck.

Turning his attention from the vehicles to the building, Nate stared up at his former apartment, the kitchen lights spilling out onto the deck and dripping a path of shadows across the snowy lawn.

Distant voices came from inside. The rest of the building was dark, save for the Christmas lights on the front deck.

An arctic wind knifed from the woods, assaulting Nate not only with its frigid bite but also with memories. He watched the shed, arms crossed, remembering everything that had happened in there. Though he was standing still, he found himself out of breath. He'd begun sweating profusely and shivering, a conflict of hot and cold he'd only experienced when sick.

Tonight he was sick with dread. Unable to catch his breath, he felt like he would vomit. This couldn't be happening. For a moment it seemed like a dream, but the darkness of reality crept into his heart like a disease. It was all real, such a turbulent night with the snow surging in, but inside there was a far stronger storm gathering. Uncle Mike, Dave Strait, and Blake Grafton were all in there somewhere – and now little Jocey Marie had joined the fray, challenging a force of seemingly limitless strength.

Nate had no idea what to do. The logical decision was announcing his presence to whoever was in unit four, but they didn't know what was really happening. Mike and Dave certainly hadn't told them, and Nate had no time to explain a situation to people who would never believe it.

Instead he ran to Joss's car and, using his cell phone flashlight, followed her footprints across the front lawn, down the walkway, and around the side of the building to the back lawn, closer, closer – *No, please, no* – but yes, the footprints took him straight to the shed.

Chapter 9

Feeling as small as a child in the shadow of the shed, Joss recited the Lord's Prayer before studying the door. The padlock had been opened, probably the work of Nate's uncle and his friend. A lucky break – now Joss would be able to walk right in.

I'm almost there, Max. Just hang on a little longer.

Voices. Increasing in volume. They came from the second floor, originating in Nate's old apartment. Joss ignored them. After a few deep breaths, followed by another prayer and a sign of the cross, she pulled open the door.

For a moment she just stood there, staring into the darkness and listening to the battering of her heart. An impulse told her to run back to her car, but thoughts of Max held her in place. She reached into her pocket and pulled out her cell phone, though she wouldn't need it. The shed suddenly filled with bright bluish light. It emanated from a series of pendant lights suspended from the ceiling, a line that stretched into the passageway as if to illuminate the way for her.

But who had lit the path?

Joss felt a fleeting hope that Max was responsible. Then she realized it had to be Shepherd's doing, thoughts of a torn black dress capering through her head. Shepherd had all the power in this place – and now she was back inside the building where she'd nearly been killed. Again she remembered being tied up on the stage. Again she recalled precisely what she'd felt, a panicked, breathless fear for her own life and for that of her boyfriend.

Chaotic ambivalence tugged at her. She was not only risking her life but endangering Nate as well. He had undoubtedly followed her and would arrive at any moment.

She took a few backward steps, thinking entirely of Nate. But she stopped at the thought of Max, sharp and agonizing. His life was over. No wedding, no children, no nothing – only isolation in these walls and possibly Hell for a final destination. What if Mason was wrong? What if he'd been trying to protect Joss by saying Max would go to Heaven? How could he know for sure?

A rough rub beneath her clothes, the chafe of a familiar garment.

Disregarding it, knowing it was only in her mind, Joss dashed down the passageway and came to a staircase. She tried not to think, tried not to listen to anything but her own footfalls.

Just keep moving!

She coached herself up the stairs, memories of Max impelling her farther. A landing. More stairs. Aching with fear, almost out of breath, she reached the top and followed the pendant lights past a pair of doors, arriving at a junction with another hallway.

At the far end of this new hallway was a door bathed in red. The sight of it halted her. She somehow knew what lurked behind it. Shepherd.

He was waiting for her.

"Our Father, who art in Heaven," she began, pulling her cross out from beneath layers of clothes.

Yet again she felt the starchy, terrifying scratch of the undermost layer, but she refused to look. Clutching her cross, she continued the prayer and slowly approached the door. By the time she uttered, "Amen", she was filled with a strangely powerful courage. It warmed her, coursing its way downward until her entire body felt strengthened. Her previously shaky legs were solid. Her teeth no longer chattered. Even her heart settled.

She was ready to open the door.

Still holding the cross with her left hand, she twisted the silver knob and pushed the door open. A theater waited on the other side, a white, glowing screen at the far end. It was about half the size of a movie theater, rows of seats marking a slight gradient.

Stunned but remarkably unafraid, guided by the increasing warmth of faith, Joss carefully approached the screen, passing four rows before stopping.

I should go back – I'll never find him. No, keep going! You've come this far!

When she reached the first row, movement captured her attention. Someone stood, then abruptly fell back into the seat and…evaporated. Now there was nothing left except for clothes, black and crumpled and lonely. It happened again in the fourth row, then again in the seventh or eighth row, shadows rising and falling.

The screen came to life in black and white, music exploding throughout the theater. It was organ music, a familiar song. Where had Joss heard it? The screen provided the answer with a short clip of Carl Larose playing before one of his Friday night crowds – but soon Max dominated the screen.

"Jesus," Joss murmured, watching with horror as her brother held a bottle of pills in his apartment. She suddenly realized what was about to happen, her tears uncontrollable.

Shepherd was replaying Max's suicide.

Pop! Max opened the bottle, shook a handful of pills out, looking oddly peaceful. He put two or three in his mouth, washed them down with beer. More pills, more beer. Joss fell to her knees, shoved a hand over her mouth, the inner warmth suddenly replaced by frigidity. More pills. More and more and more. Max finally collapsed to the bedroom floor and laughed…and now an image of his casket superimposed the footage of his last moments.

A voice cracked over the sound system. Shepherd's voice. "All of your memories, all of his memories, everything you've ever done or felt – it all belongs to me. You belong to me, Jocelyne."

Joss spun around, searching the dark theater.
Empty.

"Are you ready for the exchange, Joss?" Shepherd rasped, his words causing her to flinch. But faith made an unexpected resurgence, casting her fears out and replacing them with self-assurance. She could do this. Dad had always said that anything is possible if you believe. Anything. Now that she'd come this far, she wouldn't run. Wouldn't back down or hide. Wouldn't be the victim. She would harness her innermost strength and confront the demon.

The door at the back of the room flung open. Joss steeled herself, ready to face that which had driven her to alcohol over the last three months. But Shepherd didn't enter. Someone else appeared in the doorway, scanning the rows of seats just as Joss had done a few minutes earlier. His face was too dark for Joss to identify, but he instantly recognized her.

"Jocey!" shouted a voice she'd feared she would never hear again.

Though she'd wanted so desperately to remain strong in the heat of the unexpected, Joss fainted upon seeing her brother rush toward her.

Chapter 10

As Mike and the others watched the perplexing exchange between the levitating battery and whoever was on the other side of the wall, a door to their left creaked open. Beyond it, an eruption of sound and colorful flashing lights cascaded out of an otherwise dark room.

Gripping his gun, Mike led the group to the door and pushed it fully open. At the end of a long, dark entry runway, music crashed in sonorous waves, vibrating the walls and thrumming in the floor, drawing them forth with each resounding blast.

"You think it's a trap?" Dave said.

Mike stopped, glancing back at Max and Gerald. "Have either of you seen this room before?"

Gerald shook his head, but where was Max? He'd been there just a second ago.

Dave slammed a hand against the wall. "Christ, he led us into a fucking trap!"

"It's not his fault," Gerald said. "We don't have any control in here. We're like puppets on a string. Thank God my son got away from this place."

Mike didn't know what to do. The lights ahead seemed to call to him. What if Blake was down there, just a short distance away from his potential rescuers?

The lights sizzled in bursts of brilliant blue, reminding Mike of a bug zapper. Cautiously, he pressed forward toward the end of the runway and beheld a small theater, rows of seats flooded with pulses of luminosity emanating from what was likely a screen out of sight. The entire room seemed energized by the promise of impending doom.

As they crept closer, more of the theater came into view. There was indeed a large screen angled to their left; it showed a black and white film, the scene portraying a graphic battle between pioneers and Indians, the music exceedingly dramatic.

"Let's just stay here for a while and watch," Mike said, turning away from the screen.

Movement, Dave the first to notice it. Mike's immediate thought was of Blake Grafton, but the person Dave had spotted standing in the far aisle was no child.

It was Joss Leclaire!

***

Max tried to follow the group as they approached the door, but he collided with an invisible wall, the same barrier that had restricted him when Blake was taken away.

Max hollered for them to come back, but they couldn't hear him, the wall stifling sound and hope.

"Fuck!" he shouted, fearing he would be imprisoned yet again. "Fuck, fuck, fuck!!"

The wall, however, only denied his progress in one direction. He was able to run the other way, expecting to see the hovering battery but instead finding a new door that hadn't been there before. It swung open as if greeted by heavy winds.

Another trick, Max thought. *Another game.*

Yet he found himself passing through the door and entering a theater. He didn't notice what was on the screen, too focused on searching the rows for Blake. He had to find him, had to save him from Shepherd.

Instead, he found Jocey.

***

Mike couldn't believe what happened next.

"Jocey!" a voice shouted from the far aisle, Max dashing in from a rear entrance.

Joss jumped at the sight of her brother. There was a moment of comprehension that seemed to last an hour. Then she fell backward, collapsing, but Max somehow made it in time to catch her.

***

To hold her. To hold his sister again…Max couldn't believe it was real. He looked up, thanked the God he'd renounced so long ago. Thanked Him repeatedly, his hands shaking with joy.

Jocey was unconscious. She'd fainted, but her pulse was strong. For a moment she was the little girl Max had comforted on countless occasions. He squeezed her hand, tears pooling in his eyes.

The others gathered around him. "I remember her from before," Gerald said. "I made a bad mistake that day. Shepherd told me to drug her boyfriend, said I'd get to be with my wife again if I did. But he only wanted this girl. Had her all tied up – I still don't know how she got out."

Max was hardly listening. He stroked Jocey's cheeks and hair, unaware of fast approaching footsteps.

"Nate!" Mike gasped. "Jesus, what are you guys doing here?" He pointed to Jocey. "She fainted when she saw her brother, but I think she's gonna be all right."

Nate knelt beside Jocey, then noticed Max. "Holy fuck...Max! It's true! You're really in here!"

"This is some reunion," Dave remarked. "Who's the next person we're gonna see in this damn place, Jimmy Hoffa? Mikey, we've found everyone *but* the kid we came here for."

Mike checked Jocey's pulse, but there was no need. Her eyes fluttered open, dazed and oddly peaceful, slowly processing her surroundings. Max could easily identify the moment of recognition, her eyes igniting so fiercely that they became an even deeper blue.

"Max!" Her voice was soft, barely above a whisper. She sat up and touched his cheeks disbelievingly, her hands shaking as the tears came.

"I knew I'd find you," she cried, hugging him, Max ecstatic yet terrified that it would all end in disaster. "Why did you leave us, Max? I've been so messed up. I don't know how to go on without you."

Mike came between them, tapping Jocey's shoulder. "Joss, you and Nate need to get out of here right now! *Right now!*"

"No!" Jocey refused. "Not unless I know Max is safe."

"Uncle Mike's right," Nate said, scowling at Jocey. "Shepherd only brought Max here because of us, and you did exactly what he wanted!" He turned to Mike. "What's going on with you guys? Have you seen Blake?"

"Still no luck," Dave said, glancing about the theater. "We've been walking around for hours."

"What about Aunt Sue? She's gotta be freaking out. It's almost midnight."

"Midnight?" Mike checked his watch, incredulous.

"Joss and I couldn't wait any longer. I was gonna come on my own, but she beat me to it."

"And luckily she did," another voice added.

Seated in the first row was Shepherd. In the seat immediately to the right of the hooded monster, his hands bound together and mouth taped, was Blake Grafton.

"I'm glad you've all made it," Shepherd said. "It's time for the exchange."

THE INHABITANTS II

Part VIII: Who Survives 99 Deepwoods Drive?

"I'd love to tell you I had some deep revelation on my way down, that I came to terms with my own mortality, laughed in the face of death, et cetera. The truth? My only thought was: Aaaaggghhhhh!"
~ Rick Riordan

Chapter 1

Katie followed her parents and Whit down the deck to the staircase. She wanted to stay, but Sgt. Fitzgerald had been adamant about ejecting them from the apartment.

Dad led them down the stairs. "Come on, let's get to the parking lot," he urged. "We'll wait down there for the cops to figure things out."

A barrage of thoughts and fears came to Katie, colliding in a massive wreck. She remembered Blake's nightmare, which hadn't been a nightmare at all. Then there was the warning taped to her car; the organ music; her son's screams; Whit's visit from someone who looked identical to Mason Blackwell; the mystery of unit nine; the dark past of the building…and on top of everything was the chaos of the last ten minutes. The lights had gone out. The walls had been repeatedly pounded by someone on the other side. The young cop had clearly seen something that shocked him in the kitchen, his face whiter than a dry-erase board. And Fitzgerald had ordered them all out.

Katie stopped at the base of the staircase. Her parents and Whit were halfway to the parking lot, but she refused to follow them any further. Instead, she raced back up the stairs. Whatever the police were discussing about her apartment, she had the right to know about it.

Back on the deck, Katie demanded answers. Fitzgerald, fully immersed in his talk with the young cop, didn't notice her until she spoke.

"Please, Ms. Grafton, just give us some space to get the situation under control. The feds are on their way," Fitzgerald said, pointing impatiently to the parking lot.

The other two cops joined them on the deck, everyone's face blanched with mystification. The youngest cop still looked disoriented and frightened. He blinked rapidly and glanced often back at the apartment.

The snow had intensified, unnoticed by Katie, whose anger was also strengthening. "What do you mean, *get the situation under control*? None of you could figure out where the knocks were coming from? What did you see?" Now her focus was squarely on the young cop.

He glanced warily away from her to Fitzgerald, deferring to his superior.

"I don't know what to tell you, Ms. Grafton," Fitzgerald said. "I'm so sorry, but we couldn't identify the source." He turned to one of his officers. "Notify the electric company about the power outage. And I want the landlord here now!"

"Yes, sir," the cop said, taking the opportunity to escape down the stairs.

Before Katie could say anything further, Fitzgerald placed a thick hand on her shoulder. "We'll stay here all night until we figure out what's happening – you have my word on that. The feds'll be swarming this place in minutes."

Meanwhile, the youngest cop was trying to get Fitzgerald's attention, repeating the word, "Sir, Sir, Sir", until Fitzgerald finally spun around.

"What?" the sergeant snapped.

The cop leaned over the railing and pointed toward the parking lot. "Sir, that car with the headlights on – it wasn't there when we got here."

Katie's gaze angled to the lot, where a sedan's headlights magnified the fluffy snowflakes. Her father and Whit were examining it, Dad peering through the back windows.

"Well, what are you two waiting for? Go check it out!" Fitzgerald barked with an angry backhand wave that sent the remaining officers scrambling down the stairs.

Fitzgerald then spoke into his radio, confirmed something with the dispatcher, and finally returned his focus to Katie. "Look, Ms. Grafton, this building isn't safe right now with…whatever's going on in there. Clearly there was, or still is, someone in the building. Our best bet is to surround it, but if one of the suspects is in there, we don't want you and your family in harm's way. The safest place for you to be right now is in the parking lot, preferably in your vehicles with the doors locked."

Katie nodded, realizing that continued questions would only delay Fitzgerald's intended course of action. Although she desperately wanted to search every unit for Blake, she had to leave the job to the professionals and stop wasting their time. If Blake's abductors were still inside the building, they couldn't be allowed to get away.

Yet a fear, hot and striking, though not new, told Katie the house itself had taken her son, trapping him within its walls.

Chapter 2

With decades of law enforcement experience between them, it was impossible for Mike and Dave to not reach for their guns when Shepherd spoke. Based on Nate's and Joss's descriptions of him – or, more accurately, it – Mike identified Shepherd as soon as he saw the robe and veiled hood.

"Let the kid go!" Mike ordered.

"Do it now!" added Dave, his Glock's laser sight beaming a red track to Shepherd's veil.

Gurgling laughter escaped the veil. It sounded like Shepherd was laughing with a mouthful of water. Finally the fiend said, "Stop wasting time with your toys and listen to my offer. A simple exchange – you get the boy, and I get Nate and Joss."

An added emphasis was given to the final two letters of Joss's name, reminding Mike of the half-raven, half-serpent visage he knew lurked behind that veil.

"Never!" Max shouted, charging in front of Mike and Dave. "You can never have her, never!" He was shaking with rage, but Shepherd dismissed him with laughter.

Patting Blake on the head, enjoying the boy's tears, Shepherd continued, "I have no use for this child. He's merely a bargaining chip. Nate and Joss, however, are extremely important for my plans."

"No deal," Mike said, lowering his weapon. He was suddenly infused with confidence in their situation. If Shepherd was offering an exchange, then clearly it wasn't omnipotent.

"Your time here is done." Dave held his gun level, the laser barely moving. "Now give up the kid and move on."

More laughter, this time extending for several seconds. Before Shepherd spoke again, the rear door opened and a tall man entered. Holding a candle in each hand, his slow approach was marked by a fury of biblical verses. He spoke with the booming voice of an orator. "And when Jesus entered Peter's house, he saw his mother-in-law lying sick with a fever. He touched her hand, and the fever left her – and she *rose* and began to serve him. That evening, they brought to him many who were oppressed by demons, and he cast out the spirits with a word and healed all who were sick!"

Mike raised his weapon once more. About fifty feet away, the old man had come to a stop, his eyes sharp with single-focused, animalistic intensity. Even before Gerald Blackwell shouted, "Johansen, you son of a bitch!", Mike recognized this newest entrant from the proceedings earlier that night.

Johansen began to speak again, but Blackwell rushed him with a rapidity that startled Mike. It was almost as if he'd flown at Johansen and tackled him, candles hurtling through the air. One of them landed on a seat in the third row, igniting the upholstery.

Shepherd's laughter intensified. "Now look what you've done, Gerald. Starting fires isn't wise unless you can put them out."

Blackwell quickly overwhelmed Johansen, repeatedly punching the old man until he was flat on his back and motionless. But Mike's attention was drawn to the back of the theater, where three additional men slowly entered, their faces lit by pale white glows.

They broke into a sprint, forcing Mike and Dave into action. The reverberating gunfire bounced around the theater like thunderclaps. Two attackers dropped, their facial glimmers blinking out, but the third managed to slip through and lunge at Joss.

Chapter 3

Joss screamed when the creature leaped at her, fangs sprouting, but the combination of Max and Nate dropped it to the floor.

Her ears still ringing from the gunshots, Joss watched as her boys clobbered the would-be assailant, a tall, pale, gruesome thing without hair or eyebrows, its face flaccid and slimy. It flailed and screeched unavailingly, tried to bite their arms, but they were too strong, pressing its throat to the floor and choking the air from its lungs.

"Stand back!" Mike Overbrook shouted at Nate and Max, and the cops filled the corpses with bullets.

Shock had numbed Joss severely, the violence like that of a movie scene – but there was something else working on her, churning darkly up from within, betrayed only by its feel against her skin, tight and abrasive.

Smoke rapidly filled the room, Joss coughing on the oppressive air…and now the fire was leaping in every direction, claiming more seats, relentless in its pursuit of victims to devour. Yet the flames didn't approach Shepherd or Blake, allowing them a clearance of ten feet on all sides.

Wide-eyed, Blake made strained, suffocated inhalations. Because of the tape on his mouth, he could only breathe through his nose, the air he received smoke-poisoned and insufficient, Joss left to imagine his suffering, like being dunked underwater and coming up for a gasp, only to be shoved down again.

"We need to get everyone out of here!" Nate urged his uncle. "This place will go up quick!"

Mike nodded, glanced at Shepherd, whose grip on the boy's arm suddenly shattered Joss's shock and filled her with rage, a snap felt on her shoulders, the awful garment falling thinly downward beneath her clothes.

"Get away from him!" Joss screamed, wanting nothing more than to pry evil's grip from Blake. The sight disgusted her beyond anything she'd ever glimpsed.

Joss rushed forward, emboldened by the need to protect, vaguely aware of the others at her sides. They covered their faces with their arms, desperate to shield themselves from the smoke.

"Give us the boy!" Mike shouted.

"It's over!" said Dave Strait.

But it wasn't over, far from it. Though outnumbered, Shepherd was not at the disadvantage, a realization that didn't reach Joss until the hooded monstrosity burst into a black, swirling mist that shot upward and outward.

And now Joss and the others were outnumbered.

Bats descended on them from the mist, ruthlessly biting and swooping back down for additional attacks. Joss fell to her knees, threw her hands up to cover herself. She could feel them in her hair, rustling and swishing and entangling themselves, chittering greedily, their hooked claws like needles. One of them found its way inside her clothes, somehow slipping beneath the layers and raking against her chest and stomach before escaping back into the tumultuous fray.

"Joss and Nate for the boy!" erupted Shepherd's voice. "Joss and Nate for the boy!" The smoke was becoming overwhelming, stinging Joss's eyes.

"An even better deal – Joss for the boy. A simple exchange and it's all over. One for one, just hand your soul to me, Jocey Marie, and Blake goes free. Max, too. Your brother goes to Heaven, Jocey Marie."

The voice was no longer coming from an external source but rising from within. Only Joss could hear it, Shepherd burrowing into her soul, the darkness of this place creeping in as it had often done before, the rough straps sliding back over her shoulders.

Laughter, endless laughter. Flooding smoke. Bats pounding against her. Choking, can't breathe. A sharp pain on her right hand – a bat had bitten her. Panicking. Lungs filling with smoke…CAN'T BREATHE…and a thought flared in her heart, induced by fear for the others. Could she die for them? Could she suffer for eternity for them? Even at the height of chaos, she thought of Mason. He'd risked the fires of Hell for her, and now it was coming full circle in a maddening rush.

"Death. They're all dying, Joss. Dying! Will you let them die, Jocey Marie? Will you let your brother burn? And Nate? Don't you love them?"

The voice no longer came from Shepherd – it was deeper, more frightening, the voice of something else, the voice of...oh God, the voice of evil itself, the voice of fire, the voice of the blackness that threatened to consume her, a blackness that ruled the most wicked hours, when there was nothing but wind and hatred, marauders peering in at sleeping souls, hoping to get at them before sunrise.

"Don't do it!" came a faint urge. Mason's voice, but Joss had already murmured yes.

"Your soul is mine!" the other voice clattered. "Say it! Give it to me!"

White sparkling light suffused the fire-torn darkness, drifting down in luminous flakes like snow and setting the room aglow. A new room, Joss its only occupant. She suddenly knew what she needed to do, knew it absolutely, unequivocally. Back in September, she'd said she would die for Nate, but she hadn't entirely embraced the implications of those words; she'd only said them reflexively, anything to keep Nate alive. But now she did embrace the sacrifice. This was but one stop, one chapter, not the end, not eternity. She would rise one day, rise to Heaven like Mason, where she would spend forever with those she loved.

Let them burn, came a sickening menace of a thought. Like a shadow springing from a previously unseen hollow, it had leapt from some black, enigmatic, ever-expanding chamber in her heart, leaving her cold with atavistic fear.

"Ignore the darkness!" Mason exhorted. "You have to save Blake and get everyone else out!"

For a hectic flash Joss could see herself at Blake's age, smiling and happy, one year before Dad died. That had been an insufferably dark day, but what Blake endured now was even darker. He should have known nothing of evil, yet its tendrils had snatched him away from his home. Now he was restrained by Shepherd, just as Joss had been. She remembered her colossal fear – praying for a miracle, begging for survival – and with that memory came a redoubled determination to prevent Blake Grafton from suffering another minute of terror.

Yes, she realized, she was strong enough to die for this boy. She could withstand temporary suffering, because at the end of every tunnel was the light, the same light felt by Mason and Max and–

But what if there is only darkness?

"I will go with you, Shepherd, but my soul will always belong to God!" she shouted, if only to silence her indefatigable thoughts. "Now let the others go! Please, let them all go!"

Chapter 4

A flaming beam fell from the ceiling, nearly crushing Uncle Mike. Its landing generated even more smoke, fanning it into their eyes and mouths. Nate reached for Joss's arm, but more beams rained down, one of them striking Joss on the shoulder and knocking her to the floor.

"Joss!" Nate screamed, but a downpour of fiery debris fell atop her and Max.

As Nate tried to pull one of the heavy beams off, searching for assistance, he noticed Mike and Dave in the first row. They'd gotten to Blake, Mike carrying him into the aisle.

Heat lashed at Nate's hands. "Help me get these off! Joss is pinned under here!"

But just as Mike arrived, the entire ceiling rattled with thunderous quakes.

"The roof's coming down!" By the time Mike said that final word, the crash had already begun, no way to escape.

They tried to cover each other, Nate diving to protect Joss, Mike shielding Nate. The ear-shattering chaos was so prodigious that it was hard to believe a roof had fallen and not an asteroid.

CRASH! CRASH! CRASH! CRASH! CRASH!

Somehow Nate was still alive, still hearing the deafening sounds. More debris buried them in a grave of agony, the fire roaring, the smoke and dust combining in a toxic cloud. Distantly, organ music began to play.

And then, finally, there was darkness. But not nothingness – this was the conscious blackness Nate had known on countless mornings between presses of the snooze button, bringing with it awareness of where he was and things to come.

He strained his eyes.

Saw only blackness.

Felt the rising pain and terror.

Chapter 5

Mike awoke in bed. His first thought was that of a horrible nightmare, so vivid as to be real.

Then he realized he wasn't in his bedroom. Wasn't even in his house. What the hell was going on?

He left the bed and ventured out of a small room into an unfamiliar hallway, his head throbbing, fragments of memory returning. A light was on in the distance. He came to a larger room and was filled with joy at what he saw.

"Mikey, you made it! Jesus Christ, you're alive!"

Dave was sitting beside Blake Grafton on a sofa.

"Dave, how'd you get out of there? Where are we?"

His friend shook his head, spoke softly. "I have no idea, man – just woke up a few minutes ago. All of my stuff is gone…my weapons, everything. But we're alive, and Blake appears none the worse for wear, at least physically. He doesn't remember anything, though."

Mike slowly approached the boy and kneeled before him. He looked worried but not frightened. "Are you okay, Blake? Does anything hurt?"

A headshake. "Where's Mom? I want to go home."

"Okay, we'll get you to your mom real soon, I promise," Mike said. "But first, can you tell me who took you from home?"

Blake looked confused. "No one took me. I was playing outside, and…I don't remember how I got here."

Mike and Dave exchanged wary glances.

"Where's Nate and Joss?" Mike gasped, remembering even more from their ordeal.

Dave's face grew pale. "What if…my God, Mikey, what if they didn't make it out?"

Chapter 6

Following her talk with Sgt. Fitzgerald, Katie had just reached her father's car in the parking lot when it happened.

There was a deafening WHOOMP mixed with a tinkling of broken glass. Facing Dad's car, dropping reflexively to her knees, Katie didn't need to turn around to know something had exploded. The heat against her neck and the orange reflection in the windshield were more than enough proof.

She turned slowly, dreading what she'd see. And when she did behold the damage, it was infinitely worse than her expectations.

"Holy shit!" Dad was out of the car, grabbing Katie by the arm and pulling her away.

Mom and Whit raced to the edge of the woods. Dad led Katie back there as well, and they all stared in shock through the snow at the devastation.

The shed was gone, blown away like an arm blown off a body, exposing a gaping, flaming maw. Fire raged through the roof, spreading to the third floor deck.

Fitzgerald, who'd hurried around front after their conversation, was huddling behind a pickup truck, speaking frantically into his radio. Two of the other cops had joined him, but the third one was missing.

He came into view a short while later, though it wasn't the sight of the youngest officer that sent Katie sprinting across the slippery, snow-slickened parking lot...but instead the person he was carrying.

"Blake! Oh my God, Blake!"

Wrapped in a large blanket, Blake spotted her and smiled. Katie, suddenly speechless, could only scoop him out of the officer's arms and cry.

A hand on her shoulder. Fitzgerald's hand. "Let's get to the road, Ms. Grafton. It's not safe here."

Behind them, the blaze continued to eat away at the building. In the distance, a fire engine wailed, but Katie's focus was fixed on Blake. For a dizzy moment she wondered if this was actually happening, tears tracking down her face as they came to the edge of Deepwoods Drive, police cars flashing in a sea of blue.

"Why are you crying, Mom?" Blake said in a small, worried voice.

Katie didn't understand. She set Blake down, held his cheeks. Was he in shock?

"Baby, you've been gone a long time. Who took you? Where have you been?"

"No one took me. I went outside to play, and I fell asleep." He brightened. "When's supper? I'm hungry."

Katie felt exceedingly cold, fearing her son's reply to the next question.

"Blake, do you know what day it is, baby?"

"It's Monday," he said without hesitation. "Can we go inside? I'm cold."

Chapter 7

Mike and Dave searched as much of the place as they safely could, but Nate and Joss were gone, vanished just like Blake Grafton on Monday night.

The cave where the shed had been was spouting flames like the mouth of a dragon, the apartment units above it afire as well, perhaps to collapse in on the initial point of explosion. The roof was burning. The third floor deck at the rear of the building was burning. Soon everything would be burning.

Mike was panting, crushed by the fear of never seeing Nate again. Mike and Dave had just searched unit one, which for the moment was unaffected. "He took them, Dave! What are we gonna do?"

Dave spoke into his radio, informing Fitzgerald of their position. To Mike, he said, "Do you think they agreed to the exchange?" His face was shadowed ominously in flickering orange light.

Mike shook his head, wondering if Nate and Joss had indeed gone through with it. He tried to remember those last few chaotic moments.

Horn ripping the night, a fire engine blared into the parking lot. Dave told the first firefighter off the truck that two people were inside, their last known location the shed, which was now just a flaming, smoking ruin.

Mike squeezed back the tears. He felt an abysmal wrath take hold of him, its grip ineluctable. Looking up at the building, angry waves of heat clashing with snowflakes against his face, it seemed that Shepherd had undoubtedly won. The bastard hadn't been able to get Nate and Joss the first time, but now he had them, the two people he'd been after all along.

Blake Grafton had been just a bargaining chip. Shepherd had really wanted the two who'd gotten away in September.

Chapter 8

Working swiftly and effectively, the fire crews were able to knock down the blaze in relatively short order. Now the building stood smoking and spectral beneath increasingly steady snowfall, its midsection destroyed and roof charred.

The third floor deck was black as well, buckled and bowed, and for a few seconds Katie spotted a trio of hooded men standing upon it. Although they were partially obscured by the snow, their dimly glowing faces were momentarily visible as they looked down on the parking lot, staring directly at Katie in her car, their hatred as hot as the flames which had gutted the building.

Then the deck was empty again.

Chilled to her marrow, Katie watched from the driver's seat as firemen continued to assail troublesome patches of orange with arcs of water, ensuring that none of the old wood got rekindled. Katie had been asked to move her car to the edge of the woods near the dumpster to make room for more fire trucks, and now her vehicle was flanked by state troopers keeping guard. Yet still Katie felt defenseless against whatever was in that building.

Back here, the house looked even taller and more frightening, like stepping back from a skyscraper and gazing up at its prominence – except this place was nothing to behold in admiration, hellish with its sporadic fiery glows.

"Are you okay, sweetie?" Katie asked Blake for perhaps the hundredth time, wanting to get as far as possible from 99 Deepwoods Drive. The ambulance that would take them to the hospital couldn't arrive soon enough.

Blake was in the passenger seat, enjoying the full blast of the heater. Whit was in the back seat texting someone. Mom and Dad, meanwhile, were trying to gather information from the cops in the parking lot. Katie had asked them to give her and Whit a few minutes with Blake, and they'd set out into the storm in search of answers.

Watching snowflakes pile up on the windshield and then disperse with each pass of the wipers, Katie reached across the center console and held her son's hand. There didn't appear to be anything wrong with him – and that was the greatest terror of all. He remained under the impression that it was Monday evening and he'd fallen asleep, Katie deciding it was best not to question him too intensely. But not knowing what her son had been through was agonizing. She could only pray he hadn't suffered anything beyond the sheer horror of his ordeal…but even that would be enough to thoroughly damage a seven-year-old.

"We're gonna get through this, okay, sweetie?" Katie said, squeezing his hand and kissing his head. "Mommy's here for you now. No one can hurt you."

Blake was confused again. "Why would anyone hurt me?"

"Never mind, baby." Katie rubbed her eyes before the tears came again. "I love you, Blake."

"Love you, too, Mommy."

Katie watched the falling snow, her fear steadily building. The questions far outnumbered the answers at this point, but all that mattered was their reunion, mother and son – and together they would find a way to get through the coming days and weeks. No matter how difficult it was, Katie would help Blake through it.

The evil inside this house would not break them. Katie would pick up the pieces and continue building a future that had been temporarily derailed at 99 Deepwoods Drive. She would put this wicked place behind them and never look back, concentrating only on the joys that lay ahead.

It was time to leave Deepwoods Drive…and begin the rest of their lives.

Chapter 9

Gerald Blackwell ran without thinking, letting adrenaline carry him as he'd done in the war.

Following one corridor after another, the fire chasing him like a predator – its heat always pressing against his back – Gerald flashed with memories of Dachau, where the corpses had been piled up like heaps of garbage, a sickening testament to evil's depths. Every sound had been amplified, every sight and smell exceedingly vivid, and now Gerald was at war again almost seventy years later.

Except this time he wasn't confronting the enemy – he was fleeing like a coward. He'd once been courageous and purposeful, but now he feared that only Hell awaited a man who'd sinned as he had. It was inescapable, inevitable, yet still Gerald ran from the flames, hoping to delay that which would eventually claim him.

He continued to run, the hungry fire roaring behind him. He didn't dare look back. He'd already tried challenging evil along with the others, but the Devil had won.

NO!!!

No more running. No more hiding. Mason had gotten to Heaven, and Gerald could accept condemnation knowing that much. He could face his fate, just as the Dachau survivors had been forced to do – the ones who'd thought their liberation meant a life in the U.S. or England or France, only to be returned to their blown out villages of desolation.

Gerald forced himself to stop, an act requiring as much courage as any command he'd taken in war. Slowly, he spun around. "Have me, if you must," he muttered, but there was no fire, only misty darkness.

A voice in the distance, calling from the depths of evil's lair.

"There's still a chance for you to see Mason again," Shepherd said with a rumble of laughter. "You simply need to follow orders like the good soldier you've always been."

***

Nate awoke to the sounds of a television. Across the room, Alex Trebek was reading a Daily Double answer.

Nate reached for the remote on the sofa, flicked off the TV. It took an achy moment for recognition to set in. Then he realized where he was – the living room of his old apartment.

"What the fuck?" He kicked in the sofa's recliner. *His* sofa!

In fact, everything was his, the room fully furnished with his belongings. Textbooks from first semester rested on the desk – books he'd recently sold online.

His laptop was open, a Microsoft Word page glowing on the screen. A can of Pepsi stood beside it. On the walls were his photos and posters, the guys from Metallica staring at him from the wall behind the television.

Before he could begin to piece together what had happened, soft cries startled him from beyond the living room door. Joss's cries.

Nate raced through the door, found her kneeling on the bedroom floor, hands covering her face. "Joss! Thank God you're okay!"

She looked up at him, cheeks red and puffy, then leaped into his arms. "I'm so sorry, Nate, but we're trapped in here. Shepherd, he…" She couldn't continue, claimed by her tears.

Nate jerked free of his girlfriend's embrace, terror swelling in his chest. "How can we be trapped?" He dashed into the kitchen and tried to yank open the door. It wouldn't move.

Joss was right behind him, still crying hysterically. "I already tried – we can't get out. Nate, please forgive me – it's all my fault!"

Nate tried to remain calm, but his breaths were quickening. Panicked, he hurried to the near corner, grabbed a broom, and slammed the side window with its handle.

When the glass failed to shatter or even crack, a twinge of dreadful knowingness glided down his back. They were indeed trapped, but how could Shepherd have altered time? How could they be seeing unit four as it had appeared three months ago?

Joss sobbed into her hands, Nate noticing that her bandage was gone.

Did we go back to the...? How is this happening?

They still wore their winter clothes. This was just another deception, Nate assumed, another layer of Shepherd's realm they had to fight through.

"How do we get out?" Nate said, more to himself than to Joss.

"I...I don't know," she replied with an underlying tone of resignation that made Nate shudder.

The wind flared up outside, rattling the weak walls. The refrigerator purred, a look inside revealing sodas and delis and half a grinder from Earl's Sandwich and Salad Shop at the corner of 119 and 202. Upstairs, Carl Larose's organ began to play.

Reaching for each other, holding hands, Nate and Joss gazed up to the ceiling with wild, frightened eyes, prisoners of a place they'd thought would forever remain in their past.

The bathroom door swung open, a frail old wraith of a woman emerging from the darkness with a tray of food and drinks in hand. "Time to eat, my dears.

Jocey, as you well know, one should never go to sleep on an empty stomach."

Chapter 10

Monday, December 20

I fear the fallout from the disaster at 99 Deepwoods
Drive will never end. At least there was one miracle
on that terrible night, Blake Grafton's reappearance,
but it was offset by the disappearances of three
more individuals.

The FBI has taken over the investigation. Initial
reports suggest that the same suspects who took
Blake also abducted Nathan Overbrook, Jocelyne
Leclaire, and Peter Dobyns. I don't know what they
were doing there, any of them, but I know it had
something to do with what I saw in that place. The
faces. So many faces!

I've just gotten back from another interview with
the feds, although they seem more like
interrogations than interviews. Luckily, I haven't
told them about what I saw. Sgt. Fitzgerald asked
me about it again in private this morning, but I
retracted my claims, explaining them away as
products of extreme stress on my first night on the
job. But there was something in his eyes that
betrayed his secrets. He knows what's really going
on, and so does Chief Strait. They're hiding
something, perhaps the truth of the haunting. They
keep saying things like, *You did a good job, Zach*
and *You were part of the effort that brought Blake
home*…but no amount of praise will allow me to
forget what I saw. I'm a total mess. I can't sleep,
and when I do the nightmares are overwhelming.

Those faces will never leave me. Were they ghosts? Messengers?

Or were they demons? Some say the Devil lives at 99 Deepwoods Drive, and maybe before long I'll find out for sure.

Epilogue

Monday night, December 20

The last two days had been utter chaos.

Mike had slept only a few hours, almost every waking minute dedicated to searching for Nate and Joss. It had seemed pointless, however, to search the surrounding woods when he and Dave both knew where those two kids really were: somewhere in the burnt building that had once been Nate's residence.

99 Deepwoods Drive had been scoured countless times, and no evidence of human remains had been found amidst the rubble of the shed. That had been the only positive news, confirming that Nate and Joss were trapped deep within the building's dark parallel plane. There was no getting back inside, though, not even for Dave. The FBI had come in and blocked off the entire building with temporary fencing, even throwing down a barricade at the entrance to the parking lot. No one besides the feds got in or out.

His eyes so heavy that he had trouble keeping them open, Mike stepped before the podium and produced a folder of notes.

"Thanks for coming, everyone," he said, adjusting the microphone and scanning two rows of apprehensive faces.

Among them was Sue. Earlier, she had been immensely understanding and comforting when Mike shared revelations that would have made most spouses furious. Now they were in a conference room at Anya Leclaire's university. Members of both the Overbrook and Leclaire families had been asked to attend, no reporters or feds allowed.

Mike peeked over his right shoulder at Dave. "What Chief David Strait, of the Hollisville Police Department, and I are about to tell you is going to sound impossible – but it's the truth. Nate and Joss didn't disappear into the woods, and they most certainly weren't abducted, at least not by a living, breathing entity." The room was suddenly alive with gasps and murmurs. "I assure you that everything you'll hear from us tonight is the God's honest truth. We saw everything ourselves."

"That's right," Dave said. "You won't believe it at first, but we can tell you with one hundred percent confidence it's true."

"Just tell them already!" shouted John Overbrook, who'd reeked of alcohol on the way in. Having learned the truth yesterday, John had at first adamantly rejected it, then proceeded to give in to the booze yet again.

Mike took a deep breath. "They were trapped by a supernatural force that calls itself Shepherd. It haunts 99 Deepwoods Drive."

The room exploded into pandemonium, the loudest voice belonging to Anya Leclaire. "Oh, Lord, I knew this would happen! I knew it!" she wailed. "I knew that girl would be taken by the Devil for her sins!" Mike had revealed the truth to Anya yesterday as well, and apparently there'd been more than enough time for her religious zealotry to take over. "This is what happens when you sin – you expose yourself to the darkness!"

"Quiet! Quiet down, everyone!" Mike hollered. "If we have any chance of getting them back, we need to work together. Blake Grafton was taken by Shepherd as well, and he's now home safe with his mother. The same can be true for Nate and Joss, but it's gonna take a lot of work on our part. No excuses, no backing down – only positivity and persistence."

The questions flew from there, piling up like yesterday's snow.

***

The FBI investigation initially focused on the disappearances of Nathan Overbrook, Jocelyne Leclaire, and reporter Peter Dobyns. Soon, however, it expanded to cover a host of other incidents occurring in and around the building over the last year, including the suspicious suicides of Jane Keppel and Blake Gaudreau, the abduction of Blake Grafton, and the brief September abduction of Jocelyne Leclaire.

In the initial stages of the investigation, several key discoveries were made, the most important of which surrounded the renters of unit nine, Theodore and

Constance Rendell. The landlord had given their names and contact information, but the couple was nowhere to be found. Their landline was disconnected. Aside from basic furniture, their apartment was oddly bare. According to the landlord, they'd paid the security deposit and rent in cash, otherwise keeping to themselves.

When Agent Jeremy Russo searched the system for the Rendells, nothing came up. No driver's licenses, no social security numbers, no tax records, no marriage license, and no financial transactions. Nothing.

After several minutes of dogged searching, Agent Russo arrived at the conclusion that Theodore and Constance Rendell didn't exist.

So who the hell had paid the rent for unit nine and supplied fake names to the police?

***

Fire overwhelmed Max, a sea of roaring flames. It consumed him, though there was no pain, only eventual darkness.

When he awoke, he was slumped in a yellow upper deck seat, the only occupant of a place he knew well – Olympic Stadium in Montreal. The massive roof loomed above him, the field a dull green. The foul lines and batter's boxes had been neatly chalked, the pitcher's mound raked and dampened. The scent of popcorn pervaded the air, the center field scoreboard brightly illuminated. Though the stadium was empty, Max sensed imminent action, as if thousands of fans would flood through the entrances and the players would charge onto the field.

Crack! Max glanced down to the field and spotted a baseball arcing toward the wall.

"How many games did we see in this place?" came a voice to his left.

Max slowly turned, dreading what he'd find. For a moment he was speechless, unable to believe his father was really there – he was much younger, in his twenties, but it was undoubtedly Jean-Philippe Leclaire.

"Dad!" Max stumbled out of the seat, into his father's embrace.

"You've made it, son."

Max pulled away, remembering all that had happened. "What about Jocey? Did she get out? Is she safe?"

Dad frowned, darkness sliding into his stare. "She's still trapped in there, Max, but she has the strength to get herself out. She just has to find her way."

***

Nate and Joss didn't waver in their search for an escape until thundering booms rattled the night. An

echo of familiarity vibrating in his heart, Nate
kneeled on the sofa and lifted the blinds behind it.

Looked beyond the treetops.

Knew what he'd see – the fireworks from that first
September night he'd brought Joss here.

The colors exploded into the night, Lake
Monomonac glimmering below. The past was the
present, everything damaged and distorted, but at
least they were together.

Kneeling on the sofa beside him, Joss took his hand.
Staring hopelessly out at the fireworks, she said,
"Do you hate me?"

He turned to her, the weight of her words too much
to carry. He kissed her forehead, kissed her lips,
desperate to keep her close. "I could never hate you,
Joss – you're the best thing that's ever happened to
me. We're gonna get out of here, I promise. No
matter what we have to do, we're getting out, and
when we do I'm gonna marry you, I swear to God."

Her lips trembled into a smile, tears streaming down
her cheeks. "I love you, Nate."

"I love you, too, Jocey Marie."

Behind them, three shadows advanced from the
doorway, gliding silently, steadily closer.

MEET THE AUTHOR

A lifelong resident of Massachusetts, Kevin Flanders has written over ten novels and multiple short stories. In 2010, he graduated from Franklin Pierce University with a degree in mass communications, then served as a reporter for several newspapers.

When he isn't writing, Flanders enjoys spending time with his family and dog, playing ice hockey, and traveling to a new baseball stadium with his father each summer. He also takes part in several functions and mentors student writers.

But no matter where Flanders travels or who he meets along the way, he's always searching for inspiration for the next project.

The author resides in Monson, MA.

For more information about upcoming works, visit www.kmflanders.wordpress.com.

Made in the USA
Lexington, KY
05 November 2019